PENGUIN BOOKS

Still Me

To darling Saskia:
wear your own stripy tights with pride

Still Me

JOJO MOYES

PENGUIN BOOKS

PENGUIN BOOKS

UK | USA | Canada | Ireland | Australia
India | New Zealand | South Africa

Penguin Books is part of the Penguin Random House group of companies
whose addresses can be found at global.penguinrandomhouse.com.

First published by Michael Joseph 2018
Published in Penguin Books 2019
001

Copyright © Jojo's Mojo Ltd, 2018

The moral right of the author has been asserted

Set in 12.02/14.25 pt Garamond MT Std
Typeset by Jouve (UK), Milton Keynes
Printed and bound in Great Britain by Clays Ltd, Elcograf S.p.A.

A CIP catalogue record for this book is available from the British Library

B FORMAT ISBN: 978–1–405–92420–7
A FORMAT ISBN: 978–1–405–92422–1

www.greenpenguin.co.uk

Know, first, who you are; and then adorn
yourself accordingly.

Epictetus

I

It was the moustache that reminded me I was no longer in England: a solid, grey millipede firmly obscuring the man's upper lip; a Village People moustache, a cowboy moustache, the miniature head of a broom that meant business. You just didn't get that kind of moustache at home. I couldn't tear my eyes from it.

'Ma'am?'

The only person I had ever seen with a moustache like that at home was Mr Naylor, our maths teacher, and he collected Digestive crumbs in his – we used to count them during algebra.

'Ma'am?'

'Oh. Sorry.'

The man in the uniform motioned me forward with a flick of his stubby finger. He did not look up from his screen. I waited at the booth, long-haul sweat drying gently into my shirt. He held up his hand, waggling four fat fingers. This, I grasped after several seconds, was a demand for my passport.

'Name.'

'It's there,' I said.

'Your name, ma'am.'

'Louisa Elizabeth Clark.' I peered over the counter. 'Though I never use the Elizabeth bit. Because my mum realized after they named me that that would make me Lou Lizzy. And if you say that really fast it sounds like lunacy. Though my dad says that's kind of fitting. Not that I'm a

I

lunatic. I mean, you wouldn't want lunatics in your country. Hah!' My voice bounced nervously off the Perspex screen.

The man looked at me for the first time. He had solid shoulders and a gaze that could pin you like a Tazer. He did not smile. He waited until my own faded.

'Sorry,' I said. 'People in uniform make me nervous.'

I glanced behind me at the immigration hall, at the snaking queue that had doubled back on itself so many times it had become an impenetrable, restless sea of people. 'I think I'm feeling a bit odd from standing in that queue. That is honestly the longest queue I've ever stood in. I'd begun to wonder whether to start my Christmas list.'

'Put your hand on the scanner.'

'Is it always that size?'

'The scanner?' He frowned.

'The queue.'

But he was no longer listening. He was studying something on his screen. I put my fingers on the little pad. And then my phone dinged.

Mum: *Have you landed?*

I went to tap an answer with my free hand but he turned sharply towards me. 'Ma'am, you are not permitted to use cell-phones in this area.'

'It's just my mum. She wants to know if I'm here.' I surreptitiously tried to press the thumbs-up emoji as I slid the phone out of view.

'Reason for travel?'

What is that? came Mum's immediate reply. She had taken to texting like a duck to water and could now do it faster than she could speak. Which was basically warp speed. *You know my phone doesn't do the little pictures. Is that an SOS? Louisa tell me you're okay.*

'Reasons for travel, ma'am?' The moustache twitched with

irritation. He added, slowly: 'What are you doing here in the United States?'

'I have a new job.'

'Which is?'

'I'm going to work for a family in New York. Central Park.'

Just briefly, the man's eyebrows might have raised a millimetre. He checked the address on my form, confirming it. 'What kind of job?'

'It's a bit complicated. But I'm sort of a paid companion.'

'A *paid companion.*'

'It's like this. I used to work for this man. I was his companion, but I would also give him his meds and take him out and feed him. That's not as weird as it sounds, by the way – he had no use of his hands. It wasn't like something pervy. Actually it ended up as more than that, because it's hard not to get close to people you look after and Will – the man – was amazing and we . . . Well, we fell in love.' Too late, I felt the familiar welling of tears. I wiped my eyes briskly. 'So I think it'll be sort of like that. Except for the love bit. And the feeding.'

The immigration officer was staring at me. I tried to smile. 'Actually, I don't normally cry talking about jobs. I'm not like an actual lunatic, despite my name. Hah! But I loved him. And he loved me. And then he . . . Well, he chose to end his life. So this is sort of my attempt to start over.' The tears were now leaking relentlessly, embarrassingly, from the corners of my eyes. I couldn't seem to stop them. I couldn't seem to stop anything. 'Sorry. Must be the jetlag. It's something like two o'clock in the morning in normal time, right? Plus I don't really talk about him any more. I mean, I have a new boyfriend. And he's great! He's a paramedic! And hot! That's like winning the boyfriend lottery, right? A hot paramedic?'

I scrabbled around in my handbag for a tissue. When I looked up the man was holding out a box. I took one. 'Thank you. So, anyway, my friend Nathan – he's from New Zealand – works here and he helped me get this job and I don't really know what it involves yet, apart from looking after this rich man's wife who gets depressed. But I've decided this time I'm going to live up to what Will wanted for me, because I didn't get it right, before. I just ended up working in an airport.'

I froze. 'Not – uh – that there's anything wrong with working in an airport! I'm sure immigration is a very important job. *Really* important. But I have a plan. I'm going to do something new every week that I'm here and I'm going to say yes.'

'Say yes?'

'To new things. Will always said I shut myself off from new experiences. So this is my plan.'

The officer studied my paperwork. 'You didn't fill the address section out properly. I need a zip code.'

He pushed the form towards me. I checked the number on the sheet that I had printed out and filled it in with trembling fingers. I glanced to my left, where the queue at my section was growing restive. At the front of the next queue a Chinese family was being questioned by two officials. As the woman protested, they were led into a side room. I felt suddenly very alone.

The immigration officer peered at the people waiting. And then, abruptly, he stamped my passport. 'Good luck, Louisa Clark,' he said.

I stared at him. 'That's it?'

'That's it.'

I smiled. 'Oh, thank you! That's really kind. I mean, it's quite weird being on the other side of the world by yourself for the first time, and now I feel a bit like I just met my first nice new person and —'

'You need to move along now, ma'am.'

'Of course. Sorry.'

I gathered up my belongings and pushed a sweaty frond of hair from my face.

'And, ma'am . . .'

'Yes?' I wondered what I had got wrong now.

He didn't look up from his screen. 'Be careful what you say yes to.'

Nathan was waiting in Arrivals, as he had promised. I scanned the crowd, feeling oddly self-conscious, secretly convinced that nobody would come, but there he was, his huge hand waving above the shifting bodies around him. He raised his other arm, a smile breaking across his face, and pushed his way through to meet me, picking me up off my feet in a gigantic hug. 'Lou!'

At the sight of him, something in me constricted unexpectedly — something linked to Will and loss and the raw emotion that comes from sitting on a slightly-too-bumpy flight for seven hours — and I was glad that he was holding me tightly so that I had a moment to compose myself. 'Welcome to New York, Shorty! Not lost your dress sense, I see.'

Now he held me at arms' length, grinning. I straightened my 1970s tiger print shirt. I had thought it might make me look like Jackie Kennedy, the Onassis Years. If Jackie Kennedy had spilled half her airline coffee on her lap. 'It's so good to see you.'

He swept up my leaden suitcases like they were filled with feathers. 'C'mon. Let's get you back to the house. The Prius is in for servicing so Mr G lent me his car. Traffic's terrible, but you'll get there in style.'

*

Mr Gopnik's car was sleek and black and the size of a bus, and the doors closed with that emphatic, discreet *thunk* that signalled a six-figure price tag. Nathan shut my cases into the boot and I settled into the passenger seat with a sigh. I checked my phone, answered Mum's fourteen texts with one that told her simply that I was in the car and would call her tomorrow, then replied to Sam's, which told me he missed me, with *Landed xxx*.

'How's the fella?' said Nathan, glancing at me.

'He's good, thanks.' I added a few more xxxxs just to make sure.

'Wasn't too sticky about you heading over here?'

I shrugged. 'He thought I needed to come.'

'We all did. Just took you a while to find your way, is all.'

I put my phone away, sat back in my seat and gazed out at the unfamiliar names that dotted the highway: Milo's Tire Shop, Richie's Gym, the ambulances and U-Haul trucks, the rundown houses with their peeling paint and wonky stoops, the basketball courts, and drivers sipping from oversized plastic cups. Nathan turned on the radio and I listened to someone called Lorenzo talking about a baseball game and felt, briefly, as if I were in some kind of suspended reality.

'So you've got tomorrow to get straight. Anything you want to do? I thought I might let you sleep in, then drag you out to brunch. You should have the full NY diner experience on your first weekend here.'

'Sounds great.'

'They won't be back from the country club till tomorrow evening. There's been a bit of strife this last week. I'll fill you in when you've had some sleep.'

I stared at him. 'No secrets, right? This isn't going to be –'

'They're not like the Traynors. It's just your average dysfunctional multimillionaire family.'

6

'Is she nice?'

'She's great. She's . . . a handful. But she's great. He is too.'

That was as good a character reference as you were likely to get from Nathan. He lapsed into silence – he never was big on gossip – and I sat in the smooth, air-conditioned Mercedes GLS and fought the waves of sleep that kept threatening to wash over me. I thought about Sam, now fast asleep several thousand miles away in his railway carriage. I thought of Treena and Thom, tucked up in my little flat in London. And then Nathan's voice cut in. 'There you go.'

I looked up through gritty eyes and there it was across the Brooklyn Bridge, Manhattan, shining like a million jagged shards of light, awe-inspiring, glossy, impossibly condensed and beautiful, a sight that was so familiar from television and films that I couldn't quite accept I was seeing it for real. I shifted upright in my seat, dumbstruck as we sped towards it, the most famous metropolis on the planet.

'Never gets old, that view, eh? Bit grander than Stortfold.'

I don't think it had actually hit me until that point. *My new home.*

'Hey, Ashok. How's it going?' Nathan wheeled my cases through the marble lobby as I stared at the black and white tiles and the brass rails, and tried not to trip, my footsteps echoing in the cavernous space. It was like the entrance to a grand, slightly faded hotel: the lift in burnished brass, the floor carpeted in a red and gold livery, the reception a little darker than was comfortable. It smelt of beeswax and polished shoes and money.

'I'm good, man. Who's this?'

'This is Louisa. She'll be working for Mrs G.'

The uniformed porter stepped out from behind his desk and held out a hand for me to shake. He had a wide smile and eyes that looked like they had seen everything.

'Nice to meet you, Ashok.'

'A Brit! I have a cousin in London. Croy-down. You know Croy-down? You anywhere near there? He's a big fella, you know what I'm saying?'

'I don't really know Croydon,' I said. And when his face fell: 'But I'll keep an eye out for him the next time I'm passing through.'

'Louisa. Welcome to the Lavery. You need anything, or you want to know anything, you just let me know. I'm here twenty-four seven.'

'He's not kidding,' said Nathan. 'Sometimes I think he sleeps under that desk.' He gestured to a service elevator, its doors a dull grey, near the back of the lobby.

'Three kids under five, man,' said Ashok. 'Believe me, being here keeps me sane. Can't say it does the same for my wife.' He grinned. 'Seriously, Miss Louisa. Anything you need, I'm your man.'

'As in drugs, prostitutes, houses of ill-repute?' I whispered, as the service lift doors closed around us.

'No. As in theatre tickets, restaurant tables, best places to get your dry-cleaning,' Nathan said. 'This is Fifth Avenue. Jesus. What have you been doing back in London?'

The Gopnik residence comprised seven thousand square feet on the second and third floors of a red-brick Gothic building, a rare duplex in this part of New York, and testament to generations of Gopnik family riches. This, the Lavery, was a scaled-down imitation of the famous Dakota building, Nathan told me, and was one of the oldest co-ops on the Upper East Side. Nobody could buy or sell an apartment here without the approval of a board of residents who were staunchly resistant to change. While the glossy condominiums across the park housed the new money: Russian oligarchs, pop stars, Chinese steel magnates and tech billionaires – with communal restaurants, gyms, childcare and infinity pools, the residents of the Lavery liked things Old School.

These apartments were passed down through generations; their inhabitants learnt to tolerate the 1930s plumbing system, fought lengthy and labyrinthine battles for permission to alter anything more extensive than a light switch, and looked politely the other way as New York changed around them, just as one might ignore a beggar with a cardboard sign.

I barely glimpsed the grandeur of the duplex itself, with its parquet floors, elevated ceilings and floor-length damask curtains, as we headed straight to the staff quarters, which were tucked away at the far end of the second floor, down a long, narrow corridor that led off the kitchen – an anomaly left over from a distant age. The newer or refurbished buildings had no staff quarters: housekeepers and nannies would travel in from Queens or New Jersey on the dawn train and return after dark. But the Gopnik family had owned these tiny rooms since the building was first constructed. They could not be developed or sold, but were tied through deeds to the main residence, and lusted after as storage rooms. It wasn't hard to see why they might naturally be considered storage.

'There.' Nathan opened a door and dropped my bags.

My room measured approximately twelve feet by twelve feet. It housed a double bed, a television, a chest of drawers and a wardrobe. A small armchair, upholstered in beige fabric, sat in the corner, its sagging seat testament to previous exhausted occupants. A small window might have looked south. Or north. Or east. It was hard to tell, as it was approximately six feet from the blank brick rear of a building so tall that I could see the sky only if I pressed my face to the glass and craned my neck.

A communal kitchen sat nearby on the corridor, to be

shared by me, Nathan and a housekeeper, whose own room was across the corridor.

On my bed sat a neat pile of five dark-green polo shirts and what looked like black trousers, bearing a cheap Teflon sheen.

'They didn't tell you about the uniform?'

I picked up one of the polo shirts.

'It's just a shirt and trousers. The Gopniks think a uniform makes it simpler. Everyone knows where they stand.'

'If you want to look like a pro golfer.'

I peered into the tiny bathroom, tiled in limescale-encrusted brown marble, which opened off the bedroom. It housed a loo, a small basin that looked like it dated from the 1940s and a shower. A paper-wrapped soap and a can of cockroach killer sat on the side.

'It's actually pretty generous by Manhattan standards,' Nathan said. 'I know it looks a little tired but Mrs G says we can give it a splosh of paint. A couple of extra lamps and a quick trip to Crate and Barrel and it'll –'

'I love it,' I said. I turned to him, my voice suddenly shaky. 'I'm in New York, Nathan. I'm actually here.'

He squeezed my shoulder. 'Yup. You really are.'

I managed to stay awake just long enough to unpack, eat some takeaway with Nathan (he called it takeout, like an actual American), flick through some of the 859 channels on my little television, the bulk of which seemed to be on an ever-running loop of American football, adverts for digestion issues, or badly lit crime shows I hadn't heard of, and then I zonked out. I woke with a start at four forty-five a.m. For a few discombobulating minutes I was confused by the distant sound of an unfamiliar siren, the low whine of a reversing truck, then flicked on the light switch, remembered where I was, and a jolt of excitement whipped through me.

I pulled my laptop from my bag and tapped out a chat message to Sam. *You there? xxx*

I waited, but nothing came back. He had said he was back on duty, and was too befuddled to work out the time difference. I put my laptop down and tried briefly to get back to sleep (Treena said when I didn't sleep enough I looked like a sad horse). But the unfamiliar sounds of the city were a siren call, and at six I climbed out of bed and showered, trying to ignore the rust in the sputtering water that exploded out of the shower head. I dressed (denim pinafore sundress and a vintage turquoise short-sleeved blouse with a picture of the Statue of Liberty) and went in search of coffee.

I padded along the corridor, trying to remember the location of the staff kitchen that Nathan had shown me the previous evening. I opened a door and a woman turned and stared at me. She was middle-aged and stocky, her hair set in neat dark waves, like a 1930s movie star. Her eyes were beautiful and dark but her mouth dragged down at the edges, as if in permanent disapproval.

'Um . . . good morning!'

She kept staring at me.

'I – I'm Louisa? The new girl? Mrs Gopnik's . . . assistant?'

'She is not Mrs Gopnik.' The woman left this statement hanging in the air.

'You must be . . .' I racked my jetlagged brain but no name was forthcoming. *Oh, come on*, I willed myself. 'I'm so sorry. My brain is like porridge this morning. Jetlag.'

'My name is Ilaria.'

'Ilaria. Of course, that's it. Sorry.' I stuck out my hand. She didn't take it.

'I know who you are.'

'Um . . . can you show me where Nathan keeps his milk? I just wanted to get a coffee.'

'Nathan doesn't drink milk.'

'Really? He used to.'

'You think I lie to you?'

'No. That's not what I was s–'

She stepped to the left and gestured towards a wall cupboard that was half the size of the others and ever so slightly out of reach. 'That is yours.' Then she opened the fridge door to replace her juice, and I noticed the full two-litre bottle of milk on her shelf. She closed it again and gazed at me implacably. 'Mr Gopnik will be home at six thirty this evening. Dress in uniform to meet him.' And she headed off down the corridor, her slippers slapping against the soles of her feet.

'Lovely to meet you! I'm sure we'll be seeing loads of each other!' I called after her.

I stared at the fridge for a moment, then decided it probably wasn't too early to go out for milk. After all, this was the city that never slept.

New York might be awake, but the Lavery was cloaked in a silence so dense it suggested communal doses of zopiclone. I walked along the corridor, closing the front door softly behind me and checking eight times that I had remembered both my purse and my keys. I figured the early hour and the sleeping residents gave me licence to look a little more closely at where I had ended up.

As I tiptoed along, the plush carpet muffling my steps, a dog started to bark from inside one of the doors – a yappy, outraged protest – and an elderly voice shouted something that I couldn't make out. I hurried past, not wanting to be responsible for waking up the other residents, and, instead of taking the main stairs, headed down in the service lift.

There was nobody in the lobby so I let myself out onto the

street and stepped straight into a clamour of noise and light so overwhelming that I had to stand still for a moment just to stay upright. In front of me the green oasis of Central Park extended for what looked like miles. To my left, the side streets were already busy – enormous men in overalls unloaded crates from an open-sided van, watched by a cop with arms like sides of ham crossed over his chest. A road sweeper hummed industriously. A taxi driver chatted to a man through his open window. I counted off the sights of the Big Apple in my head. Horse-drawn carriages! Yellow taxis! Impossibly tall buildings! As I stared, two weary tourists with children in buggies pushed past me clutching Styrofoam coffee cups, still operating perhaps on some distant time zone. Manhattan stretched in every direction, enormous, sun-tipped, teeming and glowing.

My jetlag evaporated with the last of the dawn. I took a breath and set off, aware that I was grinning but quite unable to stop myself. I walked eight blocks without seeing a single convenience store. I turned into Madison Avenue, past huge glass-fronted luxury stores with their doors locked and, dotted between them, the occasional restaurant, windows darkened like closed eyes, or a gilded hotel whose liveried doorman didn't look at me as I passed.

I walked another five blocks, realizing gradually that this wasn't the kind of area where you could just nip into the grocer's. I had pictured New York diners on every corner, staffed by brassy waitresses and men with white pork-pie hats, but everything looked huge and glossy and not remotely as if a cheese omelette or a mug of tea might be waiting behind its doors. Most of the people I passed were tourists, or fierce, jogging hard-bodies, sleek in Lycra and oblivious between earphones, stepping nimbly around homeless men, who glared from furrowed, lead-stained faces. Finally I stumbled on a large coffee bar, one of a chain, in which half of New York's early risers seemed to have congregated, bent over their phones in booths or feeding preternaturally cheerful toddlers as generic easy-listening music filtered through speakers on the wall.

I ordered cappuccino and a muffin, which, before I could say anything, the barista sliced in two, heated, then slathered with butter, all the while never breaking his conversation about a baseball game with his colleague.

I paid, sat down with the muffin, wrapped in foil, and took a bite. It was, even without the clawing jetlag hunger, the most delicious thing I had ever eaten.

I sat in a window seat staring out at the early-morning Manhattan street for half an hour or so, my mouth alternately filled with claggy, buttery muffin or scalded by hot, strong coffee, giving free rein to my ever-present internal monologue (*I am drinking New York coffee in a New York coffee house! I am walking along a New York street! Like Meg Ryan! Or Diane Keaton! I am in actual New York!*) and, briefly, I understood exactly what Will had been trying to explain to me two years previously: for those few minutes, my mouth full of unfamiliar food, my eyes filled with strange sights, I existed only in the moment. I was fully present, my senses alive, my whole being open to receive the new experiences around me. I was in the only place in the world I could possibly be.

And then, apropos of apparently nothing, two women at the next table launched into a fist fight, coffee and bits of pastry flying across the tables, baristas leaping to pull them apart. I dusted the crumbs off my dress, closed my bag, and decided it was probably time to return to the peace of the Lavery.

2

Ashok was sorting huge bales of newspapers into numbered piles as I walked back in. He straightened up with a smile. 'Well, good day, Miss Louisa. And how was your first morning in New York?'

'Amazing. Thank you.'

'Did you hum "Let The River Run" as you walked down the street?'

I stopped in my tracks. 'How did you know?'

'Everyone does that when they first come to Manhattan. Hell, even I do it some mornings and I don't look nothing *like* Melanie Griffith.'

'Are there no grocery stores around here? I had to walk about a million miles to get a coffee. And I have no idea where to buy milk.'

'Miss Louisa, you should have told me. C'mere.' He gestured behind his counter and opened a door, beckoning me into a dark office, its scruffiness and cluttered décor at odds with the brass and marble outside. On a desk sat a bank of security screens and among them an old television and a large ledger, along with a mug, some paperback books and an array of photographs of beaming, toothless children. Behind the door stood an ancient fridge. 'Here. Take this. Bring me one later.'

'Do all doormen do this?'

'No doormen do this. But the Lavery is different.'

'So where do people do their shopping?'

He pulled a face. 'People in this building don't do shopping, Miss Louisa. They don't even *think* about shopping.

I swear half of them think that food arrives by magic, cooked, on their tables.' He glanced behind him, lowering his voice. 'I will wager that eighty per cent of the women in this building have not cooked a meal in five years. Mind you, half the women in this building don't eat meals, period.'

When I stared at him he shrugged. 'The rich do not live like you and me, Miss Louisa. And the New York rich . . . well, they do not live like *anyone*.'

I took the carton of milk.

'Anything you want you have it delivered. You'll get used to it.'

I wanted to ask him about Ilaria and Mrs Gopnik, who apparently wasn't Mrs Gopnik, and the family I was about to meet. But he was looking away from me up the hallway.

'Well, good morning to you, Mrs De Witt!'

'What *are* all these newspapers doing on the floor? The place looks like a wretched newsstand.' A tiny old woman tutted fretfully at the piles of *New York Times* and *Wall Street Journal* that he was still unpacking. Despite the hour, she was dressed as if for a wedding, in a raspberry pink duster coat, a red pillbox hat and huge tortoiseshell sunglasses that obscured her tiny, wrinkled face. At the end of a lead a wheezy pug, with bulbous eyes, gazed at me belligerently (at least I thought it was gazing at me: it was hard to be sure as its eyes veered off in different directions). I stooped to help Ashok clear the newspapers from her path but as I bent down the dog leapt at me with a growl so that I sprang back, almost falling over the *New York Times*.

'Oh, for goodness' sake!' came the quavering, imperious voice. 'And now you're upsetting the dog!'

My leg had felt the whisper of the pug's teeth. My skin sang with the near contact.

'Please make sure this – this *debris* is cleared by the time we return. I have told Mr Ovitz again and again that the building is going downhill. And, Ashok, I've left a bag of refuse outside my door. Please move it immediately or the whole corridor will smell of stale lilies. Goodness knows who sends lilies as a gift. Funereal things. Dean Martin!'

Ashok tipped his cap. 'Certainly, Mrs De Witt.' He waited until she'd gone. Then he turned and peered at my leg.

'That dog tried to bite me!'

'Yeah. That's Dean Martin. Best stay out of his way. He's the most bad-tempered resident in this building, and that's saying something.' He bent back towards his papers, heaving the next lot onto the desk, then pausing to shoo me away. 'Don't you worry about these, Miss Louisa. They're heavy and you've got enough on your plate with them upstairs. Have a nice day now.'

He was gone before I could ask him what he meant.

The day passed in a blur. I spent the rest of the morning organizing my little room, cleaning the bathroom, putting up pictures of Sam, my parents, Treena and Thom to make it feel more like home. Nathan took me to a diner near Columbus Circle where I ate from a plate the size of a car tyre and drank so much strong coffee that my hands vibrated as we walked back. Nathan pointed out places that might be useful to me – this bar stayed open late, that food truck did really good falafel, this was a safe ATM for getting cash . . . My brain spun with new images, new information. Some time mid-afternoon I felt suddenly woozy and leaden-footed, so Nathan walked me back to the apartment, his arm through mine. I was grateful for the quiet, dark interior of the building, for the service lift that saved me from the stairs.

'Take a nap,' he advised, as I kicked off my shoes. 'I wouldn't sleep more than an hour, though, or your body clock will be even more messed up.'

'What time did you say the Gopniks will be back?' My voice had started to slur.

'Usually around six. It's three now so you've got time. Go on, get some shut-eye. You'll feel human again.'

He closed the door and I sank gratefully back on the bed. I was about to sleep, but realized suddenly that if I waited I wouldn't be able to speak to Sam, and reached for my laptop, briefly lifted from my torpor. *Are you there?* I typed into the messenger app.

A few minutes later, with a little bubbling sound, the picture expanded and there he was, back in the railway carriage, his huge body hunched towards the screen. Sam. Paramedic. Man-mountain. All-too-new-boyfriend. We grinned at each other like loons.

'Hey, gorgeous! How is it?'

'Good!' I said. 'I could show you my room but I might bump the walls as I turn the screen.' I twisted the laptop so that he could see the full glory of my little bedroom.

'Looks good to me. It's got you in it.'

I stared at the grey window behind him. I could picture it exactly, the rain thrumming on the roof of the railway carriage, the glass that steamed comfortingly, the wood, the damp and the hens outside sheltering under a dripping wheelbarrow. Sam was gazing at me, and I wiped my eyes, wishing suddenly that I had remembered to put on some make-up.

'Did you go into work?'

'Yeah. They reckon I'll be good to start back on full duties in a week. Got to be fit enough to lift a body without busting my stitches.' He instinctively placed his hand on his abdomen, where the gunshot had hit him just a matter of weeks previously – the routine callout that had nearly killed him, and cemented our relationship – and I felt something unbalancing and visceral.

'I wish you were here,' I said, before I could stop myself.

'Me too. But you're on day one of your adventure and it's going to be great. And in a year you will be sitting here –'

'Not there,' I interrupted. 'In your finished house.'

'In my finished house,' he said. 'And we'll be looking at your pictures on your phone and I'll be secretly thinking, Oh, God, there she goes, whanging on about her time in New York again.'

'So will you write to me? A letter full of love and longing, sprayed with lonely tears?'

'Ah, Lou. You know I'm not really a writer. But I'll call. And I'll be there with you in just four weeks.'

'Right,' I said, as my throat constricted. 'Okay. I'd better grab a nap.'

'Me too,' he said. 'I'll think of you.'

'In a disgusting porny way? Or in a romantic Nora Ephron-y kind of way?'

'Which of those is not going to get me into trouble?' He smiled. 'You look good, Lou,' he said, after a minute. 'You look . . . giddy.'

'I feel giddy. I feel like a really, really tired person who also slightly wants to explode. It's a little confusing.' I put my hand on the screen, and after a second he put his up to meet it. I could imagine it on my skin.

'Love you.' I still felt a little self-conscious saying it.

'You too. I'd kiss the screen but I suspect you'd only get a view of my nasal hair.'

I shut my computer, smiling, and within seconds I was asleep.

*

Somebody was shrieking in the corridor. I woke groggily, sweatily, half suspecting I was in a dream, and pushed myself upright. There really was a woman screaming on the other side of my door. A thousand thoughts sped through my addled brain, headlines about murders, New York and how to report a crime. What was the number you were meant to call? Not 999 like England. I racked my brain and came up with nothing.

'Why should I? Why should I sit there and smile when those witches are insulting me? You don't even hear half of what they say! You are a man! It is like you wear blinkers on your ears!'

'Darling, please calm down. Please. This is not the time or the place.'

'There is never a time or place! Because there is always someone here! I have to buy my own apartment just so I have somewhere to argue with you!'

'I don't understand why you have to get so upset about it all. You have to give it –'

'No!'

Something smashed on the hardwood floor. I was fully awake now, my heart racing.

There was a weighty silence.

'Now you're going to tell me this was a family heirloom.'

A pause.

'Well, yes, yes, it was.'

A muffled sob. 'I don't care! I don't care! I'm choking in your family history! You hear me? Choking!'

'Agnes, darling. Not in the corridor. Come on. We can discuss this later.'

I sat very still on the edge of my bed.

There was more muffled sobbing, then silence. I waited, then stood and tiptoed to the door, pressing my ear against it. Nothing. I looked at the clock – four forty-six p.m.

I washed my face and changed briskly into my uniform. I brushed my hair, then let myself quietly out of my bedroom and walked around the corner of the corridor.

And I stopped.

Further up the corridor beside the kitchen, a young woman was curled into a foetal ball. An older man had his arms wrapped around her, his back pressed against the wood panelling. He was almost seated, one knee up and one extended, as if he had caught her and been brought down by the weight. I couldn't see her face, but a long, slim leg stuck out inelegantly from a navy dress and a sheet of blonde hair obscured her face. Her knuckles were white from where she was holding on to him.

I stared and gulped, and he looked up and saw me. I recognized Mr Gopnik.

'Not now. Thank you,' he said, softly.

My voice sticking in my throat, I backed swiftly into my room and closed the door, my heart thumping in my ears so loudly that I was sure they must be able to hear it.

I stared, unseeing, at the television for the next hour, an image of those entwined people burned onto the inside of my head. I thought about texting Nathan but I wasn't sure what I would say. Instead, at five fifty-five, I walked out, tentatively making my way towards the main apartment through the connecting door. I passed a vast empty dining room, what looked like a guest bedroom and two closed doors, following the distant murmur of conversation, my feet soft on the parquet floor. Finally I reached the drawing room and stopped just outside the open doorway.

Mr Gopnik was in a window seat, on the telephone, the sleeves of his pale blue shirt rolled up and one hand resting behind his head. He motioned me in, still talking on the phone. To my left a blonde woman – Mrs Gopnik? – sat on a rose-coloured antique sofa tapping restlessly on an iPhone. She appeared to have changed her clothes and I was momentarily confused. I waited awkwardly until he ended his call and stood, I noticed, with a little wince of effort. I took another step towards him, to save him coming further, and shook his hand. It was warm, his grip soft and strong. The young woman continued to tap at her phone.

'Louisa. Glad you got here okay. I trust you have everything you need.'

He said it in the way people do when they don't expect you to ask for anything.

'It's all lovely. Thank you.'

'This is my daughter, Tabitha. Tab?'

The girl raised a hand, offering the hint of a smile, before turning back to her phone.

'Please excuse Agnes not being here to meet you. She's gone to bed for an hour. Splitting headache. It's been a long weekend.'

A vague weariness shadowed his face, but it was gone within a moment. Nothing in his manner betrayed what I had seen less than two hours previously.

He smiled. 'So . . . tonight you're free to do as you please, and from tomorrow morning you will accompany Agnes wherever she wants to go. Your official title is "assistant", and you'll be there to support her in whatever she needs to do in the day. She has a busy schedule – I've asked my assistant to loop you in on the family calendar and you'll get emailed with any updates. Best to check at around ten p.m. – that's when we tend to make late changes. You'll meet the rest of the team tomorrow.'

'Great. Thank you.' I noted the word 'team' and had a brief vision of footballers trekking through the apartment.

'What's for dinner, Dad?' Tabitha spoke as if I wasn't there.

'I don't know, darling. I thought you said you were going out.'

'I'm not sure I can face going back across town tonight. I might just stay.'

'Whatever you want. Just make sure Ilaria knows. Louisa, do you have any questions?'

I tried to think of something useful to say.

'Oh, and Mom told me to ask you if you'd found that little drawing. The Miró.'

'Sweetheart, I'm not going over that again. The drawing belongs here.'

'But Mom said she chose it. She misses it. You never even liked it.'

'That's not the point.'

I shifted my weight between my feet, not sure if I had been dismissed.

'But it *is* the point, Dad. Mom misses something terribly and you don't even care for it.'

'It's worth eighty thousand dollars.'

'Mom doesn't care about the money.'

'Can we discuss this later?'

'You'll be busy later. I promised Mom I would sort this out.'

I took a surreptitious step backwards.

'There's nothing to sort. The settlement was finalized eighteen months ago. It was all dealt with then. Oh, darling, there you are. Are you feeling better?'

I looked round. The woman who had just entered the room was strikingly beautiful, her face free of make-up and her pale blonde hair scraped back into a loose knot. Her high cheekbones were lightly freckled and the shape of her eyes suggested a Slavic heritage. I guessed she was about the same age as me. She padded barefoot over to Mr Gopnik and kissed him, her hand trailing across the back of his neck. 'Much better, thank you.'

'This is Louisa,' he said.

She turned to me. 'My new ally,' she said.

'Your new assistant,' said Mr Gopnik.

'Hello, Louisa.' She reached out a slender hand and shook mine. I felt her eyes run over me, as if she were working something out, and then she smiled, and I couldn't help but smile in return.

'Ilaria has made your room nice?' Her voice was soft and held an Eastern European lilt.

'It's perfect. Thank you.'

'Perfect? Oh, you are very easily pleased. That room is like a broom cupboard. Anything you don't like you tell us and we will make it nice. Won't we, darling?'

'Didn't you used to live in a room even smaller than that, Agnes?' said Tab, not looking up from her iPhone. 'I'm sure Dad told me you used to share with about fifteen other immigrants.'

'Tab.' Mr Gopnik's voice was a gentle warning.

Agnes took a little breath and lifted her chin. 'Actually, my room was smaller. But the girls I shared with were very nice. So it was no trouble at all. If people are nice, and polite, you can bear anything, don't you think, Louisa?'

I swallowed. 'Yes.'

Ilaria walked in and cleared her throat. She was wearing the same polo shirt and dark trousers, covered by a white apron. She didn't look at me. 'Dinner is ready, Mr Gopnik,' she said.

'Is there any for me, Ilaria darling?' said Tab, her hand resting along the back of the sofa. 'I think I might stay over.'

Ilaria's expression was filled with instant warmth. It was as if a different person had appeared in front of me. 'Of course, Miss Tabitha. I always cook extra on Sundays in case you decide to stay.'

Agnes stood in the middle of the room. I thought I saw a flicker of panic cross her face. Her jaw tightened. 'Then I would like Louisa to eat with us too,' she said.

There was a brief silence.

'Louisa?' said Tab.

'Yes. It would be nice to get to know her properly. Do you have plans for this evening, Louisa?'

'Uh – no,' I stuttered.

'Then you eat with us. Ilaria, you say you cook extra, yes?'

Ilaria looked directly at Mr Gopnik, who appeared to be engrossed in something on his phone.

'Agnes,' said Tab, after a moment. 'You do understand we don't eat with staff?'

'Who is this "we"? I did not know that there was a rulebook.' Agnes held out her hand and inspected her wedding band with studied calm. 'Darling? Did you forget to give me a rulebook?'

'With respect, and while I'm sure Louisa is perfectly nice,' said Tab, 'there are boundaries. And they exist for everybody's benefit.'

'I'm happy to do whatever . . .' I began. 'I don't want to cause any . . .'

'Well, *with respect*, Tabitha, I would like Louisa to eat supper with me. She is my new assistant and we are going to spend every day together. So I cannot see the problem in me getting to know her a little.'

'There's no problem,' said Mr Gopnik.

'Daddy –'

'There's no problem, Tab. Ilaria, please could you set the table for four? Thank you.'

Ilaria's eyes widened. She glanced at me, her mouth a thin line of suppressed rage, as if I had engineered this travesty of the domestic hierarchy, then disappeared to the dining room from where we could hear the emphatic clattering of cutlery and glassware. Agnes let out a little breath and pushed her hair back from her head. She flashed me a small, conspiratorial smile.

'Let's go through,' said Mr Gopnik, after a minute. 'Louisa, perhaps you'd like a drink.'

Dinner was a hushed, painful affair. I was overawed by the grand mahogany table, the heavy silver cutlery and the crystal glasses, out of place in my uniform. Mr Gopnik was largely silent and disappeared twice to take calls from his office. Tab flicked through her iPhone, studiously declining to engage with anybody, and Ilaria delivered chicken in a red wine sauce with all the trimmings and removed serving dishes afterwards with a face, as my mother would put it, like a smacked arse. Perhaps only I noticed the hard clunk with which my own plate was placed in front of me, the audible sniff that came every time she passed my chair.

Agnes barely picked at hers. She sat opposite me and chatted gamely as if I were her new best friend, her gaze periodically sliding towards her husband.

'So this is your first time in New York,' she said. 'Where else have you been?'

'Um . . . not very many places. I'm sort of late to travelling. I backpacked around Europe a while ago, and before that . . . Mauritius. And Switzerland.'

'America is very different. Each state has a unique feel, I think, to we Europeans. I have only been to a few places with Leonard, but it was like going to different countries entirely. Are you excited to be here?'

'Very much so,' I said. 'I'm determined to take advantage of everything New York has to offer.'

'Sounds like you, Agnes,' said Tab, sweetly.

Agnes ignored her, keeping her eyes on me. They were hypnotically beautiful, tapering to fine, upward-tilted points at the corners. Twice I had to remind myself to close my mouth while staring at her.

'And tell me about your family. You have brothers? Sisters?'

I explained my family as best I could, making them sound a little more Waltons than Addams.

'And your sister now lives in your apartment in London? With her son? Will she come visit you? And your parents? They will miss you?'

I thought of Dad's parting shot: 'Don't hurry back, Lou! We're turning your old bedroom into a jacuzzi!'

'Oh, yes. Very much.'

'My mother cried for two weeks when I left Kraków. And you have a boyfriend?'

'Yes. His name's Sam. He's a paramedic.'

'A paramedic! Like a doctor? How lovely. Please show me picture. I love to see pictures.'

I pulled my phone from my pocket and flicked through until I found my favourite picture of Sam, sitting on my roof terrace in his dark green uniform. He had just finished work, and was drinking a mug of tea, beaming at me. The sun was low behind him and I could remember, looking at it, exactly how it had felt up there, my tea cooling on the ledge behind me, Sam waiting patiently as I took picture after picture.

'So handsome! And he is coming to New York too?'

'Um, no. He's building a house so it's a bit complicated just now. And he has a job.'

Agnes's eyes widened. 'But he must come! You cannot live in different countries! How you can love your man if he is not here with you? I could not be away from Leonard. I don't even like it when he goes on two-day business trip.'

'Yes, I suppose you *would* want to make sure you're never too far away,' said Tab. Mr Gopnik glanced up from his dinner, his gaze flickering between his wife and daughter, but said nothing.

'Still,' Agnes said, arranging her napkin on her lap, 'London is not so far away. And love is love. Isn't that right, Leonard?'

'It certainly is,' he said, and his face briefly softened at her smile. Agnes reached out a hand and stroked his, and I looked quickly at my plate.

The room fell silent for a moment.

'Actually, I think I might head home. I seem to be feeling slightly nauseous.' With a loud scrape, Tab pushed her chair back and dropped her napkin on her plate, where the white linen immediately began to soak up the red wine sauce. I had to fight the urge to rescue it. She stood and kissed her father's cheek. He reached up a free hand and touched her arm fondly.

'I'll speak to you during the week, Daddy.' She turned. 'Louisa . . . Agnes.' She nodded curtly, and left the room.

Agnes watched her go. It's possible she muttered something under her breath, but Ilaria was gathering up my plate and cutlery with such a savage clatter that it was hard to tell.

With Tab gone, it was as if all the fight left Agnes. She seemed to wilt in her seat, her shoulders suddenly bowed, the sharp hollow of her collarbone visible as her head drooped over it. I stood. 'I think I might head back to my room now. Thank you so much for supper. It was delicious.'

Nobody protested. Mr Gopnik's arm was resting along the mahogany table now, his fingers stroking his wife's hand. 'We'll see you in the morning, Louisa,' he said, not looking at me. Agnes was gazing up at him, her face sombre. I backed out of the dining room, speeding past the kitchen door to my room so that the virtual daggers I could feel Ilaria hurling my way from the kitchen wouldn't have a chance to hit me.

An hour later Nathan sent me a text. He was having a beer with friends in Brooklyn. *Heard you got the full baptism of fire. You all right?*

I didn't have the energy to come back with something witty. Or to ask him how on earth he knew.

It'll be easier once you get to know them. Promise.

See you in the morning, I replied. I had a brief moment of misgiving – what had I just signed up for? – then had a stern word with myself, and fell heavily to sleep.

That night I dreamt of Will. I dreamt of him rarely – a source of some sadness to me in the early days when I had missed him so much that I felt as if someone had blasted a hole straight through me. The dreams had stopped when I met Sam. But there he was again, in the small hours, as vivid as if he were standing before me. He was in the back seat of a car, an expensive black limousine, like Mr Gopnik's, and I saw him from across a street. I was instantly relieved that he was not dead, not gone after all, and knew instinctively that he should not go wherever he was headed. It was my job to stop him. But every time I tried to cross the busy road an extra lane of cars seemed to appear in front of me, roaring past so that I couldn't get to him, the sound of the engines drowning my shouting of his name. There he was, just out of reach, his skin that smooth caramel colour, his faint smile playing around the edges of his mouth, saying something to the driver that I couldn't hear. At the last minute he caught my eye – his eyes widened just a little – and I woke, sweating, the duvet knotted around my legs.

3

To: Samfielding1@gmail.com
From: BusyBee@gmail.com

Writing this in haste – Mrs G is having her piano lesson – but I'm going to try and email you every day so that at least I can feel like we're chatting. I miss you. Please write back. I know you said you hate emails but just for me. Pleeeease. (You have to imagine my pleading face here.) Or, you know, LETTERS! Love you, Lxxxxxx

'Well, good morning!'

A very large African American man in very tight scarlet Lycra stood in front of me, his hands on his hips. I froze, blinking, in the kitchen doorway in my T-shirt and knickers, wondering if I was dreaming and whether if I closed the door and opened it again he would still be there.

'You must be Miss Louisa?' A huge hand reached out and took mine, pumping it so enthusiastically that I bobbed up and down involuntarily. I checked my watch. No, it really was a quarter past six.

'I'm George. Mrs Gopnik's trainer. I hear you're coming out with us. Looking forward to it!'

I had woken after a fitful few hours, struggling to shake off the tangled dreams that had woven themselves through my sleep, and stumbled down the corridor on automatic pilot, a caffeine-seeking zombie.

'Okay, Louisa! Gotta stay hydrated!' He picked up two

water bottles from the side. And he was gone, jogging lightly down the corridor.

I poured myself a coffee, and as I stood there sipping it, Nathan walked in, dressed and scented with aftershave. He gazed at my bare legs.

'I just met George,' I said.

'Nothing he can't teach you about glutes. You got your running shoes, right?'

'Hah!' I took a sip of my coffee but Nathan was looking at me expectantly. 'Nathan, nobody said anything about running. I'm not a runner. I mean, I am the anti-sport, the sofa-dweller. You know that.'

Nathan poured himself a black coffee and replaced the jug in the machine.

'Plus I fell off a building earlier this year. Remember? Lots of bits of me went crack.' I could joke about that night now when, still grieving Will, I had drunkenly slipped from the parapet of my London home. But the twinges in my hip were a constant reminder.

'You're fine. And you're Mrs G's assistant. Your job is to be at her side at all times, mate. If she wants you to go running, then you're running.' He took a sip of his coffee. 'Ah, don't look so panicked. You'll love it. You'll be fit as a butcher's dog within a few weeks. Everyone here does it.'

'It's a quarter past six in the morning.'

'Mr Gopnik starts at five. We've just finished his physio. Mrs G likes a bit of a lie-in.'

'So we run at what time?'

'Twenty to seven. Meet them in the main hallway. See you later!' He lifted a hand, and was gone.

Agnes, of course, was one of those women who looked even better in the mornings: naked of face, a little blurred at the

31

edges, but in a sexy Vaseline-on-the-lens way. Her hair was pulled back in a loose ponytail and her fitted top and jogging pants made her seem casual in the same way that off-duty supermodels do. She loped down the corridor, like a Palomino racehorse in sunglasses, and lifted an elegant hand in greeting, as if it were simply too early for speech. I had only a pair of shorts and a sleeveless T-shirt with me, which, I suspected, made me look like a plump labourer. I was slightly anxious that I hadn't shaved my armpits and clamped my elbows to my sides.

'Good morning, Mrs G!' George appeared beside us and handed Agnes a bottle of water. 'You all set?'

She nodded.

'You ready, Miss Louisa? We're just doing the four miles today. Mrs G wants to do extra abdominal work. You've done your stretches, right?'

'Um, I . . .' I had no water and no bottle. But we were off.

I had heard the expression 'hit the ground running' but until George I had never truly understood what it meant. He set off down the corridor at what felt like forty miles an hour, and just when I thought we would at least slow for the lift, he held open the double doors at the end so that we could sprint down the stairs that took us to the ground floor. We were out through the lobby and past Ashok in a blur, me just able to catch his muffled greeting.

Dear God, but it was too early for this. I followed the two of them, jogging effortlessly like a pair of carriage horses, while I sprinted behind, my shorter stride failing to match theirs, my bones jarring with the impact of each footfall, muttering my apologies as I swerved between the kamikaze pedestrians who walked into my path. Running had been my ex Patrick's thing. It was like kale – one of those things you know exists and is possibly good for you but, frankly, life is always going to be too short to get stuck in.

Oh, come on, you can do this, I told myself. This is your first *say yes!* moment. *You are jogging in New York! This is a whole new you!* For a few glorious strides I almost believed it. The traffic stopped, the crossing light changed, and we paused at the kerbside, George and Agnes bouncing lightly on their toes, me unseen behind them. Then we were across and into Central Park, the path disappearing beneath our feet, the sounds of the traffic fading as we entered the green oasis at the heart of the city.

We were barely a mile in when I realized this was not a good idea. Even though I was now walking as much as running, my breath was already coming in gasps, my hip protesting all-too-recent injuries. The furthest I had run in years was fifteen yards for a slowing bus, and I'd missed that. I glanced up to see that George and Agnes were talking while they jogged. I couldn't breathe, and they were holding an honest-to-God conversation.

I thought about a friend of Dad's who had had a heart attack while running. Dad had always used it as a clear illustration of why sport was bad for you. Why had I not explained my injuries? Was I going to cough a lung out right here in the middle of the park?

'You okay back there, Miss Louisa?' George turned so that he was jogging backwards.

'Fine!' I gave him a cheery thumbs-up.

I had always wanted to see Central Park. But not this way. I wondered what would happen if I keeled over and died on my first day in the job. How would they get my body home? I swerved to avoid a woman with three identical meandering toddlers. *Please, God*, I willed the two people running effortlessly in front of me, silently. *Just one of you fall over. Not to break a leg exactly, just a little sprain. One of those things that lasts twenty-four hours and requires lying on a sofa with your leg up watching daytime telly.*

They were pulling away from me now and there was nothing I could do. What kind of park had hills in it? Mr Gopnik would be furious with me for not sticking with his wife. Agnes would realize I was a silly, dumpy Englishwoman, rather than an ally. They would hire someone slim and gorgeous with better running clothes.

It was at this point that the old man jogged past me. He turned his head to glance at me, then consulted his fitness tracker and kept going, nimble on his toes, his headphones plugged into his ears. He must have been seventy-five years old.

'Oh, *come on*.' I watched him speed away from me. And then I caught sight of the horse and carriage. I pushed forward until I was level with the driver. 'Hey! Hey! Any chance you could just trot up to where those people are running?'

'What people?'

I pointed to the tiny figures now in the far distance. He peered towards them, then shrugged. I climbed up on the carriage and ducked down behind him while he urged his horse forward with a light slap of the reins. Yet another New York experience that wasn't quite as planned, I thought, as I crouched behind him. We drew closer, and I tapped him to let me out. It could only have been about five hundred yards but at least it had got me closer to them. I made to jump down.

'Forty bucks,' said the driver.

'What?'

'Forty bucks.'

'We only went five hundred yards!'

'That's what it costs, lady.'

They were still deep in conversation. I pulled two twenty-dollar notes from my back pocket and hurled them at him, then ducked behind the carriage and started to jog, just in time for George to turn around and spot me. I gave him another cheery thumbs-up as if I'd been there all along.

George finally took pity on me. He spotted me limping and jogged back while Agnes did stretches, her long legs extending like some double-jointed flamingo. 'Miss Louisa! You okay there?'

At least, I thought it was him. I could no longer see because of the sweat leaking into my eyes. I stopped, my hands resting on my knees, my chest heaving

'You got a problem? You're looking a little flushed.'

'Bit . . . rusty,' I gasped. 'Hip . . . problem.'

'You got an injury? You should have said!'

'Didn't want to . . . miss any of it!' I said, wiping my eyes with my hands. It just made them sting more.

'Where is it?'

'Left hip. Fracture. Eight months ago.'

He put his hands on my hip, then moved my left leg backwards and forwards so that he could feel it rotating. I tried not to wince.

'You know, I don't think you should do any more today.'

'But I –'

'No, you head on back, Miss Louisa.'

'Oh, if you insist. How disappointing.'

'We'll meet you at the apartment.' He clapped me on the back so vigorously that I nearly fell onto my face. And then, with a cheery wave, they were gone.

'You have fun, Miss Louisa?' said Ashok, as I hobbled in forty-five minutes later. Turned out you could get lost in Central Park after all.

I paused to pull my sweat-soaked T-shirt away from my back. 'Marvellous. Loving it.'

35

When I got into the apartment I discovered that George and Agnes had returned home a full twenty minutes before me.

Mr Gopnik had told me that Agnes's schedule was busy. Given his wife didn't have a job, or any offspring, she was in fact the busiest person I had ever met. We had a half-hour for breakfast after George left (there was a table laid for Agnes with an egg-white omelette, some berries and a silver pot of coffee; I bolted down a muffin that Nathan had left for me in the staff kitchen), then we had half an hour in Mr Gopnik's study with Mr Gopnik's assistant, Michael, pencilling in the events Agnes would be attending that week.

Mr Gopnik's office was an exercise in studied masculinity: all dark panelled wood and loaded bookshelves. We sat in heavily upholstered chairs around a coffee table. Behind us, Mr Gopnik's oversized desk held a series of phones and bound notepads and periodically Michael begged Ilaria for more of her delicious coffee and she complied, saving her smiles for him alone.

We went over the likely contents of a meeting about the Gopniks' philanthropic foundation, a charity dinner on Wednesday, a memorial lunch and a cocktail reception on Thursday, an art exhibition and concert at the Metropolitan Opera at the Lincoln Center on Friday. 'A quiet week, then,' said Michael, peering at his iPad.

Today Agnes's diary showed she had a hair appointment at ten (these occurred three times a week), a dental appointment (routine cleaning) and an appointment with an interior decorator. She had a piano lesson at four (these took place twice a week), a spin class at five thirty, and then she would be out to dinner alone with Mr Gopnik at a restaurant in Midtown. I would finish at six thirty p.m.

The prospect of the day seemed to satisfy Agnes. Or perhaps it was the run. She had changed into indigo jeans and a white shirt, the collar of which revealed a large diamond pendant, and moved in a discreet cloud of perfume. 'All looks fine,' she said. 'Right. I have to make some calls.' She seemed to expect that I would know where to find her afterwards.

'If in doubt, wait in the hall,' whispered Michael, as she left. He smiled, the professional veneer briefly gone. 'When I started I never knew where to find them. Our job is to pop up when they think they need us. But not, you know, to stalk them all the way to the bathroom.'

He was probably not much older than I was, but he looked like one of those people who came out of the womb handsome, colour-coordinated and with perfectly polished shoes. I wondered if everyone in New York but me was like this. 'How long have you worked here?'

'Just over a year. They had to let go their old social secretary because . . .' He paused, seeming briefly uncomfortable. 'Well, fresh start and all that. And then after a while they decided it didn't work having one assistant for two of them. That's where you come in. So hello!' He held out his hand.

I shook it. 'You like it here?'

'I love it. I never know who I'm more in love with, him or her.' He grinned. 'He's just the smartest. And so handsome. And she's a doll.'

'Do you run with them?'

'Run? Are you kidding me?' He shuddered. 'I don't do sweating. Apart from with Nathan. Oh, my. I would sweat with him. Isn't he gorgeous? He offered to do my shoulder and I fell *instantly* in love. How on earth have you managed to work with him this long without jumping those delicious Antipodean bones?'

'I –'

'Don't tell me. If you've been there I don't want to know. We have to stay friends. Right. I need to get down to Wall Street.'

He gave me a credit card ('For emergencies – she forgets hers all the time. All statements go straight to him') and an electronic tablet, then showed me how to set up the pin code. 'All the contact numbers you need are here. And everything to do with the calendar is on here,' he said, scrolling down the screen with a forefinger. 'Each person is colour-coded – you'll see Mr Gopnik is blue, Mrs Gopnik is red, and Tabitha is yellow. We don't run her diary any more as she lives away from home but it's useful to know when she's likely to be here, and whether there are joint family commitments, like meetings of the trusts or the foundation. I've set you up a private email, and if there are changes you and I will communicate them with each other to back up any changes made on the screen. You have to double-check everything. Schedule clashes are the only thing guaranteed to make him mad.'

'Okay.'

'So you'll go through her post every morning, work out what she wants to attend. I'll cross-check with you, as sometimes there are things she says no to and he overrides her. So don't throw anything away. Just keep two piles.'

'How many invites are there?'

'Oh, you have no idea. The Gopniks are basically top tier. That means they get invited to everything and go to almost none of it. Second tier, you wish you were invited to half and go to everything you're invited to.'

'Third tier?'

'Crashers. Would go to the opening of a burrito truck. You get them even at society events.' He sighed. 'So embarrassing.'

I scanned the diary page, zooming in on this week, which

to me appeared to be a terrifying rainbow mess of colours. I tried not to look as daunted as I felt.

'What's brown?'

'That's Felix's appointments. The cat.'

'The cat has his own social diary?'

'It's just groomers, veterinary appointments, dental hygienists, that sort of thing. Ooh, no, he's got the behaviourist in this week. He must have been pooping on the Ziegler again.'

'And purple?'

Michael lowered his voice. 'The former Mrs Gopnik. If you see a purple block next to an event, that's because she will also be present.' He was about to say something else but his phone rang.

'Yes, Mr Gopnik . . . Yes. Of course . . . Yes, I will. Be right there.' He put his phone back in his bag. 'Okay. Gotta go. Welcome to the team!'

'How many of us are there?' I said, but he was already running out of the door, his coat over his arm.

'First Big Purple is in two weeks' time. Okay? I'll email you. And wear normal clothes when you're outside! Or you'll look like you work for Whole Foods.'

The day passed in a blur. Twenty minutes later we walked out of the building and into a waiting car that took us to a glossy salon a few blocks away, me trying desperately to look like the kind of person who spent her whole life getting in and out of large black cars with cream leather interiors. I sat at the edge of the room while Agnes had her hair washed and styled by a woman whose own hair appeared to have been cut with the aid of a ruler, and an hour later the car took us to the dental appointment where, again, I sat in the waiting room. Everywhere we went was hushed and tasteful and a world away from the madness on the street below.

I had worn one of my more sober outfits: a navy blouse with anchors on it and a striped pencil skirt, but I needn't have worried: at each place I became instantly invisible. It was as if I had 'STAFF' tattooed on my forehead. I started to notice the other personal assistants, pacing outside on cell-phones or racing back in with dry-cleaning and speciality coffees in cardboard holders. I wondered if I should be offering Agnes coffee, or officiously ticking things off lists. Most of the time I wasn't entirely sure why I was there. The whole thing seemed to run like clockwork without me. It was as if I were simply human armour – a portable barrier between Agnes and the rest of the world.

Back in the car, Agnes, meanwhile, was distracted, talking in Polish on her cell-phone or asking me to make notes on my tablet: 'We need to check with Michael that Leonard's grey suit was cleaned. And maybe call Mrs Levitsky about my Givenchy dress – I think I have lost a little weight since I last wear it. She maybe can take it in an inch.' She peered into her oversized Prada handbag, pulling out a plastic strip of pills from which she popped two into her mouth. 'Water?'

I cast around, finding one in the door pocket. I unscrewed it and handed it to her. The car stopped.

'Thank you.'

The driver – a middle-aged man with thick dark hair and jowls that wobbled as he moved – stepped out to open her door. When she disappeared into the restaurant, the doorman welcoming her like an old friend, I made to climb out behind her but the driver shut the door. I was left on the back seat.

I sat there for a minute, wondering what I was meant to do.

I checked my phone. I peered through the window, wondering if there were sandwich shops nearby. I tapped my foot. Finally I leant forward through the front seats. 'My dad used to leave me and my sister in the car when he went to the pub. He'd bring us out a Coke and a packet of pickled onion Monster Munch and that would be us sorted for three hours.' I tapped my knee with my fingers. 'You'd probably be done for child abuse now. Mind you, pickled onion Monster Munch was our absolute favourite. Best part of the week.'

The driver said nothing.

I leant forward a bit further, so that my face was inches from his.

'So. How long does this usually take?'

'As long as it takes.' His eyes slid away from mine in the mirror.

'And you wait here the whole time?'

'That's my job.'

I sat for a moment, then put my hand through to the front seat. 'I'm Louisa. Mrs Gopnik's new assistant.'

'Nice to meet you.'

He didn't turn around. Those were the last words he said to me. He slid a CD into the music system. *'Estoy perdido,'* said a Spanish woman's voice. *'¿Dónde está el baño?'*

'Ehs-TOY pehr-DEE-doh. DOHN-deh ehs-TA el BAH-neeo.' The driver repeated.

'¿Cuánto cuesta?'

'KooAN-to KWEHS-ta,' came his reply.

I spent the next hour sitting in the back of the car staring at the iPad, trying not to listen to the driver's linguistic exercises and wondering if I should also be doing something useful. I emailed Michael to ask but he simply responded: *That's your lunch break, sweetie. Enjoy!* xx

I didn't like to tell him I had no food. In the warmth of

41

the waiting car, tiredness began to creep over me again, like a tide. I laid my head against the window, telling myself it was normal to feel disjointed, out of my depth. *You're going to feel uncomfortable in your new world for a bit. It always does feel strange to be knocked out of your comfort zone.* Will's last letter echoed through me as if from a long distance.

And then nothing.

I woke with a start as the door opened. Agnes was climbing in, her face white, her jaw set.

'Everything okay?' I said, scrambling upright, but she didn't answer.

We drove off in silence, the still air of the interior suddenly heavy with tension.

She turned to me. I scrambled for a bottle of water and held it up to her.

'Do you have cigarettes?'

'Uh . . . no.'

'Garry, do you have cigarettes?'

'No, ma'am. But we can get you some.'

Her hand was shaking, I noticed now. She reached into her bag, pulling out a small bottle of pills and I handed over the water. She swigged some down and I noticed tears in her eyes. We pulled up outside a Duane Reade and, after a moment, I realized I was expected to get out. 'What kind? I mean, what brand?'

'Marlboro Lights,' she said, and dabbed her eyes.

I jumped out – well, more of a hobble, really, as my legs were seizing up from the morning's run – and bought a packet, thinking how odd it was to buy cigarettes from a pharmacy. When I got back into the car she was shouting at somebody in Polish on her cell-phone. She ended the call, then opened the window and lit a cigarette, inhaling deeply. She offered one to me. I shook my head.

'Don't tell Leonard,' she said, and her face softened. 'He hates me smoking.'

We sat there for a few minutes, the engine running, while she smoked the cigarette in short, angry bursts that made me fear for her lungs. Then she stubbed out the last inch, her lips curling over some internal fury, and waved for Garry to drive on.

I was left briefly to my own devices while Agnes had her piano lesson. I retreated to my room where I thought about lying down but was afraid that my stiff legs would mean I couldn't get up again so instead I sat at the little desk, wrote Sam a quick email and checked the calendar for the next few days.

As I did so, music began to echo through the apartment, first scales, then something melodic and beautiful. I stopped to listen, marvelling at the sound, wondering how it must feel to be able to create something so gorgeous. I closed my eyes, letting it flow through me, remembering the evening when Will had taken me to my first concert and begun to force the world open for me. Live music was so much more three-dimensional than recorded – it short-circuited something deep within. Agnes's playing seemed to come from some part of her that remained closed in her dealings with the world; something vulnerable and sweet and lovely. He would have enjoyed this, I thought absently. He would have loved being here. At the exact point it swelled into something truly magical, Ilaria started up the vacuum-cleaner, swamping the sound with a roar, the unforgiving bump of machinery into heavy furniture. The music stopped.

My phone buzzed.

Please tell her to stop the vacum!

I climbed off my bed and walked through the apartment until I found Ilaria, who was pushing the vacuum cleaner furiously just outside Agnes's study door, her head dipped as she wrenched it backwards and forwards. I swallowed. There was something about Ilaria that made you hesitate before confronting her, even though she was one of the few people in this zip code shorter than I was.

'Ilaria,' I said.

She didn't stop.

'Ilaria!' I stood in front of her until she was forced to notice. She kicked the off button with her heel and glared at me. 'Mrs Gopnik has asked if you would mind doing the vacuuming some other time. She can't hear her music lesson.'

'When does she think I am meant to clean the apartment?' Ilaria spat, loud enough to be heard through the door.

'Um . . . maybe at any other point during the day apart from this particular forty minutes . . . ?'

She pulled the plug from the socket and dragged the cleaner noisily across the room. She glared at me with such venom that I almost stepped backwards. There was a brief silence and the music started up again.

When Agnes finally emerged, twenty minutes later, she looked sideways at me and smiled.

That first week moved in fits and starts, like the first day, with me watching Agnes for signals in the way that Mum used to watch our old dog when her bladder got leaky. Does she need to go out? What does she want? Where should I be? I jogged with Agnes and George every morning, waving them on from about a mile in and motioning towards my hip before walking slowly back to the building. I spent a lot of time sitting in the hall, studying my iPad intently when anybody walked past, so that I might look as if I knew what I was doing.

Michael came every day and briefed me in whispered bursts. He seemed to spend his life on the run between the apartment and Mr Gopnik's Wall Street office, one of two cell-phones pressed to his ear, dry-cleaning over his arm, coffee in his hand. He was completely charming and always smiling, and I had absolutely no idea if he liked me at all.

I barely saw Nathan. He seemed to be employed to fit around Mr Gopnik's schedule. Sometimes he would work with him at five a.m., at others it was seven in the evening, disappearing to the office to help him there if necessary. 'I'm not employed for what I do,' Nathan explained. 'I'm employed for what I *can* do.' Occasionally he would vanish and I would discover that he and Mr Gopnik had jetted somewhere overnight – it could be San Francisco or Chicago. Mr Gopnik had a form of arthritis that he worked hard to keep under control so he and Nathan would swim or work out often several times each day to supplement his regime of anti-inflammatories and painkillers.

Alongside Nathan, and George the trainer, who also came every weekday morning, the other people who passed through the apartment that first week were:

– *The cleaners.* Apparently there was a distinction between what Ilaria did (housekeeping), and actual cleaning. Twice a week a team of three liveried women and one man blitzed their way through the apartment. They did not speak, except to consult briefly with each other. Each carried a large crate of eco-friendly cleaning materials, and they were gone three hours later, leaving Ilaria to sniff the air, and run her fingers along the skirting disapprovingly.
– *The florist,* who arrived in a van on Monday morning and brought enormous vases of arranged blooms to be placed at strategic intervals in the communal areas of the apartment. Several of the vases were so

large that it took two to carry them in. They removed their shoes at the door.

- *The gardener.* Yes, really. This at first made me slightly hysterical ('You do realize we're on the second floor?') until I discovered that the long balconies at the back of the building were lined with pots of miniature trees and blossoms, which the gardener would water, trim and feed before disappearing again. It did make the balcony look beautiful, but nobody ever went out there except me.
- *The pet behaviourist.* A tiny, birdlike Japanese woman appeared at ten a.m. on a Friday, watched Felix at a distance for an hour or so, then examined his food, his litter tray, the places he slept, quizzed Ilaria on his behaviour and advised on what toys he needed, or whether his scratching post was sufficiently tall and stable. Felix ignored her for the entire time she was there, breaking off only to wash his bottom with what seemed like almost insulting enthusiasm.
- *The grocery team* came twice a week and brought with them large green crates of fresh food, which they unpacked under Ilaria's supervision. I caught sight of the bill one day: it would have fed my family – and possibly half my postcode – for several months.

And that was without the manicurist, the dermatologist, the piano teacher, the man who serviced and cleaned the cars, the handyman who worked for the building and sorted out replacement light bulbs or faulty air-conditioning. There was the stick-thin redheaded woman who brought large shopping bags from Bergdorf Goodman or Saks Fifth Avenue and viewed everything Agnes tried on with a gimlet eye, stating: 'Nope. Nope. Nope. Oh, that's perfect, honey.

That's lovely. You want to wear that with the little Prada bag I showed you last week. Now, what are we doing about the Gala?'

There was the wine merchant and the man who hung the pictures and the woman who cleaned the curtains and the man who buffed the parquet floors in the main living room with a thing that looked like a lawnmower, and a few others besides. I simply got used to seeing people I didn't recognize wandering around. I'm not sure there was a single day in the first two weeks when there were fewer than five people in the apartment at any one time.

It was a family home in name only. It felt like a workspace for me, Nathan, Ilaria, and an endless team of contractors, staff and hangers-on who traipsed through it from dawn until late into the evening. Sometimes after supper a procession of Mr Gopnik's suited colleagues would stop by, disappear into his study and emerge an hour later muttering about calls to DC or Tokyo. He never really seemed to stop working, other than the time he spent with Nathan. Even at dinner his two phones were on the mahogany table, buzzing discreetly, like trapped wasps, as messages filed in.

I found myself watching Agnes sometimes as she closed the door to her dressing room in the middle of the day – presumably the only place she could disappear – and I would wonder, *When was this place ever just a home?*

This, I concluded, was why they disappeared at weekends. Unless the country residence had staff too.

'Nah. That's the one thing she's managed to sort her way,' said Nathan, when I asked him. 'She told him to give the ex their weekend place. In return she got him to downscale to a modest place on the beach. Three beds. One bathroom. No staff.' He shook his head. 'And therefore no Tab. She's not stupid.'

*

'Hey, you.'

Sam was in uniform. I did some mental calculations and worked out he had just finished his shift. He ran his hand through his hair, then leant forward, as if to see me better through the pixellated screen. A little voice said in my head, as it did every time I'd spoken to him since I'd left, *What are you doing moving to a different continent from this man?*

'You went in, then?'

'Yeah.' He sighed. 'Not the best first day back.'

'Why?'

'Donna quit.'

I couldn't hide my shock. Donna – straight-talking, funny, calm – was the yin to his yang, his anchor, his voice of sanity at work. It was impossible trying to imagine one without the other. 'What? Why?'

'Her dad got cancer. Aggressive. Incurable. She wants to be there for him.'

'Oh, God. Poor Donna. Poor Donna's dad.'

'Yeah. It's rough. And now I have to wait and see who they're going to pair me with. I don't think they'll put me with a rookie because of the whole disciplinary-issues thing. So I'm guessing it will be someone from another district.'

Sam had been up in front of the disciplinary committee twice since we had been together. I had been responsible for at least one of those and felt the reflexive twinge of guilt. 'You'll miss her.'

'Yup.' He looked a bit battered. I wanted to reach through the screen and hug him. 'She saved me,' he said.

He wasn't prone to dramatic statements, which somehow made those three words more poignant. I still remembered that night in bursts of terrifying clarity: Sam's gunshot wound bleeding out over the floor of the ambulance, Donna calm, capable, barking instructions at me, keeping that fragile thread unbroken until the other medics finally arrived. I could still taste fear, visceral and metallic, in my mouth, could still feel the obscene warmth of Sam's blood on my hands. I shivered, pushing the image aside. I didn't want Sam in the protection of anyone else. He and Donna were a team. Two people who would never let each other down. And who would probably rib each other mercilessly afterwards.

'When does she leave?'

'Next week. She got special dispensation, given her family circumstances.' He sighed. 'Still. On the bright side, your mum's invited me to lunch on Sunday. Apparently we're having roast beef and all the trimmings. Oh, and your sister asked me round to the flat. Don't look like that – she asked if I could help her bleed your radiators.'

'That's it now. You're in. My family have you like a Venus flytrap.'

'It'll be strange without you.'

'Maybe I should just come home.'

He tried to raise a smile and failed.

'What?'

'Nothing.'

'Go on.'

'I don't know . . . Feels like I just lost my two favourite women.'

A lump rose to my throat. The spectre of the third woman he'd lost – his sister, who had died of cancer two years previously – hung between us. 'Sam, you didn't lo–'

'Ignore that. Unfair of me.'

'I'm still yours. Just at a distance for a while.'

He blew out his cheeks. 'I didn't expect to feel it this badly.'

'I don't know whether to be pleased or sad now.'

'I'll be fine. Just one of those days.'

I sat there for a moment, watching him. 'Okay. So here's the plan. First you go and feed your hens. Because you always find watching them soothing. And nature is good for perspective and all that.'

He straightened up a little. 'Then what?'

'You make yourself one of those really great bolognese sauces. The ones that take for ever, with the wine and bacon and stuff. Because it's almost impossible to feel crap after eating a really great spaghetti bolognese.'

'Hens. Sauce. Okay.'

'And then you switch on the television and find a really good film. Something you can get lost in. No reality TV. Nothing with ads.'

'Louisa Clark's Evening Remedies. I'm liking this.'

'And then . . .' I thought for a moment. '. . . you think about the fact that it's only a little over three weeks until we see each other. And that means this! Ta-daa!' I pulled my top up to my neck.

With hindsight, it was a pity that Ilaria chose that exact moment to open my door and walk in with the laundry. She stood there, a pile of towels under one arm, and froze as she took in my exposed bosom, the man's face on the screen. Then she closed the door quickly, muttering something under her breath. I scrambled to cover myself up.

'What?' Sam was grinning, trying to peer to the right of the screen. 'What's going on?'

'The housekeeper,' I said, straightening my top. 'Oh, God.'

Sam had fallen back in his chair. He was properly laughing now, one hand clutching his stomach, where he still got a little protective about his scar.

'You don't understand. She hates me.'

'And now you're Madam Webcam.' He was still laughing.

'My name will be mud in the housekeeping community

from here to Palm Springs.' I wailed a bit longer, then started to giggle. Seeing Sam laugh so much it was hard not to.

He grinned at me. 'Well, Lou, you did it. You cheered me up.'

'The downside for you is that's the first and last time I show you my lady-bits over WiFi.'

Sam leant forward and blew me a kiss. 'Yeah, well,' he said. 'I guess we should just be grateful it wasn't the other way around.'

Ilaria didn't talk to me for two whole days after the webcam incident. She would turn away when I walked into a room, immediately finding something with which to busy herself, as if by merely catching her eye I might somehow contaminate her with my penchant for salacious boob exposure.

Nathan asked what had gone down between us, after she pushed my coffee towards me with an actual spatula, but I couldn't explain it without it sounding somehow worse than it was, so I muttered something about laundry and why we should have locks on our doors, and hoped that he would let it go.

4

To: KatClark!@yahoo.com
From: BusyBee@gmail.com

Hey, Stinky Arsebandit Yourself,

(Is that how a respected accountant is really meant to talk to her globetrotting sister?)

I'm good, thanks. My employer – Agnes – is my age and really nice. So that's been a bonus. You wouldn't believe the places I'm going – last night I went to a ball in a dress that cost more than I earn in a month. I felt like Cinderella. Except with a really gorgeous sister (yup, so that's a new one for me. Ha-ha-ha-ha!).

Glad Thom is enjoying his new school. Don't worry about the felt-tip thing – we can always paint that wall. Mum says it's a sign of his creative expression. Did you know she's trying to get Dad to go to night school to learn to express himself better? He's got it into his head this means she's going to get him to go tantric. God knows where he's read about that. I pretended like she'd told me that was definitely it when he called me, and now I'm feeling a bit guilty because he's panicking that he'll have to get his old fella out in front of a room full of strangers.

Write me more news. Especially about the date!!!

Miss you,
Lou xxx

According to Agnes's social diary, numerous events were highlights of the New York social calendar, but the Neil and Florence Strager Charitable Foundation Dinner teetered somewhere near the pinnacle. Guests wore yellow – the men in necktie form, unless particularly exhibitionist – and the resulting photographs were distributed in publications from the *New York Post* to *Harper's Bazaar*. Dress was formal, the yellow outfits were dazzling, and tickets cost a pocketful of small change under thirty thousand dollars a table. For the outer reaches of the room. I knew this because I had started researching each event that Agnes was due to attend, and this was a big one not just because of the amount of preparation (manicurist, hairdresser, masseur, extra George in the mornings) but because of Agnes's stress level. She physically vibrated through the day, shouting at George that she couldn't do the exercises he'd given her, couldn't run the distance. It was all *impossible*. George, who possessed an almost Buddha-like level of calm, said that was totally fine, they would walk back and the endorphins from the walk were all good. When he left he gave me a wink, as if this were entirely to be expected.

Mr Gopnik, perhaps in response to some distress call, came home at lunchtime and found her locked into her dressing room. I collected some dry-cleaning from Ashok and cancelled her teeth-whitening appointment, then sat in the hall, unsure what I should be doing. I heard her muffled voice as he opened the door: 'I don't want to go.'

Whatever she went on to say kept Mr Gopnik at home way after I might have expected. Nathan was out so I couldn't talk to him. Michael stopped by, peering around the door. 'Is he still here?' he said. 'My tracker stopped working.'

'Tracker?'

'On his phone. Only way I can work out where he is half the time.'

'He's in her dressing room.' I didn't know what else to say, how far to trust Michael. But it was hard to ignore the sound of raised voices. 'I don't think Mrs Gopnik is very keen on going out tonight.'

'Big Purple. I told you.'

And then I remembered.

'The former Mrs Gopnik. This was her big night, and Agnes knows it. Still is. All her old harpies will be there. They're not the friendliest.'

'Well, that explains a lot.'

'He's a big benefactor so he can't not show. Plus he's old friends with the Stragers. But it's one of the tougher nights of their calendar. Last year was a total wipe-out.'

'Why?'

'Aw. She walked in like a lamb to the slaughter.' He pulled a face. 'Thought they would be her new best friends. From what I heard afterwards, they *fried* her.'

I shuddered. 'Can she not just leave him to go by himself?'

'Oh, honey, you have no idea how it works here. No. No. No. She has to go. She has to put a smile on her face and be seen in the pictures. That's her job now. And she knows it. But it's not going to be pretty.'

The voices had risen. We heard Agnes protesting, then Mr Gopnik's softer voice, pleading, reasonable.

Michael looked at his watch. 'I'll head back to the office. Do me a favour? Text me when he leaves? I have fifty-eight things for him to sign before three p.m. Love ya!' He blew me a kiss and was gone.

I sat for a while longer, trying not to listen to the argument down the corridor. I scrolled through the calendar, wondering if there was anything I could do to be useful. Felix strolled past, his lifted tail a question mark, supremely unbothered by the actions of the humans around him.

And then the door opened. Mr Gopnik saw me. 'Ah, Louisa. Can you come in for a moment?'

I stood and half walked, half ran to where he was standing. It was difficult as running brought on muscle spasms.

'I wondered if you were free this evening.'

'Free?'

'To come to an event. For charity.'

'Uh . . . sure.' I had known from the start that the hours would not be regular. And at least it meant I wasn't likely to bump into Ilaria. I would download a movie onto one of the iPads and watch it in the car.

'There. What do you think, darling?' Agnes looked as if she had been crying. 'She can sit next to me?'

'I'll sort it out.'

She took a deep, shaky breath. 'Okay, then. I suppose so.'

'Sit next to . . .'

'Good. Good!' Mr Gopnik checked his phone. 'Right. I really have to go. I'll see you in the main ballroom. Seven thirty. If I can get through this conference call any sooner I'll let you know.' He stepped forward and took her face in his hands, kissing her. 'You're okay?'

'I'm okay.'

'I love you. Very much.' Another kiss, and he was gone.

Agnes took another deep breath. She put her hands on her knees, then looked up at me. 'You have a yellow ballgown?'

I stared at her. 'Um. Nope. Bit short on ballgowns, actually.'

She ran her gaze up and down me, as if trying to work out whether I could fit into anything she owned. I think we both knew the answer to that one. Then she straightened. 'Call Garry. We need to get to Saks.'

Half an hour later I was standing in a changing room while two shop assistants pushed my bosoms into a strapless dress the colour of unsalted butter. The last time I had been handled this intimately, I quipped, I had discussed getting engaged immediately afterwards. Nobody laughed.

Agnes frowned. 'Too bridal. And it makes her look thick around the waist.'

'That's because I am thick around the waist.'

'We do some very good corrective panties, Mrs Gopnik.'

'Oh, I'm not sure I –'

'Do you have anything more fifties-style?' said Agnes, flicking through her phone. 'Because this will pull in her waist and get around the height issue. We don't have time to take anything up.'

'When is your event, ma'am?'

'We have to be there seven thirty.'

'We can alter a dress for you in time, Mrs Gopnik. I'll get Terri to deliver it over to you by six.'

'Then let's try the sunflower yellow one there . . . and that one with the sequins.'

If I'd known that that afternoon would be the one time in my life I would be trying on three-thousand-dollar dresses, I might have made sure I wasn't wearing comedy knickers with a sausage dog on them and a bra that was held together with a safety pin. I wondered how many times in one week you could end up exposing your breasts to perfect strangers. I wondered if they had ever seen a body like mine before, with actual fatty bits. The shop assistants were far too polite to comment on it, beyond repeatedly offering 'corrective' underwear, but simply brought in dress after dress, wrestling me in and out, like someone wrangling livestock, until Agnes, sitting on an upholstered chair, announced, 'Yes! This is the one. What you think, Louisa? It is even perfect length for you with that tulle underskirt.'

I stared at my reflection. I wasn't sure who was staring back at me. My waist was nipped in by an inbuilt corset, my bosom hoisted upwards into a perfect embonpoint. The colour made my skin glow and the long skirt made me a foot taller and entirely unlike myself. The fact that I couldn't breathe was irrelevant.

'We will put your hair up and some earrings. Perfect.'

'And this dress is twenty per cent off,' said one of the shop assistants. 'We don't sell much yellow after the Strager event each year . . .'

I almost deflated with relief. And then I gazed at the label. The sale price was $2575. A month's wages. I think Agnes must have seen my bleached face, for she waved at one of the women. 'Louisa, you get changed. Do you have any shoes that will go? We can run to the shoe department?'

'I have shoes. Lots of shoes.' I had some gold satin-heeled dancing pumps, which would look fine. I did not want this bill going any higher.

I went back into the changing cubicle and climbed out of the dress carefully, feeling the weight of it fall expensively around me, and as I got dressed, I listened to Agnes and the assistants talking. Agnes summoned a bag and some earrings, gave them a cursory glance and was apparently satisfied. 'Charge it to my account.'

'Certainly, Mrs Gopnik.'

I met her at the cash desk. As we walked away, me clutching the bags, I said quietly, 'So do you want me to be extra careful?'

She looked at me blankly.

'With the dress.'

Still she looked blank.

I lowered my voice. 'At home we tuck the label in, then you can take it back the next day. You know, as long as there are no accidental wine stains and it doesn't stink too much of cigarettes. Maybe give it a quick squirt of Febreze.'

'Take it back?'

'To the shop.'

'Why we would do this?' she said, as we climbed back into the waiting car and Garry put the bags into the boot. 'Don't look so anxious, Louisa. You think I don't know how you feel? I have nothing when I come here. Me and my friends, we even shared our clothes. But you have to wear good dress when you sit next to me this evening. You can't wear your uniform. This evening you are not staff. And I am happy to pay for this.'

'Okay.'

'You understand. Yes? Tonight you have to not be staff. It's very important.'

I thought of the enormous carrier bag in the boot behind me as the car navigated its way slowly through the Manhattan traffic, a little dumbstruck at the direction this day was taking.

'Leonard says you looked after a man who died.'

'I did. His name was Will.'

'He says you have – discretion.'

'I try.'

'And also that you don't know anyone here.'

'Just Nathan.'

She thought about this. 'Nathan. I think he is a good man.'

'He really is.'

She studied her nails. 'You speak Polish?'

'No.' I added quickly: 'But maybe I could learn, if you –'

'You know what is difficult for me, Louisa?'

I shook my head.

'I don't know who I . . .' She hesitated, then apparently changed her mind about what she was going to say. 'I need you to be my friend tonight. Okay? Leonard . . . he will have to do his work thing. Always talking, talking with the men. But you will stay with me, yes? Right by me.'

'Whatever you want.'

'And if anybody ask, you are my old friend. From when I lived in England. We – we knew each other from school. Not my assistant, okay?'

'Got it. From school.'

That seemed to satisfy her. She nodded, and settled in her seat. She said nothing else the whole way back to the apartment.

The New York Palace Hotel, which held the Strager Foundation Gala, was so grand it was almost comical: a fairytale fortress, with a courtyard and arched windows, it was dotted with liveried footmen in daffodil silk knickerbockers. It was as if they had looked at every grand old hotel in Europe, taken notes about ornate cornicing, marble lobbies and fiddly bits of gilt and decided to add it all together, sprinkle some Disney fairy dust on it and ramp it up to camp levels all of its own. I half expected to see a pumpkin coach and the odd glass slipper on the red stair carpet. As we pulled up, I gazed into the glowing interior, the twinkling lights and sea of yellow dresses, and almost wanted to laugh, but Agnes was so tense I didn't dare. Plus my bodice was so tight I would probably have burst my seams.

Garry dropped us outside the main entrance, levering the car into a turning area thick with huge black limousines. We walked in past a crowd of onlookers on the sidewalk. A man took our coats, and for the first time Agnes's dress was fully visible.

She looked astonishing. Hers was not a conventional ballgown like mine, or like any of the other women's, but neon yellow, structured, a floor-length tube with one sculpted shoulder motif that rose up to her head. Her hair was scraped back unforgivingly, tight and sleek, and two enormous gold and yellow-diamond earrings hung from her ears. It should have looked extraordinary. But here, I realized with a faint drop to my stomach, it was somehow too much – out of place in the old-world grandeur of the hotel.

As she stood there, nearby heads swivelled, eyebrows lifting as the matrons in their yellow silk wraps and boned corsets viewed her from the corners of carefully made-up eyes.

Agnes appeared oblivious. She glanced around distractedly, trying to locate her husband. She wouldn't relax until she had hold of his arm. Sometimes I watched them together and saw an almost palpable sense of relief come over her when she felt him beside her.

'Your dress is amazing,' I said.

She looked down at me as if she had just remembered I was there. A flashbulb went off and I saw that photographers were moving among us. I stepped away to give Agnes space, but the man motioned towards me. 'You too, ma'am. That's it. And smile.' She smiled, her gaze flickering towards me as if reassuring herself I was still nearby.

And then Mr Gopnik appeared. He walked over a little stiffly – Nathan had said he was having a bad week – and kissed his wife's cheek. I heard him murmur something into her ear and she smiled, a sincere, unguarded smile. Their hands briefly clasped, and in that moment I noted that two people could fit all the stereotypes and yet there was something about them that was completely genuine, a delight in each other's presence. It made me feel suddenly wistful for Sam. But then I couldn't imagine him somewhere like this, trussed up in a dinner jacket and bow tie. He would, I thought absently, have hated it.

'Name, please?' The photographer appeared at my shoulder.

Perhaps it was thinking of Sam that made me do it. 'Um. Louisa Clark-Fielding,' I said, in my most strangulated upper-class accent. 'From England.'

'Mr Gopnik! Over here, Mr Gopnik!' I backed into the crowd as the photographers took pictures of them together, his hand resting lightly on his wife's back, her shoulders straight and chin up as if she could command the gathering. And then I saw him scan the room for me, his eyes meeting mine across the lobby.

He walked Agnes over. 'Darling, I have to talk to some people. Will you two be all right going in on your own?'

'Of course, Mr Gopnik,' I said, as if I did this kind of thing every day.

'Will you be back soon?' Agnes still had hold of his hand.

'I have to talk to Wainwright and Miller. I promised I'd give them ten minutes to go over this bond deal.'

Agnes nodded, but her face betrayed her reluctance to let him go. As she walked through the lobby Mr Gopnik leant in to me. 'Don't let her drink too much. She's nervous.'

'Yes, Mr Gopnik.'

He nodded, glanced around him as if deep in thought. Then he turned back to me and smiled. 'You look very nice.' And then he was gone.

The ballroom was jammed, a sea of yellow and black. I wore the yellow and black beaded bracelet Will's daughter Lily had given me before I'd left England – and thought privately how much I would have loved to wear my bumblebee tights too. These women didn't look like they'd had fun with their wardrobes their entire lives.

The first thing that struck me was how thin most of them were, hoicked into tiny dresses, clavicles poking out like safety rails. Women of a certain age in Stortfold tended to spread gently outwards, cloaking their extra inches in cardigans or long jumpers ('Does it cover my bum?') and paying lip service to looking good in the form of the occasional new mascara or a six-weekly haircut. In my hometown it was as if to pay too much attention to yourself was somehow suspect, or suggested unhealthy self-interest.

But the women in this ballroom looked as if they made their appearance a full-time job. There was no hair not perfectly coiffed into shape, no upper arm that was not toned into submission by some rigorous daily workout. Even the women of uncertain years (it was hard to tell, given the amount of Botox and fillers) looked as if they'd never heard of a bingo wing, let alone flapped one. I thought of Agnes, her personal trainer, her dermatologist, her hairdressing and manicurist appointments and thought, *This* is *her job now*. She has to do all that maintenance so she can turn up here and hold her own in this crowd.

Agnes moved slowly among them, her head high, smiling at her husband's friends, who came over to greet her and share a few words while I hovered uncomfortably in the background. The friends were always men. It was only men who smiled at her. The women, while not rude enough to walk away, tended to turn their faces discreetly, as if suddenly distracted by something in the distance, so that they didn't have to engage with her. Several times as we continued through the crowd, me walking behind her, I saw a wife's expression tighten, as if Agnes's presence was some kind of transgression.

'Good evening,' said a voice at my ear.

I looked up and stumbled backwards. Will Traynor stood beside me.

5

Afterwards I was glad that the room was so crowded because when I stumbled sideways into the man next to me he instinctively reached out a hand and, in an instant, several dinner-suited arms were righting me, a sea of faces, smiling, concerned. As I thanked them, apologizing, I saw my mistake. No, not Will – his hair was the same cut and colour, his skin that same caramel hue. But I must have gasped aloud because the man who was not Will said, 'I'm sorry, did I startle you?'

'I – no. No.' I put my hand to my cheek, my eyes locked on his. 'You – you just look like someone I know. Knew.' I felt my face flush, the kind of stain that starts at your chest and floods its way up to your hairline.

'You okay?'

'Oh, gosh. Fine. I'm fine.' I felt stupid now. My face glowed with it.

'You're English.'

'You're not.'

'Not even a New Yorker. Bostonian. Joshua William Ryan the Third.' He held out his hand.

'You even have his name.'

'I'm sorry?'

I took his hand. Close up, he was quite different from Will. His eyes were dark brown, his brow lower. But the similarities had left me completely unbalanced. I tore my gaze away from him, conscious that I was still hanging onto his fingers. 'I'm sorry. I'm a little . . .'

'Let me get you a drink.'

'I can't. I'm meant to be with my – my friend over there.'

He looked at Agnes. 'Then I'll get you both a drink. It'll be – uh – easy to find you.' He grinned and touched my elbow. I tried not to stare at him as he walked off.

As I approached Agnes, the man who had been talking to her was hauled away by his wife. Agnes lifted a hand as if she were about to say something in response to him and found herself talking to a broad expanse of dinner-jacketed back. She turned, her face rigid.

'Sorry. Got stuck in the crowds.'

'My dress is wrong, isn't it?' she whispered at me. 'I have made huge mistake.'

She had seen it. In the sea of bodies it looked somehow too bright, less avant-garde than vulgar. 'What am I going to do? Is disaster. I must change.'

I tried to calculate whether she could reasonably make it home and back. Even without traffic she would be gone an hour. And there was always the risk she might not come back . . .

'No! It's not a disaster. Not at all. It's just about . . .' I paused. 'You know, a dress like that, you have to style it out.'

'What?'

'Own it. Hold your head up. Like you couldn't give a crap.'

She stared at me.

'A friend once taught me this. The man I used to work for. He told me to wear my stripy legs with pride.'

'Your what?'

'He . . . Well, he was telling me it was okay to be different from everyone else. Agnes, you look about a hundred times better than any of the other women here. You're gorgeous. And the dress is striking. So just let it be a giant finger to them. You know? *I'll wear what I like.*'

She was watching me intently. 'You think so?'

'Oh, yes.'

She took a deep breath. 'You're right. I will be *giant finger.*' She straightened her shoulders. 'And no men care what dress you wear anyway, yes?'

'Not one.'

She smiled, gave me a knowing look. 'They just care what is underneath.'

'That's quite a dress, ma'am,' said Joshua, appearing at my side. He handed us each a slim glass. 'Champagne. The only yellow drink was Chartreuse and it made me feel kind of queasy just looking at it.'

'Thank you.' I took a glass.

He held out his hand to Agnes. 'Joshua William Ryan the Third.'

'You really *have* to have made up that name.'

They both turned to look at me.

'Nobody outside soap operas can actually be called that,' I said, and then realised I had meant to think it rather than say it aloud.

'Okay. Well. You can call me Josh,' he said equably.

'Louisa Clark,' I said, then added, 'The First.'

His eyes narrowed just a little.

'Mrs Leonard Gopnik. The Second,' said Agnes. 'But then you probably knew that.'

'I did indeed. You are the talk of the town.' His words could have landed hard, but he said it with warmth. I watched Agnes's shoulders relax a little.

Josh, he told us, was there with his aunt as her husband was travelling and she hadn't wanted to attend alone. He worked for a securities firm, talking to money managers and hedge funds about how best to manage risk. He specialized, he said, in corporate equity and debt.

'I don't have a clue what any of that means,' I said.

'Most days I don't either.'

He was being charming, of course. But suddenly the room felt a little less chilly. He was from Back Bay Boston, had just moved to what he described as a rabbit-hutch apartment in SoHo, and had put on two kilos since arriving in New York because the restaurants downtown were so good. He said a lot more, but I couldn't tell you what because I couldn't stop staring at him.

'And how about you, Miss Louisa Clark the First? What do you do?'

'I –'

'Louisa is a friend of mine. Just visiting from England.'

'And how are you finding New York?'

'I love it,' I said. 'I don't think my head has stopped spinning.'

'And the Yellow Ball is one of your first social engagements. Well, Mrs Leonard Gopnik the Second, you don't do things small.'

The evening was flying by, eased by a second glass of champagne. At dinner, I was placed between Agnes and a man who failed to give me his name and spoke to me only once, asking my breasts who they knew, then turning his back when it became clear that the answer was not very many people at all. I watched what Agnes drank, on Mr Gopnik's orders, and when I caught him looking at me I switched her full glass for my near-empty one, feeling relief when his subtle smile signalled approval. Agnes talked too loudly to the man on her right, her laugh a little too high, her gestures brittle and fluttery. I watched the other women at the table, all of them forty and above, and saw the way they looked at her, their eyes sliding heavily towards each other, as if to confirm some dark opinion expressed in private. It was horrible.

Mr Gopnik could not reach her from his position across the table, but I saw his eyes flickering towards her frequently, even as he smiled and shook hands and appeared, on the surface, to be the most relaxed man on the planet.

'Where is she?'

I leant in to hear Agnes more clearly.

'Leonard's ex-wife. Where is she? You have to find out, Louisa. I can't relax until I know. I can *feel* her.'

Big Purple. 'I'll check the place settings,' I said, and excused myself from the table.

I stood at the huge printed stand at the entrance to the dining room. There were around eight hundred closely printed names and I didn't know if the first Mrs Gopnik even went by Gopnik anymore. I swore under my breath just as Josh appeared behind me.

'Lost someone?'

I lowered my voice. 'I need to find out where the first Mrs Gopnik is seated. Would you happen to know if she goes by her old name? Agnes would like . . . to have an idea where she is.'

He frowned.

'She's a little stressed,' I added.

'No idea, I'm afraid. But my aunt might. She knows every-one. Stay right here.' He touched my bare shoulder lightly and strode off into the dining room, while I tried to re-arrange my facial expression into that of someone who was scanning the board to confirm the presence of half a dozen close friends, not someone whose skin had just coloured an unexpected shade of pink.

He was back within a minute.

'She's still Gopnik,' he said. 'Aunt Nancy thinks she might have seen her over by the auction table.' He ran a manicured finger down the list of names. 'There. Table 144. I walked past to check and there's a woman who fits her description. Fifty-something, dark hair, shooting poison darts from a Chanel evening bag? They've put her about as far away from Agnes as they could.'

'Oh, thank God,' I said. 'She'll be so relieved.'

'They can be pretty scary, these New York matrons,' he said. 'I don't blame Agnes for wanting to watch her back. Is English society this cut-throat?'

'English society? Oh, I don't – I'm not very big on society events,' I said.

'Me either. To be honest, I'm so worn out after work that most days it's all I can do to pick up a takeout menu. What is it you do, Louisa?'

'Um . . .' I glanced abruptly at my phone. 'Oh, gosh. I have to get back to Agnes.'

'Will I see you before you go? Which table are you at?'

'Thirty-two,' I said, before I could think about all the reasons I shouldn't.

'Then I'll see you later.' I was briefly transfixed by Josh's smile. 'I meant to say, by the way, you look beautiful.' He leant forward, and lowered his voice so that it rumbled a little by my ear. 'I actually prefer your dress to your friend's. Did you take a picture yet?'

'A picture?'

'Here.' He held up his hand, and before I worked out what he was doing, he had taken a photograph of the two of us, our heads inches apart. 'There. Give me your number and I'll send it to you.'

'You want to send me a picture of you and me together.'

'Are you sensing my ulterior motive?' He grinned. 'Okay, then. I'll keep it for myself. A memento of the prettiest girl here. Unless you want to delete it. There you go. Yours to delete.' He held out his phone.

I peered at it, my finger hovering over the button before I withdrew it. 'It seems rude to delete someone you've just met. But, um . . . thank you . . . and for the whole covert table-surveillance thing. Really kind of you.'

'My pleasure.'

We grinned at each other. And before I could say anything more I ran back to the table.

I gave Agnes the good news – at which she let out an audible sigh – then sat and ate a bit of my now-cold fish while waiting for my head to stop buzzing. *He's not Will*, I told myself. His voice was wrong. His eyebrows were wrong. He was American. And yet there was something in his manner – the confidence combined with sharp intelligence, the air that said he could cope with anything you threw at him, a way of looking at you that left me hollowed out. I glanced behind me, remembering I hadn't asked Josh where he was seated.

'Louisa?'

I glanced to my right. Agnes was looking intently at me.

'I need to go to the bathroom.'

It took me a minute to recall that this meant I should go too.

We walked slowly through the tables to the Ladies, me trying not to scan the room for Josh. All eyes were on Agnes as she went, not just because of the vivid colour of her dress but because she had magnetism, an unconscious way of drawing the eye. She walked with her chin up, her shoulders back, a queen.

And the moment we got into the Ladies, she slumped onto the chaise longue in the corner and gestured to me to give her a cigarette. 'My God. This evening. I may die if we don't leave soon.'

The attendant – a woman in her sixties – raised an eyebrow at the cigarette, then looked the other way.

'Er – Agnes, I'm not sure you can smoke in here.'

She was going to do it anyway. Perhaps when you were rich you didn't care about other people's rules. What could they do to her after all – throw her out?

She lit it, inhaled and sighed with relief. 'Ugh. This dress is so uncomfortable. And the G-string is cutting me like cheese-wire, you know?' She wriggled in front of the mirror, hauling up her dress and rummaging underneath it with a manicured hand. 'I should have worn no underwear.'

'But you feel okay?' I said.

She smiled at me. 'I feel okay. Some people have been very nice this evening. This Josh is very nice, and Mr Peterson on other side of me is very friendly. It's not so bad. Maybe finally some people are accepting that Leonard has a new wife.'

'They just need time.'

'Hold this. I need to pee-pee.' She handed me the half-smoked cigarette and disappeared into a cubicle. I held it up between two fingers, as if it were a sparkler. The cloakroom attendant and I exchanged a look and she shrugged, as if to say, *What can you do?*

'Oh, my God,' Agnes said, from inside the cubicle. 'I will need to take whole thing off. Is impossible to pull it up. You will need to help me with zipper afterwards.'

'Okay,' I said. The attendant raised her eyebrows. We both tried not to giggle.

Two middle-aged women entered the cloakroom. They looked at my cigarette with disapproval.

'The thing is, Jane, it's like a madness takes hold of them,' one said, stopping in front of the mirror to check her hair. I wasn't sure why she needed to: it was so heavily lacquered I'm not sure a force-ten hurricane would have dislodged it.

'I know. We've seen it a million times.'

'But normally at least they've got the decency just to handle it discreetly. And that's what's been so disappointing for Kathryn. The lack of discretion.'

'Yes. It would be so much easier for her if it had at least been someone with a little class.'

'Quite. He's behaved like a cliché.'

At this both women's heads swivelled to me.

'Louisa?' came a muffled voice from inside the cubicle. 'Can you come here?'

I knew then who they were talking about. I knew just from looking at their faces.

There was a short silence.

'You do realize this is a non-smoking venue,' one of the women said pointedly.

'Is it? So sorry.' I stubbed it out in the sink then ran some water over the end.

'You can help me, Louisa? My zipper is stuck.'

They knew. They put two and two together and I saw their faces harden.

I walked past them, knocked twice on the cubicle door and she let me in.

Agnes was standing in her bra, the tubular yellow dress stalled around her waist.

'What —' she began.

I put my fingers to my lips and gestured silently outside. She looked over, as if she could see through the door, and pulled a face. I turned her around. The zipper, two-thirds down, was lodged at her waist. I tried it two, three times, then pulled my phone from my evening bag and turned on the torch, trying to work out what was stopping it.

'You can fix this?' she whispered.

'I'm trying.'

'You must. I can't go out like this in front of those women.'

Agnes stood inches from me in a tiny bra, her pale flesh giving off warm waves of expensive perfume. I tried to manoeuvre around her, squinting at the zip, but it was impossible. She needed room to take the thing off so I could work on the zip or I couldn't do it up. I looked at her and shrugged. She looked briefly anguished.

'I don't think I can do it in here, Agnes. There's no room. And I can't see.'

'I can't go out like this. They will say I am whore.' Her hands flew to her face, despairing.

The oppressive silence outside told me the women were waiting on our next move. Nobody was even pretending to go to the loo. We were stuck. I stood back and shook my head, thinking. And then it came to me.

'Giant finger,' I whispered.

Her eyes widened.

I gazed at her steadily, and gave a small nod. She frowned, and then her face cleared.

I opened the cubicle door and stood back. Agnes took a breath, straightened her spine, then strolled out past the two women, like a backstage supermodel, the top of the dress around her waist, her bra two delicate triangles that barely obscured the pale breasts underneath. She stopped in the middle of the room and leant forwards so that I could ease the dress carefully over her head. Then she straightened up, now naked except for her two scraps of lingerie, a study in apparent insouciance. I dared not look at the women's faces, but as I draped the yellow dress over my arm I heard the dramatic intake of breath, felt the reverberations in the air.

'*Well*, I –' one began.

'Would you like a sewing kit, ma'am?' The attendant appeared at my side. She worked the little packet open while

Agnes sat daintily on the chaise longue, her long pale legs stretched demurely out to the side.

Two more women walked in, and their conversation stopped abruptly at the sight of the nearly-naked Agnes. One coughed, and they looked studiedly away from her, stumbling over some new conversational platitude. Agnes rested on the chair, apparently blissfully unaware.

The attendant handed me a pin, and using its point I caught the tiny scrap of thread that had entangled itself, tugging gently until I had freed it and the zip moved again. 'Got it!'

Agnes stood, held the attendant's proffered hand and stepped elegantly back into the yellow dress, which the two of us raised around her body. When it was in place I pulled the zip smoothly up until she was clad, every inch of the dress flush against her skin. She smoothed it down around her endless legs.

The attendant proffered a can of hairspray. 'Here,' she whispered. 'Allow me.' She leant forward and gave the fastening a quick spray from the can. 'That'll help it stay up.'

I beamed at her.

'Thank you. So kind of you,' Agnes said. She pulled a fifty-dollar bill from her evening bag and handed it to the woman. Then she turned to me with a smile. 'Louisa, darling, shall we go back to our table?' And, with an imperious nod to the two women, Agnes lifted her chin and walked slowly towards the door.

There was silence. Then the attendant turned to me, and pocketed the money with a wide grin. 'Now *that*,' she said, her voice suddenly audible, 'is *class*.'

6

The following morning, George didn't come. Nobody told me. I sat in the hall in my shorts, bleary and gritty-eyed, and at half seven grasped that he must have been cancelled.

Agnes did not get up until after nine, a fact that had Ilaria tutting disapprovingly at the clock. She had sent a text asking me to cancel the rest of her day's appointments. Instead, some time around mid-morning, she said she'd like to walk around the Reservoir. It was a breezy day and we walked with scarves pulled up around our chins and our hands thrust into our pockets. All night I had thought about Josh's face. I still felt unbalanced by it, found myself wondering how many of Will's doppelgängers were walking around in different countries right now. Josh's eyebrows were heavier, his eyes a different colour, and obviously his accent wasn't Will's. But still.

'You know what I used to do with my friends when we were hungover?' said Agnes, breaking into my thoughts. 'We would go to this Japanese place near Gramercy Park and we would eat noodles and talk and talk and talk.'

'Let's go, then.'

'Where?'

'To the noodle place. We can pick up your friends on the way.'

She looked briefly hopeful, then kicked a stone. 'I can't now. Is different.'

'You don't have to turn up in Garry's car. We could get a taxi. I mean, you could dress down, just turn up. It would be fine.'

'I told you. Is different.' She turned to me. 'I tried these things, Louisa. For a while. But my friends are curious. They want to know everything about my life now. And then when I tell them the truth it makes them . . . weird.'

'Weird?'

'Once we were all the same, you know? Now they say I can never know what their problems are. Because I am rich. Somehow I am not allowed to have problems. Or they are strange around me, like I am somehow different person. Like the good things in my life are an insult to theirs. You think I can moan about housekeeper to someone with no house?'

She stopped on the path. 'When I first marry Leonard, he gave me money for my own. A wedding present, so that I don't have to ask him for money all the time. And I give my best friend, Paula, some of this money. I give her ten thousand dollars to clear her debts, to make fresh start. At first she was so happy. I was happy too! To do this for my friend! So she doesn't have to worry any more, like me!' Her voice grew wistful. 'And then . . . then she didn't want to see me any more. She was different, was always too busy to meet me. And slowly I see she resents me for helping her. She didn't mean to, but when she sees me now all she can think is that she owes me. And she is proud, very proud. She does not want to live with this feeling. So . . .' she shrugged '. . . she won't have lunch with me or take my calls. I lost my friend because of money.'

'Problems are problems,' I said, when it became clear she was expecting me to say something. 'Doesn't matter whose they are.'

She stepped sideways to avoid a toddler on a scooter. She gazed after it, thinking, then turned to me. 'You have cigarettes?'

I had learnt now. I pulled the packet from my backpack and handed it to her. I wasn't sure I should be encouraging her to smoke, but she was my boss. She inhaled and blew out a long plume of smoke.

'Problems are problems,' she repeated slowly. 'You have problems, Louisa Clark?'

'I miss my boyfriend.' I said it as much as anything to re-assure myself. 'Apart from that, not really. This is . . . great. I'm happy here.'

She nodded. 'I used to feel like this. New York! Always something to see new. Always exciting. Now I just . . . I miss . . .' She tailed off.

For a moment I thought her eyes had filled with tears. But then her face stilled.

'You know she hates me?'

'Who?'

'Ilaria. The witch. She was the other one's housekeeper and Leonard will not sack her. So I am stuck with her.'

'She might grow to like you.'

'She might grow to put arsenic in my food. I see the way she looks at me. She wishes me dead. You know how it feels to live with someone who wishes you dead?'

I was pretty scared of Ilaria myself. But I didn't want to say so. We walked on. 'I used to work for someone who I was pretty sure hated me at first,' I said. 'Gradually I worked out that it was nothing to do with me. He just hated his life. And as we got to know each other we started to get along just fine.'

'Did he ever scorch your best shirt "accidentally"? Or put detergent in your underwear that he knew would make your vajajay itch?'

'Uh – no.'

'Or serve food that you tell him fifty times you do not like so you will look like you are complaining all the time? Or tell stories about you to make you seem like prostitute?'

My mouth had opened like that of a goldfish. I closed it and shook my head.

She pushed her hair off her face. 'I love him, Louisa. But

living in his life is impossible. My life is impossible . . .' Again she tailed off.

We stood, watching the people passing us on the path: the roller-bladers and the kids on wobbling scooters, the couples arm in arm and the policemen in their shades. The temperature had dropped and I gave an involuntary shiver in my tracksuit top.

She sighed. 'Okay. We go back. Let's see which piece of my favourite clothing the witch has ruined today.'

'No,' I said. 'Let's get your noodles. We can do that much at least.'

We took a taxi to Gramercy Park, to a place in a brownstone on a shady side-street that looked grubby enough to harbour some terrible intestinal bug. But Agnes seemed lighter almost as soon as we arrived. As I paid the taxi she bounded up the stairs and into the darkened interior, and when the young Japanese woman emerged from the kitchen she threw her arms round Agnes and hugged her, as if they were old friends. Then, holding Agnes by the elbow, she kept demanding to know where she had been. Agnes pulled off her beanie and muttered vaguely that she had been busy, got married, moved house, never once giving any clue to the true level of change in her circumstances. I noticed she was wearing her wedding ring but not the diamond engagement ring that was large enough to ensure a triceps workout.

And when we slid into the Formica booth, it was like I had a different woman opposite me. Agnes was funny, animated and loud, with an abrupt, cackling laugh, and I could see who Mr Gopnik had fallen in love with.

'So how did you meet?' I asked, as we slurped our way through scalding bowls of ramen.

'Leonard? I was his masseuse.' She paused, as if waiting for my scandalized reaction, and when it didn't come she put her head down and continued, 'I worked at the St Regis. And they would send masseur to his home every week – André, usually. He was very good. But André was sick this day and they ask me to go instead. And I think, *Oh, no, another Wall Street guy.* They are, so many of them, full of bullshit, you know? They don't even think of you as human. Don't bother saying hello, don't speak . . . Some, they ask for . . .' she lowered her voice '. . . happy finish. You know "happy finish"? Like you are prostitute. Ugh. But Leonard, he was kind. He shake my hand, ask me if I want English tea as soon as I come in. He was so happy when I massage him. And I could tell.'

'Tell what?'

'That she never touch him. His wife. You can tell, touching a body. She was cold, cold woman.' She looked down. 'And he is in a lot of pain some days. His joints hurt him. This is before Nathan came. Nathan was my idea. To keep Leonard fit and healthy? But anyway. I really try hard to make this good massage for him. I go over my hour. I listen to what his body is telling me. And he was so grateful after. And then he asks for me the next week. André was not so happy about this, but what can I do? So then I am going twice a week to his apartment. And some days he would ask me if I would like English tea afterwards and we talk. And then . . . Well, it is hard. Because I know I am falling in love with him. And this is something we cannot do.'

'Like doctors and patients. Or teachers.'

'Exactly.' Agnes paused to put a dumpling into her mouth. It was the most I had ever seen her eat. She chewed for a moment. 'But I cannot stop thinking about this man. So sad. And so tender. And so lonely! In the end I tell André he must go instead. I cannot go any more.'

'And what happened?' I'd stopped eating.

'Leonard comes to my home! In Queens! He somehow gets my address and his big car comes to my home. My friends and I, we are sitting on the fire escape having cigarette and I see him get out and he says, "I want to talk to you".'

'Like *Pretty Woman*.'

'Yes! It is! And I go down to the sidewalk and he is so mad. He say, "Did I offend you in some way? Did I treat you inappropriately?" And I just shake my head. And then he walks up and down and he say, "Why won't you come? I don't want André any more. I want you." And, like a fool, I start to cry.'

As I watched, her eyes brimmed with tears.

'I cry right there in the middle of the day on the street, with my friends watching. And I say, "I can't tell you." And then he gets mad. Wants to know if his wife was rude to me. Or whether something has happened at work. And then finally I tell him, "I can't come because I like you. I like you very much. And this is very unprofessional. And I can lose my job." And he looks at me for one moment and he says nothing. Nothing at all. And then he gets back in his car and his driver takes him away. And I think, *Oh, no. Now I will never see this man again, and I have lost my job*. And I go to work the next day and I am so nervous. So nervous, Louisa. My stomach hurts!'

'Because you thought he'd tell your boss.'

'Exactly this. But you know what happened when I arrive?'

'What?'

'Enormous bouquet of red roses is waiting for me. Biggest I have ever seen, with beautiful velvet scented roses. So soft you want to touch them. No name on it. But I know immediately. And then every day a new bouquet of red roses. Our apartment is filled with roses. My friends say they are sick from the smell.' She started to laugh. 'And then on the last day he comes to my house again and I go down and he asks

79

me to get in the car with him. And we sit in the back and he asks the driver to go for a walk and he tells me he is so unhappy and that from the moment we met he could not stop thinking about me and that all I have to say is one word and he will leave his wife and we will be together.'

'And you hadn't even kissed?'

'Nothing. I have massaged his buttocks, sure, but is not the same.' She breathed out, savouring the memory. 'And I knew. I knew we must be together. And I said it. I said, "Yes."'

I was transfixed.

'That night he goes home and he tells his wife that he does not want to be married any more. And she is mad. *So* mad. And she ask him why and he tells her he cannot live in marriage with no love. And that night he calls me up from hotel and asks me to come meet him and we are in this suite at the Ritz Carlton. You stayed at Ritz Carlton?'

'Uh – no.'

'I walk in and he is standing by the door, like he is too nervous to sit down, and he tells me he knows he is stereotype and he is too old for me and his body is wrecked from this arthritis but if there is a chance I really do want to be with him he will do everything he can to make me happy. Because he just has feeling about us, you know? That we are soulmates. And then we hold each other and finally we kiss, and then we stay awake all night, talking, talking about our childhoods and our lives and our hopes and dreams.'

'This is the most romantic story I've ever heard.'

'And then we fuck, of course, and my God, I can feel that this man has been frozen for years, you know?'

At this point I coughed a piece of ramen onto the table. When I looked up several people at nearby tables were watching us.

Agnes's voice lifted. She gesticulated into the air. 'You cannot believe it. It is like a hunger in him, like all this hunger from years and years is just *pulsing* through him. *Pulsing!* That first night he is *insatiable.*'

'Okay,' I squeaked, wiping my mouth with a paper napkin.

'It is magical, this meeting of our bodies. And afterwards we just hold each other for hours and I wrap myself around him and he lays his head on my breasts and I promise him he will never be frozen again. You understand?'

There was silence in the restaurant. Behind Agnes, a young man in a hooded top was staring at the back of her head, his spoon raised halfway to his mouth. When he saw me watching, he dropped it with a clatter.

'That – that's a really lovely story.'

'And he keeps his promise. Everything he says is true. We are happy together. So happy.' Her face fell a little. 'But his daughter hates me. His ex-wife hates me. She blames me for everything, even though she did not love him. She tells everyone I am a bad person for stealing her husband.'

I didn't know what to say.

'And every week I have to go to these fundraisers and cocktail evenings and smile and pretend I do not know what they are saying about me. The way these women look at me. I am not what they say I am. I speak four languages. I play piano. I did special diploma in therapeutic massage. You know what language she speaks? *Hypocrisy.* But it is hard to pretend you have no pain, you know? Like you do not care?'

'People change,' I said hopefully. 'Over time.'

'No. I don't think is possible.'

Agnes's expression was briefly wistful. Then she shrugged. 'But on bright side, they are quite old. Maybe some of them will die soon.'

That afternoon I called Sam when Agnes was taking a nap and Ilaria was busy downstairs. My head was still swimming with the previous evening's events, and with Agnes's confidences. I felt as if somehow I had moved into a new space. *I feel like you are more my friend than my assistant*, she had told me, as we walked back to the apartment. *It is so good to have somebody I can trust.*

'I got your pictures,' he said. It was evening there, and Jake, his nephew, was staying over. I could hear his music playing in the background. He moved his mouth closer to the phone. 'You looked beautiful.'

'I'll never wear a dress like that again in my life. But the whole thing was amazing. The food and the music and the ballroom ... and the weirdest thing is these people don't even notice it. They don't see what's around them! There was one entire wall made of gardenias and fairy lights. Like, a massive wall! And there was the most amazing chocolate pudding – a fondant square with white chocolate feathers on it and tiny truffles on the outside and not one woman ate hers. Not one! I walked the whole way around the tables counting, just to check. I was tempted to put some of the truffles in my clutch bag, but I thought they might melt. I bet they just threw the whole lot away. Oh, and every table had a different decoration – but they were all made of yellow feathers, and shaped like different birds. We had an owl.'

'Sounds like quite an evening.'

'There was this one barman who would make cocktails based on your character. You had to tell him three things about yourself and then he would create one.'

'Did he make one for you?'

'No. The guy I was talking to got a Salty Dog and I was afraid I'd get a Corpse Reviver or a Slippery Nipple or something. So I just stuck with champagne. Stuck with champagne! What do I sound like?'

'So who were you talking to?'

There was just the slightest pause before he said it. And, to my annoyance, just the slightest pause before I responded. 'Oh . . . just this guy . . . Josh. A suit. He was keeping me and Agnes company while we waited for Mr Gopnik to come back.'

Another pause. 'Sounds great.'

I started to gabble now. 'And the best bit is, you never even have to worry about how to get home because there's always a car outside. Even when they just go to the shops. The driver just pulls up outside, then waits, or drives around the block, and you walk out and ta-daa! There's your big black shiny car. Climb in. Put all your bags in the boot. Except they call it a trunk. No night bus! No late-night tube with people puking on your shoes.'

'The high life, eh? You won't want to come home.'

'Oh. No. It's not like it's *my* life. I'm just a hanger-on. But it's quite something to see up close.'

'I have to go, Lou. Promised Jake I'd take him out for a pizza.'

'But – but we've hardly spoken. What's going on with you? Tell me your news.'

'Some other time. Jake's hungry.'

'Okay!' My voice was too high. 'Say hi to him for me!'

'Okay.'

'I love you,' I said.

'Me too.'

'One more week! Counting the days.'

'Gotta go.'

I felt strangely wrong-footed when I put the phone down. I didn't quite understand what had just happened. I sat there motionless on the side of my bed. And then I looked at Josh's business card. He had handed it to me as we left, pressing it into my palm and closing my fingers around it.

Give me a call. I'll show you some cool places.

I had taken it and smiled politely. Which, of course, could have meant anything at all.

7

Fox's Cottage
Tuesday, 6 October

Dear Louisa,

I hope you are well and enjoying your time in New York. I believe Lily is writing to you, but I was thinking after our last conversation and I had a look in the loft and brought down some letters of Will's from his time in the city that I thought you might enjoy. You know what a great traveller he was and I thought you might enjoy retracing his footsteps.

I read a couple myself; a rather bittersweet experience. You can keep hold of them until we next see each other.

With fondest wishes,
Camilla Traynor

New York
12.6.2004

Dear Mum,

I would have called but the time difference doesn't really fit around schedules here, so I thought I'd shock you by writing. First letter since that short-lived stint at Priory Manor, I think. I wasn't really cut out for boarding school, was I?

New York is pretty amazing. It's impossible not to be infused by the energy of the place. I'm up and out by five thirty every morning.

My firm is based on Stone Street down in the Financial District.
Nigel fixed me up with an office (not corner but a good view across the
water – apparently these are the things by which we are judged in
NY) and the guys at work seem a good bunch. Tell Dad that on
Saturday I went to the opera at the Met with my boss and his
wife – (Der Rosenkavalier, bit overdone) and you'll be happy to hear
I went to a performance of Les Liaisons Dangereuses. Lot of client
lunches, lot of company softball. Not so much in the evenings: my new
colleagues are mostly married with young children so it's just me
trawling the bars . . .

I've been out with a couple of girls – nothing serious (here they
seem to 'date' as a pastime) – but mostly I've just spent my spare
hours at the gym or hanging out with old friends. Lots of people here
from Shipmans, and a few I knew at school. Turns out it's a small
world, after all . . . Most of them are quite changed here, though.
They're tougher, hungrier than I remember. Think the city brings that
out in you.

Right! Off out with Henry Farnsworth's daughter this even-
ing. Remember her? Leading light of the Stortfold Pony Club?
Has reinvented herself as some sort of shopping guru. (Don't get
your hopes up, I'm just doing it as a favour to Henry.) I'm
taking her to my favourite steakhouse, on the Upper East
Side: slabs of meat the size of a gaucho's blanket. I'm hoping
she's not vegetarian. Everyone here seems to have some sort of
food fad going on.

Oh, and last Sunday I took the F train and got off on the far
side of the Brooklyn Bridge just to walk back across the water, as
you suggested. Best thing I've done so far. Felt like I'd stepped
into an early Woody Allen movie – you know, the ones where
there was only a ten-year age gap between him and his leading
ladies . . .

Tell Dad I'll call him next week, and give the dog a hug for me.
Love, W x

With that bowl of cheap noodles, something had changed in my relationship with the Gopniks. I think I grasped a little better that I could bolster Agnes in her new role. She needed someone to lean on and to trust. This, and the strange osmotic energy of New York, meant that from then on I literally bounced out of bed in a way that I hadn't done since working for Will. It caused Ilaria to tut and roll her eyes and Nathan to view me sideways, as if I might have started taking drugs.

But it was simple. I wanted to be good at my job. I wanted to get the absolute most out of my time in New York, working for these amazing people. I wanted to suck the marrow out of each day, as Will would have done. I read that first letter again and again, and once I'd got over the strangeness of hearing his voice, I felt an unexpected kinship with him, a newcomer to the city.

I upped my game. I jogged with Agnes and George every morning, and some days I even managed to last the entire route without wanting to throw up. I got to know the places that Agnes's routines took her to, what she was likely to need to have with her, and wear, and bring home. I was ready in the hallway before she was there, and had water, cigarettes or green juice ready for her almost before she knew she wanted them. When she had to go to a lunch where the Awful Matrons were likely to be, I would make jokes beforehand to shake her out of her nerves, and I would send her cell-phone GIFs of farting pandas or people falling off trampolines to pick up during the meal. I was there in the car afterwards and listened to her when she told me tearfully what they had said or not said to her, nodded sympathetically or agreed that, yes, they were *impossible, mean creatures. Dried-up like sticks. No heart left in them.*

I became good at maintaining my poker face when Agnes told me slightly too much about Leonard's beautiful,

beautiful body, and his many, many *beeeyoootiful* skills as a lover, and I tried not to laugh when she told me Polish words, such as *cholernica,* with which she insulted Ilaria without the housekeeper understanding.

Agnes, I discovered quite quickly, had no filter. Dad always said I used to say the first thing that came into my head, but in my case it wasn't *Bitter old whore!* in Polish, or *Can you imagine that horrible Susan Fitzwalter getting waxed? Would be like scraping the beard off a closed mussel. Brr.*

It wasn't that Agnes was mean *per se.* I think she felt under such pressure to behave in a certain way, to be seen and scrutinized and not found wanting, that I became a kind of safety valve. The moment she was out of their company she would swear and curse, and then by the time Garry had driven us home she would have recovered her equanimity in time to see her husband.

I developed strategies to reintroduce a little fun into Agnes's life. Once a week, without putting it into the diary, we would disappear to the movie theatre on Lincoln Square in the middle of the day to watch silly, gross-out comedies, snorting with laughter as we shovelled popcorn into our mouths. We would dare each other to go into the high end boutiques of Madison Avenue and try on the worst designer outfits we could find, admiring each other straight-faced, and asking, *Do you have this in a brighter green?* while the sales assistants, one eye on Agnes's Hermès Birkin handbag, fluttered around, forcing compliments from the sides of their mouths. One lunchtime Agnes persuaded Mr Gopnik to meet us, and I watched as, posing like a catwalk model, she paraded a series of clown-like trouser suits in front of him, daring him to laugh, while the sides of his mouth twitched with suppressed mirth. *You are so naughty,* he said to her afterwards, shaking his head fondly.

But it wasn't just my job that had lifted my spirits. I had started to understand New York a little more and, in return, it had started to accommodate me. It wasn't hard in a city of immigrants – outside the rarefied stratosphere of Agnes's daily life, I was just another person from a few thousand miles away, running around town, working, ordering my takeout and learning to specify at least three particular things I wanted in my coffee or sandwich, just to sound like a native.

I watched, and I learnt.

This is what I learnt about New Yorkers in my first month.

1. Nobody in my building spoke to anyone else and the Gopniks spoke only to Ashok. The old woman on the second floor, Mrs De Witt, didn't talk to the couple from California in the penthouse, and the power-suited couple on the third floor walked along the corridor with their noses pressed to their iPhones, barking instructions to the microphone or at each other. Even the children on the first floor – beautifully dressed little mannequins, shepherded by a harried young Filipina – didn't say hello but kept their eyes on the plush carpet as I walked past. When I smiled at the girl, her eyes widened as if I had done something deeply suspicious.

The residents of the Lavery walked straight out and into identikit black cars that waited patiently at the kerb. They always seemed to know whose was whose. Mrs De Witt, as far as I could see, was the only person who spoke to anyone at all. She talked to Dean Martin constantly, muttering under her breath as she hobbled around the block about the 'wretched Russians, those awful Chinese' from the building behind ours who kept their own drivers waiting outside twenty-four seven, clogging up the street. She would complain noisily to Ashok or the building's management about Agnes playing the piano, and if we passed her in the corridor she would hurry by, occasionally letting slip a vaguely audible tut.

2. In contrast, in shops everyone talked to you. The assistants followed you around, their heads tilted forward as if to hear you better, always checking to see whether there was any way they could serve you better or whether they could *put this in a room for you.* I hadn't had so much attention since Treena and I had been caught shoplifting a Mars Bar from the post office when I was eight and Mrs Barker shadowed us, like an MI5 operative, every time we went in there for Sherbet Dib Dabs for the next three years.

And all New York shop assistants wanted you to have a nice day. Even if you were just buying a carton of orange juice or a newspaper. At first, encouraged by their niceness, I responded, 'Oh! Well, you have a nice day too!' and they were always a little taken aback, as if I simply didn't understand the rules of New York conversation.

As for Ashok, nobody passed the threshold without exchanging a few words with him. But that was business. He knew his job. He was always checking you were okay, that you had everything you needed. 'You can't go out in scuffed shoes, Miss Louisa!' He could pull an umbrella from his sleeve like a magician for the short walk to the kerb, accepting tips with the discreet sleight of hand of a card huckster. He could pull dollars from his cuffs, discreetly thanking the traffic cop who smoothed the way of this grocery driver or that dry-cleaning delivery, and whistle a bright yellow taxi out of thin air with a sound only dogs could hear. He was not just the gatekeeper to our building but its heartbeat, keeping things moving in and out, ensuring that everything went smoothly, a blood supply, around it.

3. New Yorkers – those who didn't take limos from our apartment building – walked really, really fast, striding along sidewalks and dipping in and out of crowds as if they had those sensors attached that automatically stop you bumping

into other people. They held phones, or Styrofoam coffee cups, and before seven a.m. at least half of them would be in workout gear. Every time I slowed I heard a muttered curse in my ear, or felt someone's bag swing into my back. I stopped wearing my more decorative shoes – the ones that made me totter, my Japanese geisha flip-flops or my seventies stripy platform boots – in favour of sneakers so that I could move with the current instead of being an obstacle that parted the waters. If you had seen me from above, I liked to think you would never have known that I didn't belong.

During those first weekends I walked too, for hours. I had initially assumed that Nathan and I would hang out together, exploring new places. But he seemed to have built a social circle of blokey men, the kind who really had no interest in female company unless they had sunk several beers first. He spent hours in the gym, and topped each weekend off with a date or two. When I suggested we go to a museum or perhaps to walk the High Line he would smile awkwardly and tell me he already had plans. So I walked alone, down through Midtown to the Meatpacking District, to Greenwich Village, to SoHo, veering off main streets, following whatever looked interesting, my map in my hand, trying to remember which way the traffic went. I saw that Manhattan had distinct districts, from the towering buildings of Midtown to the achingly cool cobbled roads around Crosby Street, where every second person looked like a model or as if they owned an Instagram feed devoted to clean eating. I walked with nowhere particular to go, and nowhere I had to be. I ate salad at a chopped-salad bar, ordering something with cilantro and black beans because I had never eaten either of them. I caught the subway, trying not to look like a tourist as I fathomed how to buy a ticket and identify the legendary crazies, and waited ten minutes for my heart rate to return to normal when I emerged back into daylight. And then I walked across the Brooklyn Bridge, as Will had done, and felt my heart lift at the sight of the glinting water below, feeling the rumble of the traffic beneath my feet, hearing once again his voice in my head. *Live boldly, Clark.*

I stopped halfway across and stood very still as I gazed across the East River, feeling briefly suspended, almost giddy with the sense of no longer being tied to any place at all. Another tick. And slowly I stopped ticking off experiences, because pretty much everything was new and strange.

On those first walks I saw:

- A man in full drag riding a bicycle and singing show tunes through a microphone and speakers. Several people applauded as he rode past.
- Four girls playing jump rope between two fire hydrants. They had two ropes going at once and I stopped to clap when they finally stopped jumping and they smiled shyly at me.
- A dog on a skateboard. When I texted my sister to tell her, she told me I was drunk.
- Robert De Niro.

At least I think it was Robert De Niro. It was early evening and I was feeling briefly homesick and he walked past me on the corner of Spring Street and Broadway, and I actually said, 'Oh, my God. Robert De Niro,' out loud before I could stop myself as he walked past and he didn't turn round and I couldn't be sure afterwards whether that was because he was just some random who thought I was talking to myself, or whether that was exactly what you would do if you were Robert De Niro and some woman on the sidewalk started bleating your name.

I decided the latter. Again, my sister accused me of being drunk. I sent her a picture from my phone but she said, *That could be the back of anyone's head, you doofus,* and added that I was not just drunk but genuinely quite stupid. It was at that point that I started to feel slightly less homesick.

I wanted to tell Sam this. I wanted to tell him all of it, in beautiful handwritten letters or at least in long, rambling emails that we would later save and print out and that would be found in the attic of our house when we had been married fifty years for our grandchildren to coo over. But I was so tired those first few weeks that all I did was email him about how tired I was.

I'm so tired. I miss you.

Me too.

No, like really, really tired. Like cry at TV advertisements and fall asleep while brushing my teeth and end up with toothpaste all over my chest tired.

Okay, now you got me.

I tried not to mind how little he emailed me. I tried to remind myself that he was doing a real, hard job, saving lives and making a difference, while I was sitting outside manicurists' studios and running around Central Park.

His supervisor had changed the rota. He was working four nights on the trot and still waiting to be assigned a new permanent partner. That should have made it easier for us to talk but somehow it didn't. I would check in on my phone in the minutes I had free every evening but that was usually the time he was heading off to begin his shift.

Sometimes I felt curiously disjointed, as if I had simply dreamt him up.

One week, he reassured me. One more week.

How hard could it be?

Agnes was playing the piano again. She played when she was happy or unhappy, angry or frustrated, picking tumultuous pieces, high in emotion, closing her eyes, as her hands roved up and down the keyboard, and swaying on the piano stool. The previous evening she had played a nocturne, and as I passed the open door of the drawing room, I'd watched for a moment as Mr Gopnik sat down beside her on the stool. Even as she became wholly absorbed in the music, it was clear that she was playing for him. I noted how content he was just to sit and turn the pages for her. When she'd finished she'd beamed at him, and he had lowered his head to kiss her hand. I tiptoed past the door as if I hadn't seen.

I was in the study going over the week's events and had got as far as Thursday (Children's Cancer Charity lunch, *Marriage of Figaro*) when I became aware of a rapping at the front door. Ilaria was with the pet behaviourist – Felix had done something unmentionable in Mr Gopnik's office again – so I walked out to the hallway and opened it.

Mrs De Witt stood in front of me, her cane raised as if to strike. I ducked instinctively and then, when she lowered it, straightened, my palms raised. It took me a second to grasp she had simply used it to rap on the door.

'Can I help you?'

'Tell her to quit that infernal racket!' Her tiny etched face was puce with fury.

'I'm sorry?'

'The masseuse. The mail-order bride. Whatever. I can hear it all the way down the corridor.' She was wearing a 1970s Pucci-style duster coat with green and pink swirls and an emerald green turban. Even as I bristled at her insults, I was transfixed. 'Uh, Agnes is actually a trained physical therapist. And it's Mozart.'

'I don't care if it's Champion the Wonder Horse playing the kazoo with his you-know-what. Tell her to pipe down.

She lives in an apartment. She should have some consideration for other residents!'

Dean Martin growled at me, as if in agreement. I was going to say something else but trying to work out which of his eyes was actually looking at me was weirdly distracting. 'I'll pass that on, Mrs De Witt,' I said, my professional smile in place.

'What do you mean "pass it on"? Don't just "pass it on". Make her *stop*. She drives me crazy with the wretched pianola. Day, night, whenever. This used to be a peaceful building.'

'But, to be fair, your dog is always bar–'

'The other one was just as bad. Miserable woman. Always with her quacking friends, *quack quack quack* in the corridor, clogging up the street with their oversized cars. Ugh. I'm not surprised he traded her in.'

'I'm not sure Mr Gopnik –'

'"Trained physical therapist". Good Lord, is that what we're calling it these days? I suppose that makes me chief negotiator at the United Nations.' She patted her face with a handkerchief.

'As I understand it, the great joy of America is that you can be whatever you want to be.' I smiled.

She narrowed her eyes. I held my smile.

'Are you English?'

'Yes.' I sensed a possible softening. 'Why? Do you have relatives there, Mrs De Witt?'

'Don't be ridiculous.' She looked me up and down. 'I just thought English girls were meant to have style.' And with that she turned and, with a dismissive wave, hobbled off down the corridor, Dean Martin casting resentful glances behind her.

*

'Was that the crazy old witch across the corridor?' Agnes called, as I closed the door softly. 'Ugh. No wonder nobody ever comes to see her. She is like horrible dried-up piece of *suszony dorsz.*'

There was a brief silence. I heard pages being turned.

And then Agnes started a thunderous, cascading piece, her fingers crashing on the keyboard, hitting the pedal so hard that I felt the wood floors vibrate.

I fixed my smile again as I walked across the hallway, and checked my watch with an internal sigh. Only two hours to go.

8

Sam was flying in that day, and staying until Monday evening. He had booked us into a hotel a few blocks from Times Square. Given what Agnes had said about how we shouldn't be apart, I had asked if she might give me some of the afternoon off. She had said *maybe* in what I felt was a positive tone, although I got the distinct feeling that Sam coming for the weekend was an irritation to her. Still, I walked to Penn Station, a bounce in my step, and a weekend bag at my heels, and caught the AirTrain to JFK. By the time I got to the airport, slightly ahead of time, I was buzzing with anticipation.

The arrivals board said Sam's flight had landed and that he was awaiting his luggage so I hurried into the Ladies to check my hair and make-up. A little sweaty from the walk and the packed train, I touched up my mascara and lipstick, and swiped at my hair with a brush. I was wearing turquoise silk culottes with a black polo-neck and black ankle boots. I wanted to look like myself, but also as if I had changed in some indefinable way, perhaps become a little more mysterious. I dodged out of the way of an exhausted-looking woman with an oversized wheelie case, gave myself a little spritz of perfume, then finally judged myself the kind of woman who meets her lover at international airports.

All the same, as I walked out, heart thumping, and peered up at the board, I felt oddly nervous. We had been apart only four weeks. This man had seen me at my worst: broken, panicked, sad, contrary, and still apparently liked me. He was still Sam, I told myself. My Sam. Nothing had changed since the first time he had rung my doorbell and asked me, ham-fistedly, through the intercom, for a date.

The sign still said: 'AWAITING LUGGAGE'.

I wedged myself into position at the barrier, checked my hair again and trained my eyes on the double doors, smiling involuntarily at the shrieks of happiness as long-separated couples found each other. I thought, *That'll be us in a minute.* I took a deep breath, noting that my palms had started to sweat. A trickle of people made their way through, and my face kept settling into what I suspected was a slightly mad-looking rictus of anticipation, eyebrows raised, delighted, like a politician fake-spotting someone in a crowd.

And then, as I rummaged in my bag for a handkerchief, I did a double-take. There, a few yards away from me in the mass of people, stood Sam, a head taller than anyone around him, scanning the crowd, just as I was. I muttered, 'Excuse me,' to the person on my right at the barrier, ducked under it, and ran towards him. He turned just as I got to him and promptly whacked me, hard, in the shin with his bag.

'Oh, shoot. Are you okay? Lou? . . . Lou?'

I clutched my leg, trying not to swear. Tears had sprung to my eyes and when I spoke it came through a gasp of pain. 'It said your luggage wasn't through!' I said, teeth clenched. 'I can't believe I missed our great reunion! I was in the loo!'

'I came hand luggage only.' He put his hand on my shoulder. 'Is your leg okay?'

'But I had it all planned! I had a sign and everything!' I wrestled it, specially laminated, out of my jacket and straightened, trying to ignore the throbbing in my shin. 'WORLD'S HANDSOMEST PARAMEDIC'. 'This was meant to be one of the defining moments of our relationship! One of those moments you look back on and go, "Aah, do you remember that time I met you at JFK?"'

'It's still a great moment,' he said hopefully. 'It's good to see you.'

'*Good to see me?*'

'Great. It's great to see you. Sorry. I'm knackered. Didn't sleep.'

I rubbed my shin. We stared at each other for a minute. 'It's no good,' I said. 'You have to go again.'

'Go again?'

'To the barrier. And then I'll do what I planned, which is hold up my sign, then run towards you and we kiss and we start it all properly.'

He stared at me. 'Seriously?'

'It'll be worth it. Go on. Please.'

It took him a moment longer to confirm that I wasn't joking, then he began to walk against the tide of arrivals. Several people turned to stare at him, and somebody tutted.

'Stop!' I yelled across the noisy concourse. 'That'll do!'

But he didn't hear me. He kept walking, all the way to the double doors – I had a fleeting fear that he might just jump back on the plane.

'*Sam!*' I yelled. '*STOP!*'

Everyone turned. Then he turned, and saw me. And as he started to walk towards me again I ducked back under the barrier. 'Here! Sam! It's me!' I waved my sign and as he walked towards me he was grinning at the ridiculousness of it all.

I dropped the sign and ran towards him, and this time he didn't bash me in the shin but let his bag fall at his feet and swept me up and we kissed like people do in the movies, fully and with absolute joy and without self-consciousness or fears about coffee breath. Or perhaps we did. I couldn't tell you. Because from the moment Sam picked me up I was oblivious to everything else, to the bags and the people and the eyes of the crowds. Oh, God, but the feel of his arms around me, the softness of his lips on mine. I didn't want to let him go. I held onto him and felt the strength of him around me and breathed in the scent of his skin and I buried my face in his neck, my skin against his, feeling like every cell in my body had missed him.

'Better, you insane person?' he said, when he finally pulled back so that he could see me properly. I think my lipstick may have been halfway across my face. I almost definitely had stubble rash. My ribs hurt where he was holding me so tightly.

'Oh, yes,' I said, unable to stop grinning. 'Much.'

We decided to drop our bags at the hotel first, me trying not to gabble with excitement. I was talking nonsense – a stream of disjointed thoughts and observations coming out of my mouth unfiltered. He watched me the way you might look at your dog if it did an unprompted dance: with faint amusement and vaguely suppressed alarm. But when the lift doors closed behind us, he pulled me towards him, took my face in his hands and kissed me again.

'Was that to stop me talking?' I said, when he released me.

'No. That was because I've wanted to do that for four long weeks and I plan to do it as many times as I can until I go home again.'

'That's a good line.'

'Took me most of the flight.'

I gazed at him as he fed the key-card into the door and, for the five-hundredth time, marvelled at my luck in finding him when I'd thought I could never love anyone again. I felt impulsive, romantic, a character in a Sunday-afternoon movie.

'Aaaand here we are.'

We stopped in the doorway. The hotel room was smaller than my bedroom at the Gopniks', carpeted in a brown plaid, and the bed, rather than the luxurious expanse of white

Frette linen I had envisaged, was a sunken double with a burgundy and orange checked bedspread. I tried not to think about when it might last have been cleaned. As Sam closed the door behind us, I set down my bag and edged around the bed until I could peer through the bathroom door. There was a shower and no bath, and when you put the light on the extractor whined, like a toddler at a supermarket checkout. The room was scented with a combination of old nicotine and industrial air freshener.

'You hate it.' His eyes scanned my face.

'No! It's perfect!'

'It's not perfect. Sorry. I got it off this booking website when I'd just finished a night shift. Want me to go downstairs and see if they have other rooms?'

'I heard her saying it was fully booked. Anyway, it's fine! It has a bed and a shower and it's in the middle of New York and it has you in it. Which means it's all wonderful!'

'Aw, crap. I should have run it past you.'

I never was any good at lying. He reached for my hand and I squeezed his.

'It's fine. Really.'

We stood and stared at the bed. And I put my hand over my mouth until I realized I couldn't not say the thing I was trying not to say.

'We should probably check for bedbugs, though.'

'Seriously?'

'There's an epidemic of them, according to Ilaria.'

Sam's shoulders sagged.

'Even some of the poshest hotels have them.' I stepped forward and pulled back the covers abruptly, scanning the white sheet before stooping to check the mattress edge. I moved closer. 'Nothing!' I said. 'So that's good! We're in a bedbug-free hotel!' I gave a small thumbs-up. 'Yay!'

There was a long silence.

'Let's go for a walk,' he said.

We went for a walk. It was, at least, a great location. We strolled half a dozen blocks down Sixth Avenue and back up Fifth, zigzagging and following where the urge took us, me trying not to talk endlessly about myself or New York, which was harder than I'd thought, given that Sam was mostly silent. He took my hand in his, and I leant against his shoulder and tried not to sneak too many glances at him. There was something unexpectedly odd about having him there. I found myself fixing on tiny details, a scratch on his hand, a slight change in the length of his hair, trying to reclaim him in my imagination.

'You've lost your limp,' I said, as we paused to look in the window of the Museum of Modern Art. I felt nervous that he wasn't talking, as if the terrible hotel room had ruined everything.

'So have you.'

'I've been running!' I said. 'I told you! I go around Central Park every morning with Agnes and George, her trainer. Here – feel my legs!' Sam squeezed my upper thigh as I held it towards him and looked suitably impressed. 'You can let go now,' I said, when people started to stare.

'Sorry,' he said. 'It's been a while.'

I had forgotten how much he preferred to listen than talk. It took a while before he offered up anything about himself. He finally had a new partner. After two false starts – a young man who'd decided he didn't want to be a paramedic, and Tim, a middle-aged union rep, who apparently hated all mankind (not a great mindset for the job) – he had been paired with a woman from North Kensington station who had recently moved house and wanted to work somewhere closer to home.

'What's she like?'

'She's not Donna,' he said, 'but she's okay. Least she seems to know what she's doing.'

He had met Donna for coffee the week previously. Her father was not responding to chemotherapy, but she had disguised her sadness under sarcasm and jokes, as Donna always did. 'I wanted to tell her she didn't have to,' he said. 'She knows what I went through with my sister. But,' he looked at me sideways, 'we all cope with these things in our own ways.'

Jake, he told me, was doing well at college. He sent his love. His dad, Sam's brother-in-law, had dropped out of grief therapy, saying it wasn't for him, even though it had stopped his compulsive bedding of strange women. 'He's eating his way through his feelings now. Put on a stone since you left.'

'And you?'

'Ah. I'm coping.'

He said it simply, but it caused something in my heart to crack a little.

'It's not for ever,' I said, as we stopped.

'I know.'

'And we're going to do loads of fun stuff while you're here.'

'What have you got planned?'

'Um, basically it's You Getting Naked. Followed by supper. Followed by more You Getting Naked. Maybe a walk around Central Park, some corny tourist stuff, like the Staten Island ferry and Times Square, and some shopping in the East Village and some really good food with added You Getting Naked.'

He grinned. 'Do I get You Getting Naked too?'

'Oh, yes, it's a two-for-one deal.' I leant my head against him. 'Seriously, though, I'd love you to come and see where I work. Maybe meet Nathan and Ashok and all the people I go on about. Mr and Mrs Gopnik will be out of town so you probably won't meet them but you'll at least get an idea of it all in your head.'

He stopped and turned me to face him. 'Lou. I don't really

care what we do as long as we're together.' He coloured a little as he said it, as if the words had surprised even him.

'That's quite romantic, Mr Fielding.'

'I tell you what, though. I need to eat something pretty fast if I'm going to fulfil this Getting Naked bit. Where can we get some food?'

We were walking past Radio City, surrounded by huge office buildings. 'There's a coffee shop,' I said.

'Oh, no,' he said, clapping his hands together. 'There's my boy. A genuine New York food truck!' He pointed towards one of the ever-present food trucks, this one advertising 'stacked burritos': *'We make 'em any way you like 'em.'* I followed him and waited while he ordered something that appeared to be the size of his forearm and smelt of hot cheese and unidentified fatty meat. 'We didn't have plans to eat out tonight, right?' He wedged the end into his mouth.

I couldn't help but laugh. 'Whatever keeps you awake. Though I suspect that's going to put you in a food coma.'

'Oh, God, this is so good. Want some?'

I did, actually. But I was wearing really nice underwear and I didn't want bits of me hanging over the top. So I waited until he had finished it, noisily licking his fingers, then tossing his napkin into the bin. He sighed with deep satisfaction. 'Right,' he said, taking my arm, and everything felt suddenly, blissfully normal. 'About this naked thing.'

We walked back to our hotel in silence. I no longer felt awkward, as if the time apart had created some unexpected distance between us. I didn't want to talk any more. I just wanted to feel his skin against mine. I wanted to be completely his again, enfolded, possessed. We headed down Sixth Avenue, past the Rockefeller Center and I no longer noticed the tourists who stood in our way. I felt locked into an invisible bubble, all my senses trained on the warm hand that had closed around mine, the arm that crept around my shoulders. His every movement felt heavy with intent. I was almost breathless with it. I could live with the absences, I thought, if the times we spent together felt as delicious as this.

We were barely in the lift when he turned and pulled me to him. We kissed, and I melted, lost myself in the feel of him against me, my blood pulsing in my ears so that I barely heard the lift doors open. We staggered out.

'Door thing,' he said, patting his pockets with some urgency. 'Door thing! Where did I put it?'

'I've got it,' I said, wrestling it out of my back pocket.

'Thank God,' he said, as he kicked the door shut behind us, his voice low in my ear. 'You have no idea how long I've been thinking about this.'

Two minutes later I was lying on the Burgundy Bedspread of Doom, sweat cooling on my skin, wondering whether it would be really bad if I reached down to get my knickers. Despite the bedbug checks, there was still something about this cover that made me want a barrier between it and any part of my bare body.

Sam's voice floated into the air beside me. 'Sorry,' he murmured. 'I knew I was pleased to see you, but not that pleased.'

'It's fine,' I said, turning to face him. He had this way of pulling me into him, like he was gathering me up, so that I was totally enclosed. I had never understood women who said a man made them feel safe – but that was how I felt with Sam. His eyes were drooping, battling sleep. I calculated it was around three in the morning for him now. He dropped a kiss on my nose. 'Give me twenty minutes and I'll be good to go.'

I ran my finger lightly along his face, tracing his lips, and shifted so that he could pull the covers over us. I placed my leg over his, so that there was almost no part of me not touching him. Even that movement caused something in me to ignite. I don't know what it was about Sam that made me unlike myself – without inhibition, full of hunger. I was not sure I could touch his skin without feeling that reflexive internal heat. I could glance over at his shoulders, the heft of his forearms, the baby-soft dark hairs where his neck became his hairline, and I would feel almost incandescent with lust.

'I love you, Louisa Clark,' he said softly.

'Twenty minutes, hmm?' I said, smiling, and hooked him in tighter.

But he dropped into sleep like someone stepping off a cliff. I watched him for a while, wondering whether it would be possible to wake him, and what means I might employ to do it, but then I remembered how disoriented and exhausted I had been when I'd arrived. And then I thought of how he had just done a week of twelve-hour shifts. And that it was only a few hours into our whole three days together. With a sigh I released him and flopped onto my back. It was dark outside now, the sounds of the distant traffic floating up to us. I felt a million things and I was disconcerted to find that one was disappointment.

Stop, I told myself firmly. My expectations for this weekend had simply risen, like a soufflé, too high for sustained contact with the atmosphere. He was here, and we were together, and in a few hours he would be awake again. Go to sleep, Clark, I told myself. I pulled his arm over me, inhaling the scent of his warm skin. And closed my eyes.

An hour and a half later, I was lying on the far side of the bed, scrolling through Facebook on my phone, marvelling at Mum's apparently infinite appetite for motivational quotes and photographs of Thom in his school uniform. It was half past ten, and sleep was uninterested in stopping by. I climbed out of bed, and used the bathroom, leaving the light off so that Sam wouldn't be woken by the screeching fan. I hesitated before climbing back in. The sagging mattress meant that Sam had tipped gently into the middle, leaving me a few inches on the edge unless I pretty much lay on top of him. I wondered idly if an hour and a half's sleep was enough. And then I climbed in, slid my body against his warm one and, after a moment's hesitation, I kissed him.

Sam's body came to before he did. His arm pulled me in, his big hand sliding the length of my body, and he kissed me back, slow, sleep-filled kisses that were tender and soft and made my body arch against his. I shifted so that his weight was on me, my hand seeking his, my fingers linking with his, a sigh of pleasure escaping me. He wanted me. He opened his eyes in the dim light and I looked into them, heavy with longing, noting with surprise that he had already broken into a sweat.

He gazed at me for a moment.

'Hello, handsome,' I whispered.

He made as if to speak but nothing came out.

He looked off to the side. And then suddenly he clambered off me.

'What?' I said. 'What did I say?'

'Sorry,' he said. 'Hold on.'

He bolted for the bathroom, hurling the door shut behind him. I heard an 'Oh, God,' and then sounds that, for once, I was grateful that the screeching extractor fan largely obscured.

I sat there, frozen, then climbed out of bed, pulling on a T-shirt. 'Sam?'

I leant into the door, pressing my ear against it, then backed away. Intimacy, I observed, could only survive so much in the way of sound effects.

'Sam? Are you okay?'

'Fine,' came his muffled voice.

He was not fine.

'What's going on?'

A long gap. The sound of flushing.

'I – uh – I think I may have food poisoning.'

'Seriously? Can I do anything?'

'No. Just – just don't come in. Okay?' This was followed by more retching and soft cursing. 'Don't come in.'

We spent almost two hours like that: him locked in some awful battle with his internal organs on one side of the door, me sitting anxiously in my T-shirt on the other. He refused to let me check on him – his pride, I think, forbade it.

The man who finally came out shortly before one o'clock was the colour of putty, with a Vaseline glaze. I scrambled to my feet as the door opened and he staggered slightly, as if surprised to see me still there. I reached out a hand, as if I had any hope of stopping someone his size falling. 'What shall I do? Do you need a doctor?'

'No. Just . . . just got to sit this one out.' He flopped onto the bed, panting and clutching his stomach. His eyes were ringed with black shadows, and he stared straight ahead. 'Literally.'

'I'll get you some water.' I stared at him. 'Actually, I'm going to run to a pharmacy and get you some Dioralyte or whatever they have here.' He didn't even speak, just toppled onto his side, staring straight ahead, his body still damp with sweat.

I got the required medication, offering up silent thanks to the City That Didn't Just Not Sleep But Offered Rehydration Powders Too. Sam chugged one down, and then, with an apology, retreated to the bathroom again. Occasionally I would pass a bottle of water through a gap in the door, and in the end I turned on the television.

'Sorry,' he muttered, when he stumbled out again, shortly before four. And then he collapsed onto the Bedspread of Doom and fell into a brief, disjointed sleep.

I slept for a couple of hours, covered with the hotel robe, and woke to find him still asleep. I showered and got dressed, letting myself out silently so that I could grab a coffee from the machine in the lobby. I felt bleary. At least, I told myself, we still had two days to go.

But when I walked back into the room Sam was in the bathroom again.

'Really sorry,' he said, when he emerged. I had pulled the curtains and in daylight he looked, if anything, greyer against the hotel sheets. 'I'm not sure I'm up to much today.'

'That's fine!' I said.

'I might be okay by this afternoon,' he said.

'Fine!'

'Maybe not the ferry trip, though. Think I don't want to be anywhere where . . .'

'. . . there are communal loos. I get it.'

He sighed. 'This is not quite the day I had in mind.'

'It's fine,' I said, climbing onto the bed beside him.

'Will you stop saying *it's fine*,' he said irritably.

I hesitated a moment, stung, then said icily, 'Fine.'

He looked at me from the corner of his eye. 'Sorry.'

'Stop apologizing.'

We sat on the bedspread, both looking straight ahead. And then his hand reached across for mine. 'Listen,' he said eventually. 'I'm probably just going to hang here for a couple of hours. Try and get my strength back. Don't feel you have to sit with me. Go shopping or something.'

'But you're only here till Monday. I don't want to do anything without you.'

'I'm good for nothing, Lou.'

He looked like he could have punched a wall, if he'd only had the strength to raise his fist.

I walked two blocks to a newsstand and bought an armful of newspapers and magazines. I then bought myself a decent coffee and a bran muffin, and a plain white bagel for when he might want to eat something.

'Supplies,' I said, dropping them on my side of the bed. 'Might as well just burrow in.' And that was how we spent the day. I read every single section of the *New York Times*, including the baseball reports. I put the Do Not Disturb sign on the door, watched him dozing and waited for colour to return to his face.

Maybe he'll feel better in time for us to have a walk in daylight.
Maybe we could grab a drink in the hotel bar.
Sitting up would be good.
Okay, so maybe he'll be better tomorrow.

At nine forty-five when I turned off the television chat show, pushed all the newspapers off the bed and burrowed down under the duvet, the only part of my body still touching his was my fingers, entwined with his at the tips.

He woke feeling a little brighter on Sunday. I think by then there was so little in his system that there was nothing left to come out. I bought him some clear soup and he ate it tentatively and pronounced himself well enough to go for a walk. Twenty minutes later we jogged back and he locked himself into the bathroom. He was really angry then. I tried to tell him it was okay but that just seemed to make him angrier. There's not much that's more pathetic than a six-foot-four man-mountain trying to be furious while he can barely lift a glass of water.

I did leave him for a bit then because my disappointment was starting to show. I needed to walk the streets and remind myself that this wasn't a sign, it didn't mean anything, and that it was easy to lose perspective when you'd had no sleep and had been stuck for forty-eight hours with a gastro-intestinally challenged man and a bathroom with deeply inadequate soundproofing.

But the fact that it was now Sunday left me heartbroken. I was back at work tomorrow. And we had done none of the things I'd planned. We hadn't gone to a ball game or on the Staten Island ferry. We hadn't climbed to the top of the Empire State or walked the High Line arm in arm. That night we sat in bed and he ate some boiled rice I had picked up from a sushi restaurant and I ate a grilled chicken sand-wich that tasted of nothing.

'On the right track now,' he murmured, as I pulled the cover over him.

'Great,' I said. And then he was asleep.

I couldn't face another evening of scrolling through my phone so I got up quietly, left him a note and headed out. I felt miserable and oddly angry. Why had he eaten something that had given him food poisoning? Why couldn't he make himself better quicker? He was a paramedic after all. Why couldn't he have picked a nicer hotel? I walked down Sixth Avenue, my hands thrust deep into my pockets, the traffic blaring around me, and before long I found myself headed towards home.

Home.

With a start, I realized that was how I now thought of it.

Ashok was under the awning, chatting to another door-man, who moved away as soon as I approached.

'Hey, Miss Louisa. Aren't you meant to be with that boy-friend of yours?'

'He's sick,' I said. 'Food poisoning.'

'You're kidding me. Where is he now?'

'Sleeping. I just . . . couldn't face sitting in that room for another twelve hours.' I felt suddenly, oddly, close to tears. I think Ashok could see it because he motioned me to come in. In his little porter's room he boiled a kettle and made me a mint tea. I sat at his desk and sipped it, while he peered out now and then to make sure Mrs De Witt wasn't around to accuse him of slacking. 'Anyway,' I said, 'why are you on duty? I thought it was the night guy.'

'He's sick too. My wife is super mad at me right now. She's meant to be at one of her library meetings but we don't have anybody to look after the kids. She says if I spend one more of my days off here she's going to have a word with Mr Ovitz herself. And nobody wants that.' He shook his head. 'My wife is a fearsome woman, Miss Louisa. You do not want to upset my wife.'

'I'd offer to help. But I think I'd better go back and check on Sam.'

'Be sweet,' he said, as I handed him his mug. 'He came a long way to see you. And I can guarantee he is feeling way worse than you are right now.'

When I got back to the room, Sam was awake, propped up on pillows and watching the grainy television. He looked up as I opened the door.

'I just went for a walk. I – I –'

'Couldn't face one more minute stuck in here with me.'

I stood in the doorway. His head was sunk into his shoulders. He looked pale and unutterably depressed.

'Lou – if you knew how hard I'm kicking myself –'

'It's fi—' I stopped myself just in time. 'Really,' I said. 'We're good.'

I ran him a shower, made him get in and washed his hair,

squeezing the last out of the tiny hotel bottle, then watched the suds slide down the huge slope of his shoulders. As I did he reached up, took my hand silently and kissed the inside of my wrist softly, a kiss of apology. I placed the towel over his shoulders and we made our way out to the bedroom. He lay back on the bed with a sigh. I changed out of my clothes and lay down beside him, wishing I didn't still feel so flat.

'Tell me something about you that I don't know,' he said.

I turned towards him. 'Oh, you know everything. I'm an open book.'

'C'mon. Indulge me.' His voice was low against my ear. I couldn't think of anything. *I still felt really oddly annoyed about this weekend even though I know that's unfair of me.*

'Okay,' he said, when it was clear I wasn't going to speak. 'I'll start then. I am never eating anything but white toast again.'

'Funny.'

He studied my face for a moment. When he spoke again his voice was unusually quiet. 'And things haven't been easy at home.'

'What do you mean?'

It took a minute before he spoke again, as if he wasn't sure even then if he should. 'It's work. You know, before I got shot I wasn't afraid of anything. I could handle myself. I guess I reckoned I was a bit of a tough guy. Now, though, what happened, it's at the back of my mind all the time.'

I tried not to look startled.

He rubbed at his face. 'Since I've been back I find myself assessing situations as we go in . . . differently, trying to work out exit routes, potential sources of trouble. Even when there's no reason to.'

'You're frightened?'

'Yeah. Me.' He laughed drily, and shook his head. 'They've

offered me counselling. Oh, I know the drill from when I was in the army. Talk it through, understand it's your mind's way of processing what happened. I know it all. But it's disconcerting.' He rolled onto his back. 'To tell you the truth, I don't feel like myself.'

I waited.

'That's why it hit so hard when Donna left because . . . because I knew she'd always look out for me.'

'But this new partner will look out for you, surely. What's her name?'

'Katie.'

'Katie will look out for you. I mean, she's experienced, and you guys must be trained to take care of each other, right?'

His gaze slid towards me.

'You won't be shot again, Sam. I *know* you won't.'

Afterwards I realized it was a stupid thing to say. I'd said it because I couldn't bear the idea of him being unhappy. I'd said it because I wanted it to be true.

'I'll be fine,' he said, quietly.

I felt as if I'd failed him. I wondered how long he'd wanted to tell me that. We lay there for a while. I ran a finger lightly along his arm, trying to work out what to say.

'You?' he murmured.

'Me what?'

'Tell me something I don't know. About you.'

I was going to tell him he knew all the important stuff. I was going to be my New York self, full of life, go-getting, impenetrable. I was going to say something to make him laugh. But he had told me his truth.

I turned so that I was facing him. 'There is one thing. But I don't want you to see me differently. If I tell you.'

He frowned.

'It's something that happened a long time ago. But you

told me a thing. So I'm going to do the same.' I took a breath then and told him. I told him the story I had only ever told Will, a man who had listened and then released me from the hold it had had over me. I told Sam the story of a girl who, ten years previously, had drunk too much and smoked too much and found to her cost that just because a gang of boys came from good families it didn't make them good. I told it in a calm voice, a little detached. These days it didn't really feel like it had happened to me, after all. Sam listened in the near dark, his eyes on mine, saying nothing.

'It's one of the reasons coming to New York and doing this was so important to me. I boxed myself in for years, Sam. I told myself that was what I needed to feel safe. And now . . . well, now I guess I need to push myself. I need to know what I'm capable of if I stop looking down.'

When I had finished he was silent for a long time, long enough that I had a momentary doubt as to whether I should have told him at all. But he reached out a hand and stroked my hair. 'I'm sorry,' he said. 'I wish I'd been there to protect you. I wish –'

'It's fine,' I said. 'It was a long time ago.'

'It's not fine.' He pulled me to him. I rested my head against his chest, absorbing the steady beat of his heart.

'Just, you know, don't look at me differently,' I whispered.

'I can't help looking at you differently.'

I tilted my head so that I could see him.

'Only in that I think you're even more amazing,' he said, and his arms closed around me. 'On top of all the other reasons to love you, you're brave, and strong, and you just reminded me . . . we all have our hurdles. I'll get over mine. But I promise you, Louisa Clark.' His voice, when it came, was low and tender. 'Nobody is ever going to hurt you again.'

9

To: SillyLily@gmail.com
From: BusyBee@gmail.com

Hey, Lily!

In haste as I'm tapping this out on the subway (I'm always in haste these days) but lovely to hear from you. Glad school is going so well, though it sounds like you were quite lucky with the smoking thing. Mrs Traynor is right – it would be a shame if you got expelled before you'd even taken your exams.

But I'm not going to lecture you. New York is amazing. I'm enjoying every moment. And, yes, it would be lovely if you came out here but I think you'd have to stay in a hotel so you might want to speak to your parents first. Also, I'm quite busy as my hours with the Gopniks are long so I wouldn't have much time to hang out just now.

Sam is fine, thanks. No, he hasn't dumped me yet. In fact he's here right now. He heads home later today. You can talk to him about borrowing his motorbike when he's back. I think that may be one for the two of you to sort out between you.

Okay – my stop is coming up. Give Mrs T my love. Tell her I've been doing the things your dad did in his letters (not all of them: I haven't been on any dates with leggy blonde PR girls).

Lou xxx

My alarm went off at six thirty a.m., a brittle micro-siren breaking the silence. I had to be back at the Gopniks' for seven thirty. I let out a soft groan as I reached across to the bedside table and fumbled to turn it off. I had figured it would take me fifteen minutes to walk back to Central Park. I mentally ran through a rapid to-do list, wondering if there was any shampoo left in the bathroom and whether I would need to iron my top.

Sam's arm reached across and pulled me towards him. 'Don't go,' he said sleepily.

'I have to.' His arm was pinning me.

'Be late.' He opened one eye. He smelt warm and sweet and he kept his gaze on mine as he slowly slid a heavy, muscular leg over me.

It was impossible to refuse him. Sam was feeling better. Quite a lot better, apparently.

'I need to get dressed.'

He was kissing my collarbone, feathery kisses that made me shiver. His mouth, light and focused, began to trace a pattern downwards. He looked up at me from under the cover, one eyebrow raised. 'I'd forgotten these scars. I really love these scars here.' He lowered his head and kissed the silvery ridges on my hip that marked my surgery, making me squirm, then disappeared.

'Sam, I need to go. Really.' My fingers closed around the bedspread. 'Sam . . . Sam . . . I really . . . oh.'

Some time later, my skin prickling with drying sweat, breathing hard, I lay on my stomach wearing a stupid smile, my muscles aching in unexpected places. My hair was over my face but I couldn't summon the energy to push it away. A strand rose and fell with my breath. Sam lay beside me. His hand felt its way across the sheet to mine. 'I missed you,' he said. He shifted and rolled over so that he was on top of me,

116

holding me in place. 'Louisa Clark,' he murmured, and his voice, impossibly deep, resonated somewhere inside me. 'You do something to me.'

'I think it was you who did something to me, if we're going to get technical about it.'

His face was filled with tenderness. I lifted my own so that I could kiss him. It was as if the last forty-eight hours had fallen away. I was in the right place, with the right man, and his arms were around me and his body was beautiful and familiar. I ran a finger down his cheek, then leant in and kissed him slowly.

'Don't do that again,' he said, his eyes on mine.

'Why?'

'Because then I won't be able to help myself and you're already late and I don't want to be responsible for you losing your job.'

I turned my head to see the alarm. I blinked. 'Quarter to *eight*? Are you kidding? *How the hell is it a quarter to eight?*' I wriggled out from under him, my arms flapping, and hopped to the bathroom. 'Oh, my God. I am so late. *Oh, no – oh, no no no no no.*'

I threw myself under a shower so rapid it's possible the droplets didn't make contact with my body, and when I emerged he stood and held out items of clothing for me so that I could slide into them.

'Shoes. Where are my shoes?'

He held them up. 'Hair,' he said, gesturing. 'You need to comb your hair. It's all . . . well . . .'

'What?'

'Matted. Sexy. Just-had-sex hair. I'll pack your things,' he said. As I ran for the door he caught me by the arm and pulled me to him. 'Or you could, you know, just be a tiny bit later.'

'I am later. So later.'

'It's just once. She's your new best mate. They're hardly going to fire you.' He put his arms around me and kissed me and ran his lips down the side of my neck so that I shivered. 'And this is my last morning here . . .'

'Sam . . .'

'Five minutes.'

'It's never five minutes. Oh, man – I can't believe I'm saying that like it's a bad thing.'

He growled with frustration. 'Dammit. I feel okay today. Like *really* okay.'

'Believe me, I can tell.'

'Sorry,' he said. And then: 'No, I'm not. Not remotely.'

I grinned at him, closed my eyes and kissed him back, feeling even then how easy it would be just to topple back onto the Burgundy Bedspread of Doom and lose myself again. 'Me either. I'll see you later, though.' I wriggled out of his arms and ran out of the room and along the corridor, listening to his yelled 'I love you!' And thinking that despite potential bedbugs, unsanitary bedspreads and inadequate bathroom soundproofing, actually, this was a very nice hotel indeed.

Mr Gopnik was suffering acute pain in his legs and had been awake half the night, which had left Agnes anxious and fractious. She had had a bad weekend at the country club, the other women freezing her out of conversation and gossiping about her in the spa. From the way Nathan whispered this as I passed him in the lobby, it sounded like thirteen-year-old girls on a toxic sleepover.

'You're late,' Agnes growled, as she returned from her run with George, mopping her face with a towel. In the next room I could hear Mr Gopnik's uncharacteristically raised voice on the telephone. She didn't look at me as she spoke.

'I'm sorry. It's because my . . .' I began, but she had already walked past.

'She's freaking out about the charity reception this evening,' murmured Michael, heading past me with an armful of dry-cleaning and a clipboard.

I racked my mental Rolodex. 'Children's Cancer Hospital?'

'The very one,' he said. 'She's meant to bring a doodle.'

'A doodle?'

'A little picture. On a special card. They auction them off at the dinner.'

'So how hard is that? She can do a smiley face or a flower or something. I'll do it if she likes. I can do a mean smiling horse. I can put a hat on it too, with the ears sticking out.' I was still full of Sam and found it hard to see the problem in anything.

He looked at me. 'Sweetheart. You think "doodle" means actual doodle? *Oh*, no. It has to be real art.'

'I got a B in GCSE art.'

'You're so sweet. No, Louisa, they don't do it themselves. Every artist between here and Brooklyn Bridge has apparently spent the weekend creating some delicious little pen-and-ink study for cold, hard cash. She only found out last night. Overheard two of the Witches talking about it before she left the club and when she asked them they told her the truth. So guess what you're doing today? Have a great morning!'

He blew me a kiss and hurried out of the door.

While Agnes showered and had breakfast I did an online search of 'artists in New York'. It was about as much use as searching 'dogs with tails'. The few who had websites and bothered to pick up the phone answered my request like I'd suggested they waltz naked around the nearest shopping mall. 'You want Mr Fischl to do a . . . *doodle*? For a *charity lunch*?' Two put the phone down on me. Artists, it turned out, took themselves very seriously.

I called everyone I could find. I called gallerists in Chelsea. I called the New York Academy of Art. All the while I tried not to think about what Sam was doing. He would be having a nice brunch in that diner we'd talked about. He would be walking the High Line, like we were meant to. I needed to be back in time to take that ferry ride with him before he left for England. To do it at dusk would be romantic. I pictured us, his arm around me, gazing up at the Statue of Liberty, dropping a kiss on my hair. I dragged my thoughts back and racked my brains. And then I thought about the only other person I knew in New York who might be able to help.

'Josh?'

'Speaking?' The sound of a million male voices behind him.

'It's – it's Louisa Clark. We met at the Yellow Ball?'

'Louisa! Great to hear from you! How are you doing?' He sounded so relaxed, as if strange women called him every day of the week. They probably did. 'Hold on. Let me take this outside . . . So what's up?'

He had this way of making you feel instantly at ease. I wondered if Americans were born with it.

'Actually, I'm in a bit of a bind and I don't know many people in New York so I wondered if you might be able to help.'

'Try me.'

I explained the situation, leaving out Agnes's mood, her paranoia, my utter stammering terror faced with the New York art scene.

'Shouldn't be too hard. When do you need this thing by?'

'That's the tricky bit. Tonight.'

A sharp intake of breath. 'Oooh-*kay*. Yeah. That's a little tougher.'

I ran a hand through my hair. 'I know. It's nuts. If I'd known about it sooner I might have been able to do something. I'm really sorry to have bothered you.'

'No, no. We'll fix this. Can I call you back?'

Agnes was out on the balcony, smoking. Turns out I wasn't the only person who used the space after all. It was cold and she was swaddled in a huge cashmere wrap, her fingers faintly pink where her hand emerged from the soft wool.

'I've put out a number of calls. I'm just waiting for someone to get back to me.'

'You know what they will say, Louisa? If I bring them stupid doodle?'

I waited.

'They will say I have no culture. What can you expect from stupid Polish masseuse? Or they will say that nobody wanted to do it for me.'

'It's only twelve twenty. We've still got time.'

'I don't know why I bother,' she said softly.

Strictly speaking, I wanted to say, it wasn't her doing the bothering. Her chief concern right now seemed to be Smoking And Looking Moody. But I knew my place. Just then my phone rang.

'Louisa?'

'Josh?'

'I think I have someone who can help. Can you get over to East Williamsburg?'

Twenty minutes later we were in the car headed towards the Midtown Tunnel.

As we sat in traffic, Garry impassive and silent in the front, Agnes called Mr Gopnik, anxious about his health, his pain. 'Is Nathan coming to the office? Did you have pain-killers? . . . Are you sure you're okay, darling? You don't want me to come bring you anything? . . . No . . . I'm in the car. I have to sort something for this evening. Yes, I'm still going. It's all fine.'

I could just make out his voice at the other end. Low, reassuring.

She hung up and gazed out of the window, heaving a long sigh. I waited a moment, then started running through my notes.

'So, apparently this Steven Lipkott is up and coming in the fine art world. He's had shows in some very important places. And he's . . .' I scanned my notes '. . . figurative. Not abstract. So you just need to tell him what you want him to draw and he'll do it. I'm not sure how much it will cost, though.'

'It doesn't matter,' said Agnes. 'Is going to be disaster.'

I turned back to the iPad and did an online search on the artist's name. With relief I noted that the drawings were indeed beautiful: sinuous depictions of the body. I handed the iPad to Agnes so that she could see and in a moment her mood lifted. 'This is good.' She sounded almost surprised.

'Yup. If you can think of what you want, we can get him to draw it and be back for . . . four maybe?' *And then I can leave*, I added silently. While she scrolled through the other images, I texted Sam.

How you doing?

Not bad. Went for a nice walk. Bought souvenir beer hat for Jake. Don't laugh.

Wish I was with you.

A pause.

So what time do you think you'll get off? I worked out I should leave for the airport by seven.

Hoping for four. Will stay in touch xxxxx

New York traffic meant it took us an hour to get to the address Josh had given me: a scruffy, featureless former office building at the back of an industrial block. Garry pulled up with a sceptical sniff. 'You sure this is the place?' he said, turning with effort in his seat.

I checked the address. 'That's what it says.'

'I will stay in car, Louisa. I am going to call Leonard again.'

The upper corridor was lined with doors, a couple of which were open, music blaring. I walked along slowly, checking the numbers. Some had tins of white emulsion paint outside, and I walked past an open door revealing a woman in baggy jeans stretching a canvas over a huge wood frame.

'Hi! Do you know where Steven is?'

She fired a battery of staples from a huge metal gun into the frame. 'Fourteen. But I think he just went out for food.'

Fourteen was at the far end. I knocked, then pushed the door tentatively and walked in. The studio was lined with canvases, two huge tables covered with sloppy trays of oil paints and battered pastel crayons. The walls were hung with beautiful oversized pictures of women in various states of undress, some unfinished. The air smelt of paint, turpentine and stale cigarette smoke.

'Hello.'

I turned to see a man holding a white plastic bag. He was around thirty, his features regular but his gaze intense, his chin unshaven, his clothes crumpled and utilitarian, as if he had barely noticed what he'd put on. He looked like a male model in a particularly esoteric fashion magazine.

'Hi. Louisa Clark. We spoke on the phone earlier? Well, we didn't – your friend Josh told me to come.'

'Oh, yeah. You want to buy a drawing.'

'Not as such. We need you to *do* a drawing. Just a small one.'

He sat down on a small stool, opened his carton of noodles and started to eat, hoicking them into his mouth with rapid strokes of his chopsticks.

'It's for a charity thing. People do these doo— small drawings,' I corrected myself. 'And apparently a lot of the top artists in New York are doing them for other people so –'

'"Top artists",' he repeated.

'Well. Yes. Apparently it's not the done thing to do your own and Agnes – my employer – really needs someone brilliant to do one for her.' My voice sounded high and anxious. 'I mean, it shouldn't take you long. We – we don't want anything fancy . . .'

He was staring at me and I heard my voice trail off, thin and uncertain.

'We – we can pay. Quite well,' I added. 'And it's for charity.'

He took another mouthful, peering intently into his carton. I stood by the window and waited.

'Yeah,' he said, when he had finished chewing. 'I'm not your man.'

'But Josh said –'

'You want me to create something to satisfy the ego of some woman who can't draw and doesn't want to be shown up in front of her ladies who lunch . . .' He shook his head. 'You want me to draw you a greetings card.'

'Mr Lipkott. Please. I probably haven't explained it very well. I –'

'You explained it just fine.'

'But Josh said –'

'Josh said nothing about greetings cards. I hate that charity dinner shit.'

'Me also.' Agnes stood in the doorway. She took a step into the room, glancing down to make sure she was not treading onto one of the tubes of paint or bits of paper that littered the floor. She held out a long, pale hand. 'Agnes Gopnik. I hate this charity shit too.'

Steven Lipkott stood slowly and then, almost as if it were an impulse from a more courtly age that he had little control over, raised his hand to shake hers. He couldn't take his eyes from her face. I had forgotten that Agnes got you like that at first meeting.

'Mr Lipkott – is that right? Lipkott? I know this is not a normal thing for you. But I have to go to this thing with room of witches. You know? Actual witches. And I draw like three-year-old in mittens. If I have to go and show them my drawing they bitch about me more than they do already.' She sat down and pulled a cigarette from her handbag. She reached across and picked up a lighter that sat on one of his painting tables and lit her cigarette. Steven Lipkott was still watching her, his chopsticks loose in his hand.

'I am not from this place. I am Polish masseuse. There is no shame in this. But I do not want to give these witches chance to look down on me again. Do you know how it is to have people look down on you?' She exhaled, gazing at him, her head tilted, so that smoke trickled horizontally towards him. I thought he might actually have inhaled.

'I – uh – yeah.'

'So it is one small thing I am asking you. To help me. I know this is not your thing and that you are serious artist, but I really need help. And I will pay you very good money.'

The room fell silent. A phone vibrated in my back pocket. I tried to ignore it. For that moment I knew I should not move. We three stood there for an eternity.

'Okay,' he said finally. 'But on one condition.'

'Name it.'

'I draw you.'

For a minute nobody spoke. Agnes raised an eyebrow, then took a slow drag of her cigarette, her eyes not leaving his. 'Me.'

'Can't be the first time someone's asked.'

'Why me?'

'Don't play the ingénue.'

He smiled then, and she kept her face straight, as if deciding whether to be insulted. Her eyes dropped to her feet, and, when she lifted them, there it was, her smile, small, speculative, a prize he believed he had won.

She stubbed out her cigarette on the floor. 'How long will it take?'

He shoved the carton of noodles to one side and reached for a white pad of thick paper. It might have been only me who noticed the way his voice lowered in volume. 'Depends how good you are at keeping still.'

Minutes later I was back in the car. I closed the door. Garry was listening to his tapes.

'Por favor, habla más despacio.'

'Pohr fah-VOR, AH-blah mahs dehs-PAHS-ee-oh.' He slapped the dashboard with a fat palm. 'Ah, crap. Lemme try that again. AHblamahsdehsPAHSeeoh.' He practised three more lines, then turned to me. 'She gonna be long?'

I stared out of the window at the blank windows of the second floor. 'I really hope not,' I said.

Agnes finally emerged at a quarter to four, an hour and three-quarters after Garry and I had run out of our already limited conversation. After watching a cable comedy show downloaded on his iPad (he didn't offer to share it with me) he had nodded off, his chins resting on the bulk of his chest as he snored lightly. I sat in the back of the car growing increasingly tense as the minutes ticked by, sending periodic messages to Sam that were variations on: *She's not back yet. Still not back. Omigod, what on earth is she doing in there?* He had had lunch in a tiny deli across town and said he was so hungry he could eat fifteen horses. He sounded cheerful, relaxed, and every word we exchanged told me I was in the wrong place, that I should be beside him, leaning against him, feeling his voice rumble in my ear. I had started to hate Agnes.

And suddenly there she was, striding out of the building with a broad smile and a flat package under her arm.

'Oh, thank God,' I said.

Garry woke with a start and hurried around the car to open the door for her. She slid in calmly, as if she had been gone two minutes instead of two hours. She brought with her the faint scents of cigarettes and turpentine.

'We need to stop at McNally Jackson on the way back. To get some pretty paper to wrap it in.'

'We have wrapping paper at the –'

'Steven told me about this special hand-pressed paper. I want to wrap it in this special paper. Garry, you know the place I mean? We can drop down to SoHo on the way back, yes?' She waved a hand.

I sat back, faintly despairing. Garry set off, bumping the limo gently over the potholed car park as he headed back to what he considered civilization.

We arrived back at Fifth Avenue at four forty. As Agnes climbed out, I hurried out beside her, clutching the bag with the special paper.

'Agnes, I – I was wondering . . . what you said about me leaving early today . . .'

'I don't know whether to wear the Temperley or the Badgley Mischka this evening. What do you think?'

I tried to recall either dress. Failed. I was trying to calculate how long it would take me to get over to Times Square, where Sam was now waiting. 'The Temperley, I think. Definitely. It's perfect. Agnes – you remember you said I might be able to leave early today?'

'But it's such a dark blue. I'm not sure this blue is a good colour on me. And the shoes that go with it rub on my heel.'

'We talked last week. Would it be okay? It's just I really want to see Sam off at the airport.' I fought to keep the irritation from my voice.

'Sam?' She nodded a greeting at Ashok.

'My boyfriend.'

She considered this. 'Mm. Okay. Oh, they are going to be so impressed with this drawing. Steven is genius, you know? Actual genius.'

'So I can go?'

'Sure.'

My shoulders sagged with relief. If I left in ten minutes I could get the subway south and be with him by five thirty. That would still give us an hour and a bit together. Better than nothing.

The lift doors closed behind us. Agnes opened a compact and checked her lipstick, pouting at her reflection. 'But maybe just stay until I'm dressed. I need second opinion on this Temperley.'

Agnes changed her outfit four times. I was too late to meet Sam in Midtown, Times Square or anywhere else. Instead I got to JFK fifteen minutes before he had to head through security. I shoved my way past the other passengers to where

I could see him standing in front of the departures board, and hurled myself through the airport doors and against his back. 'I'm sorry. I'm so, so sorry.'

We held each other for a minute.

'What happened?'

'Agnes happened.'

'Wasn't she going to let you out early? I thought she was your mate.'

'She was just obsessed by this artwork thing and it all went . . . Oh, God, it was maddening.' I threw my hands into the air. 'What am I even doing in this stupid job, Sam? She made me wait because she couldn't work out what dress to wear. At least Will actually needed me.'

He tilted his head and touched his forehead to mine. 'We had this morning.'

I kissed him, reaching around his neck so that I could place my whole self against him. We stayed there, eyes closed, as the airport moved and swayed around us.

And then my phone rang.

'I'm ignoring it,' I said, into his chest.

It continued to ring, insistently.

'It might be her.' He held me gently away from him.

I let out a low growl, then pulled my phone from my back pocket and put it to my ear. 'Agnes?'

'It's Josh. I was just calling to see how today went.'

'Josh! Um . . . oh. Yes, it was fine. Thank you!' I turned away slightly, putting my hand up to my other ear. I felt Sam stiffen beside me.

'So he did the drawing for you?'

'He did. She's really happy. Thank you so much for organizing it. Listen, I'm in the middle of something right now, but thank you. It really was incredibly kind of you.'

'Glad it worked out. Listen, give me a call, yeah? Let's grab a coffee sometime.'

'Sure!' I ended the call to find Sam watching me.

'Josh,' he said.

I put the phone back into my pocket.

'The guy you met at the ball.'

'It's a long story.'

'Okay.'

'He helped me sort this drawing for Agnes today. I was desperate.'

'So you had his number.'

'It's New York. Everyone has everyone's number.'

He dragged his hand over the top of his head and turned away.

'It's nothing. Really.' I took a step towards him, pulled him by his belt buckle. I could feel the weekend sliding away from me again. 'Sam . . . Sam . . .'

He deflated, put his arms around me. He rested his chin on the top of my head and moved his from side to side. 'This is . . .'

'I know,' I said. 'I know it is. But I love you and you love me and at least we managed to do a bit of the getting-naked thing. And it was great, wasn't it? The getting-naked thing?'

'For, like, five minutes.'

'Best five minutes of the last four weeks. Five minutes that will keep me going for the next four.'

'Except it's seven.'

I slid my hands into his back pockets. 'Don't let's end this badly. Please. I don't want you to go away angry because of some stupid call from someone who is literally nothing to me.'

His face softened when he held my gaze, as it always did. It was one of the things I loved about him, the way his features, so brutal in repose, melted when he looked at me. 'I'm not pissed off at you. I'm pissed off at myself. And airline food or burritos or whatever it was. And your woman there who can't apparently put on a dress by herself.'

'I'll be back for Christmas. For a whole week.'

Sam frowned. He took my face in his hands. They were warm and slightly rough. We stood there for a moment, and then we kissed, and some decades later he straightened up and glanced at the board.

'And now you have to go.'

'And now I have to go.'

I swallowed the lump that had risen in my throat. He kissed me once more, then swung his bag over his shoulder. I stood on the concourse, watching the space where he had been for a full minute after security had swallowed him.

In general, I'm not a moody person. I'm not very good at the whole door-slamming, scowling, eye-rolling thing. But that evening I made my way back to the city, pushed my way through the crowds on the subway platform, elbows out, and scowled like a native. Throughout the journey I found myself checking the time. *He's in the departure lounge. He'll be boarding. And . . . he's gone.* The moment his plane was due to take off I felt something sink inside me and my mood darkened even further. I picked up some takeout sushi and walked from the subway station to the Gopniks' building. When I got to my little room I sat and stared at the container, then at the wall, and knew I couldn't stay there alone with my thoughts so I knocked on Nathan's door.

'C'min!'

Nathan was watching American football, holding a beer. He was wearing a pair of surfer shorts and a T-shirt. He looked up at me expectantly, and with the faintest of delays, in the way people do when they're letting you know that they're really locked into something else.

'Can I eat my dinner in here with you?'

He tore his gaze away from the screen again. 'Bad day?'

I nodded.

'Need a hug?'

I shook my head. 'Just a virtual one. If you're nice to me I'll probably cry.'

'Ah. Your man gone home, has he?'

'It was a disaster, Nathan. He was sick for pretty much the whole thing and then Agnes wouldn't let me have the time off she promised me today so I barely got to see him and when I did it kept getting . . . awkward between us.'

Nathan turned down the television with a sigh, and patted the side of the bed. I climbed up, and placed my takeout bag on my lap where, later, I would discover soy sauce had leaked through onto my work trousers. I rested my head on his shoulder.

'Long-distance relationships are tough,' Nathan pronounced, as if he was the first person to have considered such a thing. Then he added, 'Like, really tough.'

'Right.'

'It's not just the sex, and the inevitable jealousy –'

'We're not jealous people.'

'But he's not going to be the first person you tell stuff to. The day-to-day bits and pieces. And that stuff is important.'

He proffered his beer and I took a swig, handing it back to him. 'We did know it was going to be hard. I mean we talked about all this before I left. But you know what's really bugging me?'

He dragged his gaze back from the screen. 'Go on.'

'Agnes knew how much I wanted to spend time with Sam. We'd talked about it. She was the one saying we had to be together, that we shouldn't be apart, blah-blah-blah. And then she made me stay with her till the absolute last minute.'

'That's the job, Lou. They come first.'

'But she knew how important it was to me.'

'Maybe.'

'She's meant to be my friend.'

Nathan raised an eyebrow. 'Lou. The Traynors were not normal employers. Will was not a normal employer. Neither are the Gopniks. These people may act nice, but ultimately you have to remember this is a power relationship. It's a business transaction.' He took a swig of his beer. 'You know what happened to the Gopniks' last social secretary? Agnes told Old Man Gopnik that she was talking about her behind her back, spreading secrets. So they sacked her. After twenty-two years. They sacked her.'

'And was she?'

'Was she what?'

'Spreading secrets?'

'I don't know. Not the point, though, is it?'

I didn't want to contradict him but to explain why Agnes and I were different would have meant betraying her. So I said nothing.

Nathan seemed about to say something, then changed his mind.

'What?'

'Look . . . nobody can have everything.'

'What do you mean?'

'This is a really great job, right? I mean, you might not think that tonight, but you've got a great situation in the heart of New York, a good wage and a decent employer. You get to go to all sorts of great places, and some occasional perks. They bought you a nearly-three-thousand-dollar ball dress, right? I got to go to the Bahamas with Mr G a couple of months ago. Five-star hotel, beachfront room, the lot. Just for a couple of hours' work a day. So we're lucky. But in the long term, the cost of all that might turn out to be a relationship with someone whose life is completely different and a million miles away. That's the choice you make when you head out.'

I stared at him.

'I just think you've got to be realistic about these things.'

'You're not really helping, Nathan.'

'I'm being straight with you. And, hey, look on the bright side. I heard you did a great job today with the drawing. Mr G told me he was really impressed.'

'They really liked it?' I tried to suppress my glow of pleasure.

'Aw, man. Seriously. Loved it. She's going to knock those charity ladies dead.'

I leant against him, and he switched the volume back up. 'Thanks, Nathan,' I said, and opened my sushi. 'You're a mate.'

He grimaced slightly. 'Yeah. That whole fishy thing. Any chance you could wait until you're in your own room?'

I closed my sushi box. He was right. Nobody could have everything.

10

To: MrandMrsBernardClark@yahoo.com
From: BusyBee@gmail.com

Hey, Mum,

Sorry for the late reply. It's quite busy here! Never a dull moment!

I'm glad you liked the pictures. Yes, the carpets are 100 per cent wool, some of the rugs are silk, the wood is definitely not veneer, and I asked Ilaria and they get their curtains dry-cleaned once a year while they spend a month in the Hamptons. The cleaners are very thorough but Ilaria does the kitchen floor every day herself because she doesn't trust them.

Yes, Mrs Gopnik does have a walk-in shower and also a walk-in wardrobe in her dressing room. She is very fond of her dressing room and spends a lot of time in there on the phone to her mum in Poland. I didn't have time to count the shoes like you asked but I'd say there are well over a hundred pairs. She has them stacked in boxes with pictures of them stuck to the front just so she knows which is which. When she gets a new pair it's my job to take the picture. She has a camera just for her shoe boxes!

I'm glad the art course went well and the Better Communication for Couples class sounds grand, but you must tell Dad that it's not to do with Bedroom Stuff. He's sent me three emails this week, asking if I think he could fake a heart murmur.

Sorry to hear that Granddad's been under the weather. Is he still hiding his vegetables under the table? Are you sure you have to give up your night classes? Seems like a shame.

Okay – got to go. Agnes is calling me. I'll let you know about Christmas, but don't worry, I will be there.

Love you,
Louisa xxx

PS No, I haven't seen Robert De Niro again but, yes, if I do I will definitely tell him that you liked him very much in The Mission.

PPS No, I honestly haven't spent any time in Angola and I'm not in urgent need of a cash transfer. Don't answer those ones.

I'm no expert on depression. I hadn't even understood my own after Will died. But I found Agnes's moods especially hard to fathom. My mother's friends who suffered depression – and there seemed to be a dismaying number of them – seemed flattened by life, struggling through a fog that descended until they could see no joy, no prospect of pleasure. It obscured their way forward. You could see it in the way they walked around town, their shoulders bowed, their mouths set in thin lines of forbearance. It was as if sadness seeped from them.

Agnes was different. She was boisterous and garrulous one minute, then weepy and furious the next. I'd been told that she felt isolated, judged, without allies. But that never quite fitted. Because the more time I spent with her, the more I noticed she was not really cowed by those women: she was infuriated by them. She would rage about the unfairness, scream at Mr Gopnik; she would imitate them cruelly behind his back, and mutter furiously about the first Mrs

Gopnik, or Ilaria and her scheming ways. She was mercurial, a human flame of outrage, growling about *cipa* or *debil* or *dziwka*. (I would google these in my time off until my ears went pink.)

And then, abruptly, she was someone quite different – a woman who disappeared into rooms and wept quietly, a tense, frozen face after a long phone call in Polish. Her sadness manifested itself in headaches, which I was never quite sure were real.

I talked about it to Treena in the coffee shop with the free WiFi that I had sat in on my first morning in New York. We were using FaceTime Audio, which I preferred to us looking at each other's faces as we talked – I got distracted by the way my nose looked enormous, or what someone was doing behind me. I also didn't want her to see the size of the buttered muffins I was eating.

'Perhaps she's bipolar,' Treena said.

'Yeah. I looked that up, but it doesn't seem to fit. She's never manic, as such, just sort of . . . energetic.'

'I'm not sure depression is a one-size-fits-all thing, Lou,' my sister said. 'Besides, hasn't everyone got something wrong with them in America? Don't they like to take a lot of pills?'

'Unlike England, where Mum would have you go for a nice brisk walk.'

'To take you out of yourself.' My sister sniggered.

'Turn that frown upside down.'

'Put a nice bit of lippy on. Brighten your face up. There. Who needs all those silly medications?'

Something had happened to Treena's and my relationship since I had been gone. We called each other once a week, and for the first time in our adult lives, she had stopped nagging me every time we spoke. She seemed genuinely interested in what my life was like, quizzing me about work, the places I had visited and what the people around me did all day. When I asked for advice, she generally gave me a considered reply instead of calling me a doofus, or asking if I understood what Google was for.

She liked someone, she had confided two weeks previously. They had gone for hipster cocktails at a bar in Shoreditch, then to a pop-up cinema in Clapton, and she had felt quite giddy for several days afterwards. The idea of my sister giddy was a novel one.

'What's he like? You must be able to tell me something *now*.'

'I'm not going to say anything yet. Every time I talk about these things they go wrong.'

'Not even to me?'

'For now. It's . . . Well. Anyway. I'm happy.'

'Oh. So that's why you're being nice.'

'What?'

'You're *getting* some. I thought it was because you finally approved of what I'm doing with my life.'

She laughed. My sister didn't normally laugh, unless it was at me. 'I just think it's nice that everything's working out. You have a great job in the US of A. I love my job. Thom and I are loving being in the city. I feel like things are really opening up for all of us.'

It was such an unlikely statement for my sister to make that I didn't have the heart to tell her about Sam. We talked a bit more, about Mum wanting to take a part-time job at the local school, and Granddad's deteriorating health, which meant that she hadn't applied. I finished my muffin and my coffee and realized that, while I was interested, I didn't feel homesick at all.

'You're not going to start speaking with a bloody awful transatlantic accent, though, right?'

'I'm me, Treen. That's hardly going to change,' I said, in a bloody awful transatlantic accent.

'You're such a doofus,' she said.

'Oh, goodness. You're still here.'

Mrs De Witt was just exiting the building as I arrived home, pulling on her gloves under the awning. I stepped back, neatly avoiding Dean Martin's teeth snapping near my leg, and smiled politely at her. 'Good morning, Mrs De Witt. Where else would I be?'

'I thought the Estonian lap-dancer would have sacked you by now. I'm surprised she's not frightened you'll run off with the old man, like she did.'

'Not really my modus operandi, Mrs De Witt,' I said cheerfully.

'I heard her yelling again in the corridor the other night. Awful racket. At least the other one just sulked for a couple of decades. A lot easier on the neighbours.'

'I'll pass that on.'

She shook her head, and was about to move away, but she stopped and gazed at my outfit. I was wearing a fine-pleated gold skirt, my fake fur gilet and a beanie hat coloured like a giant strawberry that Thom had been given for Christmas two years ago and refused to wear because it was 'girly'. On my feet were a pair of bright red patent brogues that I had bought from a sale in a children's shoe shop, air-punching amid the harassed mothers and screeching toddlers when I realized they fitted.

'Your skirt.'

I glanced down, and braced myself for whatever barb was coming my way.

'I have one like that from Biba.'

'It *is* Biba!' I said delightedly. 'I got it from an online auction two years ago. Four pounds fifty! Only one tiny hole in the waistband.'

'I have that exact skirt. I used to travel a lot in the sixties. Whenever I went to London I would spend hours in that store. I used to ship whole trunks of Biba dresses home to Manhattan. We had nothing like it here.'

'Sounds like heaven. I've seen pictures,' I said. 'What an amazing thing to have been able to do. What did you do? I mean, why did you travel so much?'

'I worked in fashion. For a women's magazine. It was –' She lurched forward, ambushed by a fit of coughing, and I waited while she recovered her breath. 'Well. Anyway. You look quite reasonable,' she said, putting her hand up against the wall. Then she turned and hobbled away up the street, Dean Martin casting baleful glances simultaneously at me and the kerb behind him.

The rest of the week was, as Michael would say, *interesting*. Tabitha's apartment in SoHo was being redecorated and our apartment, for a week or so, became the battle ground for a series of turf wars apparently invisible to the male gaze, but only too obvious to Agnes, whom I could hear hissing at Mr Gopnik when she thought Tabitha was out of range.

Ilaria relished her role as foot-soldier. She made a point of serving Tab's favourite dishes – spicy curries and red meat – none of which Agnes would eat, and professed herself ignorant of that when Agnes complained. She made sure Tab's laundry was done first, and left folded neatly on her bed, while Agnes raced through the apartment in a towelling robe trying to work out what had happened to the blouse she had planned to wear that day.

In the evenings Tab would plant herself in the sitting room while Agnes was on the phone to her mother in Poland.

She would hum noisily, scrolling through her iPad, until Agnes, silently enraged, would get up and decamp to her dressing room. Occasionally Tab invited girlfriends to the apartment and they took over the kitchen or the television room, a gaggle of noisy voices, gossiping, giggling, a ring of blonde heads that fell silent if Agnes happened to walk past.

'It's her house too, my darling,' Mr Gopnik would say mildly, when Agnes protested. 'She did grow up here.'

'She treats me like I am temporary fixture.'

'She'll get used to you in time. She's still a child in many ways.'

'She's *twenty-four*.' Agnes would make a low growling noise, a sound I was quite sure no Englishwomen had ever mastered (I did try a few times) and throw up her hands in exasperation. Michael would walk past me, his face frozen, his eyes sliding towards mine in mute solidarity.

Agnes asked me to send a parcel to Poland via FedEx. She wanted me to pay cash, and keep hold of the receipt. The box was large, square and not particularly heavy, and we had the conversation in her study, which she had taken to locking, to Ilaria's disgust.

'What is it?'

'Just present for my mother.' She waved a hand. 'But Leonard thinks I spend too much on my family so I don't want him to know everything that I send.'

I humped it down to the FedEx office at West 57th Street and waited in line. When I filled out the form with the assistant, he asked: 'What are the contents? For Customs purposes?' and I realized I didn't know. I texted Agnes and she responded swiftly: *Just say is gifts for family.*

'But what kind of gifts, ma'am?' said the man, wearily.

I texted again. There was an audible sigh from someone in the queue behind me.

Tchotchkes.

I stared at the message. Then I held out my phone. 'Sorry. I can't pronounce that.'

He peered at it. 'Yeah, lady. That's not really helping me.'

I texted Agnes.

Tell him mind his own business! What business of him what I want to send my mother!

I shoved my phone into my pocket. 'She says it's cosmetics, a jumper and a couple of DVDs.'

'Value?'

'A hundred and eighty-five dollars and fifty-two cents.'

'Finally,' muttered the FedEx employee. And I handed over the money and hoped nobody could see the crossed fingers on my other hand.

On Friday afternoon, when Agnes began her piano lesson, I retreated to my room and called England. As I dialled Sam's number, I felt the familiar flutter of excitement just at the prospect of hearing his voice. Some days I missed him so much I carried it round like an ache. I sat and waited as it rang.

And a woman answered.

'Hello?' she said. She was well-spoken, her voice slightly raspy at the edges, as if she had smoked too many cigarettes.

'Oh, I'm sorry. I must have dialled the wrong number.' I briefly pulled the phone from my ear and stared at the screen.

'Who are you after?'

'Sam? Sam Fielding?'

'He's in the shower. Hold on, I'll get him.' Her hand went over the receiver and she yelled his name, her voice briefly muffled. I went very still. There were no young women in Sam's family. 'He's just coming,' she said, after a moment. 'Who shall I say is calling?'

'Louisa.'

'Oh. Okay.'

Long-distance phone calls make you oddly attuned to slight variations in tone and emphasis and there was something in that 'Oh' that made me uneasy. I was about to ask whom I was talking to when Sam picked up.

'Hey!'

'Hey!' It came out strangely broken, as my mouth had dried unexpectedly. and I had to say it twice.

'What's up?'

'Nothing! I mean nothing urgent. I – I just, you know, wanted to hear your voice.'

'Hold on. I'll close this door.' I could picture him in the little railway carriage, pulling the bedroom door to. When he came back on he sounded cheery, quite unlike the last time we had spoken. 'So what's going on? Everything okay with you? What's the time there?'

'Just after two. Um, who was that?'

'Oh. That's Katie.'

'Katie.'

'Katie Ingram. My new partner?'

'Katie! Okay! So . . . uh . . . what's she doing in your house?'

'Oh, she's just giving me a lift to Donna's leaving do. Bike's gone into the garage. Problem with the exhaust.'

'She really is looking after you, then!' I wondered, absently, if he was wearing a towel.

'Yeah. She only lives down the road so it made sense.' He said it with the casual neutrality of someone aware he was being listened to by two women.

'So where are you all off to?'

'That tapas place in Hackney? The one that used to be a church? I'm not sure we ever went there.'

143

'A church! Ha-ha-ha! So you'll all have to be on your best behaviour!' I laughed, too loudly.

'Bunch of paramedics on a night out? I doubt it.'

There was a short silence. I tried to ignore the knot in my stomach. Sam's voice softened. 'You sure you're okay? You sound a little –'

'I'm fine! Totally! Like I said. I just wanted to hear your voice.'

'Sweetheart, it's great to speak to you but I have to go. Katie did me a big favour giving me a lift and we're late already.'

'Okay! Well, have a lovely evening! Don't do anything I wouldn't!' I was talking in exclamation marks. 'And give Donna my best!'

'Will do. We'll speak soon.'

'Love you.' It sounded more plaintive than I'd intended. 'Write to me!'

'Ah, Lou . . .' he said.

And then he was gone. And I was left staring at my phone in a too-silent room.

I organized a private view of a new film at a small screening room for the wives of Mr Gopnik's business associates, and the hors d'oeuvres that would go with it. I disputed a bill for flowers that had not been received and then I ran down to Sephora and picked up two bottles of nail varnish that Agnes had seen in *Vogue* and wanted to take with her to the country.

And two minutes after my shift finished and the Gopniks departed for their weekend retreat, I said no thank you to Ilaria's offer of leftover meatballs and ran back to my room.

Reader, I did the stupid thing. I looked her up on Facebook.

It didn't take more than forty minutes to filter this Katie Ingram from the other hundred or so. Her profile was unlocked, and contained the logo for the NHS. Her job description said: 'Paramedic: Love My Job!!!' She had hair that could have been red or strawberry blonde, it was hard to tell from the photographs, and she was possibly in her late twenties, pretty with a snub nose. In the first thirty photographs she had posted she was laughing with friends, frozen in the middle of Good Times. She looked annoyingly good in a bikini (Skiathos 2014!! What a laugh!!!!), she had a small hairy dog, a penchant for vertiginously high heels and a best friend with long dark hair who was fond of kissing her cheek in pictures (I briefly entertained the hope that she was gay but she belonged to a Facebook group called: *Hands up if you're secretly delighted that Brad Pitt is single again!!*).

Her 'relationship status' was set to single.

I scrolled back through her feed, secretly hating myself for doing so, but unable to stop myself. I scanned her photographs, trying to find one where she looked fat, or sulky, or perhaps the recipient of some terrible scaly skin disease. I clicked and I clicked. And just as I was about to close my laptop I stopped. There it was, posted three weeks previously. Katie Ingram stood on a bright winter's day, in her dark green uniform, her pack proudly at her feet, outside the ambulance station in east London. This time her arm was around Sam, who stood in his uniform, arms folded, smiling at the camera.

'Best partner in the WORLD,' read the caption. 'Loving my new job!'

Just below it, her dark-haired friend had commented: 'I wonder why . . . ?!' and added a winky face.

Here is the thing about jealousy. It's not a good look. And the rational part of you knows that. You are not the jealous sort! That sort of woman is awful! And it makes no sense! If someone likes you, they will stay with you; if they don't like you enough to stay with you, they aren't worth being with anyway. You know that. You are a sensible, mature woman of twenty-eight years. You have read the self-help articles. You have watched *Dr Phil*.

But when you live 3,500 miles from your handsome, kind, sexy paramedic boyfriend and he has a new partner who sounds and looks like Pussy Galore – a woman who spends at least twelve hours a day in close proximity to the man you love, a man who has confessed already to how hard he is finding the physical separation – then the rational part of you gets firmly squashed by the gigantic, squatting toad that is your irrational self.

It didn't matter what I did, I couldn't scrub that image of the two of them from my mind. It lodged itself, a white on black negative, somewhere behind my eyes and haunted me: her lightly tanned arm tight around his waist, her fingers resting lightly on the waistband of his uniform. Were they side by side at a late bar, her nudging him at some shared joke? Was she the kind of touchy-feely woman who would reach over and pat his arm for emphasis? Did she smell good, so that when he left her each day he would feel, in some indefinable way, he was missing something?

I knew this was the way to madness yet I couldn't stop myself. I thought about calling him, but nothing says stalky, insecure girlfriend like someone who calls at four a.m. My thoughts whirred and tumbled and fell in a great toxic cloud. And I hated myself for them. And they whirred and fell some more.

'Oh, why couldn't you just have been partnered with a nice middle-aged man?' I murmured to the ceiling. And some time in the small hours I finally fell asleep.

On Monday we ran (I stopped only once), then went shopping in Macy's and bought a bunch of children's clothes for

Agnes's niece. I sent them off to Kraków from the FedEx office, this time confident of the contents.

Over lunch she spoke to me about her sister, how she had been married too young, to the manager of a local brewery, who treated her with little respect, and how she now felt so downtrodden and worthless that Agnes could not persuade her to leave. 'She cries to my mother every day because of what he says to her. She's fat or she's ugly or he could have done better. That stinking dickhead piece of chickenshit. A dog would not piss on his leg if it had drunk a hundred buckets of water.'

Her ultimate aim, she confided, over her chard and beetroot salad, was to bring her sister to New York, away from that man. 'I think I can get Leonard to give her a job. Maybe as secretary in his office. Or, better, housekeeper in our apartment! Then we could get rid of Ilaria! My sister is very good, you know. Very conscientious. But she doesn't want to leave Kraków.'

'Maybe she doesn't want to disrupt her daughter's education. My sister was very nervous about moving Thom to London,' I said.

'Mm,' said Agnes. But I could tell she didn't really think that was an obstacle. I wondered if rich people just didn't see obstacles to anything.

We had barely been back half an hour before she glanced at her phone and announced we were going to East Williamsburg.

'The artist? But I thought –'

'Steven is teaching me to draw. Drawing lessons.'

I blinked. 'Okay.'

'Is surprise for Leonard so you must not say anything.'

She didn't look at me for the whole journey.

*

147

'You're late,' said Nathan, when I arrived home. He was heading off to play basketball with some friends from his gym, his kit-bag slung over his shoulder and a hoodie over his hair.

'Yeah.' I dropped my bag and filled the kettle. I had a carton of noodles in a plastic bag and put them on the counter.

'Been anywhere nice?'

I hesitated. 'Just . . . here and there. You know what she's like.' I switched on the kettle.

'You okay?'

'I'm fine.'

I could feel his gaze on me until I turned and forced a smile. Then he clapped me on the back and turned to head out. 'Some days, eh?'

Some days, indeed. I stared at the kitchen worktop. I didn't know what to say to him. I didn't know how to explain the two and a half hours Garry and I had waited in the car for her, my eyes flicking repeatedly up to the light at the obscured window and back to my phone. After an hour Garry, bored of his language tapes, had texted Agnes to say he was being moved on by a parking attendant and she should text him as soon as she needed to go, but she didn't respond. We drove around the block and he filled the car with fuel, then suggested we get a coffee. 'She didn't say how long she'd be. That usually means she'll be a coupla hours at least.'

'This has happened before?'

'Mrs G does as she pleases.'

He bought me a coffee in a near-empty diner, where the laminated menu showed poorly lit photographs of every single dish, and we sat in near-silence, each monitoring our phones, in case she called, and watching the Williamsburg dusk turn gradually to a neon-lit night. I had moved to the most exciting city on earth, yet some days I felt my life had shrunk: limo to apartment; apartment back to limo.

'So have you worked for the Gopniks for long?'

Garry slowly stirred two sugars into his coffee, screwing up the wrappers in a fat fist. 'Year and a half.'

'Who did you work for before?'

'Someone else.'

I took a sip of my coffee, which was surprisingly good. 'You never mind it?'

He looked up at me from under heavy brows.

'All the hanging around?' I clarified. 'I mean – does she do this often?'

He kept stirring his coffee, his eyes back on his mug. 'Kid,' he said, after a minute. 'I don't mean to be rude. But I can see you ain't been in this business long, and you'll last a whole lot longer if you don't ask questions.' He sat back in his chair, his bulk spreading gently across his lap. 'I'm the driver. I'm there when they need me. I speak when I'm spoken to. I see nothing, hear nothing, forget everything. That's why I've stayed in this game thirty-two years, and how I've put two ungrateful kids through college. In two and a half years, I take early retirement and move to my beach property in Costa Rica. That's how you do it.' He wiped his nose with a paper napkin, making his jowls judder. 'You get me?'

'See nothing, hear nothing . . .'

'. . . forget everything. You got it. You want a doughnut? They do good doughnuts here. Make 'em fresh throughout the day.' He got up and moved heavily over to the counter. When he came back he said nothing more to me, just nodded, satisfied, when I told him that, yes, the doughnuts were very good indeed.

Agnes said nothing when she rejoined us. After a few minutes, she asked, 'Did Leonard call? I accidentally turn my phone off.'

'No.'

'He must be at the office. I will call him.' She straightened her hair, then settled back in her seat. 'That was very good lesson. I really feel like I'm learning many things. Steven is very good artist,' she announced.

It took me until we were halfway home to notice she wasn't carrying any drawings.

11

Dear Thom,

*I'm sending you a baseball cap because Nathan and I went to a
real-life baseball game yesterday and all the players wore them
(actually, they wore helmets but this is the traditional version). I got
one for you and one for someone else I know. Get your mum to take a
picture of you in it and I can put it on my wall!*

*No, I'm afraid there aren't any cowboys in this part of America
sadly – but today I am going to a country club so I will keep an eye
out in case one rides by.*

*Thank you for the very nice picture of my bum-bum with my
imaginary dog. I hadn't realized my backside was that shade of
purple underneath my trousers, but I shall bear that in mind if I ever
decide to walk naked past the Statue of Liberty like in your picture.*

*I think your version of New York may be even more exciting than
the real thing.*

*Lots of love,
Auntie Lou xxx*

Grand Pines Country Club sprawled across acres of lush
countryside, its trees and fields rolling so perfectly and in
such a vivid shade of green they might have sprung from the
imagination of a seven-year-old with crayons.

On a crisp, clear day Garry drove us slowly up the long
drive, and when the car pulled up in front of the sprawling

white building, a young man in a pale blue uniform stepped forward and opened Agnes's door.

'Good morning, Mrs Gopnik. How are you today?'

'Very good, thank you, Randy. And how are you?'

'Couldn't be better, ma'am. Getting busy in there already. Big day!'

Mr Gopnik having been detained at work, it had fallen to Agnes to present Mary, one of the long-serving staff at his country club, with a retirement gift. Agnes had made her feelings clear for much of the week about having to do this. She hated the country club. The former Mrs Gopnik's cronies would be there. And Agnes hated speaking in public. She could not do it without Leonard. But, for once, he was immovable. *It will help you claim your place, darling. And Louisa will be with you.*

We practised her speech and we made a plan. We would arrive in the Great Room as late as possible, at the last moment before the starters were served so that we could sit down with apologies, blaming Manhattan traffic. Mary Lander, the retiree in question, would stand after the coffee at two p.m., and a few people would say nice words about her. Then Agnes would stand, apologize for Mr Gopnik's unavoidable absence, and say a few more nice words about Mary before handing over her retirement gift. We would wait a diplomatic half-hour longer then leave, pleading important business in the city.

'You think this dress is okay?' She was wearing an unusually conservative two-piece: a shift dress in fuchsia with a paler short-sleeved jacket and a string of pearls. Not her usual look, but I understood that she needed to feel as if she were wearing armour.

'Perfect.' She took a breath and I nudged her, smiling. She took my hand briefly and squeezed it.

'In and out,' I said. 'Nothing to it.'

'Two giant fingers,' she murmured, and gave me a small smile.

The building itself was sprawling and light, painted magnolia, with huge vases of flowers and reproduction antique furniture everywhere. Its oak-panelled halls, its portraits of founders on the walls and silent staff moving from room to room were accompanied by the gentle hush of quiet conversation, the occasional clink of a coffee cup or glass. Every view was beautiful, every need seemingly already met.

The Great Room was full, sixty or so round, elegantly decorated tables, filled with well-dressed women, chatting over glasses of still mineral water or fruit punch. Hair was uniformly perfectly blow-dried, and the preferred mode of dress was expensively elegant – well-cut dresses with bouclé jackets, or carefully matched separates. The air was thick with a heady mix of perfume. At some tables a solitary man sat flanked by women, but they seemed oddly neutered in such a largely female room.

To the casual observer – or perhaps an average man – almost nothing would have seemed amiss. A faint movement of heads, a subtle dip in the noise level as we passed, the slight pursing of lips. I walked behind Agnes, and she faltered suddenly, so that I almost collided with her back. And then I saw the table setting: Tabitha, a young man, an older man, two women I did not recognize and, beside me, an older woman who lifted her head and looked Agnes square in the eye. As the waiter stepped forward and pulled out her seat, Agnes was seated opposite the Big Purple herself, Kathryn Gopnik.

'Good afternoon,' Agnes said, offering it up to the table as a whole and managing not to look at the first Mrs Gopnik as she did so.

'Good afternoon, Mrs Gopnik,' the man who was seated on my side of the table replied.

'Mr Henry,' said Agnes, her smile wavering. 'Tab. You didn't say you were coming today.'

'I'm not sure we have to inform you of all our movements, do we, Agnes?' Tabitha said.

'And who might you be?' The elderly gentleman on my right turned to me. I was about to say I was Agnes's friend from London, but realized that was now going to be impossible. 'I'm Louisa,' I said. 'Louisa Clark.'

'Emmett Henry,' he said, holding out a gnarled hand. 'Delighted to meet you. Is that an English accent?'

'It is.' I looked up to thank a waitress who was pouring me some water.

'How very delightful. And are you over visiting?'

'Louisa works as Agnes's assistant, Emmett.' Tabitha's voice lifted across the table. 'Agnes has developed the most extraordinary habit of bringing her staff to social occasions.'

My cheeks flooded with colour. I felt the burn of Kathryn Gopnik's scrutiny, along with the eyes of the rest of the table.

Emmett considered this. 'Well, you know, my Dora took her nurse Libby with her absolutely everywhere for the last ten years. Restaurants, the theatre, wherever we went. She used to say old Libby was a better conversationalist than I was.' He patted my hand and chuckled, and several other people at the table joined in obligingly. 'I dare say she was right.'

And, just like that, I was saved from social ignominy by an eighty-six-year-old man. Emmett Henry chatted to me through the shrimp starter, telling me about his long association with the country club, his years as a lawyer in Manhattan, his retirement to a senior citizens' facility a short distance away.

'I come here every day, you know. It keeps me active, and there are always people to talk to. It's my home from home.'

'It's beautiful,' I said, peering behind me. Several heads immediately turned away. 'I can see why you'd want to come.'

Agnes seemed outwardly composed but I could detect a slight tremor to her hands.

'Oh, this is a very historic building, dear.' Emmett was gesturing to the side of the room where a plaque stood. 'It dates from . . .' he paused to ensure I had the full impact, then pronounced carefully '. . . 1937.'

I didn't like to tell him that on our street in England we had council housing older than that. I think Mum might even have a pair of tights older than that. I nodded, smiled, ate my chicken with wild mushrooms and wondered if there was any way I could move closer to Agnes, who was clearly miserable.

The meal dragged. Emmett told me endless tales of the club, and amusing things said and done by people I had never heard of, and occasionally Agnes looked up and I smiled at her, but I could see her sinking. Glances flickered surreptitiously towards our table and heads dipped towards heads. *The two Mrs Gopniks sitting inches away from each other! Can you imagine!* After the main course, I excused myself from my seat.

'Agnes, would you mind showing me where the Ladies is?' I said. I figured even ten minutes away from this room would help.

Before she could answer, Kathryn Gopnik placed her napkin on the table and turned to me. 'I'll show you, dear. I'm headed that way.' She picked up her handbag and stood beside me, waiting. I glanced at Agnes, but she didn't move.

Agnes nodded. 'You go. I'll – finish my chicken,' she said.

I followed Mrs Gopnik through the tables of the Great Room and out into the hallway, my mind racing. We walked along a carpeted corridor, me a few paces behind her, and stopped at the Ladies. She opened the mahogany door and stood back, allowing me in before her.

'Thank you,' I muttered, and headed into a cubicle. I didn't even want to wee. I sat on the seat: if I stayed there long enough she might leave before I came out, but when I emerged she was at the basins, touching up her lipstick. Her gaze slid towards me as I washed my hands.

'So you live in my old home,' she said.

'Yes.' There didn't seem much point in lying about it.

She pursed her lips, then, satisfied, closed her lipstick. 'This must all feel rather awkward for you.'

'I just do my job.'

'Mm.' She took out a small hairbrush and dragged it lightly over her hair. I wondered if it would be rude to leave, or if etiquette said I should also return to the table with her. I dried my hands and leant toward the mirror, checking under my eyes for smudges and taking as much time as possible.

'How is my husband?'

I blinked.

'Leonard. How is he? Surely you're not betraying any great confidence by telling me that.' Her reflection looked out at me.

'I . . . I don't see him much. But he seems fine.'

'I was wondering why he wasn't here. Whether his arthritis had flared up again.'

'Oh. No. I think he has a work thing today.'

'A "work thing". Well. I suppose that's good news.' She placed her hairbrush carefully back in her bag and pulled out a powder compact. She patted her nose once, twice, on each side, before closing it. I was running out of things to do. I rummaged in my bag, trying to remember if I had brought a powder compact with me. And then Mrs Gopnik turned to face me. 'Is he happy?'

'I'm sorry?'

'It's a straightforward question.'

My heart bumped awkwardly against my ribcage.

Her voice was mellifluous, even. 'Tab won't talk to me about him. She's quite angry at her father still, though she loves him desperately. Always was a daddy's girl. So I don't think it's possible for her to paint an accurate picture.'

'Mrs Gopnik, with respect I really don't think it's my place to –'

She turned her head away. 'No. I suppose not.' She placed her compact carefully in her handbag. 'I'm pretty sure I can guess what you've been told about me, Miss . . . ?'

'Clark.'

'Miss Clark. And I'm sure you're also aware that life is rarely black and white.'

'I am.' I swallowed. 'I also know Agnes is a good person. Smart. Kind. Cultured. And not a gold-digger. As you say, these things are rarely clear-cut.'

Her eyes met mine in the glass. We stood for a few seconds longer, then she closed her handbag and, after a last glance at her reflection, she gave a tight smile. 'I'm glad Leonard is well.'

We returned to the table just as the plates were being cleared. She said not another word to me for the rest of the afternoon.

The desserts were served alongside the coffee, the conversation ebbed and lunch dragged to a close. Several elderly women were helped to the Ladies, their walking frames extricated with gentle commotions from chair legs as they went. The man in the suit stood on the small podium at the front, sweating gently into his collar, thanked everybody for coming, then said a few words about upcoming events at the club, including a charity night in two weeks, which was apparently sold out (a round of applause greeted this news). Finally, he said, they had an announcement to make, and nodded towards our table.

Agnes let out a breath and stood, the room's eyes upon her.

She walked to the podium, taking the manager's place at the microphone. As she waited, he brought an older African American woman in a dark suit to the front of the room. The woman fluttered her hands as if everyone were making an unnecessary fuss. Agnes smiled at her, took a deep breath, as I had instructed her, then laid her two small cards carefully on the stand, and began to speak, her voice clear and deliberate.

'Good afternoon, everybody. Thank you for coming today, and thank you to all the staff for such a delicious lunch.'

Her voice was perfectly modulated, the words polished like stones over hours of practice the previous week. There was an approving murmur. I glanced at Mrs Gopnik, whose expression was unreadable.

'As many of you know, this is Mary Lander's last day at the club. We would like to wish her a very happy retirement. Leonard wishes me to tell you, Mary, he is so very sorry not to be able to come today. He appreciates everything you have done for the club and he knows that everyone else here does too.' She paused, as I had instructed her. The room was silent, the women's faces attentive. 'Mary started here at Grand Pines in 1967 as a kitchen attendant and rose up to become assistant house manager. Everybody here has very much enjoyed your company and your hard work over the years, Mary, and we will all miss you very much. We – and the other members of this club - would like to offer you a small token of our appreciation and we sincerely hope that your retirement is most enjoyable.'

There was a polite round of applause and Agnes was handed a glass sculpture of a scroll, with Mary's name engraved on it. She handed it to the older woman, smiling, and stood still as some people took pictures. Then she moved to the edge of the platform and returned to our table, her face flashing relief as she was allowed to leave the limelight.

I watched as Mary smiled for more pictures, this time with the manager. I was about to lean over to Agnes to congratulate her when Kathryn Gopnik stood.

'Actually,' she said, her voice cutting across the chatter, 'I'd like to say a few words.'

As we watched, she made her way up onto the podium, where she walked past the stand. She took Mary's gift from her and handed it to the manager. Then she clasped Mary's hands in her own. 'Oh, Mary,' she said, and then, turning so that they were facing outward: 'Mary, Mary, Mary. What a *darling* you've been.'

There was a spontaneous burst of applause across the room. Mrs Gopnik nodded, waiting until it died down. 'Over the years my daughter has grown up with you watching over her – and us – during the hundreds, no, *thousands* of hours we've spent here. Such happy, happy times. If we've had the slightest problem you've always been there, sorting things out, bandaging scraped knees or putting endless ice packs on bumped heads. I think we all remember the incident in the boathouse!'

There was a ripple of laughter.

'You've especially loved our children, and this place always felt like a sanctuary to Leonard and me because it was the one place we knew our family would be safe and happy. Those beautiful lawns have seen so many great times, and been witness to so much laughter. While we'd be off playing golf or having a delicious cocktail with friends there at the sidelines, you'd be watching over children or handing out glasses of that inimitable iced tea. We all love Mary's special iced tea, don't we, friends?'

There was a cheer. I watched as Agnes grew rigid, clapping robotically as if she wasn't quite sure what else to do.

Emmett leant into me. 'Mary's iced tea is quite a thing. I don't know what she puts into it but, my goodness, it's *lethal*.' He raised his eyes to the heavens.

'Tabitha came out specially from the city, like so many of us today, because I know that she thinks of you not just as staff at this club, but as part of the *family*. And we all know there's no substitute for family!'

I dared not look at Agnes now, as the applause broke out again.

'Mary,' Kathryn Gopnik said, when it had died down, 'you have helped perpetuate the true values of this place – values that some may find old fashioned but which we feel make this country club what it is: consistency, excellence and *loyalty*. You have been its smiling face, its beating heart. I know I speak for everyone when I say it simply won't be the same without you.' The older woman was now beaming, her eyes glittering with tears. 'Everyone, charge your glasses and raise them to our wonderful *Mary*.'

The room erupted. Those who were able to stand stood. As Emmett clambered unsteadily to his feet, I glanced around, and then, feeling somehow treacherous, I did too. Agnes was the last to rise from her chair, still clapping, her smile a glossy rictus on her face.

There was something comforting about a truly heaving bar, one where you had to thrust your arm through a queue three deep to get the attention of a bar-tender, and where you'd be lucky if two-thirds of your drink remained in the glass by the time you'd fought your way back to your table. Balthazar, Nathan told me, was something of a SoHo institution: always jammed, always fun, a staple of the New York bar scene. And tonight, even on a Sunday, it was packed, busy enough for the noise, the ever-moving barmen, the lights and the clatter to drive the day's events from my head.

We sank a couple of beers each, standing at the bar, and Nathan introduced me to the guys he knew from his gym, whose names I forgot almost immediately but who were funny and nice and just needed one woman as an excuse to bounce cheerful insults off each other. Eventually we fought our way to a table where I drank some more and ate a cheeseburger and felt a bit better. At around ten o'clock, when the boys were busy doing grunting impressions of other gym-goers, complete with facial expressions and bulging veins, I got up to go to the bathroom. I stayed there for ten minutes, relishing the relative silence as I touched up my make-up and ruffled my hair. I tried not to think about what Sam was doing. It had stopped being a comfort to me, and had instead started to give me a knot in my stomach. Then I headed back out.

'Are you stalking me?'

I spun round in the corridor. There stood Joshua Ryan in a shirt and jeans, his eyebrows raised.

'What? Oh. Hi!' My hand went instinctively to my hair. ' No – no, I'm just here with some friends.'

'I'm kidding you. How are you, Louisa Clark? Long way from Central Park.' He stooped to kiss my cheek. He smelt delicious, of limes and something soft and musky. 'Wow. That was almost poetic.'

'Just working my way through all the bars in Manhattan. You know how it is.'

'Oh, yeah. The "try something new" thing. You look cute. I like the whole . . .' he gestured towards my shift dress and short-sleeved cardigan '. . . preppy vibe.'

'I had to go to a country club today.'

'It's a good look on you. Want to grab a beer?'

'I – I can't really leave my friends.' He looked momentarily disappointed. 'But, hey,' I added, 'come and join us!'

'Great! Let me just tell the people I'm with. I'm tagging along on a date – they'll be glad to shake me. Where are you?'

I fought my way back to Nathan, my face suddenly flushed

and a faint buzzing in my ears. It didn't matter how wrong his accent, how different his eyebrows, the slant at the edge of his eyes that went the wrong way, it was impossible to look at Josh and not see Will there. I wondered if it would ever stop jolting me. I wondered at my unconscious internal use of the word 'ever'.

'I bumped into a friend!' I said, just as Josh appeared.

'A friend,' said Nathan.

'Nathan, Dean, Arun, this is Josh Ryan.'

'You forgot "the Third".' He grinned at me, like we'd exchanged a private joke. 'Hey.' Josh held out a hand, leant forward and shook Nathan's. I saw Nathan's eyes travel over him and flicker towards me. I raised a bright, neutral smile, as if I had loads of good-looking male friends dotted all over Manhattan who might just want to come and join us in bars.

'Can I buy anyone a beer?' said Josh. 'They do great food here too if anyone's interested.'

'A "friend"?' murmured Nathan, as Josh stepped up to the bar.

'Yes. A friend. I met him at the Yellow Ball. With Agnes.'

'He looks like –'

'I know.'

Nathan considered this. He looked at me, then at Josh. 'That whole "saying yes" thing of yours. You haven't . . .'

'I love Sam, Nathan.'

'Sure you do, mate. I'm just saying.'

I felt Nathan's scrutiny during the rest of the evening. Josh and I somehow ended up on the edge of the table away from everyone else, where he talked about his job and the insane mixture of opiates and anti-depressants his work colleagues shovelled into themselves every day just to cope with the demands of the office, and how hard he was trying not to offend his easily offended boss, and how he kept failing, and the apartment he never had time to decorate and what had happened when his clean-freak mother visited from Boston. I nodded and smiled and listened and tried to make sure that when I found myself watching his face it was in an appropriate, interested way rather than a slightly obsessive, wistful oh-but-you're-so-like-him way.

'And how about you, Louisa Clark? You've said almost nothing about yourself all evening. How's the holiday going? When do you have to head back?'

The job. I realized, with a lurch, that the last time we had met I had lied about who I was. And also that I was too drunk to maintain any kind of lie, or to feel as ashamed as I probably should about confessing. 'Josh. I have to tell you something.'

He leant forward. 'Ah. You're married.'

'Nope.'

'Well, that's something. You have an incurable disease? Weeks left to live?'

I shook my head.

'You're bored? You're bored. You'd really rather talk to someone else now? I get it. I've barely drawn breath.'

I started to laugh. 'No. Not that. You're great company.' I looked down at my feet. 'I'm . . . not who I told you I was. I'm not Agnes's friend from England. I just said that because she needed an ally at the Yellow Ball. I'm, well, I'm her assistant. I'm just an assistant.'

When I looked up he was gazing at me.

'And?'

I stared at him. His eyes had tiny flecks of gold in them.

'Louisa. This is New York. Everyone talks themselves up. Every bank teller is a junior vice president. Every bar-tender has a production company. I guessed you had to work for Agnes because of the way you were running around after her. No friend would do that. Unless they were, like, really stupid. Which you plainly are not.'

'And you don't mind?'

'Hey. I'm just glad you're not married. Unless you *are* married. That bit wasn't a lie too, was it?'

He had taken hold of one of my hands. I felt my breath give slightly in my chest, and I had to swallow before I spoke. 'No. But I do have a boyfriend.'

He kept his eyes on mine, perhaps searching to see whether there was some punch-line coming, then released my hand reluctantly. 'Ah. Well, that's a pity.' He leant back in his chair, and took a sip of his drink. 'So how come he isn't here?'

'Because he's in England.'

'And he's coming over?'

'No.'

He pulled a face, the kind of face people make when they think you're doing something stupid but don't want to say so out loud. He shrugged. 'Then we can be friends. You know everyone dates here, right? Doesn't have to be a thing. I'll be your incredibly handsome male walker.'

'Do you mean dating as in "having sex with"?'

'Woah. You English girls don't mince your words.'

'I just don't want to lead you down the garden path.'

'You're telling me this isn't going to be a friends-with-benefits thing. Okay, Louisa Clark. I get it.'

I tried not to smile. And failed.

'You're very cute,' he said. 'And you're funny. And direct. And not like any girl I've ever met.'

'And you're very charming.'

'That's because I'm a little bit enraptured.'

'And I'm a little bit drunk.'

'Oh, now I'm wounded. Really wounded.' He clutched at his heart.

It was at this point that I turned my head and saw Nathan watching. He gave a faint lift of his eyebrow, then tapped his wrist. It was enough to bring me back to earth. 'You know – I really have to go. Early start.'

'I've gone too far. I've frightened you off.'

'Oh, I'm not that easily frightened. But I do have a tricky day at work tomorrow. And my morning run doesn't work so well on several pints of beer and a tequila chaser.'

'Will you call me? For a platonic beer? So I can moon at you a little?'

'I have to warn you, "mooning" means something quite different in England.' I told him and he exploded with laughter.

'Well, I promise not to do that. Unless, of course, you want me to.'

'That's quite the offer.'

'I mean it. Call me.'

I walked out, feeling his eyes on my back the whole way. As Nathan hailed a yellow taxi, I turned as the door was closing. I could only just make him out through a tiny gap as it swung shut, but it was enough to see he was still watching me. And smiling.

I called Sam. 'Hey,' I said, when he picked up.

'Lou? Why am I even asking? Who else would ring me at four forty-five in the morning?'

'So what are you doing?' I lay back on my bed, and let my shoes drop from my feet onto the carpeted floor.

'Just back off a shift. Reading. How are you? You sound cheerful.'

'Been to a bar. Tough day. But I feel a lot better now. And I just wanted to hear your voice. Because I miss you. And you're my boyfriend.'

'And you're drunk.' He laughed.

'I might be. A little. Did you say you were reading?'

'Yup. A novel.'

'Really? I thought you didn't read fiction.'

'Oh, Katie got it for me. Insisted I'd enjoy it. I can't face the endless inquisitions if I keep not reading it.'

'She's buying you books?' I pushed myself upright, my good mood suddenly dissipating.

'Why? What does buying me a book mean?' He sounded half amused.

'It means she fancies you.'

'It does not.'

'It totally does.' Alcohol had loosened my inhibitions. I felt the words coming before I could stop them. 'If women try to make you read something it's because they fancy you. They want to be in your head. They want to make you think of stuff.'

I heard him chuckle. 'And what if it's a motorcycle repair manual?'

'Still counts. Because then she'd be trying to show you what a cool, sexy, motorbike-loving kind of chick she is.'

'Well, this isn't about motorbikes. It's some French thing.'

'French? This is bad. What's the title?'

'Madame de.'

'Madame de what?'

'Just *Madame de*. It's about a general and some earrings and . . .'

'And what?'

'He has an affair.'

'She's making you read books about French people who have affairs? Oh, my God. She totally fancies you.'

'You're wrong, Lou.'

'I know when someone fancies someone, Sam.'

'Really.' He had begun to sound tired.

'So, a man made a pass at me tonight. I knew he fancied me. So I told him straight off I was with someone. I headed it off.'

'Oh, you did? Who was that, then?'

'His name is Josh.'

'*Josh*. Would that be the same Josh who called you when I was leaving?'

Even through my slightly drunken fug I had begun to realize this conversation was a bad idea. 'Yes.'

'And you just happened to bump into him in a bar.'

'I did! I was there with Nathan. And I literally ran into him outside the Ladies.'

'So what did he say?' His voice now held a faint edge.

'He . . . he said it was a pity.'

'And is it?'

'What?'

'A pity?'

There was a short silence. I felt suddenly, horribly sober. 'I'm just telling you what he said. I'm with you, Sam. I'm literally just using this as an example of how I could tell that someone fancied me and how I headed it off before he could get the wrong idea. Which is a concept you seem to be unwilling to grasp.'

'No. Seems to me you're calling me up in the middle of the night to have a go at me about my work partner who has lent me a book, but you're fine with you going out and having drunk conversations with this Josh about relationships. Jesus. You wouldn't even admit we were *in* a relationship until I pushed you into it. And now you'll happily talk about intimate stuff to some guy you just met in a bar. *If* you really just met him in a bar.'

'It just took me time, Sam! I thought you were playing around!'

'It took you time because you were still in love with the

memory of another guy. A dead guy. And you're now in New York because, well, he wanted you to go there. So I have no idea why you're being weird and jealous about Katie. You never minded how much time I spent with Donna.'

'Because Donna didn't fancy you.'

'You've never even met Katie! How could you possibly know whether she fancies me or not?'

'I've seen the pictures!'

'*What pictures?*' he exploded.

I was an idiot. I closed my eyes. 'On her Facebook page. She has pictures. Of you and her.' I swallowed. 'A picture.'

There was a long silence. The kind of silence that says, *Are you serious?* The kind of ominous silence that comes while somebody quietly adjusts his view of who you are. When Sam spoke again his voice was low and controlled. 'This is a ridiculous discussion and I've got to get some sleep.'

'Sam, I –'

'Go to sleep, Lou. We'll speak later.' He rang off.

12

I barely slept, all the things I wished I had and hadn't said whirring around my head in an endless carousel, and woke groggily to the sound of knocking. I stumbled out of bed, and opened my door to find Mrs De Witt standing there in her dressing-gown. She looked tiny and frail without her make-up and set hair, and her face was twisted with anxiety.

'Oh, you're *there*,' she said, like I would have been any-where else. 'Come. Come. I need your help.'

'Wh-what? Who let you in?'

'The big one. The Australian. Come on. No time to waste.'

I rubbed my eyes, struggling to come to.

'He's helped me before but said he couldn't leave Mr Gopnik. Oh, what does it matter? I opened my door this morning to put my trash out and Dean Martin ran out and he's somewhere in the building. I have no idea where. I can't find him by myself.' Her voice was quavering yet imperious, and her hands fluttered around her head. 'Hurry. Hurry now. I'm afraid somebody will open the doors downstairs and he'll get out onto the sidewalk.' She wrung her hands together. 'He's not good by himself outdoors. And someone might steal him. He's a pedigree, you know.'

I grabbed my key and followed her out into the hall, still in my T-shirt.

'Where have you looked?'

'Well, nowhere, dear. I'm not good at walking. That's why I need you to do it. I'm going to go and get my stick.' She looked at me as if I had said something particularly stupid. I sighed, trying to imagine what I would do if I were a small, wonky-eyed pug with an unexpected taste of freedom.

'He's all I have. You have to find him.' She started to cough, as if her lungs couldn't cope with the tension.

'I'll try the main lobby first.'

I ran downstairs, on the basis that Dean Martin was unlikely to be able to call the lift, and scanned the corridor for a small, angry canine. Empty. I checked my watch, noting with mild dismay that this was because it was not yet six a.m. I peered behind and under Ashok's desk, then ran to his office, which was locked. I called Dean Martin's name softly the whole time, feeling faintly stupid as I did so. No sign. I ran back up the stairs and did the same thing on our floors, checking the kitchen and back corridors. Nothing. I did the same on the fourth floor, before rationalizing that if I was now out of breath, the chances of a small fat pug being able to run up that many flights of stairs at speed was pretty unlikely. And then outside I heard the familiar whine of the refuse truck. And I thought about our old dog, who had a spectacular ability to tolerate – and even enjoy – the most disgusting smells known to humanity.

I headed to the service entrance. There, entranced, stood Dean Martin, drooling, as the men wheeled the huge, stinking bins backwards and forwards from our building to their truck. I approached him slowly, but the noise was so great and his attention so locked on the rubbish that he didn't hear me until the exact moment I reached down and grabbed him.

Have you ever held a raging pug? I haven't felt anything squirm that hard since I had to pin a two-year-old Thom down on a sofa while my sister extricated a rogue marble from his left nostril. As I wrestled Dean Martin under my arm, the dog threw himself left and right, his eyes bulging with fury, his outraged yapping filling the silent building. I had to wrap my arms around him, my head at an angle to stop his snapping jaw reaching me. From upstairs I heard Mrs De Witt calling down: 'Dean Martin? Is that him?'

It took everything I had to hold him. I ran up the last flight of stairs, desperate to hand him over.

'Got him!' I gasped. Mrs De Witt stepped forward, her arms outstretched. She had a lead ready and she reached out and snapped it onto his collar, just as I lowered him to the ground. At which point, with a speed wholly incommensurate with his size and shape, he whipped round and sank his teeth into my left hand.

If there had been anyone left in the building who hadn't already been woken by the barking, my scream would probably have done it. It was at least loud enough to shock Dean Martin into letting go. I bent double over my hand and swore, the blood already blistering on the wound. 'Your dog bit me! He bloody bit me!'

Mrs De Witt took a breath and stood a little straighter. 'Well, of course he did, with you holding him that tightly. He was probably desperately uncomfortable!' She shooed the little dog inside, where he continued to growl at me, teeth bared. 'There, see?' she said, gesturing towards him. 'Your shouting and screaming frightened him. He's terribly agitated now. You have to learn about dogs if you're going to handle them correctly.'

I couldn't speak. My jaw had dropped, cartoon-style. It was at this moment that Mr Gopnik, in tracksuit bottoms and a T-shirt, threw open his front door.

'What on earth is this racket?' he said, striding out into the corridor. I was startled by the ferocity of his voice. He took in the scene before him, me in my T-shirt and knickers, clutching my bleeding hand, and the old woman in her dressing-gown, the dog snapping at her feet. Behind Mr Gopnik I could just make out Nathan in his uniform, a towel raised to his face. 'What the hell is going on?'

'Oh, ask the wretched girl. She started it.' Mrs De Witt scooped Dean Martin up in her thin arms again, then wagged a finger at Mr Gopnik. 'And don't you dare lecture *me* on noise in this building, young man! Your apartment is a veritable Vegas casino with the amount of to-ings and fro-ings. I'm amazed nobody has complained to Mr Ovitz.' With her head high, she turned and shut the door.

Mr Gopnik blinked twice, looked at me, then back at the closed door. There was a short silence. And then, unexpectedly, he began to laugh. '"Young man"! Well,' he said, shaking his head, 'it's a long time since anyone called me *that*.' He turned to Nathan behind him. 'You must be doing something right.'

From somewhere inside the apartment a muffled voice lifted in response:

'Don't flatter yourself, Gopnik!'

Mr Gopnik sent me in the car with Garry to get a tetanus shot from his personal physician. I sat in a waiting room that resembled the lounge of a luxury hotel, and was seen by a middle-aged Iranian doctor, who was possibly the most solicitous person I had ever met. When I glanced at the bill, to be paid by Mr Gopnik's secretary, I forgot the bite and thought I might pass out instead.

Agnes had already heard the story by the time I got back. I was apparently the talk of the building. 'You must sue!' she said cheerfully. 'She is awful, troublemaking old woman. And that dog is plainly dangerous. I am not sure is safe for us to live in same building. Do you need time off? If you need time off maybe I can sue her for lost services.'

I said nothing, nursing my dark feelings towards Mrs De

Witt and Dean Martin. 'No good deed goes unpunished, eh?' Nathan said, when I bumped into him in the kitchen. He held up my hand, checking out the bandage. 'Jeez. That little dog is ropeable.'

But even as I felt quietly furious with her, I kept remembering what Mrs De Witt had said when she had first come to my door. *He's all I have.*

Although Tabitha moved back into her apartment that week, the mood in the building remained fractious, muted, and marked with occasional explosions. Mr Gopnik continued to spend long hours at work while Agnes filled much of our time together on the phone to her mother in Polish. I got the feeling there was some kind of family crisis going on. Ilaria burnt one of Agnes's favourite shirts – a genuine accident, I believed, as she had been complaining about the temperature controls on the new iron for weeks – and when Agnes screamed at her that she was disloyal, a traitor, a *suka* in her house, and hurled the damaged shirt at her, Ilaria finally erupted and told Mr Gopnik that she could not work here any more, it was impossible, nobody could have worked harder and for less reward over these years. She could no longer stand it and was handing in her notice. Mr Gopnik, with soft words and an empathetic head-tilt, persuaded her to change her mind (he might also have offered hard cash) and this apparent act of betrayal caused Agnes to slam her door hard enough to topple the second little Chinese vase from the hall table with a musical crash, and for her to spend an entire evening weeping in her dressing room.

When I appeared the next morning Agnes was seated beside her husband at the breakfast table, her head resting on his shoulder as he murmured into her ear, their fingers entwined. She apologized formally to Ilaria as he watched, smiling, and when he left for work she swore furiously, in Polish, for the whole time it took us to jog around Central Park.

That evening she announced she was going to Poland for a long weekend, to see her family, and I felt a faint relief when I gathered she did not want me to come too. Sometimes being in that apartment, enormous as it was, with Agnes's ever-changing moods and the swinging tensions between her and Mr Gopnik, Ilaria and his family felt impossibly claustrophobic. The thought of being alone for a few days felt like a little oasis.

'What would you like me to do while you're gone?' I said.

'Have some days off!' she said, smiling. 'You are my friend, Louisa! I think you must have a nice time while I am away. Oh, I am so excited to see my family. So excited.' She clapped her hands. 'Just to Poland! No stupid charity things to go to! I am so happy.'

I remembered how reluctant she had been to leave her husband even for a night when I had arrived. And pushed the thought away.

When I walked back into the kitchen, still pondering this change, Ilaria was crossing herself.

'Are you okay, Ilaria?'

'I'm praying,' she said, not looking up from her pan.

'Is everything all right?'

'Is fine. I'm praying that that *puta* doesn't come back again.'

I emailed Sam, the germ of an idea flooding me with excitement. I would have rung him, but he had been silent since our phone call and I was afraid he was still annoyed with me. I told him I had been given an unexpected three-day weekend, had looked up flights and thought I might splurge on an unexpected trip home. So how about it? What else were wages for? I signed it with a smiley face, an aeroplane emoji, some hearts and kisses.

The answer came back within an hour.

Sorry. I'm working flat out and Saturday night I promised to take Jake to the O2 to see some band. It's a nice idea but this isn't a great weekend. S x

I stared at the email and tried not to feel chilled. *It's a nice idea*. It was as if I'd suggested a casual stroll around the park.

'Is he cooling on me?'

Nathan read it twice. 'No. He's telling you he's busy and this isn't a great time for you to come home unexpectedly.'

'He's cooling on me. There's nothing in that email. No love, no . . . *desire*.'

'Or he might have been on his way to work when he wrote it. Or on the john. Or talking to his boss. He's just being a bloke.'

I didn't buy it. I knew Sam. I stared at those two lines again and again, trying to dissect their tone, their hidden intent. I went on Facebook, hating myself for doing so, and checked to see whether Katie Ingram had announced that she was doing something special that weekend. (Annoyingly, she hadn't posted anything at all. Which was *exactly* what you would do if you were planning to seduce someone else's hot paramedic boyfriend.) And then I took a breath and wrote him a response. Well, several responses, but this was the only one I didn't delete.

No problem. It was a long shot! Hope you have a lovely time with Jake. Lx

And then I pressed 'send', marvelling at how far the words of an email could deviate from what you actually felt.

*

Agnes left on the Thursday evening, laden with gifts. I waved her off with big smiles and collapsed in front of the television.

On Friday morning I went to an exhibition of Chinese opera costumes at the Met Costume Institute and spent an hour admiring the intricately embroidered, brightly coloured robes, the mirrored sheen of the silks. From there, inspired, I travelled to West 37th to visit some fabric and haberdashery stores I had looked up the previous week. The October day was cool and crisp, heralding the onset of winter. I took the subway, and enjoyed its grubby, fuggy warmth. I spent an hour scanning the shelves, losing myself among the bolts of patterned fabric. I had decided to put together my own mood board for Agnes for when she returned, covering the little chaise longue and the cushions with bright, cheerful colours – jade greens and pinks, gorgeous prints with parrots and pineapples, far from the muted damasks and drapes that the expensive interior decorators kept offering her. Those were all First Mrs Gopnik colours. Agnes needed to put her own stamp on the apartment – something bold and lively and beautiful. I explained what I was doing, and the woman at the desk told me about another shop, in the East Village – a second-hand clothes outfit where they kept bolts of vintage fabric at the back.

It was an unpromising storefront – a grubby 1970s exterior that promised a 'Vintage Clothes Emporium, all decades, all styles, low prices'. But I walked in and stopped in my tracks. The shop was a warehouse, set with carousels of clothes in distinct sections under homemade signs that said '1940s', '1960s', 'Clothes That Dreams Are Made Of', and 'Bargain Corner: No Shame In A Ripped Seam'. The air smelt musky, of decades-old perfume, moth-eaten fur and long-forgotten evenings out. I gulped in the scent like oxygen, feeling as if I had somehow recovered a part of myself I had barely known I was missing. I trailed around the store, trying on armfuls of clothes by designers I had never heard of, their names a whispered echo of some long-forgotten age – Tailored by Michel, Fonseca of New Jersey, Miss Aramis – running my fingers over invisible stitching, placing Chinese silks and chiffon against my cheek. I could have bought a dozen things, but I finally settled on a teal blue fitted cocktail dress with huge fur cuffs and a scoop neck (I told myself fur didn't count if it dated from sixty years ago), a pair of vintage denim railroad dungarees and a checked shirt that made me want to chop down a tree or maybe ride a horse with a swishy tail. I could have stayed there all day.

'I've had my eye on that dress for *soooo* long,' said the girl at the checkout desk, as I placed it on the counter. She was heavily tattooed, her dyed black hair swept up in a huge chignon and her eyes lined with dark kohl. 'But I couldn't get my tush into it. You looked cute.' Her voice was raspy, thickened by cigarettes and impossibly cool.

'I have no idea when I'll wear it, but I have to have it.'

'That's how I feel about clothes all the time. They talk to you, right? That dress has been screaming at me: *Buy me you idiot! And maybe lay off the potato chips!*' She stroked it. 'Bye-bye, little blue friend. I'm sorry I let you down.'

'Your store is amazing.'

'Oh, we're hanging in here. Buffeted by the cruel winds of rent rises and Manhattanites who would rather go to TJ Maxx than buy something original and beautiful. Look at that quality.' She held up the lining of the dress, pointing to the tiny stitches. 'How are you going to get work like that out of some sweat shop in Indonesia? Nobody in the whole of New York state has a dress like this.' She raised her eyebrows. 'Except you, British lady. Where is that beauty from?'

I was wearing a green military greatcoat that my dad joked smelt like it had been in the Crimean War, and a red beanie.

Underneath I had my turquoise Dr Martens boots, a pair of tweed shorts and tights.

'I'm loving that look. You ever wanna offload that coat, I could sell it like that.' She snapped her fingers so loudly that my head shot backwards. 'Military coats. Never get tired. I have a red infantry coat that my grandma swears she stole from a guardsman at Buckingham Palace. I cut the back off and turned it into a bum-freezer. You know what a bum-freezer is, right? You wanna see a picture?'

I did. We bonded over that short jacket the way other people bond over pictures of babies. Her name was Lydia and she lived in Brooklyn. She and her sister, Angelica, had inherited the store from their parents seven years previously. They had a small but loyal clientele, and were mostly kept afloat by visits from TV and film costume designers who would buy things to rip apart and re-tailor. Most of their clothes, she said, came from estate sales. 'Florida is the best. You have these grandmas with huge air-conditioned closets stuffed full of cocktail dresses from the 1950s that they never got rid of. We fly down every couple of months and mostly restock from grieving relatives. But it's getting harder. There's so much competition, these days.' She gave me a card with their website and email. 'You ever have anything you want to sell, you just give me a call.'

'Lydia,' I said, when she had packed my clothes with tissue, and placed them in a bag. 'I think I'm a buyer more than a seller. But thank you. Your store is the greatest. You're the greatest. I feel like . . . I feel like I'm at home.'

'You are adorable.' She said this with no change in her facial expression whatsoever. She held up a finger, then stooped below the counter. She came up bearing a pair of vintage sunglasses, dark with pale blue plastic frames.

'Someone left these here months ago. I was going to put

them up for sale but it just occurred to me they would look fabulous on you, especially in that dress.'

'I probably shouldn't,' I began. 'I've already spent so —'

'Ssh! A gift. So you're now indebted to us and have to come back. There. How cute do you look in those?' She held up a mirror.

I had to admit, I did look cute. I adjusted the shades on my nose. 'Well, this is officially my best day in New York. Lydia, I'll see you next week. And basically spend all my money in here from now on.'

'Cool! This is how we emotionally blackmail our customers into keeping us afloat!' She lit a Sobranie and waved me off.

I spent the afternoon putting together the mood board, and trying on my new clothes, and suddenly it was six o'clock and I was sitting on my bed tapping my fingers on my knees. I had been thrilled with the idea of having time to myself, but now the evening stretched in front of me like a bleak, featureless landscape. I texted Nathan, who was still with Mr Gopnik, to see if he wanted to go out for a bite to eat after work, but he had a date, and said so nicely, but in the way that people do when they really don't need a gooseberry tagging along.

I thought about calling Sam again, but I no longer had faith that our phone calls were going to happen in real life the way they happened in my head, and although I kept staring at the phone my fingers never quite made it to the digits. I thought about Josh, and wondered whether if I called him up and asked to meet him for a drink he would think It Meant Something. And then I wondered if the fact that I wanted to meet him for a drink did Actually Mean Something. I checked Katie Ingram's Facebook page, but she still hadn't posted. And then I headed into the kitchen before I could do anything else that stupid and asked Ilaria if she wanted any help making supper, which caused her to rock on her black-slippered heels and stare at me suspiciously for a full ten seconds. 'You want to help me make supper?'

'Yes,' I said, and smiled.

'No,' she said, and turned away.

Until that evening I hadn't realized quite how few people I knew in New York. I had been so busy since I'd arrived and my life had been so comprehensively based around Agnes, her schedule and needs, that it hadn't occurred to me that I hadn't made any friends of my own. But there was something about a Friday night in the city with no plans that made you feel like . . . well, like a bit of a loser.

I walked to the good sushi place and bought miso soup and some sashimi I hadn't had before and tried not to think, *Eel! I'm actually eating eel!* and drank a beer, then lay on my bed, flicked through the channels and pushed away thoughts of other things, such as what Sam was doing. I told myself I was in New York, the centre of the universe. So what if I was having a Friday night in? I was simply resting after a week of my demanding New York job. I could go out any night of the week, if I really wanted to. I told myself this several times. And then my phone pinged.

You out exploring New York's finest bars again?

I knew who it was without looking. Something inside me lurched. I hesitated a moment before responding.

Just having a night in, actually.

Fancy a friendly beer with an exhausted corporate wage slave? If nothing else, you could make sure I don't go home with an unsuitable woman.

I started to smile. And then I typed: *What makes you think I'm any kind of defence?*

Are you saying we look like we could never be together? Oh, that's harsh.

I meant what makes you think I'd stop you going home with someone else?

The fact that you're even responding to my messages? (He added a smiley face to this.)

I stopped typing, feeling suddenly disloyal. I stared at my phone, watching the cursor wink impatiently. In the end he typed, *Did I blow it? I just blew it, didn't I? Damn, Louisa Clark. I just wanted a beer with a pretty girl on a Friday night and I was prepared to overlook the feeling of vague dejection that comes with knowing she's in love with someone else. That's how much I enjoy your company. Come for a beer? One beer?*

I lay back on the pillow, thinking. I closed my eyes and groaned. And then I sat up and typed, *I'm really sorry, Josh. I can't. x*

He didn't respond. I had offended him. I would never hear from him again.

And then my phone pinged. *Okay. Well, if I get myself in trouble I'm texting you first thing tomorrow morning to come get me and pretend to be my crazy jealous girlfriend. Be prepared to hit hard. Deal?*

I found I was laughing. *The least I can do. Have a good night. X*

You too. Not too good, though. The only thing keeping me going right now is the thought of you secretly regretting not coming out with me. X

I did regret it a little. Of course I did. There are only so many episodes of *The Big Bang Theory* a girl can watch. I turned the television off and I stared at the ceiling and I thought about my boyfriend on the other side of the world and I thought about an American who looked like Will Traynor and actually wanted to spend time with me, not a girl with wild blonde hair who looked like she wore sequined G-strings under her uniform. I thought about ringing my sister but I didn't want to disturb Thom.

For the first time since I had arrived in America I had an almost physical sense of being in the wrong place, as if I were being tugged by invisible cords to somewhere a million miles away. At one point I felt so bad that when I walked into my bathroom and saw a large chestnut-coloured cockroach on the sink I didn't scream, like I had previously, but briefly considered making it a pet, like a character in a children's novel. And then I realized that I was now officially thinking like a madwoman and sprayed it with Raid instead.

At ten, irritable and restless, I walked to the kitchen and stole two of Nathan's beers, leaving an apologetic note under his door, and drank them, one after the other, gulping so fast that I had to suppress a huge belch. I felt bad about that damned cockroach. What was he doing after all? Just going about his cockroachy business. Maybe he'd been lonely. Maybe he'd wanted to make friends with *me*. I went and peered under the basin where I'd kicked him but he was definitely dead. This made me irrationally angry. I'd thought you weren't meant to be able to kill cockroaches. I'd been lied to about cockroaches. I added this to my list of things to feel furious about.

I put my earphones in and sang my way drunkenly through some Beyoncé songs that I knew would make me feel worse, but somehow I didn't care. I scrolled through my phone, looking at the few pictures I had of Sam and me together, trying to detect the strength of his feelings from the way he put his arm around me, or the way he bent his head towards mine. I stared at them and tried to recall what it was that had made me feel so sure, so secure in his arms. Then I picked up my laptop, clicked open an email and addressed it to him.

Do you still miss me?

And I pressed send, realizing, as it whooshed into the ether, that I had now condemned myself to unknown hours of email-related anxiety while I waited for him to respond.

13

I woke feeling sick, and it wasn't the beer. It took fewer than ten seconds for the vague feeling of nausea to seep along a synapse and connect with the memory of what I had done the previous evening. I opened my laptop slowly and balled my fists into my eyes when I discovered that, yes, I had indeed sent it and, no, he hadn't responded. Even when I pressed 'refresh' fourteen times.

I lay in the foetal position for a bit, trying to make the knot in my stomach go away. And then I wondered about calling him and explaining lightly that *Hah! I'd been a bit merry and homesick and I'd just wanted to hear his voice and you know, sorry* . . . but he had told me he would be working all Saturday, which meant that right now he would be in the rig with Katie Ingram. And something in me balked at having that conversation with her in earshot.

For the first time since I had come to work for the Gopniks, the weekend stretched out in front of me like an interminable journey over bleak terrain.

So I did what every girl does when she's far from home and a little sad. I ate half a packet of chocolate Digestives and called my mother.

'Lou! Is that you? Hold on, I'm in the middle of washing Granddad's smalls. Let me turn the hot water off.' I heard my mother walking to the other side of the kitchen, the radio, humming distantly in the background, abruptly silenced, and I was instantly transported to our little house in Renfrew Road.

'Hello! I'm back! Is everything all right?' She sounded breathless. I pictured her untying her apron. She always removed her apron for important calls.

'Fine! I've barely had a minute to talk properly so I thought I'd give you a ring.'

'Is it not fearful expensive? I thought you only wanted to send emails. You're not going to be hit with one of those thousand-pound bills, are you? I saw a whole thing on the television about people getting caught out using their phones on holiday. You'd have to sell your house when you got home, just to get them off your back.'

'I checked the rates. It's good to hear your voice, Mum.'

Mum's delight at speaking to me made me feel a little ashamed for not having called before. She rattled on, telling me about how she planned to start the poetry night classes when Granddad was feeling better, and the Syrian refugees who had moved in at the end of the street – she was giving them English lessons. 'Of course I can't understand a thing they're saying half the time but we draw pictures, you know? And Zeinah – that's the mother – she always cooks me a little something to say thank you. What she can do with flaky pastry you wouldn't believe. Really, they're awful nice, the bunch of them.'

She said that Dad had been told to lose weight by the new doctor; Granddad's hearing was going and the television was on so loud that every time he turned it on she nearly did a little wee; and Dymphna from two doors down was having a baby and they could hear her retching morning, noon and night. I sat in my bed, and listened and felt oddly comforted that life continued, as normal, somewhere else in the world.

'Have you spoken to your sister?'

'Not for a couple of days, why?'

She lowered her voice, as if Treena were in the room instead of forty miles away. 'She has a man.'

'Oh, yeah, I know.'

'You know? What's he like? She won't tell us a thing. She's after going out with him two or three times a week now. She keeps humming and smiling when I talk about him. It's very *odd*.'

'Odd?'

'To have your sister smiling so much. I've been quite unnerved. I mean, it's lovely and all, but she's not herself. Lou, I went down to London to spend the night with her and Thom so she could go out, and when she came back she was *singing*.'

'Woah.'

'I know. Almost in tune too. I told your dad and he accused me of being unromantic. Unromantic! I told him only someone who truly believed in romance could stay married after washing his undercrackers for thirty years.'

'Mum!'

'Oh, Lord. I forgot. You wouldn't have had your breakfast yet. Well. Anyway. If you speak to her try and get some information out of her. How's your fella, by the way?'

'Sam? Oh, he's . . . fine.'

'That's grand. He came to your flat a couple of times after you'd gone. I think he just wanted to feel close to you, bless him. Treena said he was awful sad. Kept looking for jobs to do around the place. Came up here for a roast dinner with us too. But he hasn't been by for a while now.'

'He's really busy, Mum.'

'I'm sure he is. That's a job and a half, isn't it? Right, well, I must let you go before this call bankrupts the both of us. Did I tell you I'm seeing Maria this week? The toilet attendant from that lovely hotel we went to back in August? I'm going to London to see Treena and Thom on Friday, and I'm going to pop in and have lunch with Maria first.'

'In the toilets?'

'Don't be ridiculous. There's a two-for-one pasta deal at that Italian chain near Leicester Square. I can't remember the name. She's very fussy about where she goes – she says you should judge a restaurant kitchen by the cleanliness of the Ladies. This one has a very good maintenance schedule, apparently. Every hour on the hour. Is everything good with you? How's the glamorous life of Fifth Street?'

'Avenue. Fifth Avenue, Mum. It's great. It's all . . . amazing.'

'Don't forget to send me some more pictures. I showed Mrs Edwards that one of you at the Yellow Ball and she said you looked like a film star. Didn't say which one, but I know she meant well. I was telling Daddy we should come and visit you before you're too important to know us!'

'Like that's going to happen.'

'We're awful proud, sweetheart. I can't believe I have a daughter in New York high society, riding in limousines and hobnobbing with the flash Harrys.'

I looked around my little room, with the 1980s wallpaper and the dead cockroach under the basin. 'Yeah.' I said. 'I'm really lucky.'

Trying not to think about the significance of Sam no longer stopping by my flat just to feel close to me, I got dressed, drank a coffee and went downstairs. I would head back to the Vintage Clothes Emporium. I had the feeling Lydia wouldn't mind if I just hung out.

I had picked my clothes carefully – this time I wore a Chinese mandarin-style blouse in turquoise with black wool culottes and a pair of red ballet slippers. Just the act of creating a look that didn't involve a polo shirt and nylon slacks made me feel more like myself. I tied my hair into two plaits, joined at the back with a little red bow, then added the sunglasses Lydia had given me and some earrings in the shape of the Statue of Liberty that had been irresistible, despite coming from a stall of tourist tat.

I heard the commotion as I headed down the stairs. I wondered briefly what Mrs De Witt was up to now, but when I turned the corner I saw that the raised voice was coming from a young Asian woman, who appeared to be thrusting a small child at Ashok. 'You said this was my day. You promised. I have to go on the march!'

'I can't do it, baby. Vincent is off. They got nobody to mind the lobby.'

'Then your kids can sit here while you do it. I'm going on this march, Ashok. They need me.'

'I can't mind the kids here!'

'The library is going to *close*, baby. You understand that? You know that is the one place with air-con I can go in the summer! And it is the one place I can feel sane. You tell me where else in the Heights I'm supposed to take these kids when I'm alone eighteen hours a day.'

Ashok looked up as I stood there. 'Oh, hi, Miss Louisa.'

She turned. I'm not sure what I had expected of Ashok's wife, but it was not this fierce-looking woman in jeans and a bandanna, her curly hair tumbling down her back.

'Morning.'

'Good morning.' She turned away. 'I'm not discussing this any further, baby. You told me Saturday was mine. I am going on the march to protect a valuable public resource. That is *it*.'

'There's another march next week.'

'We have to keep up the pressure! This is the time when the city councillors decide funding! If we're not out there now, the local news doesn't report it, and then they think nobody cares. You know how PR works, baby? You know how the world works?'

'I will *lose my job* if my boss comes down here and sees three kids. Yes, I love you, Nadia. I do love you. Don't cry, sweetheart.' He turned to the toddler in his arms and kissed her wet cheek. 'Daddy just has to do his job today.'

'I'm going now, baby. I'll be back early afternoon.'

'Don't you go. Don't you dare – hey!'

She walked away, her palm up, as if to ward off further protest and swung out of the building, stooping to pick up a placard she'd left by the door. As if perfectly choreographed, all three small children began to cry. Ashok swore softly. 'What the Sam Hill am I supposed to do now?'

'I'll do it.' I'd said it before I knew what I was doing.

'What?'

'Nobody's in. I'll take them upstairs.'

'Are you serious?'

'Ilaria goes to see her sister on Saturdays. Mr Gopnik's at his club. I'll park them in front of the television. How hard can it be?'

He looked at me. 'You don't have children, do you, Miss Louisa?' And then he recovered himself. 'But, man, that would be a lifesaver. If Mr Ovitz stops by and sees me with these three I'll be fired before you can say, uh . . .' He thought for a moment.

'You're fired?'

'Exactly. Okay. Lemme come up with you and I'll explain who is who and who likes what. Hey, kids, you're gonna have an adventure upstairs with Miss Louisa! How cool is that?' Three children stared at me with wet, snotty faces. I smiled brightly at them. And, in tandem, all three began to cry again.

*

If you ever find yourself in a melancholy state of mind, removed from your family and a little unsure about the person you love, I can highly recommend being left in temporary charge of three small strangers, at least two of whom are still unable to go to the lavatory unaided. The phrase 'living in the moment' only really made sense to me once I'd found myself chasing a crawling baby, whose obscenely filled nappy hung half off, across a priceless Aubusson rug, while simultaneously trying to stop a four-year-old chasing a traumatized cat. The middle child, Abhik, could be pacified with biscuits, and I parked him in front of cartoons in the TV room, shovelling crumbs with fat hands into his dribbling mouth, while I tried to shepherd the other two into at least the same twenty-square-foot radius. They were funny and sweet and mercurial and exhausting, squawking and running and colliding repeatedly with furniture. Vases wobbled, books were hauled from shelves and hastily shoved back. Noise – and various unsavoury scents – filled the air. At one point I sat on the floor clutching two around their waists while Rachana, the eldest, poked me in the eye with sticky fingers and laughed. I laughed too. It was kind of funny, in a *thank God this will be over soon* kind of way.

After two hours, Ashok came up and told me his wife was caught up in her protest and could I do another hour? I said yes. He wore the wide-eyed look of the truly desperate and, after all, I had nothing else to do. I did, however, take the precaution of moving them into my room, where I put on some cartoons, tried to keep them from opening the door and accepted, with some distant part of me, that the air in this part of the building might never smell the same again. I was just trying to stop Abhik putting cockroach spray into his mouth when there was a knock on my door.

'*Hold on, Ashok,*' I yelled, trying to wrestle the canister off the child before his father saw.

But it was Ilaria's face that appeared round my door. She stared at me, then at the children, then back at me. Abhik briefly stopped crying, gazing at her with huge brown eyes.

'Um. Hi, Ilaria!'

She said nothing.

'I'm – I'm just helping Ashok out for a couple of hours. I know it's not ideal but, um, please don't say anything. They'll only be here a tiny bit longer.'

She eyed the scene, then sniffed the air.

'I'll fumigate the room afterwards. Please don't tell Mr Gopnik. I promise it won't happen again. I know I should have asked first but there was nobody here and Ashok was desperate.' As I spoke, Rachana ran wailing towards the older woman and hurled herself like a rugby ball at her stomach. I winced, as Ilaria staggered backwards. 'They'll be gone any minute. I can call Ashok right now. Really. Nobody has to know . . .'

But Ilaria simply adjusted her blouse, then scooped the little girl up in one arm. 'You are thirsty, *compañera*?' Without a backward glance she shuffled off, Rachana huddled against her huge chest, her little thumb plugged into her mouth.

As I sat there, Ilaria's voice echoed down the corridor. 'Bring them to the kitchen.'

Ilaria fried a batch of banana fritters, handing the children small pieces of banana to keep them occupied while she cooked, and I refilled cups of water and tried to stop the smaller children toppling off the kitchen chairs. She didn't talk to me, but kept up a low croon, her face filled with unexpected sweetness, her voice low and musical as she chatted to them. The children, like dogs responding to an efficient trainer, were immediately quiet and biddable, holding out dimpled hands for another piece of banana, remembering their pleases and thank-yous, according to Ilaria's instructions. They ate and ate, growing smiley and placid, the baby rubbing balled fists into her eyes as if she were ready for bed.

'Hungry,' Ilaria said, nodding towards the empty plates.

I tried to recall whether Ashok had told me about food in the baby's rucksack but I had been too distracted to look. I was just grateful to have a grown-up in the room. 'You're brilliant with kids,' I said, chewing a piece of fritter.

She shrugged. But she looked quietly gratified. 'You should change the little one. We can make a bed for her in your bottom drawer.'

I stared at her.

'Because she will fall out of your bed?' She rolled her eyes, as if this should have been obvious.

'Oh. Sure.'

I took Nadia back to my room and changed her, wincing. I drew the curtains. And then I pulled out my bottom drawer, arranged my jumpers so that they lined it, and laid Nadia down inside them, waiting for her to go to sleep. She fought it at first, her big eyes staring at me, her fat dimpled hands reaching up for mine, but I could tell it was a battle she would lose. I tried to copy Ilaria and softly sang a lullaby. Well, it wasn't strictly speaking a lullaby: the only thing I could remember the words to was 'The Molahonkey Song', which just made her chuckle, and another about Hitler having only one testicle that Dad had sung when I was small. But the baby seemed to like it. Her eyes began to close.

I heard Ashok's footsteps in the hall, and the door open behind me.

'Don't come in,' I whispered. 'She's nearly there ... *Himmler had something similar . . .*'

Ashok stayed where he was.

'*But poor old Goebbels had no balls at all.*'

And just like that she was asleep. I waited a moment, placed my turquoise cashmere round-neck over her to keep her from getting chilly, and then I climbed to my feet.

'You can leave her in here, if you like,' I whispered. 'Ilaria's in the kitchen with the other two. I think she's –'

I turned and let out a yelp. Sam stood in my doorway, his arms folded and a half-smile on his face. A holdall sat on the floor between his feet. I blinked at him, wondering if I was hallucinating. And then my hands rose slowly to my face.

'Surprise!' he mouthed silently, and I stumbled across the room and pushed him out into the hall where I could kiss him.

He had planned it the night I had told him about my unexpected free weekend, he told me. Jake had been no problem – there was no shortage of friends happy to take a free concert ticket – and he had reorganized his work, begging favours and swapping shifts. Then he had booked a last-minute cheap flight and come to surprise me.

'You're lucky I didn't decide to do the same to you.'

'The thought did cross my mind, at thirty thousand feet. I had this sudden vision of you flying in the opposite direction.'

'How long have we got?'

'Only forty-eight hours, I'm afraid. I have to leave early Monday morning. But, Lou, I just – I didn't want to wait another few weeks.'

He didn't say any more but I knew what he meant. 'I'm so happy you did. Thank you. Thank you. So who let you in?'

'Your man at Reception. He warned me about the kids. Then asked me whether I'd recovered from my food poisoning.' He raised an eyebrow.

'Yeah. There are no secrets in this building.'

'He also told me that you were a doll and the nicest person

here. Which I knew already, of course. And then some little old lady with a yappy dog came along the corridor and started yelling at him about refuse collection so I left him to it.'

We drank coffee until Ashok's wife arrived and took the children back. Her name was Meena and, glowing with the residual energy of her community march, she thanked me wholeheartedly and told us about the library in Washington Heights they were trying to save. Ilaria didn't seem to want to hand Abhik back to her: she was busy chuckling to him, gently pinching his cheeks and making him laugh. The whole time we stood there with the two women, chatting, I felt Sam's hand on the small of my back, his huge frame filling our kitchen, his free hand around one of our coffee cups, and I felt suddenly as if this place were a few degrees more my home because I would now be able to picture him in it.

'Very pleased to meet you,' he had said to Ilaria, holding out his hand, and instead of her normal look of blank suspicion, she had smiled, a small smile, and shaken it. I realised how few people took the trouble to introduce themselves to her. She and I were invisibles, most of the time, and Ilaria – perhaps by virtue of her age, or nationality – even more so than me.

'Make sure Mr Gopnik doesn't see him,' she muttered, as Sam went to the bathroom. 'No boyfriends allowed in the building. Use the service entrance.' She shook her head as if she couldn't believe she was acceding to something so immoral.

'Ilaria, I won't forget this. Thank you,' I said. I put my arms out as if to hug her but she gave me the gimlet stare. I stopped in my tracks and turned it into a sort of double thumbs-up instead.

We ate pizza – with safe vegetarian toppings – and then we stopped in a dark, grubby bar where baseball blared from a small TV screen over our heads and sat at a tiny table with our knees pressed together. Half the time I had no idea what we were talking about because I couldn't believe Sam was there, in front of me, leaning back in his chair, laughing at things I said and running his hand over his head. As if by mutual consent we kept off the topics of Katie Ingram and Josh, and instead we talked about our families. Jake had a new girlfriend and was rarely at Sam's any more. He missed him, he said, even as he understood that no seventeen-year-old boy really wanted to be hanging around with his uncle. 'He's a lot happier, and his dad still hasn't sorted himself out, so I should just be glad for him. But it's weird. I got used to having him around.'

'You can always go and see my family,' I said.

'I know.'

'Can I just tell you for the fifty-eighth time how happy I am that you're here?'

'You can tell me anything you like, Louisa Clark,' he said softly, and lifted my knuckles to his lips.

We stayed at the bar until eleven. Oddly, despite the amount of time we had together, neither of us felt the panicky urgency we'd had last time to make the most of every minute. That he was there was such an unexpected bonus that I think we had both silently agreed just to enjoy being around each other. There was no need to sightsee, to tick off experiences or to run to bed. It was, as the young people say, all good.

We fell out of the bar wrapped around each other, as happy drunks do, and I stepped onto the kerb, put two fingers into my mouth and whistled, not flinching as the yellow cab screeched to a halt in front of me. I turned to motion Sam in, but he was staring at me.

'Oh. Yeah. Ashok taught me. You have to kind of put your fingers underneath your tongue. Look – like this.'

I beamed at him, but something about his expression troubled me. I thought he'd enjoy my little taxi-summoning flourish, but instead it was as if he suddenly didn't recognize me.

We arrived back to a silent building. The Lavery stood hushed and majestic overlooking the park, rising out of the noise and chaos of the city as if it were somehow above that kind of thing. Sam stopped as we reached the covered walkway that extended from the front door and gazed up at the structure towering above him, at its monumental brick façade, its Palladian-style windows. He shook his head, almost to himself, and we walked in. The marble lobby was hushed, the night man dozing in Ashok's office. We ignored the service lift and walked up the staircase, our feet muffled on the huge sweep of royal blue carpet, our hands sliding along the polished brass balustrade, then walked up another flight until we were on the Gopniks' corridor. In the distance Dean Martin started to bark. I let us in and closed the huge door softly behind us.

Nathan's light was off, and along the corridor Ilaria's TV burbled distantly. Sam and I tiptoed through the large hall, past the kitchen and down to my room. I changed into a T-shirt, wishing, suddenly, that I slept in something a little more sophisticated, then went into the bathroom and started to clean my teeth. I wandered out, still brushing, to find Sam sitting on the bed, staring at the wall. I looked at him as quizzically as you can, when you have a mouthful of peppermint-flavoured foam.

'What?'

'It's . . . strange,' he said.

'My T-shirt?'

'No. Being here. In this place.'

I turned back to the bathroom, spat and rinsed my mouth.

'It's fine,' I began, turning off the tap. 'Ilaria is cool and Mr Gopnik won't be back until Sunday evening. If you're really uncomfortable tomorrow I'll book us a room in this little hotel Nathan knows two blocks down and we can –'

He shook his head. 'Not *this*. You. Here. When we were at the hotel it was just like you and me as normal. We were just in a different location. Here, I can finally see how everything has changed for you. You live on Fifth Avenue, for crying out loud. One of the most expensive addresses in the world. You work in this crazy building. Everywhere smells of money. And it's totally normal to you.'

I felt oddly defensive. 'I'm still me.'

'Sure,' he said. 'But you're in a different place now. Literally.'

He said it evenly, but there was something in the conversation that made me feel uneasy. I padded up to him in my bare feet, put my hands on his shoulders and said, with a little more urgency than I had intended, 'I'm still just Louisa Clark, your slightly wonky girl from Stortfold.' When he didn't speak, I added, 'I'm just the hired help here, Sam.'

He looked into my eyes, then reached a hand up and stroked my cheek. 'You don't get it. You can't see how you've changed. You're different, Lou. You walk around these city streets like you own them. You hail taxis with a whistle and they come. Even your stride is different. It's like . . . I don't know. You've grown into yourself. Or maybe you've grown into someone else.'

'See, now you're saying a nice thing and yet somehow it sounds like a bad thing.'

'Not bad,' he said. 'Just . . . different.'

I moved then so that I was astride him, my bare legs pressed against his jeans. I put my face up close to his, my nose against his, my mouth inches from his own. I looped my arms around his neck, so that I could feel the softness of his short dark hair against my skin, his warm breath on my chest. It was dark, and a cold neon light beamed a narrow ray across my bed. I kissed him, and with that kiss I tried to convey something of what he meant to me, the fact that I could hail a million taxis with a whistle and still know that he was the only person I would want to climb into one with. I kissed him, my kisses increasingly deep and intense, pressing into him, until he gave in to me, until his hands closed around my waist and slid upwards, until I felt the exact moment he stopped thinking. He pulled me sharply into him, his mouth crushing mine, and I gasped as he twisted, pushing me back down, his whole being reduced to one intention.

That night I gave something to Sam. I was uninhibited, unlike myself. I became someone other than myself because I was so desperate to show him the truth of my need for him. It was a fight, even if he didn't know it. I hid my own power and made him blind with his. There was no tenderness, no soft words. When our eyes met I was almost angry with him. *It is still me*, I told him silently. *Don't you dare doubt me. Not after all this.* He covered my eyes, placed his mouth against my hair, and he possessed me. I let him. I wanted him half mad with it. I wanted him to feel like he'd taken everything. I have no idea what sounds I made but when it was over my ears were ringing.

'That was . . . different,' he said, when we could breathe again. His hand slid across me, tender now, his thumb gently stroking my thigh. 'You've never been like that before.'

'Maybe I never missed you that much before.' I leant over and kissed his chest. It left salt on my lips. We lay there in the dark, blinking at the neon strip across the ceiling.

'It's the same sky,' he said, into the dark. 'That's what we have to keep remembering. We're still under the same sky.'

In the distance a police siren started, followed by another in a discordant descant. I never really registered them any more: the sounds of New York had become familiar, fading into unheard white noise. Sam turned to me, his face shadowed. 'I started to forget things, you know. All the little parts of you that I love. I couldn't remember the scent of your hair.' He lowered his head to mine and breathed in. 'Or the shape of your jaw. Or the way your skin shivers when I do this . . .' He ran a finger lightly down from my collarbone and I half smiled at my body's involuntary reaction. 'That lovely dazed way you look at me afterwards . . . I had to come here, to remind myself.'

'I'm still me, Sam,' I said.

He kissed me, his lips landing softly, four, five times on mine, a whisper. 'Well, whichever you you are, Louisa Clark, I love you,' he said, and rolled slowly, with a sigh, onto his back.

But it was at that point I had to acknowledge an uncomfortable truth. I had been different with him. And it wasn't just because I wanted to show him how much I wanted him, how much I adored him, though that had been part of it.

On some dark, hidden level, I had wanted to show him I was better than *her*.

14

We slept until after ten, then walked downtown to the diner near Columbus Circle. We ate until our stomachs hurt, drank gallons of stewed coffee and sat opposite each other with our knees entwined.

'Glad you came over?' I said, like I didn't know the answer.

He reached out a hand and placed it gently behind my neck, leaning forward across the table until he could kiss me, oblivious to the other diners, until I had all the answer I needed. Around us sat middle-aged couples with weekend newspapers, groups of outlandishly dressed nightclubbers who hadn't been to bed yet, talking over each other, exhausted couples with cranky children.

Sam sat back in his chair and let out a long sigh. 'My sister always wanted to come here, you know. Seems stupid that she never did.'

'Really?' I reached for his hand and he turned his palm upwards to take mine, then closed his fingers over it.

'Yeah. She had this whole list of things she wanted to do, like go to a baseball game. The Kicks? The Knicks? Some team she wanted to see. And eat in a New York diner. And most of all she wanted to go to the top of the Rockefeller Center.'

'Not the Empire State?'

'Nah. She said the Rockefeller was meant to be better — some glass observatory thing you could look through. Apparently you can see the Statue of Liberty from there.'

I squeezed his hand. 'We could go today.'

'We could,' he said. 'Makes you think, though, doesn't it?' He reached for his coffee. 'You have to take your chances when you can.'

A vague melancholy settled over him. I didn't attempt to shake it. I knew better than anyone how sometimes you just needed to be allowed to feel sad. I waited a moment, then said, 'I feel that every day.'

He turned back to me.

'I'm going to say a Will Traynor thing now.' I said it like a warning.

'Okay.'

'There's almost not a day that I'm here when I don't think he'd be proud of me.'

I felt the tiniest bit anxious as I said it, conscious of how I had tested Sam in the early days of our relationship by going on and on about Will, about what he had meant to me, about the Will-shaped hole he had left behind. But he just nodded. 'I think he would too.' He stroked his thumb down my finger. 'I know I am. Proud of you. I mean, I miss you like hell. But, jeez, you're amazing, Lou. You've come to a city you didn't know and you've made this job, with its millionaires and billionaires, work for you, and you've made friends, and you've created this whole *thing* for yourself. People live their whole lives without doing one tenth of that.' He gestured around him.

'You could do it too.' It just fell out of my mouth. 'I looked it up. The New York authorities always need good paramedics. But I'm sure we could get round that.' I said it jokingly but as soon as the words were out I realized how badly I wanted it to happen. I leant forward over the table. 'Sam. We could rent a little apartment out in Queens or somewhere and then we could be together every night, depending on who was working what insane hours, and we could do this every Sunday morning. We could be *together*. How amazing would that be?'

You only get one life. I heard the words ringing in my ears. *Say yes*, I told him silently. *Just say yes.*

He reached across for my hand. Then he sighed. 'I can't, Lou. My house isn't built. Even if I decided to rent it out, I'd have to finish it. And I can't leave Jake just yet. He needs to know I'm still around. Just a bit longer.'

I forced my face into a smile, the kind of smile that said I hadn't taken it at all seriously. 'Sure! It was just a stupid idea.'

He pressed his lips against my palm. 'Not stupid. Just impossible right now.'

We decided by unspoken agreement not to mention potentially difficult subjects again, and that killed a surprising number – his work, his home life, our future – and we walked the High Line, then peeled off to go to the Vintage Clothes Emporium where I greeted Lydia like an old friend and dressed up in a 1970s pink sequined jumpsuit, then a 1950s fur coat and a sailor cap and made Sam laugh.

'Now *this*,' he said, as I came out of the changing room in a pink and yellow nylon psychedelic shift dress, 'is the Louisa Clark I know and love.'

'Did she show you the blue cocktail dress yet? The one with the sleeves?'

'I can't decide between this and the fur.'

'Sweetheart,' said Lydia, lighting a Sobranie, 'you can't wear fur on Fifth Avenue. People won't realize you're doing it ironically.'

When I finally left the changing room, Sam was standing at the counter. He held out a package.

'It's the sixties dress,' Lydia said helpfully.

'You bought it for me?' I took it from him. 'Really? You didn't think it was too loud?'

'It's totally insane,' Sam said, straight-faced. 'But you looked so happy wearing it . . . so . . .'

'Oh, my, he's a keeper,' whispered Lydia, as we headed out, her cigarette wedged into the corner of her mouth. 'Also, next time get him to buy you the jumpsuit. You looked like a total boss.'

We went back to the apartment for a couple of hours and napped, fully dressed and wrapped around each other chastely, overloaded with carbohydrates. At four we rose groggily and agreed we should head out and do our last excursion, as Sam had to catch the eight a.m. flight from JFK the following day. While he packed up his few things I went to make tea in the kitchen where I found Nathan mixing some kind of protein shake. He grinned. 'I hear your man is here.'

'Is absolutely nothing private in this corridor?' I filled the kettle and flicked the switch.

'Not when the walls are this thin, mate, no,' he said. 'I'm kidding!' he said, as I flushed to my hairline. 'Didn't hear a thing. Nice to know from the colour of your face that you had a good night, though!'

I was about to hit him when Sam appeared at the door. Nathan stopped in front of him, reached out a hand. 'Ah. The famous Sam. Nice to finally meet you, mate.'

'And you.'

I waited anxiously to see if they were going to get all alpha male with each other. But Nathan was naturally too laid back and Sam was still sweetened from twenty-four hours of food and sex. They just shook hands, grinned at each other and exchanged pleasantries.

'Are you guys going out tonight?' Nathan swigged at his drink as I handed Sam a mug of tea.

'We thought we might head up to the top of 30 Rockefeller. It's kind of a mission.'

'Aw, mates. You don't want to be standing in tourist queues on your last night. Come to the Holiday Cocktail Lounge over in the East Village. I'm meeting my mates there – Lou, you met the guys last time we headed out. They're doing some promo there tonight. It's always a good buzz.'

I looked over at Sam. He shrugged. We could pop by for a half-hour, I said. Then maybe we could go up to Top of the Rock by ourselves. It was open till eleven fifteen.

Three hours later we were wedged around a cluttered table, my brain spinning gently from the cocktails that had landed, one after another, on its surface. I had worn my psychedelic shift dress because I wanted to show Sam how much I loved it. He, meanwhile, in the way that men who love the company of other men do, had bonded with Nathan and his friends. They were loudly running down each other's musical choices and comparing gig horror stories from their youth.

With one part of my being I smiled and joined in the conversation and with the other I made mental calculations as to how often I could contribute financially so that Sam could come here twice as much as we had originally planned. Surely he could see how good this was. How good we were together.

Sam got up to buy the next round. 'I'll get a couple of menus,' he mouthed. I nodded. I knew I should probably eat something if only so I didn't disgrace myself later on.

And then I felt a hand on my shoulder.

'You really are stalking me!' Josh beamed down at me, white teeth in a wide smile. I stood abruptly, flushing. I turned, but Sam was at the bar, his back to us. 'Josh! Hi!'

'You know this is pretty much my other favourite bar, right?' He was wearing a soft, striped blue shirt, the sleeves rolled up.

'I didn't!' My voice was too high, my speech too fast.

'I believe you. You want a drink? They do an Old-Fashioned that is something else.' He reached out and touched my elbow.

I sprang back as if he'd burnt me. 'Yes, I know. And no. Thank you. I'm here with friends and . . .' I turned just in time for Sam to arrive back, holding a tray of drinks, a couple of menus under his arm.

'Hey,' he said, and glanced at Josh, before he placed the tray on the table. Then he straightened up slowly and really looked at him.

I stood, my hands stiff by my side. 'Josh, this is Sam, my – my boyfriend. Sam, this is – this is Josh.'

Sam was staring at Josh, as if he was trying to take something in. 'Yeah,' Sam said finally. 'I think I could have worked that out.' He looked at me, then back at Josh.

'Do – do you guys want a drink? I mean, I can see you've got some but I'd be glad to line up some more.' Josh gestured towards the bar.

'No. Thanks, mate,' said Sam, who had remained standing so that he was a good half-head taller than Josh. 'I think we're good here.'

There was an awkward silence.

'Okay then.' Josh looked at me, and nodded. 'Great to meet you, Sam. You here for long?'

'Long enough.' Sam's smile didn't stretch as far as his eyes. I had never seen him quite so prickly.

'Well, then . . . I'll leave you guys to it. Louisa – I'll see you around. Have a great evening.' He held up his palms, a pacifying gesture. I opened my mouth but there was nothing to say that sounded right, so I waved, a weird, fluttering gesture with my fingers.

Sam sat down heavily. I glanced across the table at Nathan,

whose face was a study in neutrality. The other guys didn't appear to have noticed anything and were still talking about ticket prices at their last gig. Sam was briefly lost in thought. He finally looked up. I reached for his hand but he didn't squeeze mine back.

The mood didn't recover. The bar was too noisy for me to talk to him, and I wasn't sure what I wanted to say. I sipped my cocktail and ran through a hundred looping arguments in my head. Sam swigged his drink and nodded and smiled at the guys' jokes, but I saw the tic in his jaw and knew his heart was no longer in it. At ten we peeled off and got a taxi towards home.

I let him hail it.

We went up in the service lift, as instructed, and listened before we crept into my room. Mr Gopnik appeared to be in bed. Sam didn't speak. He went into the bathroom to change and closed the door behind him, his back rigid. I heard him brush his teeth and gargle as I crept into bed, feeling wrong-footed and angry at the same time. He seemed to be in there for ever. Finally, he opened the door and stood there in his boxers. His scars still ran livid red across his stomach. 'I'm being a dick.'

'Yes. Yes, you are.'

He let out a huge breath. He looked at my photograph of Will, nestled between the one of himself and the one of my sister with Thom, whose finger was up his nose. 'Sorry. It just threw me. How much he looks like . . .'

'I know. But you might as well say you spending time with my sister and her looking like me is weird.'

'Except she doesn't look like you.' He raised his eyebrows. '. . . what?'

'I'm waiting for you to say I'm miles better-looking.'

'You are miles better-looking.'

I pushed the covers back to let him in and he climbed in beside me.

'You're much better-looking than your sister. Heaps better. You're basically a supermodel.' He placed a hand on my hip. It was warm and heavy. 'But with shorter legs. How's that working for you?'

I tried not to smile. 'Better. But quite rude about my short legs.'

'They're beautiful legs. My favourite legs. Supermodel legs are just – boring.' He moved across so that he was over me. Every time he did that it was like bits of me sparked into involuntary life and I had to work hard not to wriggle. He rested on his elbows, pinning me in place and looking down at my face, which I was trying to make stern even though my heart was thumping.

'I think you may have frightened the life out of that poor man,' I said. 'You looked like you slightly wanted to hit him.'

'That's because I slightly did.'

'You are an idiot, Sam Fielding.' I reached up and kissed him, and when he kissed me back he was smiling again. His chin was thick with stubble where he hadn't bothered to shave.

This time he was tender. Partly because we now believed the walls were thin and he wasn't really meant to be there. But I think we were both careful of each other after the unexpected events of the evening. Every time he touched me it was with a kind of reverence. He told me he loved me, his voice low and soft, and he looked straight into my eyes when he said it. The words reverberated through me like little earthquakes.

I love you.

I love you.

I love you too.

*

We had set the alarm for a quarter to five, and I woke cursing, dragged from sleep by the shrill sound. Beside me Sam groaned and pulled a pillow over his head. I had to push him awake.

I propelled him, grumbling, into the bathroom, turned on the shower, and padded to the kitchen to make us both coffee. When I came back I heard the *thunk* of the water being turned off. I sat on the side of the bed, sipped my coffee and wondered whose smart idea it had been to drink strong cocktails on a Sunday evening. The bathroom door opened just as I flopped back down.

'Can I blame you for the cocktails? I need someone to blame.' My head was thumping. I raised and lowered it gently. 'What even was in those things?' I placed my fingertips against my temples. 'They must have been double measures. I don't normally feel this grim. Oh, man. We should have just gone to 30 Rock.'

He didn't say anything. I turned my head so that I could see him. He was standing in the doorway of the bathroom. 'You want to talk to me about this?'

'About what?' I pushed myself upright. He was wearing a towel around his waist and holding a small white rectangular box. For a brief moment I thought he was trying to give me jewellery, and I almost laughed. But when he held the box towards me he wasn't smiling.

I took it from him. And stared, disbelieving, at a pregnancy test. The box was opened, and the white plastic wand was loose inside. I checked it, some distant part of me noting that there were no blue lines, then looked up at him, temporarily lost for words.

He sat down heavily on the side of the bed. 'We used a condom, right? The last time I was over. We used a condom.'

'Wha— where did you find that?'

'In your bin. I just went to put my razor in there.'

'It's not mine, Sam.'

'You share this room with someone else?'

'No.'

'Then how can you not know whose it is?'

'I don't know! But – but it's not mine! I haven't had sex with anyone else!' I realized as I was protesting that the mere act of insisting you hadn't had sex with someone else made you sound like you were trying to hide the fact that you had had sex with someone else. 'I know how it looks but I have no idea why that thing is in my bathroom!'

'Is this why you're always on at me about Katie? Because you're actually feeling guilty about seeing someone else? What is it they call it? Transference? Is – is that why you were so . . . so different the other night?'

The air disappeared from the room. I felt as if I'd been slapped. I stared at him. 'You really think that? After everything we've been through?'

He didn't say anything.

'You – you really think I'd cheat on you?'

He was pale, as shocked as I felt. 'I just think if it looks like a duck and it quacks like a duck then, you know . . . it's usually a duck.'

'I am not a bloody *duck* . . . Sam. Sam.'

He turned his head reluctantly.

'I wouldn't cheat on you. It's not mine. You have to believe me.'

His eyes scanned my face.

'I don't know how many times I can say it. It's not mine.'

'We've been together such a short time. And so much of it has been spent apart. I don't . . .'

'You don't what?'

'It's one of those situations, you know? If you told your mates in the pub? They'd give you that look like – *mate* . . .'

'Then don't talk to your bloody mates in the pub! Listen to *me*!'

'I want to, Lou!'

'Then what the hell is your problem?'

'*He looked just like Will Traynor!*' It burst out of him like it had nowhere else to go. He sat down. He put his head in his hands. And then he said it again, quietly. 'He looked just like Will Traynor.'

My eyes had filled with tears. I wiped them away with the heel of my hand, knowing that I had probably now smudged yesterday's mascara all over my cheeks but not really caring. When I spoke my voice was low and severe and didn't really sound like mine.

'I'm going to say this one more time. I am not sleeping with anyone else. If you don't believe me I . . . Well, I don't know what you're doing here.'

He didn't reply but I felt as if his answer floated silently between us: *Neither do I.* He stood and walked over to his bag. He pulled some pants from inside and put them on, yanking them up with short, angry movements. 'I have to go.'

I couldn't say anything else. I sat on the bed and watched him, feeling simultaneously bereft and furious. I said nothing while he dressed and threw the rest of his belongings into his bag. Then he slung it over his shoulder, walked to the door and turned.

'Safe trip,' I said. I couldn't smile.

'I'll call you when I'm home.'

'Okay.'

He stooped and kissed my cheek. I didn't look up when he opened the door. He stood there a moment longer and then he left, closing it silently behind him.

*

Agnes came home at midday. Garry picked her up from the airport and she arrived back oddly subdued, as if she were reluctant to be there. She greeted me from behind sunglasses with a cursory hello, and retreated to her dressing room, where she stayed with the door locked for the next four hours. At teatime she emerged, showered and dressed, and forced a smile when I entered her study bearing the completed mood boards. I talked her through the colours and fabrics, and she nodded distractedly, but I could tell she hadn't really registered what I had done. I let her drink her tea, then waited until I knew Ilaria had gone downstairs. I closed the study door so that she glanced up at me.

'Agnes,' I said quietly. 'This is a slightly odd question, but did you put a pregnancy test in my bathroom?'

She blinked at me over her teacup. And then she put her cup down on its saucer and pulled a face. 'Oh. That. Yes, I was going to tell you.'

I felt anger rise up in me like bile. 'You were going to tell me? You know my boyfriend found it?'

'Your boyfriend came for the weekend? That's so nice! Did you have lovely time?'

'Right up until he found a used pregnancy test in my bathroom.'

'But you tell him it's not yours, yes?'

'I did, Agnes. But, funnily enough, men tend to get a little shirty when they find pregnancy tests in their girlfriends' bathrooms. Especially girlfriends who live three thousand miles away.'

She waved her hand, as if shooing my concerns away. 'Oh, for goodness' sake. If he trusts you he will be fine. You are not cheating on him. He should not be so stupid.'

'But why? Why would you put a pregnancy test in my bathroom?'

She stopped. She glanced around me, as if to check that the study door really was closed. And suddenly her expression grew serious. 'Because if I had left it in my bathroom Ilaria would have found it,' she said flatly. 'And I cannot have Ilaria seeing this thing.' She lifted her hands as if I were being spectacularly dim. 'Leonard was very clear when we marry. No children. This was our deal.'

'Really? But that's not . . . What if you decide you want them?'

She pursed her lips. 'I won't.'

'But – but you're my age. How can you know for sure? I can't tell most days if I'm going to want to stick with the same brand of hair conditioner. Lots of people change their mind when –'

'I am not having children with Leonard,' she snapped. 'Okay? Enough with the talk of children.'

I stood, a little reluctantly, and her head whipped around, her expression fierce. 'I'm sorry. I'm sorry if I caused you trouble.' She pushed at her brow with the heel of her palm. 'Okay? I'm sorry. Now I am going for a run. On my own.'

Ilaria was in the kitchen when I walked in a few moments later. She was pushing a huge lump of dough around a mixing bowl with fierce, even strokes and she didn't look up.

'You think she is your friend.'

I stopped, my mug halfway to the coffee machine.

She pushed the dough with particular force. 'The *puta* would sell you down the river if it meant she saved herself.'

'Not helpful, Ilaria,' I said. It was perhaps the first time I had ever answered her back. I filled my mug and walked to the door. 'And, believe it or not, you don't know everything.'

I heard her snort from halfway down the hall.

*

I headed down to Ashok's desk to pick up Agnes's dry-cleaning, stopping to chat for a few moments to try to push aside my dark mood. Ashok was always even, always upbeat. Talking with him was like having a window on a lighter world. When I arrived back at the apartment there was a small, slightly wrinkled plastic bag propped up outside the front door. I stooped to pick it up and found, to my surprise, that it was addressed to me. Or at least to '*Louisa I think her name is*'.

I opened it in my room. Inside, wrapped in recycled tissue paper, was a vintage Biba scarf, decorated with a print of peacock feathers. I opened it out and draped it around my neck, admiring the subtle sheen of the fabric, the way it shimmered even in the dim light. It smelt of cloves and old perfume. Then I reached into the bag and pulled out a small card. The name at the top read, in looping dark blue print: Margot De Witt. Underneath, in a shaky scrawl, was written: *Thank you for saving my dog.*

15

To: MrandMrsBernardClark@yahoo.com
From: BusyBee@gmail.com

Hi, Mum,

Yes, Halloween is kind of a big deal here. I walked around the city and it was very sweet. There were lots of little ghosts and witches carrying baskets of sweets, with their parents following at a distance with torches. Some of them had even dressed up too. And people here seem to really get into it, not like our street where half the neighbours turn their lights out or hide in the back room to stop kids knocking. All the windows are full of plastic pumpkins or fake ghosts and everyone seems to love dressing up. Nobody even egged anyone else that I could see.

But no trick-or-treaters in our building. We're not really in the kind of neighbourhood where people knock on each other's doors. Maybe they'd call out to each other's drivers. Also they'd have to get past the night man and he can be kind of scary in himself.

It's Thanksgiving next. They'd barely cleared away the ghost silhouettes before the adverts for turkey started. I'm not entirely sure even what Thanksgiving's about – mostly eating, I think. Most holidays here seem to be.

I'm fine. I'm sorry I haven't called much. Give my love to Dad and Granddad.

I miss you.
Lou x

Mr Gopnik, newly sentimental about family gatherings in the way that recently divorced men often are, had decreed that he wanted a Thanksgiving dinner at the apartment with his closest family present, capitalizing on the fact that the former Mrs Gopnik was headed to Vermont with her sister. The prospect of this happy event – along with his schedule of eighteen-hour working days – was enough to send Agnes into a persistent funk.

Sam sent me a text message on his return – twenty-four hours after his return, actually – to say he was tired and this was harder than he'd thought. I answered with a simple *yes* because in truth I was tired too.

I ran with Agnes and George early in the morning. When I didn't run I woke in the little room with the sounds of the city in my ears and a picture of Sam, standing in my bathroom doorway, in my head. I would lie there, shifting and turning, until I was tangled in the sheets, my mood blackened. The whole day would be tarnished before it had even started. When I had to get up and out in my running shoes, I woke up already on the move, forced to contemplate other people's lives, the pull in my thighs, the cold air in my chest, the sound of my breathing in my ears. I felt taut, strong, braced to bat away whatever crap the day was likely to greet me with.

And that week there was significant crap. Garry's daughter dropped out of college, putting him in a foul mood, so that every time Agnes left the car he would rail about ungrateful children who didn't understand sacrifice or the value of a working man's dollar. Ilaria was reduced to constant mute fury by Agnes's more bizarre habits, such as ordering food she subsequently decided she didn't want to eat, or locking her dressing room when she wasn't in it, so that Ilaria couldn't put her clothes away. 'She wants me to put her underwear in the hallway? She wants her sexytime outfits on full display to the grocery man? What is she hiding in there anyway?'

Michael flitted through the apartment like a ghost, wearing the exhausted, harried expression of a man doing two jobs – and even Nathan lost some of his equanimity and snapped at the Japanese cat lady when she suggested that the unexpected deposit in Nathan's shoe was the result of his 'bad energy'. 'I'll give her bad ruddy energy,' he grumbled, as he dropped his running shoes into a bin. Mrs De Witt knocked on our door twice in a week to complain about the piano, and in retaliation Agnes put on a recording of a piece called 'The Devil's Staircase', and turned it up loud just before we went out. 'Ligeti,' she sniffed, checking her make-up in her compact as we headed down in the lift, the hammering, atonal notes climbing and receding above us. I quietly texted Ilaria in private and asked her to turn it off once we had gone.

The temperature dropped, the sidewalks became even more congested, and the Christmas displays began to creep into the shopfronts, like a gaudy, glittering rash. I booked my flights home with little anticipation, no longer knowing what kind of welcome I'd be returning to. I called my sister, hoping she wouldn't ask too many questions. I needn't have worried. She was as talkative as I had ever known her, chatting about Thom's school projects, his new friends from the estate, his football prowess. I asked her about her boyfriend and she grew uncharacteristically quiet.

'Are you going to tell us *anything* about him? You know it's driving Mum nuts.'

'Are you still coming home at Christmas?'

'Yup.'

'Then I might introduce you. If you can manage not to be a complete eejit for a couple of hours.'

'Has he met Thom?'

'This weekend,' she said, her voice suddenly a little less confident. 'I've kept them separate till now. What if it doesn't work? I mean, Eddie loves kids but what if they don't –'

'Eddie!'

She sighed. 'Yes. Eddie.'

'Eddie. Eddie and Treena. *Eddie and Treena sitting in a tree. K-I-S-S-I-N-G.*'

'You are such a child.'

It was the first time I had laughed all week. 'They'll be fine,' I said. 'And once you've done that you can take him to meet Mum and Dad. Then you'll be the one Mum keeps asking about wedding bells and I can take a Maternal Guilt Trip Vacation.'

'It's "holiday". You're not American. And like that's ever going to happen. You know she's worried you'll be too grand to talk to them at Christmas? She thinks you won't want to get in Daddy's van from the airport because you've got used to riding in limousines.'

'It's true. I have.'

'Seriously, what's going on? You've said nothing about what's happening with you.'

'Loving New York,' I said, smooth as a mantra. 'Working hard.'

'Oh, crap. I've got to go. Thom's woken up.'

'Let me know how it goes.'

'I will. Unless it goes badly, in which case I'll be emigrating without saying a word to anyone ever for the rest of my life.'

'That's our family. Always a proportionate response.'

Saturday served itself up cold, with a side order of gales. I hadn't known quite how brutal the winds could be in New York. It was as if the tall buildings funnelled any breeze, polishing it hard and fast into something icy and fierce and solid.

I frequently felt as if I were walking in some kind of sadistic wind tunnel. I kept my head down, my body at an angle of forty-five degrees and, occasionally reaching out to clutch at fire hydrants or lamp posts, I caught the subway to the Vintage Clothes Emporium, stayed for a coffee to thaw out and bought a zebra-print coat at the marked-down bargain price of twelve dollars. In truth, I lingered. I didn't want to go back to my silent little room, with Ilaria's news programme burbling down the corridor, its ghostly echoes of Sam and the temptation to check my email every fifteen minutes. I got home when it was already dark and I was cold and weary enough not to be restless or submerged in that persistent New York feeling – that staying in meant I was missing out on something.

I sat and watched TV in my room and thought about writing Sam an email but I was still angry enough not to feel conciliatory and wasn't sure what I had to say was about to make anything better. I'd borrowed a novel by John Updike from Mr Gopnik's shelves but it was all about the complexities of modern relationships, and everyone in it seemed unhappy or was lusting madly after someone else, so in the end I turned off the light and slept.

The next morning when I came down Meena was in the lobby. She was minus children this time, but accompanied by Ashok, who was not in his uniform. I startled a little at the sight of him in civvies, rootling under his desk. It occurred to me suddenly how much easier it was for the rich to refuse to know anything about us when we weren't dressed as individuals.

'Hey, Miss Louisa,' he said. 'Forgot my hat. Had to pop in before we head to the library.'

'The one they want to close?'

'Yup,' Ashok said. 'You want to come with us?'

'Come help us save our library, Louisa!' Meena clapped me on the back with a mitten-clad hand. 'We need all the help we can get!'

I had been planning to go to the coffee shop, but I had nothing else to do and Sunday stretched ahead of me like a wasteland, so I agreed. They handed me a placard, saying 'A LIBRARY IS MORE THAN BOOKS', and checked that I had a hat and gloves. 'You're good for an hour or two, but you get really chilled by the third,' Meena said, as we walked out. She was what my father would have called ballsy – a voluptuous, big-haired sexy New Yorker, who had a smart retort for everything her husband said, and loved to rib him about his hair, his handling of their children, his sexual prowess. She had a huge, throaty laugh and took no crap from anyone. He plainly adored her. They called each other 'baby' so often that I occasionally wondered if they had forgotten each other's names.

We caught the subway north to Washington Heights and talked about how he had taken the job as a temporary measure when Meena first got pregnant, and how when the children were school age he was going to start looking around for something else, something with office hours, so that he could help out more. ('But the health benefits are good. Makes it hard to leave.') They had met at college – I was ashamed to admit I had assumed they were an arranged marriage.

When I'd told her, Meena had exploded into laughter. *Girl? You think I wouldn't have made my parents pick me better than him?*

Ashok: *You didn't say that last night, baby.*

Meena: *That's because I was focused on the TV.*

When we finally laughed our way up the subway steps at 163rd Street I was suddenly in a very different New York.

*

The buildings in this part of Washington Heights looked exhausted: boarded-up shop fronts with sagging fire escapes, liquor shops, fried-chicken shops, and beauty salons with curled and faded pictures of outdated hairstyles in the windows. A softly cursing man walked past us, pushing a shopping trolley full of plastic bags. Groups of kids slouched on corners, catcalling to each other, and the kerb was punctuated by refuse bags that lay stacked in unruly heaps, or vomited their contents onto the road. There was none of the gloss of Lower Manhattan, none of the purposeful aspiration that was shot through the very air of Midtown. The atmosphere here was scented with fried food and disillusionment.

Meena and Ashok appeared not to notice. They strode along, their heads bent together, checking phones to make sure Meena's mother wasn't having problems with the kids. Meena turned to see if I was with them and smiled. I glanced behind me, tucked my wallet deeper inside my jacket, and hurried after them.

We heard the protest before we saw it, a vibration in the air that gradually became distinct, a distant chant. We rounded a corner and there, in front of a sooty red-brick building, stood around a hundred and fifty people, waving placards and chanting, their voices mostly aimed towards a small camera crew. As we approached, Meena thrust her sign into the air. '*Education for all!*' she yelled. '*Don't take away our kids' safe spaces!*' We pierced the crowd and were swiftly swallowed by it. I had thought New York was diverse, but now I realized all I had seen was the colour of people's skin, the styles of their clothes. Here was a very different range of people. There were old women in knitted caps, hipsters with babies strapped to their backs, young black men with their hair neatly braided, and elderly Indian women in saris. People were animated, joined in a common purpose, and utterly, communally intent on getting their point across. I joined in with the chanting, seeing Meena's beaming smile, the way she hugged fellow protesters as she moved through the crowd.

'They said it'll be on the evening news.' An elderly woman turned to me, nodding with satisfaction. 'That's the only thing the city council takes any notice of. They all wanna be on the news.'

I smiled.

'Every year it's the same, right? Every year we have to fight a little harder to keep the community together. Every year we have to hold tighter to what's ours.'

'I – I'm sorry. I don't really know. I'm just here with friends.'

'But you came to help us. That's what matters.' She placed a hand on my arm. 'You know my grandson does a mentoring programme here? They pay him to teach other young folk the computers. They actually pay him. He teaches adults too. He helps them apply for jobs.' She clapped her gloved hands together, trying to keep warm. 'If the council close it, all those people will have nowhere to go. And you can bet the city councillors will be the first people complaining about the young folk hanging around on street corners. You know it.' She smiled at me as if I did.

Ahead, Meena was holding up her sign again. Ashok, beside her, stooped to greet a friend's small boy, picking him up and lifting him above the crowd so that he could see better. He looked completely different in this crowd without his doorman outfit. For all we talked, I had only really seen him through the prism of his uniform. I hadn't wondered about his life beyond the lobby desk, how he supported his family or how long he travelled to work or what he was paid. I surveyed the crowd, which had grown a little quieter once the camera crew departed, and felt oddly ashamed at how little I had really explored New York. This was as much the city as the glossy towers of Midtown.

We kept up our chant for another hour. Cars and trucks beeped in support as they passed and we would cheer in return. Two librarians came out and offered trays of hot drinks to as many as they could. I didn't take one. By then I had noticed the ripped seams on the old lady's coat, the threadbare, well-worn quality of the clothes around me. An Indian woman and her son walked across the road with large foil trays of hot pakoras and we dived on them, thanking her profusely. 'You are doing important work,' she said. 'We thank you.' My pakora was full of peas and potato, spicy enough to make me gasp and absolutely delicious. 'They bring those out to us every week, God bless them,' said the old lady, brushing pastry crumbs from her scarf.

A squad car crawled by two, three times, the officer's face blank as he scanned the crowd. 'Help us save our library, sir!' Meena yelled at him. He turned his face away but his colleague smiled.

At one point Meena and I went inside to use the loos and I got a chance to see what I was apparently fighting for. The building was old, with high ceilings, visible pipework and a hushed air; the walls were covered with posters offering adult education, meditation sessions, help with CVs and payment of six dollars per hour for mentoring classes. But it was full of people, the children's area thick with young families, the computer section humming with adults clicking carefully on keyboards, not yet confident in what they were doing. A handful of teenagers sat chatting quietly in a corner, some reading books, several wearing earphones. I was surprised to see two security guards standing by the librarians' desk.

'Yeah. We get a few fights. It's free to anyone, you know?'

whispered Meena. 'Drugs usually. You're always gonna get some trouble.' We passed an old woman as we headed back down the stairs. Her hat was filthy, her blue nylon coat creased and street-worn, with rips in the shoulders, like epaulettes. I found myself staring after her as she levered her way up, step by step, her battered slippers barely staying on her feet, clutching a bag from which one solitary paperback poked out.

We stayed outside for another hour – long enough for a reporter and another news crew to stop by, asking questions, promising they would do their best to get the story to run. And then, at one, the crowd started to disperse. Meena, Ashok and I headed back to the subway, the two of them chatting animatedly about whom they had spoken to and the protests planned for the following week.

'What will you do if it does close?' I asked them, when we were on the train.

'Honestly?' said Meena, pushing her bandanna back on her hair. 'No idea. But they'll probably close it in the end. There's another, better-equipped, building two miles away and they'll say we can take our children there. Because obviously everyone round here has a car. And it's good for the old people to walk two miles in the ninety-degree heat.' She rolled her eyes. 'But we keep fighting till then, right?'

'You gotta have your places for community.' Ashok raised a hand emphatically, slicing the air. 'You gotta have places where people can meet and talk and exchange ideas and it not just be about money, you know? Books are what teach you about life. Books teach you *empathy*. But you can't buy books if you barely got enough to make rent. So that library is a vital resource! You shut a library, Louisa, you don't just shut down a building, you shut down *hope*.'

There was a brief silence.

'I love you, baby,' said Meena, and kissed him full on the mouth.

'I love you too, baby.'

They gazed at each other and I brushed imaginary crumbs from my coat and tried not to think about Sam.

Ashok and Meena headed over to her mother's apartment to pick up their children, hugging me and making me promise to come next week. I took myself to the diner where I had a coffee and a slice of pie. I couldn't stop thinking about the protest, the people in the library, the grimy, potholed streets that surrounded it. I kept picturing the rips in that woman's coat, the elderly woman beside me and her pride in her grandson's mentoring wages. I thought about Ashok's impassioned plea for community. I recalled how my life had been changed by our library back home, the way Will had insisted that 'knowledge is power'. How each book I now read – almost every decision I made – could be traced back to that time.

I thought about the way that every single protester in the crowd had known somebody else or was linked to somebody else or bought them food or drink or chatted to them, how I had felt the energy rush and pleasure that came from a shared goal.

I thought about my new home where, in a silent building of perhaps thirty people nobody spoke to anyone, except to complain about some small infringement of their own peace, where nobody apparently either liked anyone or could be bothered to get to know them enough to find out.

I sat until my pie grew cold in front of me.

When I got back I did two things: I wrote a short note to Mrs De Witt thanking her for the beautiful scarf, telling her the gift had made my week, and that if she ever wanted further help with the dog I would be delighted to learn more about canine care. I put it into an envelope and slid it under her door.

I knocked on Ilaria's door, trying not to be intimidated when she opened it and stared at me with open suspicion. 'I passed the coffee shop where they sell the cinnamon cookies you like so I bought you some. Here.' I held out the bag to her.

She eyed it warily. 'What do you want?'

'Nothing!' I said. 'Just . . . thanks for the whole thing with the kids the other day. And, you know, we work together and stuff so . . .' I shrugged. 'It's just some cookies.'

I held them a few inches closer to her so that she was obliged to take them from me. She looked at the bag, then at me, and I had the feeling she was about to thrust it back at me, so before she could I waved and hurried back to my room.

That evening I went online and looked up everything I could find out about the library: the news stories about its budget cuts, threatened closures, small success stories – *Local teen credits library for college scholarship* – printing out key pieces and saving all the useful information into a file.

And at a quarter to nine, an email popped into my inbox. It was titled SORRY.

Lou,

I've been on lates all week and I wanted to write when I had more than five minutes and knew I wasn't going to mess things up more. I'm not great with words. And I'm guessing only one word is really important here. I'm sorry. I know you wouldn't cheat. I was an idiot even for thinking it.

The thing is it's hard being so far apart and not knowing what's going on in your life. When we meet it's like the volume's turned up too high on everything. We can't just relax with each other.

I know your time in New York is important to you and I don't want
you to stay still.

I'm sorry, again.

Your Sam
xxx

It was the closest thing he'd sent me to a letter. I stared at
the words for a few moments, trying to unpick what I felt.
Finally I opened up an email and typed:

I know. I love you. When we see each other at Christmas hopefully
we'll have time just to relax around each other. Lou xxx

I sent it, then answered an email from Mum and wrote one
to Treena. I typed them on autopilot, thinking about Sam
the whole time. *Yes, Mum, I will check out the new pictures of the
garden on Facebook. Yes, I know Bernice's daughter pulls that duck
face in all her pictures. It's meant to be attractive.*

I logged onto my bank, and then onto Facebook and
found myself smiling, despite myself, at the endless pictures
of Bernice's daughter with her rubberized pout. I saw Mum's
pictures of our little garden, the new chairs she had bought
from the garden centre. Then, almost on a whim, I found
myself flicking to Katie Ingram's page. Almost immediately
I wished I hadn't. There, in glorious technicolour, were seven
recently uploaded pictures of a paramedics' night out, possibly the one they had been headed to when I had called.

Or, worse, possibly not.

There was Katie, in a dark pink shirt that looked like silk,
her smile wide, her eyes knowing, leaning across the table to
make a point, or her throat bared as she threw back her head
in a laugh. There was Sam, in his battered jacket and a grey

T-shirt, his big hand clasping a glass of what looked like lime cordial, a few inches taller than everyone else. In every picture the group was happy, laughing at shared jokes. Sam looked utterly relaxed and completely at home. And in every picture, Katie Ingram was pressed up next to him, nestled into his armpit as they sat around the pub table, or gazing up at him, one hand resting lightly on his shoulder.

16

'I have project for you.' I was seated in the corner at her super-trendy hairdresser's, waiting while Agnes had her hair coloured and blow-dried. I had been watching the local news reports of the library-closure protest, and switched my phone off hurriedly when she approached, her hair in carefully folded layers of tin foil. She sat down beside me, ignoring the colourist who clearly wanted her back in her seat.

'I want you to find me very small piano. To ship to Poland.'

She said this as if she was asking me to buy a packet of gum from Duane Reade.

'A very small piano.'

'A very special small piano for child to learn on. Is for my sister's little girl,' she said. 'It must be very good quality, though.'

'Are there no small pianos you can buy in Poland?'

'Not this good. I want it to come from Hossweiner and Jackson. These are best pianos in the world. And you must organize special shipping with climate control so it is not affected by cold or moisture as this will alter the tone. But the shop should be able to help with this.'

'How old is your sister's kid again?'

'She is four.'

'Uh . . . okay.'

'And it needs to be the best so she can hear the difference. There is huge difference, you know, between tones. Is like playing Stradivarius compared to cheap fiddle.'

'Sure.'

'But here is thing.' She turned away, ignoring the now

frantic colourist, who was gesturing at her head from across the salon and tapping at a non-existent watch. 'I do not want this to appear on my credit card. So you must withdraw money every week to pay for this. Bit by bit. Okay? I have some cash already.'

'But . . . Mr Gopnik wouldn't mind, surely?'

'He thinks I spend too much on my niece. He doesn't understand. And if Tabitha discovers this she twist everything to make me look like bad person. You know what she is like, Louisa. So you can do this?' She looked at me intently from under the layers of foil.

'Uh, okay.'

'You are wonderful. I am so happy to have friend like you.' She hugged me abruptly so that the foils crushed against my ear and the colourist immediately ran over to see what damage my face had done.

I called the shop and got them to send me the costs for two varieties of miniature piano plus shipping. Once I'd finished blinking, I printed out the relevant quotes and showed them to Agnes in her dressing room.

'That's quite a present,' I said.

She waved a hand.

I swallowed. 'And the shipping is another two and a half thousand dollars on top.'

I blinked. Agnes didn't. She walked over to her dresser and unlocked it with a key she kept in her jeans. As I watched, she pulled out an untidy wedge of fifty-dollar bills as fat as her arm. 'Here. This is eight thousand five hundred. I need you to go every morning and get the rest from the ATM. Five hundred a time. Okay?'

I didn't feel entirely comfortable with the idea of extracting so much money without Mr Gopnik's knowledge. But I knew that Agnes's links to her Polish family were intense, and I also knew better than most how you could long to feel close to those who were far away. Who was I to question how she was spending her money? I was pretty sure she owned dresses that cost more than that little piano, after all.

For the next ten days, at some point during daylight hours, I dutifully walked to the ATM on Lexington Avenue and collected the money, stuffing the notes deep into my bra before walking back, braced to fight off muggers who never materialized. I would give the money to Agnes when we were alone, and she would add it to the stash in the dresser, then lock it again. Eventually I took the whole lot to the piano store, signed the requisite form and counted it out in front of a bemused shop assistant. The piano would arrive in Poland in time for Christmas.

It was the only thing that seemed to give Agnes any joy. Every week we drove over to Steven Lipkott's studio for her art lesson, and Garry and I would silently overdose on caffeine and sugar in the Best Doughnut Place, or I would murmur agreement with his views on ungrateful adult children, and caramel sprinkle doughnuts. We would pick up Agnes a couple of hours later and try to ignore the fact that she had no drawings with her.

Her resentment at the relentless charity circuit had grown ever greater. She had stopped trying to be nice to the other women, Michael told me, in whispers over snatched coffees in the kitchen. She just sat, beautiful and sullen, waiting for each event to be over. 'I guess you can't blame her, given how bitchy they've been to her. But it's driving him a little nuts. It's important for him to have, well, if not a trophy wife, someone who's at least prepared to smile occasionally.'

Mr Gopnik looked exhausted by work and by life in general. Michael told me things at the office were difficult. A huge deal to prop up a bank in some emerging economy had gone wrong and they were all working around the clock to try to save it. At the same time – or perhaps because of it – Nathan said Mr Gopnik's arthritis had flared up and they were doing extra sessions to keep him moving normally. He took a lot of pills. A private doctor saw him twice a week.

'I hate this life,' Agnes said to me, as we walked across the park. 'All this money he gives away and for what? So we can sit four times a week and eat dried-up canapés with dried-up people. And so these dried-up women can bitch about me.' She stopped for a minute and looked back at the building and I saw that her eyes had filled with tears. Her voice dropped. 'Sometimes, Louisa, I think I cannot do this any more.'

'He loves you,' I said. I didn't know what else to say.

She wiped her eyes with the palm of her hand and shook her head, as if she were trying to rid herself of the emotion. 'I know.' She smiled at me, and it was the least convincing smile I'd ever seen. 'But it is a long time since I believed love solved everything.'

On impulse, I stepped forward and hugged her. Afterwards I realized I couldn't say whether I'd done it for her or myself.

It was shortly before the Thanksgiving dinner that the idea first occurred to me. Agnes had refused to get out of bed all day, faced with a mental-health charity do that evening. She said she was too depressed to attend, apparently refusing to see the irony.

I thought about it for as long as it took me to drink a mug of tea, and then I decided I had little to lose.

'Mr Gopnik?' I knocked on his study door and waited for him to invite me in.

He looked up, his pale blue shirt immaculate, his eyes dragged downwards with weariness. Most days I felt a little sorry for him, in the way that you can feel sorry for a caged bear while maintaining a healthy and slightly fearful respect for it.

'What is it?'

'I – I'm sorry to bother you. But I had an idea. It's something I think might help Agnes.'

He leaned back in his leather chair and signalled to me to close the door. I noticed there was a lead glass tumbler of brandy on his desk. That was earlier than usual.

'May I speak frankly?' I said. I felt a little sick with nerves.

'Please do.'

'Okay. Well, I couldn't help but notice Agnes is not as, um, happy as she might be.'

'That's an understatement,' he said quietly.

'It seems to me that a lot of her issues relate to being plucked from her old life and not really integrating with her new one. She told me she can't spend time with her old friends because they don't really understand her new life, and from what I've seen, well, a lot of the new ones don't seem that keen to be friends with her either. I think they feel it would be . . . disloyal.'

'To my ex-wife.'

'Yes. So she has no job, and no community. And this building has no real community. You have your work, and people around you you've known for years, who like you and respect you. But Agnes doesn't. I know she finds the charity circuit particularly hard. But the philanthropic side of things is really important to you. So I had an idea.'

'Go on.'

'Well, there's this library up in Washington Heights which is threatened with closure. I've got all the information here.' I pushed my file across his desk. 'It's a real community library, used by all different nationalities and ages and types of people, and it's absolutely vital for the locals that it stays open. They're fighting so hard to save it.'

'That's an issue for the city council.'

'Well, maybe. But I spoke to one of the librarians and she said that in the past they've received individual donations that have helped keep them going.' I leant forward. 'If you just went there, Mr Gopnik, you'd see – there are mentoring programmes and mothers keeping their children warm and safe and people really trying to make things better. In a practical way. And I know it's not as glamorous as the events you attend – I mean, there's not going to be a ball there, but it's still charity, right? And I thought maybe . . . well, maybe you could get involved. And even better, if Agnes got involved she could be part of a community. She could make it her own project. You and she could do something amazing.'

'Washington Heights?'

'You should go there. It's a very mixed area. Quite different from . . . here. I mean some bits of it are gentrified but this bit –'

'I know Washington Heights, Louisa.' He tapped his fingers on the desk. 'Have you spoken to Agnes about this?'

'I thought I should probably mention it to you first.'

He pulled the file towards him and flicked it open. He frowned at the first sheet – a newspaper cutting of one of the early protests. The second was a budget statement I had pulled from the city council's website, showing its latest financial year.

'Mr Gopnik, I really think you could make a difference. Not just to Agnes but to a whole community.'

It was at this point that I realised he appeared unmoved, dismissive even. It wasn't a sea-change in his expression, but a faint hardening, a lowering of his gaze. And it occurred to me that to be as wealthy as he was, was probably to receive a hundred such requests for money each day, or suggestions as to what he should do with it. And that perhaps, by being part of that, I had stepped over some invisible employee/employer line.

'Anyway. It was just an idea. Possibly not a great one. I'm sorry if I've said too much. I'll get back to work. Don't feel you have to look at that stuff if you're busy. I can take it with me if you –'

'It's fine, Louisa.' He pressed his fingers to his temples, his eyes closed.

I stood, not sure if I was being dismissed.

Finally he looked up at me. 'Can you go and talk to Agnes, please? Find out whether I'm going to have to go to this dinner alone?'

'Yes. Of course.' I backed out of the room.

She went to the mental-health dinner. We didn't hear any fighting when they got home but the next day I discovered she had slept in her dressing room.

In the two weeks before I was due to head home for Christmas I developed an almost obsessive Facebook habit. I found myself checking Katie Ingram's page morning and evening, reading the public conversations she had with her friends, checking for new photographs she might have posted. One of her friends had asked how she was enjoying her job and she had written, 'I LOVE it!' with a winky face (she was irritatingly fond of winky faces). Another day she had posted: 'Really tough day today. Thank God for my amazing partner! #blessed'

She posted one more picture of Sam, at the wheel of the ambulance. He was laughing, lifting his hand as if to stop her, and the sight of his face, the intimacy of the shot, the way it placed me in the cab with them, took my breath away.

We had scheduled a call for the previous evening, his time, and when I'd called he hadn't picked up. I'd tried again, twice, with no answer. Two hours later, just as I was getting worried, I received a text message: *Sorry – you still there?*

'Are you okay? Was it work?' I said, when he called me.

There was the faintest hesitation before he responded. 'Not exactly.'

'What do you mean?' I was in the car with Garry, waiting while Agnes had a pedicure, and I was conscious that he might be listening in, no matter how engrossed he appeared to be in the sports pages of his *New York Post*.

'I was helping Katie with something.'

My stomach dropped merely at the mention of her name. 'Helping her with what?' I tried to keep my voice light.

'Just a wardrobe. Ikea. She bought it and couldn't put it together by herself so I said I'd give her a hand.'

I felt sick. 'You went to her house?'

'Flat. It was just to help her with a piece of furniture, Lou. She doesn't have anyone else. And I only live down the road.'

'You took your toolbox.' I remembered how he used to come to my flat and fix things. It had been one of the first things I'd loved about him.

'Yes. I took my toolbox. And all I did was help her with an Ikea wardrobe.' His voice had grown weary.

'Sam?'

'What?'

'Did you offer to go there? Or did she ask you?'

'Does it matter?'

I wanted to tell him it did, because it was obvious that she was trying to steal him from me. She was alternately playing the helpless female, the fun party girl, the understanding best friend and work colleague. He was either blind to it or, worse, he wasn't. There wasn't a single picture that she had posted online in which she wasn't glued to his side, like some kind of lipsticked leech. Sometimes I wondered if she'd guessed I'd be looking at them, and if she got satisfaction from knowing the discomfort this caused me, whether in fact this was part of her plan, to make me miserable and paranoid. I wasn't sure men would ever understand the infinitely subtle weaponry women used against each other.

The silence between us on the phone opened up and became a sinkhole. I knew I couldn't win. If I tried to warn him about what was happening, I became a jealous harpy. If I didn't, he'd carry on walking blindly into her mantrap. Until the day he suddenly realized he was missing her as much as he had ever missed me. Or he found her soft hand creeping into his at the pub as she leant on him for comfort after a tough day. Or they bonded over some shared adrenalin rush, some near-death incident, and found themselves kissing and –

I closed my eyes.

'So when do you get back?'

'Christmas Eve.'

'Great. I'll try and move some shifts. I'll be working for some of the Christmas period, though, Lou. You know the job. It doesn't stop.'

He sighed There was a pause before he spoke again. 'Listen. I was thinking. Maybe it would be a good idea if you and Katie met each other. Then you can see she's okay. She's not trying to be anything other than a mate.'

Like hell she isn't.

'Great! Sounds lovely,' I said.

'I think you'll like her.'

'Then I'm sure I will.'

Like I'd like Ebola virus. Or grating off my own elbows. Or maybe eating that cheese that has live bugs in it.

He sounded relieved when he said, 'Can't wait to see you. You're back for a week, right?'

I lowered my head, trying to muffle my voice a little. 'Sam,

235

does – does Katie really want to meet me? Is this, like, something you've discussed?'

'Yeah.' And then, when I said nothing, he added, 'I mean, not in any . . . We didn't talk about what happened with you and me or anything. But she gets that it must be hard for us.'

'I see.' I felt my jaw tighten.

'She thinks you sound great. Obviously I told her she's got that wrong.'

I laughed, and I'm not sure the world's worst actor could have made it sound less convincing.

'You'll see when you meet her. Can't wait.'

When he rang off, I looked up to find Garry was looking at me in the rear-view mirror. Our eyes met for a moment, then his slid away.

Given that I lived in one of the world's busiest metropolises, I had begun to understand that the world as I knew it was actually very small, shrink-wrapped around the demands of the Gopniks from six in the morning often until late evening. My life had become completely intertwined with theirs. Just as I had with Will, I'd become attuned to Agnes's every mood, able to detect from the subtlest signs whether she was depressed, angry or simply in need of food. I now knew when her periods were due, and marked them in my personal diary so that I could be braced for five days of heightened emotion or extra-emphatic piano playing. I knew how to become invisible during times of family conflict or when to be ever-present. I became a shadow, so much so that sometimes I felt almost evanescent – useful only in relation to someone else.

My life before the Gopniks had receded, become a faint, ghostly thing, experienced through odd phone calls (when Gopnik schedules allowed) or sporadic emails. I failed to ring my sister for two weeks and cried when my mother sent me a handwritten letter with photographs of her and Thom at a theatre matinee 'just in case you've forgotten what we look like'.

It could get a little much. So as a balance, even though I was exhausted, I travelled to the library every weekend with Ashok and Meena – once even going by myself when their children were ill. I got better at dressing for the cold and made my own placard – *Knowledge is power!* – with its private nod to Will. I would head back on the train and afterwards make my way down to the East Village to have a coffee at the Vintage Clothes Emporium and look over whatever new items Lydia and her sister had in stock.

Mr Gopnik never mentioned the library again. I realized with mild disappointment that charity could mean something quite different here; that it was not enough to give, you had to be seen to be giving. Hospitals bore the names of their donors in six-foot-high letters above the door. Balls were named after those who funded them. Even buses bore lists of names alongside their rear windows. Mr and Mrs Leonard Gopnik were known as generous benefactors because they were visible in society as being so. A scruffy library in a rundown neighbourhood offered no such kudos.

Ashok and Meena had invited me for Thanksgiving at their apartment in Washington Heights, horrified when I revealed I had no plans. 'You can't spend Thanksgiving on your own!' Ashok said, and I decided not to mention that few people in England even knew what it was. 'My mother makes the turkey – but don't expect it to be done American-style,' Meena said. 'We can't stand all that bland food. This is going to be some serious tandoori turkey.'

It was no effort to say yes to something new: I was quite excited. I bought a bottle of champagne, some fancy chocolates and some flowers for Meena's mother, then put on my blue cocktail dress with the fur sleeves, figuring an Indian Thanksgiving would be a suitable first outing for it – or, at least, one with no discernible dress code. Ilaria was flat out preparing for the Gopniks' family dinner and I decided not to disturb her. I let myself out, checking that I had the instructions Ashok had given me.

As I headed down the corridor I noticed Mrs De Witt's door was open. I heard the television burbling from deep inside the apartment. A few feet from the door Dean Martin stood in the hallway glaring at me. I wondered if he was about to make another break for freedom, and rang the doorbell.

Mrs De Witt emerged into the corridor.

'Mrs De Witt? I think Dean Martin may be about to go for a walk.' The dog pottered back towards her. She leaned against the wall. She looked frail and tired. 'Can you shut the door, dear? I must have not closed it properly.'

'Will do. Happy Thanksgiving, Mrs De Witt,' I said.

'Is it? I hadn't noticed.' She disappeared back into the room, the dog behind her, and I closed the front door. I had never seen her with so much as a casual caller and felt a brief sadness at the thought of her spending Thanksgiving alone.

I was just turning to leave when Agnes came down the corridor in her gym kit. She seemed startled to see me. 'Where are you going?'

'To dinner?' I didn't want to say who I was going with. I didn't know how the employers of the building would feel if they thought the staff were getting together without them. She looked at me in horror.

'But you can't go, Louisa. Leonard's family is coming here. I can't do this by myself. I told them you would be here.'

'You did? But –'

'You must stay.'

I looked at the door. My heart sank.

And then her voice dropped. 'Please, Louisa. You're my friend. I need you.'

I rang Ashok and told him. My one consolation was that, doing the job he did, he grasped the situation immediately. 'I'm so sorry,' I whispered into the phone. 'I really wanted to come.'

'Nah. You got to stay. Hey, Meena's yelling to tell you she's going to save some turkey for you. I'll bring it with me tomorrow . . . Baby, I told her! I did! She says drink all their expensive wine. Okay?'

I felt, briefly, on the edge of tears. I had looked forward to an evening full of giggling children, delicious food and laughter. Instead I was going to be a shadow again, a silent prop in an icy room.

My fears were justified.

Three other members of the Gopnik family came to Thanksgiving: his brother, an older, greyer, more anaemic version of Mr Gopnik, who apparently did something in law. Probably ran the US Department of Justice. He brought with him their mother, who sat in a wheelchair, refused to take off her fur coat for the entire evening and complained loudly that she couldn't hear what anyone was saying. Mr Gopnik's brother's wife, a former violinist apparently of some note, accompanied them. She was the only person there who bothered to ask what I did. She greeted Agnes with two kisses and the kind of professional smile that could have been meant for anyone.

Tab made up the numbers, arriving late and bringing with her the air of someone who has spent their cab ride in deep telephone discussion about how much they did not want to be there. Moments after she arrived we were seated to eat in the dining room – which was off the main living room and dominated by a long oval mahogany dining table.

It is fair to say the conversation was stilted. Mr Gopnik and his brother fell immediately into conversation about the legal restrictions in the country where he was currently doing business, and the two wives asked each other a few stiff questions, like people practising small-talk in a foreign language.

'How have you been, Agnes?'

'Fine, thank you. And you, Veronica?'

'Very well. You look very well. That's a very nice dress.'

'Thank you. You also look very nice.'

'Did I hear that you had been to Poland? I'm sure Leonard said you were visiting your mother.'

'I was there two weeks ago. It was lovely to see her, thank you.'

I sat between Tab and Agnes, watching Agnes drink too much white wine and Tab flick mutinously through her phone and occasionally roll her eyes. I sipped at the pumpkin and sage soup, nodded, smiled, and tried not to think longingly of Ashok's apartment and the joyful chaos there. I would have asked Tab about her week – anything to move the stuttering conversation along – but she had made so many acid asides about the horror of having 'staff' at family events that I didn't have the nerve.

Ilaria brought out dish after dish. 'The Polish *puta* does not cook. So somebody has to give up their Thanksgiving,' she muttered afterwards. She had laid on a feast of turkey, roast potatoes and a bunch of things I had never seen served as an accompaniment but suspected were about to leave me with instantaneous Type 2 diabetes – candied sweet potato casserole with marshmallow topping, green beans with honey and bacon, roasted acorn squash with bacon drizzled in maple syrup, buttery cornbread, and carrots roasted with honey and spice. There were also popovers – a kind of Yorkshire pudding – and I peered at them surreptitiously to see if they were draped with syrup too.

Of course only the men ate much of it. Tab pushed hers around her plate. Agnes ate some turkey and almost nothing else. I had a little of everything, grateful for something to do and also that Ilaria no longer slammed dishes down in front of me. In fact, she looked at me sideways a few times as if to express silent sympathy for my predicament. The men kept talking business, unaware or unwilling to acknowledge the permafrost at the other end of the table.

Occasionally the silence was broken by the elderly Mrs Gopnik demanding somebody help her to some potato or asking loudly, for the fourth time, what on earth the woman had done to the carrots. Several people would answer her at once, as if relieved to have a focus, no matter how irrational.

'That's an unusual dress, Louisa,' said Veronica, after a particularly long silence. 'Very striking. Did you buy it in Manhattan? One doesn't often see fur sleeves these days.'

'Thank you. I bought it in the East Village.'

'Is it Marc Jacobs?'

'Um, no. It's vintage.'

'Vintage,' snorted Tab.

'What did she say?' said Mrs Gopnik, loudly.

'She's talking about the girl's dress, Mother,' said Mr Gopnik's brother. 'She says it's vintage.'

'Vintage what?'

'What is problem with "vintage", Tab?' said Agnes, coolly.

I shrank backwards into my seat.

'It's such a meaningless term, isn't it? It's just a way of saying "second hand". A way of dressing something up to pretend it's something it's not.'

I wanted to tell her that vintage meant a whole lot more than that, but I didn't know how to express it – and suspected I wasn't meant to. I just wanted the whole conversation to move forwards and away from me.

'I believe vintage outfits can be quite the fashion now,' said Veronica, addressing me directly with a diplomat's skill. 'Of course, I'm far too old to understand the young people's trends these days.'

'And far too polite to say such things,' muttered Agnes.

'I'm sorry?' said Tab.

'Oh, now you are sorry?'

'I meant, what did you just say?'

Mr Gopnik looked up from his plate. His eyes darted warily from his wife to his daughter.

'I mean why you have to be so rude to Louisa. She is my guest here, even if she is staff. And you have to be rude about her outfit.'

'I wasn't being rude. I was simply stating a fact.'

'This is how being rude is these days. *I tell it like I see it. I'm just being honest.* The language of the bully. We all know how this is.'

'What did you just call me?'

'Agnes. Darling.' Mr Gopnik reached across and placed his hand over hers.

'What are they saying?' said Mrs Gopnik. 'Tell them to speak up.'

'I said Tab is being very rude to my friend.'

'She's not your friend, for crying out loud. She's your *paid assistant*. Although I suspect that's all you can get in the way of friends, these days.'

'Tab!' her father said. 'That's a horrible thing to say.'

'Well, it's true. Nobody wants anything to do with her. You can't pretend you don't see it wherever we go. You know this family is a laughing stock, Daddy? You have become a cliché. She is a walking cliché. And for what? We all know what her plan is.'

Agnes removed her napkin from her lap and screwed it into a ball. 'My plan? You want to tell me what my plan is?'

'Like every other sharp-elbowed immigrant on the make. You've somehow managed to convince Dad to marry you. Now you're no doubt doing everything possible to get pregnant and pop out a baby or two, then within five years you'll divorce him. And you're made for life. Boom! No more massages. Just Bergdorf Goodman, a driver and lunch with your Polish coven all the way.'

Mr Gopnik leant forward over the table. 'Tabitha, I don't want you ever using the word "immigrant" in a derogatory manner in this house again. Your great-grandparents were immigrants. You are the descendant of immigrants –'

'Not *that* kind of immigrant.'

'What does this mean?' said Agnes, her cheeks flushed.

'Do I have to spell it out? There are those who achieve their goals through hard work and there are those who do it by lying on their –'

'Like you?' yelled Agnes. 'Like you who lives off trust-fund allowance at age of nearly twenty-five? You who have barely held a job in your life? I am meant to take example from you? At least I know what hard work is –'

'Yes. Straddling strange men's naked bodies. *Quite* the employment.'

'That's enough!' Mr Gopnik was on his feet. 'You are quite, quite wrong, Tabitha, and you must apologize.'

'Why? Because I can see her without rose-coloured spectacles? Daddy, I'm sorry to say this but you are totally blind to what this woman really is.'

'No. You are the one who is wrong!'

'So she's never going to want children? She's twenty-eight years old, Dad. Wake up!'

'What are they talking about?' said old Mrs Gopnik, querulously, to her daughter-in-law. Veronica whispered something in her ear. 'But she said something about naked men. I heard her.'

'Not that it's any of your business, Tabitha, but there will be no more children in this house. Agnes and I agreed this point before I married her.'

Tab pulled a face. '*Oooh*. She *agreed*. Like that means anything at all. A woman like her would say anything to marry you! Daddy, I hate to say it but you are being hopelessly naïve. In a year or so there will be some little "accident" and she'll persuade –'

'There will be no accidents!' Mr Gopnik slammed his hand on the table so hard the glassware rattled.

'How can you know?'

'Because I had a goddamn vasectomy!' Mr Gopnik sat down. His hands were shaking. 'Two months before we got married. At Mount Sinai. With Agnes's full agreement. Are you satisfied now?'

The room fell silent. Tab gaped at her father.

The old woman looked from left to right, and then said, peering at Mr Gopnik, 'Leonard had an appendectomy?'

A low hum had started somewhere in the back of my head. As if in the distance I heard Mr Gopnik insisting that his daughter apologize, then watched her push back her chair and leave the table without doing so. I saw Veronica exchange looks with her husband and take a long, weary swig of her drink.

And then I looked at Agnes, who was staring mutely at her plate on which her food was congealing in honeyed, bacon-strewn portions. As Mr Gopnik reached out a hand and squeezed hers my heart thumped loudly in my ears.

She didn't look at me.

17

I flew home on 22 December, laden with presents and wearing my new vintage zebra-print coat, which, I would later discover, was strangely and adversely affected by the circulation of recycled air in the 767 and smelt, by the time I reached Heathrow, like a deceased equid.

I had actually not been due to fly until Christmas Eve but Agnes had insisted I go sooner as she was making an unheralded short stop back to Poland to see her mother, who was unwell, and there was apparently no point in my staying there to do nothing when I could be with my family. Mr Gopnik had paid for the change to my ticket. Agnes had been both overly nice and distant with me since the Thanksgiving dinner. In turn, I was professional and amenable. Sometimes my head would spin with the information it held. But I would think of Garry's words way back in the autumn when I'd arrived: *See nothing, hear nothing, forget everything.*

Something had happened in the run-up to Christmas, some lightening of my mood. Perhaps I was just relieved to be leaving that house of dysfunction. Or perhaps the act of buying Christmas presents had resurrected some buried sense of fun in my relationship with Sam. When had I last had a man to buy Christmas presents for, after all? For the last two years of our relationship Patrick had simply sent me emails with links to specific pieces of fitness equipment he wanted. *Don't bother wrapping them, babe, in case you get it wrong and I need to send them back.* All I had done was press a button. I had never spent Christmas with Will. Now I went shoulder to shoulder with the other shoppers in Saks, trying to imagine my boyfriend in the cashmere sweaters, my face pressed against them, the soft checked shirts he liked to wear in the garden, thick outdoor socks from REI. I bought toys for Thom, getting a sugar high from the scents in the M&M store in Times Square. I bought stationery for Treena from McNally Jackson and a beautiful dressing gown for Granddad from Macy's. Feeling flush, as I had spent so little over the past months, I bought Mum a little bracelet from Tiffany and a wind-up radio for Dad to use in his shed.

And then, as an afterthought, I bought a stocking for Sam. I filled it with small gifts: aftershave, novelty gum, socks and a beer holder in the shape of a woman in denim hotpants. Finally I went back to the toy store where I had bought Thom's presents and bought a few pieces of doll's house furniture – a bed, a table and chairs, a sofa and bathroom suite. I wrapped them and wrote on the label: *Until the real one is finished*. I found a tiny medical kit and included that too, marvelling at the detail contained within it. And suddenly Christmas felt real and exciting, and the prospect of almost ten days away from the Gopniks and the city felt like a gift in itself.

I arrived at the airport, praying silently that the weight of my gifts hadn't pushed me over the limit. The woman at check-in took my passport and asked me to lift my suitcase onto the scales – and frowned as she looked at the screen.

'Is there a problem?' I said, when she glanced at my passport, then behind her. I mentally calculated how much I might have to pay for the added weight.

'Oh, no, ma'am. You shouldn't be in this line.'

'You're kidding.' My heart sank as I looked over at the heaving queues behind me. 'Well, where should I be?'

'You're in business class.'

'Business?'

'Yes, ma'am. You've been upgraded. You should be checking in over there. But it's no problem. I can do it for you here.'

I shook my head. 'Oh, I don't think so. I . . .'

And then my phone dinged. I looked down. *You should be at the airport by now! Hope this makes your journey home a bit more pleasant. Little gift from Agnes. See you in the New Year, comrade! Michael x*

I blinked. 'That's fine. Thank you.' I watched my oversized suitcase disappear down the conveyor-belt and put my phone back into my bag.

The airport had been heaving, but in the business-class section of the plane everything was calm and peaceful, a little oasis of collective smugness removed from the holiday-related chaos outside. On board, I investigated my washbag of complimentary overnight goodies, pulled on my free socks and tried not to talk too much to the man in the next seat, who eventually put his eye mask on and lay back. I had just one hiccup with the reclining seat when my shoe got caught in the foot rest but the steward was perfectly lovely and showed me how to get it out. I ate duck in a sherry glaze and lemon tart, and thanked all the staff who brought me things. I watched two films and realized I should really try to sleep for a bit. But it was hard when the whole experience was so delightful. It was exactly the kind of thing I would have written home about – except, I thought, with butterflies in my stomach, now I was going to get to tell everyone in person.

I was returning home a different Louisa Clark. That was what Sam had said, and I had decided to believe it. I was more confident, more professional, a long way from the sad, conflicted, physically broken person of six months ago. I thought about Sam's face when I would surprise him, just as he had surprised me. He had sent me a copy of his rota for the next fortnight so that I could plan my visits to my parents, and I had calculated that I could drop my belongings at the flat, grab a few hours with my sister, then head over to his and be there to meet him for the end of his shift.

This time, I thought, we would get it right. We had a decent length of time to spend together. And this time we would settle into some kind of routine – a way of existing with no trauma or misunderstandings. The first three months were always going to be the hardest. I pulled my blanket over me and, already too far over the Atlantic for it to be of use, tried and failed to sleep, my stomach tight and my mind buzzing as I watched the tiny winking plane slide its way slowly across my pixellated screen.

I arrived at my flat shortly after lunchtime and let myself in, fumbling with my keys. Treena was at work, Thom was still at school, and London's grey was punctured by glitter, Christmas lights and the sound of shops playing Christmas carols I'd heard a million times before. I walked up the stairs of my old building, breathing in the familiar scent of cheap air freshener and London damp, then opened my front door, dropped my suitcase the few inches to the floor and let out a breath.

Home. Or something like it.

I walked down the hall, shedding my jacket, and let myself into the living room. I had been a little afraid of returning here – remembering the months in which I had been sunk in depression, drinking too much, its empty, unloved rooms a self-inflicted rebuke for my failure to save the man who had given it to me. But this, I grasped immediately, was not the same flat: in three months it had been utterly transformed. The once-bare interior was now full of colour, paintings by Thom pinned to every wall. There were embroidered cushions on the sofa and a new upholstered chair and curtains and a shelf bursting with DVDs. The kitchen was crammed with food packets and new crockery. A cereal bowl and Coco Pops on a rainbow placemat spoke of a hurriedly abandoned breakfast.

I opened the door to my spare room – now Thom's – smiling at the football posters and cartoon-printed duvet. A new wardrobe was stuffed with his clothes. Then I walked through to my bedroom – now Treena's – and found a rumpled quilt, a new bookshelf and blind. Still not much in the way of clothes, but she'd added a chair and a mirror, and the little dressing table was covered with the moisturisers, hairbrushes and cosmetics that told me my sister might have changed beyond recognition even in the few short months I had been gone. The only thing that told me it was Treena's room was the bedside reading: *Tolley's Capital Allowances* and *An Introduction to Payroll*.

I knew I was overtired but I felt wrong-footed all the same. Was this how Sam had felt when he flew out and saw me the second time? Had I seemed so familiar and unfamiliar at the same time?

My eyes were gritty with exhaustion, my internal clock haywire. There were still three hours before they'd get home. I washed my face, took off my shoes and lay down on the sofa with a sigh, the sound of London traffic slowly receding.

I woke to a sticky hand patting my cheek. I blinked, trying to bat it away, but there was a weight on my chest. It moved. A hand patted me again. And then I opened my eyes and found myself staring into Thom's.

'Auntie Lou! Auntie Lou!'

I groaned. 'Hey, Thom.'

'What did you get me?'

'Let her at least open her eyes first.'

'You're on my boob, Thom. Ow.'

Released, I pushed myself upright and blinked at my nephew, who was now bouncing up and down.

'What did you get me?'

My sister stooped and kissed my cheek, leaving one hand on my shoulder, which she squeezed. She smelt of expensive perfume and I pulled back slightly to see her better. She was wearing make-up. Proper make-up, subtly blended, rather than the one blue eyeliner she had received free with a magazine in 1994 and kept in a desk drawer to be used on every 'dressing-up' occasion for the next ten years.

'You made it, then. Didn't get the wrong plane and end up in Caracas. Me and Dad had a bit of a bet on.'

'Cheek.' I reached up and held her hand for a moment longer than either of us had expected. 'Wow. You look pretty.'

She did. She'd had her hair trimmed to shoulder length and it hung in blow-dried waves rather than the usual scraped-back ponytail. That, the well-cut shirt and the mascara actually made her look beautiful.

'Well. It's work, really. You have to make the effort in the City.' She turned away as she said this so I didn't believe her.

'I think I need to meet this Eddie,' I said. 'I certainly never had this much of an effect on what you wore.'

She filled the kettle and switched it on. 'That's because you only ever dress like someone gave you a two-pound voucher for a jumble sale and you decided to blow the lot.'

It was growing dark outside. My jetlagged brain suddenly registered what this meant. 'Oh, wow. What time is it?'

'Time you gave me my presents?' Thom's gappy smile swam in front of me, both hands raised in prayer.

'You're fine,' said Treena. 'You've got another hour before Sam finishes, plenty of time. Thom – Lou will give you whatever she's got once she's had a cup of tea and found her deodorant. Also, what the bloody hell is that stripy coat thing you dropped in the hall? It smells like old fish.'

Now I was home.

'Okay, Thom,' I said. 'There may be some pre-Christmas bits for you in that blue bag. Bring it over here.'

It took a shower and fresh make-up before I felt human again. I put on a silver mini-skirt, a black polo-neck and suede wedge-heeled shoes I had bought at the clothes emporium, Mrs De Witt's Biba scarf and a spritz of La Chasse aux Papillons, the perfume Will had convinced me to buy, which always gave me confidence. Thom and Treena were eating when I was ready to leave. She had offered me some pasta with cheese and tomato but my stomach had started to work its way into knots and my body clock was screwed up.

'I like that thing you've done with your eyes. Very seductive.' I said to her.

She pulled a face. 'Are you going to be okay to drive? You plainly can't see properly.'

'It's not far. I've had a power nap.'

'And when will we expect you home? This new sofa-bed is bloody amazing, in case you're wondering. Proper sprung mattress. None of your two inches of foam rubbish.'

'I'm hoping I won't need to use the sofa-bed for a day or two.' I gave her a cheesy smile.

'What's that?' Thom swallowed his mouthful and pointed at the parcel under my arm.

'Ah. That's a Christmas stocking. Sam's working on Christmas Day and I won't see him till the evening so I thought I'd give him something to wake up with.'

'Hmm. Don't ask to see what's in there, Thom.'

'There's nothing in it that I couldn't give to Granddad. It's just a bit of fun.'

She actually winked at me. I offered silent thanks to Eddie and his miracle-working ways.

'Text me later, yeah? Just so I know whether to put the chain on.'

I kissed them both and headed for the front door.

'Don't put him off with your terrible half-arsed American accent!' I held up a middle finger as I exited the flat. 'And don't forget to drive on the left! And don't wear the coat that smells like a mackerel!'

I heard her laughing as I shut the door.

For the past three months I had either walked, hailed a taxi or been chauffeured by Garry in the huge black limousine. Getting used to being behind the wheel of my little hatchback with its dodgy clutch and biscuit crumbs in the passenger seat took a surprising amount of concentration. I set out into the last of the evening rush-hour traffic, put the radio on and tried to ignore the hammering in my chest, not sure whether it was the fear of driving or the prospect of seeing Sam again.

The sky was dark, the streets thick with shoppers and strung with Christmas lights, and my shoulders dropped slowly from somewhere around my ears as I braked and lurched my way to the suburbs. The pavements became verges and the crowds thinned and disappeared, just the odd person glimpsed instead through brightly lit windows as I passed. And then, shortly after eight, I slowed to a crawl, peering forward over the wheel to make sure I had the right place in the unlit lane.

The railway carriage sat glowing in the middle of the dark field, casting a golden light out through its windows onto the mud and grass. I could just make out his motorbike on the far side of the gate, tucked into its little shed behind the hedge. He had even put a little spray of Christmas lights in the hawthorn at the front. He really was home.

I pulled the car into the passing place, cut the lights, and looked at it. Then, almost as an afterthought, I picked up my phone. *Really looking forward to seeing you* I typed. *Not long now! XXX*

There was a short pause. And then the response pinged back. *Me too. Safe flight. xx*

I grinned. Then I climbed out, realizing too late I had parked over a puddle so the cold, muddy water washed straight over my shoes. 'Oh, thanks, Universe,' I whispered. 'Nice touch.'

I placed my carefully purchased Santa hat on my head and pulled his stocking from the passenger seat, then shut the door softly, locking it manually so that it didn't beep and alert him to the fact that I was there.

My feet squelched as I tiptoed forward, and I recalled the first time I had come here, how I had been soaked by a sudden shower and ended up in his clothes, my own steaming in the fuggy little bathroom as they dried. That had been an extraordinary night, as if he had peeled off all the layers that Will's death had built up around me. I had a sudden flashback to our first kiss, to the feel of his huge socks soft on my chilled feet, and a hot shiver ran through me.

I opened the gate, noting with relief that he had made a rudimentary path of paving slabs over to the railway carriage since I had last been there. A car drove past, and in the brief illumination of its headlights I glimpsed Sam's partially built house ahead of me, its roof now on and windows already fitted. Where one was still missing, blue tarpaulin flapped gently over the gap so that it seemed suddenly, startlingly, a real thing, a place we might one day live.

I tiptoed a few more paces, then paused just outside the door. The smell of something wafted out of an open window – a casserole of some sort? – rich and tomatoey, with a hint of garlic. I felt unexpectedly hungry. Sam never ate packet noodles or beans out of a tin: everything was made from scratch, as if he drew pleasure from doing things methodically. Then I saw him – his uniform still on – a tea-towel slung over his shoulder as he stooped to see to a pan and just for a moment I stood, unseen, in the dark and felt utterly calm. I heard the distant breeze in the trees, the soft cluck of the hens locked nearby in their coop, the distant hum of traffic headed towards the city. I felt the cool air against my skin and the tang of Christmassy anticipation in the air I breathed.

Everything was possible. That was what I had learnt, these last few months. Life might have been complicated, but ultimately there was just me and the man I loved and his railway carriage and the prospect of a joyous evening ahead. I took a breath, letting myself savour that thought, stepped forward and put my hand on the door handle.

And then I saw her.

She walked across the carriage saying something unclear, her voice muffled by the glass, her hair clipped up and tumbling in soft curls around her face. She was wearing a man's T-shirt – his? – and holding a wine bottle, and I saw him shake his head. And then, as he bent over the stove, she walked up behind him and placed her hands on his neck, leaning towards him and rubbing the muscles around it with small circular motions of her thumbs, a movement that seemed born of familiarity. Her thumbnails were painted deep pink. As I stood there, my breath stalled in my chest, he leant his head back, his eyes closed, as if surrendering himself to her fierce little hands.

And then he turned to face her, smiling, his head tilted to one side, and she stepped back, laughing, and raised a glass to him.

I didn't see anything else. My heart thumped so loudly in my ears that I thought I might pass out. I stumbled backwards, then turned and ran back down the path, my breath too loud, my feet icy in my wet shoes. Even though my car was probably fifty yards away I heard her sudden burst of laughter echo through the open window, like a glass shattering.

I sat in my car in the car park behind my building until I could be sure Thom had gone to bed. I couldn't hide what I felt and I couldn't bear to explain it to Treena in front of him. I glanced up periodically, watching as his bedroom light went on and then, half an hour later, went off again. I turned off the engine and let it tick down. As it faded, so did every dream I had been clinging on to.

I shouldn't have been surprised. Why would I? Katie Ingram had laid her cards on the table from the start. What had shocked me was that Sam had been complicit. He hadn't shrugged her off. He had answered me, and then he had cooked her a meal and let her rub his neck, and it was preparation for . . . what?

Every time I pictured them I found myself clutching my stomach, doubled over, as if I'd been punched. I couldn't shake the image of them from my head. The way he tilted his head back at the pressure of her fingers. The way she had laughed confidently, teasingly, as if at some shared joke between them.

The strangest thing was that I couldn't cry. What I felt

was bigger than grief. I was numb, my brain humming with questions – *How long? How far? Why?* – and then I would find myself doubled over again, wanting to be sick with it, this new knowledge, this hefty blow, this pain, this pain, this pain.

I'm not sure how long I sat there, but at around ten I walked slowly upstairs and let myself into the flat. I was hoping Treena had gone to bed but she was in her pyjamas watching the news, her laptop on her knee. She was smiling at something on her screen and jumped when I opened the door.

'Jesus, you nearly frightened the life out of me – Lou?' She pushed her laptop to one side. 'Lou? Oh, no . . .'

It's always the kindnesses that finish you off. My sister, a woman who found adult physical contact more discomfiting than dental treatment, put her arms around me and, from some unexpected place that felt like it was located in the deepest part of me, I began to sob, huge, breathless, snotty tears. I cried in a way I hadn't cried since Will had died, sobs that contained the death of dreams and the dread knowledge of months of heartbreak ahead. We sank slowly down onto the sofa and I buried my head in her shoulder and held her, and this time my sister rested her head against mine and she held me and didn't let me go.

18

Neither Sam nor my parents had expected to see me so for the next two days it was easy to hide in the flat and pretend I wasn't there. I wasn't ready to see anyone. I wasn't ready to speak to anyone. When Sam texted I ignored it, reasoning that he would believe I was running around like a headless chicken back in New York. I found myself gazing repeatedly at his two messages – *What do you fancy doing Christmas Eve? Church service? Or too tired?* and *Are we seeing each other Boxing Day?* – and I would marvel that this man, this most straight-forward and honourable of men, had acquired such a blatant ability to lie to me.

For those two days I painted on a smile while Thom was in the flat, folding away the sofa-bed as he chatted over breakfast and disappearing into the shower. The moment he had gone I would return to the sofa and lie there, gazing up at the ceiling, tears trickling from the corners of my eyes, or coldly mulling over the many ways I appeared to have got it all wrong.

Had I leapt head first into a relationship with Sam because I was still grieving Will? Had I ever really known him at all? We see what we want to see, after all, especially when blinded by physical attraction. Had he done what he did because of Josh? Because of Agnes's pregnancy test? Did there even have to be a reason? I no longer trusted my own judgement enough to tell.

For once, Treena didn't badger me to get up or do something constructive. She shook her head, disbelieving, and cursed Sam out of Thom's earshot. Even in the depths of my misery I was left mulling over Eddie's apparent ability to instil in my sister something resembling empathy.

She didn't once say it wasn't a huge surprise, given I was living so many thousands of miles away, or that I must have done something to push him into Katie Ingram's arms, or that any of this was inevitable. She listened when I told her the events that had led up to that night, she made sure I ate, washed and got dressed. And although she wasn't much of a drinker, she brought home two bottles of wine and said she thought I was allowed a couple of days of wallowing (but added that if I was sick I had to clear it up myself).

By the time Christmas Eve arrived, I had grown a hard shell, a carapace. I felt like an ice statue. At some point, I realized, I was going to have to speak to him, but I wasn't ready yet. I wasn't sure I ever would be.

'What will you do?' said Treena, sitting on the loo while I had a bath. She wasn't seeing Eddie until Christmas Day, and was painting her toenails a pale pink in preparation, although she wouldn't admit as much. Out in the living room Thom had the television turned up to deafening volume and was leaping on and off the sofa in a pre-Christmas frenzy.

'I was thinking I might just tell him I missed the flight. And that we'd speak after Christmas.'

She pulled a face. 'You don't just want to speak to him? He's not going to believe that.'

'I don't really care what he believes right now. I just want to have Christmas with my family and no drama.' I sank under the water so that I couldn't hear Treena shouting at Thom to turn the sound down.

He didn't believe me. His text message said: *What? How could you miss the flight?*

— *I just did,* I typed. *I'll see you Boxing Day.*

I observed too late I hadn't put any kisses on it. There was a long silence, and then a single word in response: *Okay*.

Treena drove us to Stortfold, Thom bouncing in the rear seat for the full hour and a half it took us to get there. We listened to Christmas carols on the radio and spoke little. We were a mile out of town when I thanked her for her consideration, and she whispered that it wasn't for me: Eddie hadn't actually met Mum and Dad either so she was feeling nauseous at the thought of Christmas Day.

'It'll be fine,' I told her. The smile she flashed me wasn't very convincing.

'C'mon. They liked that accountant bloke you dated earlier this year. And to be honest, Treen, you've been single so long I think you could probably bring home anyone who wasn't Attila the Hun right now and they'd be delighted.'

'Well, that theory is about to be tested.'

We pulled up before I could say any more and I checked my eyes, which were still pea-sized from the amount of crying I'd done, and climbed out of the car. My mother burst out of the front door and ran down the path, like a sprinter off the starting blocks. She threw her arms around me, holding me so tightly I could feel her heart thumping.

'Look at you!' she exclaimed, holding me at arms' length before pulling me in again. She pushed a lock of hair from my face and turned to my father, who stood on the step, his arms crossed, beaming. 'How wonderful you look! Bernard! See how grand she looks! Oh, we've missed you so much! Have you lost weight? You look like you've lost weight. You look tired. You need to eat something. Come indoors. I'll bet they didn't give you breakfast on that plane. I've heard it's all powdered egg anyhow.'

She hugged Thom, and before my father could step

forward, she grabbed my bags and marched back up the path, beckoning us all to follow.

'Hello, sweetheart,' said Dad, softly, and I stepped into his arms. As they closed around me, I finally allowed myself to exhale.

Granddad hadn't made it as far as the step. He had had another small stroke, Mum whispered, and now had trouble standing up or walking, so spent most of his daylight hours in the upright chair in the living room. ('We didn't want to worry you.') He was dressed smartly in a shirt and pullover in honour of the occasion and smiled lopsidedly when I walked in. He held up a shaking hand and I hugged him, noting with some distant part of me how much smaller he seemed.

But, then, everything seemed smaller. My parents' house, with its twenty-year-old wallpaper, its artwork chosen less for aesthetic reasons than because it had been given by someone nice or covered certain dents in the wall, its sagging three-piece suite, its tiny dining area, where the chairs hit the wall if you pushed them back too far, and a ceiling light that started only a few inches above my father's head. I found myself comparing it distantly to the grand apartment with its acres of polished floors, its huge, ornate ceilings, the clamorous sweep of Manhattan outside our door. I had thought I might feel comforted at being home.

Instead I felt untethered, as if suddenly it occurred to me that, at the moment, I belonged in neither place.

We ate a light supper of roast beef, potatoes, Yorkshire puddings and trifle, just a little something Mum had 'knocked together' before tomorrow's main event. Dad was keeping the turkey in the shed as it wouldn't fit in the fridge and went out to check every half an hour that it hadn't fallen into the clutches of Houdini, next door's cat. Mum gave us a run-down on the various tragedies that had befallen our neighbours: 'Well, of course, that was before Andrew's shingles. He showed me his stomach – put me quite off my Weetabix – and I've told Dymphna she needs to put those feet up before the baby's born. Honestly, her varicose veins are like a B-road map of the Chilterns. Did I tell you Mrs Kemp's father died? He's the one did four years for armed robbery before they discovered it had been that bloke from the post office who had the same hair plugs.' Mum rattled on.

It was only when she was clearing the plates that Dad leant over to me and said, 'Would you believe she's nervous?'

'Nervous of what?'

'You. All your achievements. She was half afraid you wouldn't want to come back here. That you'd spend Christmas with your fella and head straight back to New York.'

'Why would I want to do that?'

He shrugged. 'I don't know. She thought you might have outgrown us. I told her she was being daft. Don't take that the wrong way, love. She's bloody proud of you. She prints out all your pictures and puts them in a scrapbook and bores the neighbours rigid showing them off. To be honest, she bores me rigid, and I'm related to you.' He grinned and squeezed my shoulder.

I felt briefly ashamed at how much time I'd intended spending at Sam's. I'd planned to leave Mum to handle all the Christmas stuff, my family and Granddad, like I always did.

I left Treena and Thom with Dad and took the rest of the plates through to the kitchen where Mum and I washed up in companionable silence for a while. She turned to me. 'You do look tired, love. Have you the jetlag?'

'A bit.'

'You sit down with the others. I'll take care of this.'

I forced my shoulders back. 'No, Mum. I haven't seen you for months. Why don't you tell me what's going on? How's your night school? And what's the doctor saying about Granddad?'

The evening stretched and the television burbled in the corner of the room and the temperature rose until we were all semi-comatose and cradling our bellies, like someone heavily pregnant, in the way one did after one of my mother's light suppers. The thought that we would do this again tomorrow made my stomach turn gently in protest. Granddad dozed in the chair and we left him there while we went to midnight mass. I stood in the church surrounded by people whom I had known since I was small, nudging and smiling at me, and I sang the carols I remembered and mouthed the ones I didn't and tried not to think about what Sam was doing at that exact moment, as I did approximately 118 times a day. Occasionally Treena would catch my eye from along the pew and give me a small, encouraging smile and I gave one back, as if to say, *I'm fine, all good*, even though I wasn't and nothing was. It was a relief to peel off to the box room when we got back. Perhaps it was because I was in my childhood home, or I was exhausted from three days of high emotion, but I slept soundly for the first time since I had arrived in England.

I was dimly aware of Treena being woken at five a.m. and some excited thudding, then Dad yelling at Thom that it was still the middle of the ruddy night and if he didn't go back to bed he would tell Father Ruddy Christmas to come and take all the ruddy presents back again. The next time I woke, Mum was putting a mug of tea on my bedside table and telling me that if I could get dressed we were about to start opening the presents. It was a quarter past eleven.

I picked up the little clock, squinted, and shook it.

'You needed it,' she said, stroked my head, then went off to see to the sprouts.

I descended twenty minutes later in the comedy reindeer jumper with the illuminated nose I had bought in Macy's because I knew Thom would enjoy it. Everyone else was already down, dressed and breakfasted. I kissed them all and wished them a happy Christmas, turned my reindeer nose on and off, then distributed my own gifts, all the while trying not to think of the man who should have been the recipient of a cashmere sweater and a really soft checked flannel shirt, which were languishing at the bottom of my case.

I wouldn't think about him today, I told myself firmly. Time with my family was precious and I wouldn't ruin it by feeling sad.

My gifts went down a treat, apparently given an extra layer of desirability by having come from New York, even if I was fairly sure you could have got pretty much the same things from Argos. 'All the way from New York!' Mum would say in awe, after every item was unwrapped, until Treena rolled her eyes and Thom started mimicking her. Of course, the gift that went down best was the cheapest: a plastic snow globe I had bought at a tourist stall in Times Square. I was pretty sure it would be leaking quietly into Thom's chest of drawers before the week was out.

In return I received:

- Socks from Granddad (99 per cent sure these had been chosen and bought by Mum)
- Soaps from Dad (ditto)

- A small silver frame with a picture of our family already fitted into it ('So you can take us with you wherever you go' – Mum. Dad: 'Why the heck would she want to do that? She went to ruddy New York to get away from us all.')
- A device that removed nostril hair, from Treena. ('Don't look at me like that. You're getting to that age.')
- A picture of a Christmas tree with a poem underneath it from Thom. On close questioning, it turned out he hadn't actually made it himself. 'Our teacher says we don't stick the decorations on the right places so she does them and we just put our names on them.'

I received a gift from Lily, dropped in the previous day before she and Mrs Traynor went skiing – 'She looks well, Lou. Though she runs Mrs Traynor pretty ragged from what I've heard' – a vintage ring, a huge green stone in a silver setting that fitted perfectly on my little finger. I had sent her a pair of silver earrings that looked like cuffs, assured by the fearsomely trendy SoHo shop assistant that they were perfect for a teenage girl. Especially one now apparently prone to piercings in unexpected places.

I thanked everyone and watched Granddad nod off. I smiled and I think I put on a pretty good impression of someone who was enjoying the day. Mum was smarter than that.

'Is everything okay, love? You seem very flat.' She ladled goose fat over the potatoes and stepped back as it sprayed out in an angry mist. 'Oh, will you look at those? They're going to be lovely and crisp.'

'I'm fine.'

'Is it the jetlag still? Ronnie from three doors down said when he went to Florida it took him three weeks to stop walking into walls.'

'That's pretty much it.'

'I can't believe I have a daughter who gets jetlag. I'm the envy of everyone at the club, you know.'

I looked up. 'You've been there again?'

After Will had ended his life, my parents had been ostracized at the social club they'd belonged to for years, blamed vicariously for my actions in going along with his plan. It was one of the many things I had felt guilty about.

'Well, that Marjorie has moved to Cirencester. You know she was the worst for the gossip. And then Stuart from the garage told Dad he should come down and have a game of pool some time. Just casual-like. And it was all fine.' She shrugged. 'And, you know, all that business was a couple of years ago now. People have other things to think about.'

People have other things to think about. I don't know why that innocent statement caught me by the throat, but it did. As I was trying to swallow a sudden wave of grief, Mum shoved the tray of potatoes back into the oven. She shut the door with a satisfied clunk, then turned to me, pulling the oven gloves from her hands.

'I almost forgot – the strangest thing. Your man called this morning to say what were we going to do about your flight Boxing Day and did we mind if he picked you up himself?'

I froze. 'What?'

She lifted a lid on a pan, released a burp of steam, and put it down again. 'Well, I told him he must have been mistaken and you were here already, so he said he'd pop over later. Honestly, the shifts must be taking it out of him. I heard a thing on the radio where they said working nights can be awful bad for your brain. You might want to tell him.'

'What – when's he coming?'

Mum glanced at the clock. 'Um . . . I think he said he was finishing mid-afternoon and he'd head over afterwards. All that way on Christmas Day! Here, have you met Treena's fellow yet? Have you noticed the way she's dressing these days?' She glanced behind her at the door and her voice was full of wonder. 'It's almost like she's becoming a normal person.'

I sat through Christmas lunch on high alert, outwardly calm but flinching every time someone passed our door. Every bite of my mother's cooking turned to powder in my mouth. Every bad cracker joke my father read out went straight over my head. I couldn't eat, couldn't hear, couldn't feel. I was locked in a bell jar of miserable anticipation. I glanced at Treena but she seemed preoccupied too, and I realized she was waiting on Eddie's arrival. How hard could it be? I thought, grimly. At least her boyfriend wasn't cheating on her. At least he *wanted* to be with her.

It began to rain, and the drops spat meanly on the windows, the sky darkening to fit my mood. Our little house, strung with tinsel and glitter-strewn greetings cards, shrank around us, and I felt alternately as if I couldn't breathe in it and terrified of anything that lay beyond it. Occasionally I saw Mum's eyes slide towards me, as if she was wondering what was going on, but she didn't say anything and I didn't volunteer it.

I helped clear the dishes and chatted – I thought convincingly – about the joys of grocery delivery in New York, and finally the doorbell went and my legs turned to jelly.

Mum turned to look at me. 'Are you okay, Louisa? You've gone quite pale.'

'I'll tell you later, Mum.'

My mother stared at me hard, then her face softened. 'I'll be here.' She reached out and tucked a strand of hair behind my ear. 'Whatever this is all about, I'll be here.'

Sam stood on the front step in a soft cobalt jumper I hadn't seen before. I wondered who had given it to him. He gave me a half-smile but didn't stoop to kiss me, or throw his arms around me like in our previous meetings. We gazed warily at each other.

'Do you want to come in?' My voice sounded oddly formal.

'Thanks.'

I walked in front of him down the narrow corridor, waited while he greeted my parents through the living-room door, then led him into the kitchen, closing the door behind us. I felt acutely aware of his presence, as if we were both mildly electrified.

'Would you like some tea?'

'Sure . . . Nice jumper.'

'Oh . . . Thanks.'

'You've . . . left your nose on.'

'Right.' I reached down and turned it off, not willing to indulge anything that might soften the mood between us.

He sat down at the table, his body somehow too big for our kitchen chairs, his eyes still on me, and clasped his hands on its surface, like someone awaiting a job interview. In the living room I could hear Dad laughing at some film, and Thom's shrill voice demanding to know what was funny. I busied myself making tea but I could feel his eyes burning into my back the whole time.

'So,' Sam said, when I handed him a mug and sat down, 'you're here.'

I nearly buckled then. I looked across the table at his handsome face, at the broad shoulders and the hands wrapped gently around the mug and a thought popped into my head: *I cannot bear it if he leaves me.*

But then I found myself standing again on that chilly step, her slim fingers on his neck, my feet icy in my wet shoes, and I grew cold again.

'I got back two days ago,' I said.

The briefest of pauses. 'Okay.'

'I thought I'd come and surprise you. Thursday evening.' I scratched at a mark on the tablecloth. 'Turns out it was me who got the surprise.'

I watched realization dawn slowly across his face: his slight frown, his eyes growing distant, then their faint closure when he grasped what I might have seen. 'Lou, I don't know what you saw, but –'

'But what? "It's not what you think"?'

'Well, it is and it isn't.'

It was like a punch.

'Let's not do this, Sam.'

He looked up.

'I'm pretty clear about what I saw. If you try and convince me it wasn't what I think, I'll want to believe you so badly that I might actually do it. And what I've realized these last two days is that this . . . this isn't good for me. It isn't good for either of us.'

Sam put his mug down. He dragged his hand over his face and looked off to the side. 'I don't love her, Lou.'

'I don't really care what you feel about her.'

'Well, I want you to know. Yes, you were right about Katie. I may have misread the signals. She does like me.'

I let out a bitter laugh. 'And you like her.'

'I don't know what I think about her. You're the person

268

who's in my head. You're the person I wake up thinking about. But the thing is, you're –'

'Not here. Don't you blame this on me. Don't you *dare* blame this on me. You told me to go. *You told me to go.*'

We sat in silence for a few moments. I found myself staring at his hands – the strong, battered knuckles, the way they looked so hard, so powerful, but were capable of such tenderness. I stared determinedly at the mark on the cloth.

'You know, Lou, I thought I'd be fine by myself. I've been on my own a long time, after all. But you cracked something open in me.'

'Oh, so it's my fault.'

'I'm not saying that!' he burst out. 'I'm trying to explain. I'm saying – I'm saying I'm no longer as good at being on my own as I thought I was. After my sister died I didn't want to feel anything for anyone again, okay? I had room to care for Jake, but nobody else. I had my job and my half-built house, and my chickens, and that was fine. I was just . . . getting on with it all. And then you came along and fell off that bloody building, and literally the first time you held onto my hand I felt something give in me. And suddenly I had someone I looked forward to talking to. Someone who understood how I felt. Really, really understood. I could drive past your flat and know that at the end of a crap day I was going to be able to call up to you or pop in later and feel better. And, yes, I know we had some issues, but it just felt – deep down – like there was something *right* in there, you know?'

His head was bowed over his tea, his jaw clenched.

'And then just as we were close – closer than I've ever felt to another living soul – you were . . . you were just *gone*. And I felt like – like someone had given me this gift, this key to everything, with one hand, then snatched it away with the other.'

'Then why did you let me go?'

His voice exploded into the room. 'Because – because I'm not that man, Lou! I'm not the man who's going to insist that you stay. I'm not the man who's going to stop you having the adventures and growing and doing all the stuff that you're doing out there. I'm not that guy!'

'No – you're the guy who hooks up with someone else as soon as I've gone! Someone in the same zip code!'

'It's a *postcode*! You're in England, for Christ's sake!'

'Yup, and you have no idea how much I wish I wasn't.'

Sam turned away from me, clearly struggling to contain himself. Beyond the kitchen doors, although the television was still on, I was dimly aware of silence in the front room.

After a few minutes I said quietly. 'I can't do this, Sam.'

'You can't do what?'

'I can't be worrying about Katie Ingram and her attempts to seduce you – because whatever happened that night I could see what *she* wanted, even if I don't know what you wanted. It's making me crazy and it's making me sad, and worse . . .' I swallowed hard '. . . it's making me hate you. And I can't imagine how in three short months I've got to that point.'

'Louisa –'

There was a discreet knock at the door. My mother's face appeared. 'I'm sorry to disturb you both but would you mind very much if I quickly made some tea? Granddad's gasping.'

'Sure.' I kept my face turned away.

She bustled in and filled the kettle, her back to us. 'They're watching some film about aliens. Not very Christmassy. I remember when Christmas Day was all *Wizard of Oz* or *The Sound of Music* or something that everyone could watch together. Now they're watching all this whiz-bam-shooting nonsense and Granddad and I can't understand a word anyone's saying.'

My mother rattled on, plainly mortified at having to be there, tapping the work surface with her fingers as she waited for the kettle to boil. 'You know we haven't even watched the Queen's Speech? Daddy put it on the old recording box thing. But it's not the same if you watch it afterwards, is it? I like to watch it when everyone else is watching it. The poor old woman, wedged in all those video boxes until everyone's finished the aliens and the cartoons. You'd think after sixty-odd years of service – how long has she been on that throne? – the least we could do is watch her do her thing when she does it. Mind you, Daddy tells me I'm being ridiculous as she probably recorded it weeks ago. Sam, will you have some cake?'

'Not for me, thanks, Josie.'

'Lou?'

'No. Thanks, Mum.'

'I'll leave you to it.' She smiled awkwardly, loaded a fruitcake the size of a tractor wheel onto the tray and hurried out. Sam got up and closed the door behind her.

We sat in silence, listening to the kitchen clock ticking, the air leaden. I felt crushed under the weight of the things unsaid between us.

Sam took a long swig of his tea. I wanted him to leave. I thought I might die if he did.

'I'm sorry,' he said finally. 'About the other night. I never wanted to . . . Well, it was badly judged.'

I shook my head. I couldn't speak any more.

'I didn't sleep with her. If you won't hear anything else, I do need you to hear that.'

'You said –'

He looked up.

'You said . . . nobody would ever hurt me again. You said that. When you came to New York.' My voice emerged from somewhere in my chest. 'I never thought for a moment you would be the one to do it.'

'Louisa –'

'I think I'd like you to go now.'

He stood heavily and hesitated, both hands on the table in front of him. I couldn't look at him. I couldn't see the face I loved about to disappear from my life forever. He straightened up, let out an audible breath and turned away from me.

He pulled a package from his inside pocket and placed it on the table. 'Merry Christmas,' he said. And then he walked to the door.

I followed him back down the corridor, eleven long steps, and then we were on the front porch. I couldn't look at him or I would be lost. I would plead with him to stay, promise to give up my job, beg him to change his job, not to see Katie Ingram again. I would become pathetic, the kind of woman I pitied. The kind of woman he had never wanted.

I stood, my shoulders rigid, and I refused to look any further than his stupid, oversized feet. A car pulled up. A door slammed somewhere down the street. Birds sang. And I stood, locked in my own private misery in a moment that stubbornly refused to end.

And then, abruptly, he stepped forward and his arms closed around me. He pulled me to him, and in that embrace I felt everything that we had meant to each other, the love and the pain and the bloody impossibility of it all. And my face, unseen by him, crumpled.

I don't know how long we stood there. Probably only seconds. But time briefly stopped, stretched, disappeared. It was just him and me and this awful dead feeling creeping from my head to my feet, as if I were turning to stone.

'Don't. Don't touch me,' I said, when I couldn't bear it any more. My voice was choked and unlike itself, and I pushed him back, away from me.

'Lou –'

Except it wasn't his voice. It was my sister's.

'Lou, could you just – sorry – get out of the way, please? I need to get past.'

I blinked, and turned my head. My sister, her hands raised, was trying to edge past us from the narrow doorway to the path. 'Sorry,' she said. 'I just need to . . .'

Sam released me, quite abruptly, and walked away with long strides, his shoulders hunched and rigid, just pausing as the gate opened. He didn't look back.

'Is that our Treena's new bloke arriving?' said Mum, behind me. She was wrenching off her apron and straightening her hair in one fluid movement. 'I thought he was coming at four. I haven't even put my lippy on . . . Are you all right?'

Treena turned and, through the blur of my tears, I could just make out her face as she gave a small, hopeful smile. 'Mum, Dad, this is Eddie,' she said.

And a slim black woman in a short flowery dress gave us a hesitant wave.

19

As it turns out, as a distraction from losing the second great love of your life, I can highly recommend your sister coming out on Christmas Day, especially with a young woman of colour called Edwina.

Mum covered her initial shock with a flurry of over-effusive welcomes and the promise of tea-making, shepherding Eddie and Treena into the living room, pausing momentarily to give me a look that, if my mother had been the type to swear, would have said *WTAF* before she disappeared back down the corridor to the kitchen. Thom emerged from the living room, yelled, 'Eddie!' gave our guest a huge hug, waited on jiggy feet to be handed his present and ripped it apart, then ran off with a new Lego set.

And Dad, utterly silenced, simply stared at what was unfolding before him, like someone dumped into a hallucinogenic dream. I saw Treena's uncharacteristically anxious expression, felt the rising sense of panic in the air and knew I had to act. I murmured at Dad to close his mouth, then stepped forward and held out my hand. 'Eddie!' I said. 'Hi! I'm Louisa. My sister will no doubt have told you all the bad stuff.'

'Actually,' Eddie said, 'she's only told me wonderful things. You live in New York, don't you?'

'Mostly.' I hoped my smile didn't look as forced as it felt.

'I lived in Brooklyn for two years after I left college. I still miss it.'

She shed her bronze-coloured coat, waiting while Treena

wedged it onto our over-stacked pegs. She was tiny, a porcelain doll, with the most exquisitely symmetrical features I'd ever seen and eyes that slanted upwards with extravagant black lashes. She chatted away as we went into the living room – perhaps too polite to acknowledge my parents' barely concealed shock – and stooped to shake hands with Granddad, who smiled his lopsided smile at her, then went back to staring at the television.

I had never seen my sister like this. It was as if we had just been introduced to two strangers rather than one. There was Eddie – impeccably polite, interesting, engaged, steering us with grace through these choppy conversational waters – and there was New Treena, her expression faintly unsure, her smile a little fragile, her hand occasionally reaching across the sofa to squeeze her girlfriend's as if for reassurance. Dad's jaw dropped a full three inches the first time she did it, and Mum jabbed his rib repeatedly with her elbow until he closed it again.

'So! Edwina!' said Mum, pouring the tea. 'Treena's told us – um – so little about you. How – how did you two meet?'

Eddie smiled. 'I run an interiors shop near Katrina's flat and she just popped in a few times to get cushions and fabric and we started talking. We went for a drink, and later to the cinema . . . and, you know, it turned out we had a lot in common.'

I found myself nodding, trying to work out what my sister could possibly have in common with the polished, elegant creature in front of me.

'Things in common! How lovely. Things in common are a great thing. Yes. And – and where is it you come – Oh, goodness. I don't mean . . .'

'Where do I come from? Blackheath. I know – people rarely move to north London from south. My parents moved to Borehamwood when they retired three years ago. So I'm one of those rarities – a north and south Londoner.' She beamed at Treena, as if this was some shared joke, before turning back to Mum. 'Have you always lived around here?'

'Mum and Dad will leave Stortfold in their coffins,' Treena said.

'Not too soon, we hope!' I said.

'It looks like a beautiful town. I can see why you'd want to stay,' Eddie said, holding up her plate. 'This cake is amazing, Mrs Clark. Do you make it yourself? My mother makes one with rum and she swears you have to steep the fruit for three months to get the full flavour.'

'Katrina is *gay*?' said Dad.

'It's good, Mum,' said Treena. 'The sultanas are . . . really . . . moist.'

Dad looked from one of us to the other. 'Our Treena likes girls? And nobody's saying anything? And just whanging on about fecking cushions and *cake*?'

'Bernard,' said my mother.

'Perhaps I should give you all a moment,' said Eddie.

'No, stay, Eddie.' Treena glanced at Thom, who was engrossed in the television, and said, 'Yes, Dad. I like women. Or, at least, I like Eddie.'

'Treena might be gender fluid,' said Mum, nervously. 'Is that the right expression? The young people at night school tell me a lot of them are neither one thing nor the other, these days. There's a spectrum. Or a speculum. I can never remember which.'

Dad blinked.

Mum swallowed a gulp of tea so audibly that it was almost painful.

'Well, personally,' I said, when Treena had stopped patting her on the back, 'I just think it's great that anyone would want to go out with Treena. Anyone at all. You know, anyone with eyes and ears and a heart and stuff.' Treena shot me a look of genuine gratitude.

'You did always wear jeans a lot. Growing up,' Mum mused, wiping her mouth. 'Perhaps I should have made you wear more dresses.'

'It's got nothing to do with jeans, Mum. Genes, maybe.'

'Well, it certainly doesn't run in our family,' said Dad. 'No offence, Edwina.'

'None taken, Mr Clark.'

'I'm gay, Dad. I'm gay, and I'm happier than I've ever been and it's really none of anyone else's business how I choose to be happy, but I'd really like it if you and Mum could be happy for me because I am and, more importantly, I'm hoping that Eddie will be in my and Thom's lives for a very long time.' She glanced over at Eddie, who smiled reassuringly.

There was a long silence.

'You've never said anything,' said Dad, accusingly. 'You never acted gay.'

'How's a gay person supposed to act?' Treena said.

'Well. Gay. Like . . . you never brought home a girl before.'

'I never brought home anyone before. Apart from Sundeep. That accountant. And you didn't like him because he didn't like football.'

'I like football,' said Eddie, helpfully.

Dad sat and stared at his plate. Finally he sighed, and rubbed his eyes with both palms. When he stopped, his whole face seemed dazed, like someone woken abruptly from sleep. Mum was watching him intently, anxiety writ large across her face.

'Eddie. Edwina. I'm sorry if I'm coming across as an old fart. I'm not a homophobic, really, but . . .'

'Oh, God,' said Treena. 'There's a but.'

Dad shook his head. 'But I'll probably say the wrong thing anyway and cause all sorts of offence because I'm just an aul fella who doesn't understand all the new lingo and the way things are done – my wife will tell you that. All this being said, even I know that all that matters in the long run is that these two girls of mine are happy. And if you make her happy, Eddie, like Sam makes our Lou happy, then good on you. I'm very glad to know you.'

He stood and reached a hand across the coffee table and after a moment Eddie leant forward and shook it.

'Right. Now let's have a bit of that cake.'

Mum gave a little sigh of relief and reached for the knife.

And I did the best I could to smile, then hurriedly left the room.

There is a definite hierarchy to heartbreak. I worked it out. Top of the list is the death of the person you love. There is no situation likely to elicit more shock and outright sympathy: faces will fall, a caring hand reach out to squeeze your shoulder. *Oh, God, I'm so sorry.* After that it's probably being left for someone else – the betrayal, the wickedness of the two people concerned bringing forth affirmations of outrage, of solidarity. *Oh, that must have been such a shock for you.* You could add forced separation, religious obstacles, serious illness. But *We drifted apart because we were living on separate continents* is, while true, unlikely to prompt more than a nod of acknowledgement, a pragmatic shrug of understanding. *Yeah, these things happen.*

I saw that reaction, albeit dressed up in maternal concern, in my mother's response to my news, and then my father's. *Well, that's an awful shame. But I suppose it's not a huge surprise,* and felt faintly stung in a way I couldn't express – *What do you mean not a huge surprise? I LOVED HIM.*

Boxing Day slid by slowly, the hours turgid and sad. I slept fitfully, glad of the distraction that Eddie created so that I didn't have to be the focus of attention. I lay in the bath and on the bed in the little box room, wiped away the odd tear and hoped nobody would notice. Mum brought me tea and tried not to talk too much about the radiant happiness of my sister.

And it was lovely to see. Or it would have been, had I not been so heartbroken. I watched the two of them surreptitiously holding hands under the table while Mum served supper, their heads bent together while they discussed something in a magazine, their feet touching as they watched television, Thom wedging his way between them with the confidence of the utterly loved, indifferent to who was doing the loving. Once we were past the huge surprise, it made perfect sense to me: Treena was so happy, relaxed in this woman's company in a way I had never seen. Occasionally she would cast me fleeting glances that were shy and quietly triumphant, and I would smile back, hoping it didn't look as fake as it felt.

Because all I felt was a second gigantic hole where my heart had been. Without the anger that had fuelled me for the past forty-eight hours I was a void. Sam had gone and I had as good as sent him away. To other people the end of my relationship might have been comprehensible, but to me it somehow made no sense at all.

On Boxing Day afternoon, as my family dozed on the sofa (I had forgotten how much time in our household was spent either discussing, eating or digesting food), I roused myself and walked to Stortfold Castle. It was empty, bar a brisk woman in a windcheater with her dog. She nodded hello in a way that suggested she wanted no part in any further conversation, and I made my way up the ramparts and onto a bench where I could look out over the maze and the southern half of Stortfold. I let the stiff breeze sting the tips of my ears and my feet grow cold, and I told myself that I wouldn't always feel so sad. I let myself think about Will, and how many afternoons we had spent around this castle, and how I had survived his death, and I told myself firmly that this new pain was a lesser one: I was not facing months of sadness so deep it made me feel nauseous. I would not think about Sam. I would not think about him with that woman. I would not look at Facebook. I would return to my exciting, eventful, rich new life in New York, and once I was fully away from him, the parts of me that felt scorched, destroyed, would eventually heal. Perhaps we had not been the thing I'd thought we were. Perhaps the intensity of our first meeting – who could resist a paramedic after all? – had made us believe the intensity was ours. Maybe I had just needed someone to stop me grieving. Maybe it had been a rebound relationship and I would feel better sooner than I thought.

I told myself this over and over again, but some part of me stubbornly refused to listen. And finally, when I got tired of pretending it was all going to be fine, I closed my eyes, put my head into my hands and I cried. At an empty castle on a day when everyone else was at home, I let grief course through me, and I sobbed without inhibition or fear of discovery. I cried in a way that I couldn't cry in the little house on Renfrew Road, and wouldn't be able to once I got back to the Gopniks', with anger and sadness, a kind of emotional bloodletting.

'*You fecker,*' I sobbed into my knees. '*I was only gone three months . . .*'

My voice sounded strange, strangled. And like Thom, who used to look at his own reflection deliberately when crying and then cry even harder, the sound of those words was so sad and horribly final that I made myself cry even harder. '*Damn you, Sam. Damn you for making me think it was worth the risk.*'

'So can I sit down too, or is this, like, a private grief fest?'

My head shot up. In front of me stood Lily, wrapped in a huge black parka and a red scarf, her arms folded over her chest, looking as if she might have been standing there studying me for some time. She grinned, as if somehow the sight of me in my darkest hour was actually quite amusing, then waited while I pulled myself together.

'Well, I guess I don't need to ask what's going on in *your* life,' she said, and punched me hard in the arm.

'How did you know I was here?'

'I walked round to your house to say hi as I've been home from skiing two days and you haven't even bothered to call.'

'I'm sorry,' I said. 'It's been . . .'

'It's been hard because you got dumped by Sexy Sam. Was it that blonde witch?'

I blew my nose and stared at her.

'I had a few days in London before Christmas so I went to the ambulance station to say hi and she was there, hanging off him like some kind of human mildew.'

I sniffed. 'You could tell.'

'God, yes. I was going to warn you but then I thought, *What's the point?* It's not like you could do anything about it from New York. Ugh. Men are so stupid, though. How could he not see through *that*?'

'Oh, Lily, I have missed you.' I hadn't known quite how much until that moment. Will's daughter, in all her mercurial, teenage glory. She sat down beside me and I leant against her, as if she were the adult. We gazed into the distance. I could just make out Will's home, Grantchester House.

'I mean just because she's pretty and has huge tits and one of those porny mouths that look like they're all about the blowjobs –'

'Okay, you can stop now.'

'Anyway, I wouldn't cry any more if I were you,' she said sagely. 'One, no man is worth it. Even Katy Perry will tell you that. But also your eyes go really, really small when you cry. Like, microdot kind of small.'

I couldn't help but laugh.

She stood up and held out a hand. 'C'mon. Let's walk down to yours. There's nowhere open on Boxing Day and Grandpa and Della and the Baby That Can Do No Wrong are doing my head in. I've got a whole twenty-four more hours to kill before Granny comes to pick me up. Ugh. Did you get snail trails on my jacket? You did! You are totally wiping that off.'

Over tea at our house, Lily filled me in on the news her emails hadn't covered – how she loved her new school but hadn't quite got to grips with the work as she was meant to. ('Turns out missing loads of school does have an effect. Which is actually quite irritating on the adult I-told-you-so front.') She enjoyed living with her grandmother so much that she felt able to bitch about her in the way that Lily did about people she truly loved – with humour and a kind of cheerful sarcasm. Granny was so unreasonable about her painting the walls of her room black. And she wouldn't let her drive the car, even though Lily totally knew how to drive and just wanted to get ahead before she could start lessons.

It was only when she was talking about her own mother that her upbeat demeanour fell away. Lily's mother had finally left her stepfather – 'of course' – but the architect down the road whom she had planned to make her next husband had not played ball, refusing to leave his wife. Her mother was now living a life of hysterical misery in rented accommodation in Holland Park with the twins and making her way through a succession of Filipina nannies who, despite an astonishing level of tolerance, were rarely tolerant enough to survive Tanya Houghton-Miller for more than a couple of weeks.

'I never thought I'd feel sorry for the boys, but I do,' she said. 'Ugh. I really want a cigarette. I only ever want one when I'm talking about my mum. You don't have to be Freud to work that out, right?'

'I'm sorry, Lily.'

'Don't be. I'm fine. I'm with Granny and at school. My mother's drama doesn't really touch me any more. Well, she leaves long messages on my voicemail, weeping or telling me I'm selfish for not moving back to be with her but I don't care.' She shuddered briefly. 'Sometimes I think if I'd stayed there I would have gone completely mental.' I thought back to the figure who had appeared on my doorstep all those months ago – drunk, unhappy, isolated – and felt a brief burst of quiet pleasure that by taking her in I had helped Will's daughter build this happy relationship with her grandmother.

Mum came in and out, replenishing the tray with cuts of ham, cheese and warmed mince pies, and seemed delighted that Lily was there, especially when Lily, her mouth full, gave her the run-down on goings-on in the big house. Lily didn't think Mr Traynor was very happy. Della, his new wife, was finding motherhood a challenge and fussed over the baby incessantly, flinching and weeping whenever it squawked. Which was, basically, all the time.

'Grandpa spends most of his time in his study, which just makes her even crosser. But when he tries to help she just shouts at him and tells him he's doing everything wrong. *Steven! Don't hold her like that! Steven! You've got that matinee jacket completely back to front!* I'd tell her to do one, but he's too nice.'

'He's the generation that would have had very little to do with babies,' Mum said kindly. 'I don't think your father would have changed a single nappy.'

'He always asks after Granny so I told him she had a new man.'

'Mrs Traynor has a boyfriend?' My mother's eyes rounded like saucers.

'No. Of course she doesn't. Granny says she's enjoying her freedom. But he doesn't need to know that, does he? I told Grandpa that a silver fox with an Aston Martin and all his own hair comes to take her out twice a week and I don't know his name but it's nice to see Granny looking so happy again. I can tell he really wants to ask questions but he doesn't dare while Della's there so he just nods and smiles this really fake smile and says, "Very good," and goes off to his study again.'

'Lily!' said my mother. 'You can't tell lies like that!'

'Why not?'

'Because, well, it's not true!'

'Loads of things in life aren't true. Father Christmas isn't true. But I bet you told Thom about him anyway. Grandpa's got someone else. It's good for him – and for Granny – if he thinks she's having lovely minibreaks in Paris with a hot rich pensioner. And they never speak to each other, so what's the harm?'

As logic went, it was pretty impressive. I could tell because Mum's mouth was working like someone feeling a loose tooth, but she couldn't come up with any other reason why Lily was wrong.

'Anyway,' said Lily, 'I'd better get back. Family dinner. Ho-ho-ho.'

It was at this moment that Treena and Eddie walked in, having been out to the play park with Thom. I saw Mum's sudden look of barely concealed anxiety and thought, *Oh, Lily, don't say something awful.* I gestured towards them. 'This is Lily, Eddie. Eddie, Lily. Lily is the daughter of my old employer, Will. Eddie is –'

'My girlfriend,' said Treena.

'Oh. Nice.' Lily shook Eddie's hand, then turned back to me. 'So. I'm still planning on making Granny bring me out to New York. She says she won't do it while it's this cold but she will in the spring. So be prepared to take a few days off. April totally qualifies as spring, yes? Up for it?'

'Can't wait,' I said. To the side of me, Mum deflated quietly with relief.

Lily hugged me hard, then ran from the front step. I watched her go and envied the robustness of the young.

20

To: KatrinaClark@scottsherwinbarker.com
From: BusyBee@gmail.com

Great picture, Treen! Really lovely. I liked it almost as much as the four you sent yesterday. No, my favourite is still the one you sent Tuesday. The three of you at the park. Yes, Eddie has got really nice eyes. You definitely look happy. I'm really glad.

Re your other point: I do think it might be a little early to frame one and send it to Mum and Dad but, hey, you know best.

Love to Thommo,
Lx

PS I'm fine. Thanks for asking.

I arrived back in the kind of New York blizzard that you see on the news, where only the tops of cars are visible and children sledge down normally traffic-filled streets and even the weather forecasters can't quite hide their childish glee. The wide avenues were clear, forced into compliance by the mayor, the city's huge snowploughs chugging dutifully up and down the major thoroughfares like gigantic beasts of burden.

I might normally have been thrilled to see snow like that, but my personal weather front was grey and damp, and it hung over me like a chill weight, sucking the joy from any situation.

I had never had my heart broken before, at least not by someone living. I had walked away from Patrick knowing deep down that, for both of us, our relationship had become a habit, a pair of shoes you might not really love but wore because you couldn't be bothered to get new ones. When Will had died I had thought I would never feel anything again.

It turned out there was little comfort to be had in knowing the person you'd loved and lost was still breathing. My brain, sadistic organ that it was, insisted on returning to Sam again and again throughout my day. What was he doing now? What was he thinking? Was he with her? Did he regret what had passed between us? Had he thought of me at all? I had a dozen silent arguments with him a day, some of which I even won. My rational self would butt in, telling me there was no point in thinking about him. What was done was done. I had returned to a different continent. Our futures lay thousands of miles apart.

And then, occasionally, a slightly manic self would intervene with a kind of forced optimism – *I could be whoever I wanted! I was tied to nobody! I could go anywhere in the world without feeling conflicted!* These three selves could jostle for space in my mind over a few minutes, and frequently did. It was a kind of schizophrenic existence and completely exhausting.

I drowned them. I ran with George and Agnes at dawn, not slowing when my chest hurt and my shins felt like hot pokers. I whizzed around the apartment, anticipating Agnes's needs, offering to help Michael when he looked particularly overworked, peeling potatoes alongside Ilaria and ignoring her when she harrumphed. I even offered to help Ashok shovel snow off the walkway – anything to stop me having to sit and contemplate my own life. He pulled a face and told me not to be a crazy person: did I want to see him out of a job?

Josh texted me on my third day home, while Agnes was holding up individual shoes in a children's shop and talking in Polish to her mother on the phone, apparently trying to work out which size she should be purchasing and whether her sister would approve. I felt my phone vibrate and looked down.

Hey, Louisa Clark the First. Long time no hear. Hope you had a good Christmas. Want to grab a coffee some time?

I stared. I had no reason not to, but somehow it felt wrong. I was too raw, my senses still full of a man three thousand miles away.

Hey, Josh. Bit busy right now (Agnes runs me off my feet!) but maybe sometime soon. Hope you're well. L x

He didn't respond and I felt strangely bad about it.

Garry loaded Agnes's shopping into the car and then her phone buzzed. She pulled it from her bag and stared at it. She looked out of the window for a moment, then at me. 'I forgot I had an art lesson. We have to go to East Williamsburg.'

It was patently a lie. I had a sudden memory of the awful Thanksgiving lunch, with all its revelations, and tried not to let it show on my face. 'I'll cancel the piano lesson, then,' I said evenly.

'Yes. Garry, I have art lesson. I forgot.'

Without a word, Garry pulled the limo onto the road.

Garry and I sat in silence in the car park, the engine running quietly to protect us from the chill outside. I felt quietly furious with Agnes for choosing this afternoon for one of her 'art lessons' as it meant I was left alone with my thoughts, a bunch of unwelcome houseguests who refused to leave. I put my earphones in and played myself some cheerful music. I used my iPad to organize the rest of Agnes's week. I played three online Scrabble moves with Mum. I answered an email from Treena, asking whether I thought she should take Eddie to a work dinner or if it was too soon. (I thought she should probably just get on with it.) I gazed outside at the glowering, snow-laden sky and wondered if more was going to fall. Garry watched a comedy show on his tablet, snorting alongside the canned laughter, his chin resting on his chest.

'Fancy a coffee?' I said, when I had run out of nails to chew. 'She's going to be ages, isn't she?'

'Nah. My doctor tells me I got to cut down on the doughnuts. And you know what happens if we go to the good doughnut place.'

I picked at a loose thread on my trousers. 'Want to play I Spy?'

'Are you kidding me?'

I lay back in my seat with a sigh and listened to the rest of the comedy show, then to Garry's laboured breathing as it slowed and became an occasional snore. The sky had begun to darken, an unfriendly iron grey. It was going to take hours to get back through the traffic. And then my phone rang.

'Louisa? Are you with Agnes? Her phone seems to be turned off. Can you get her for me?'

I glanced out of the window to where Steven Lipkott's studio light cast a yellow rectangle over the greying snow below.

'Uh . . . she's just . . . she's just trying some things on, Mr Gopnik. Let me run into the changing rooms and I'll get her to call you straight back.'

The downstairs door was propped open with two pots of paint, as if in the middle of a delivery. I ran up the concrete steps and along the corridor until I reached the studio. There I stopped at the closed door, breathing hard. I gazed down at my phone, then up to the heavens. I did not want to walk in. I did not want irrefutable proof of what had been suggested at Thanksgiving. I pressed my ear against the door, trying to work out if it was safe to knock, feeling furtive, as if it were I who was at fault. But all I could hear was music and muffled conversation.

With greater confidence I knocked. A couple of seconds later, I tried and opened the door. Steven Lipkott and Agnes were standing on the far side of the room with their backs to me, looking at a stack of canvases against the wall. He rested one hand on her shoulder, the other waving a cigarette towards one of the smaller canvases. The room smelt of smoke and turpentine and, faintly, of perfume.

'Well, why don't you bring me some other pictures of her?' he was saying. 'If you don't feel it really represents her, then we should –'

'Louisa!' Agnes spun around and threw up a palm, as if she were warding me off.

'I'm sorry,' I said, holding up my phone. 'It – it's Mr Gopnik. He's trying to reach you.'

'You shouldn't have come in here! Why you didn't knock?' The colour had leached from her face.

'I did. I'm sorry. I didn't have any way of . . .' It was as I was backing out of the door that I glimpsed the canvas. A child, with blonde hair and wide eyes, half turned as if about to skip away. And with a sudden and inevitable clarity I understood everything: the depression, the endless conversations with her mother, the endless toy and shoe purchases . . .

Steven stooped to pick it up. 'Look. Just take that one with you if you want. Have a think about it –'

'Shut *up*, Steven!' He flinched, as if unsure what had prompted her reaction. But that was what finally confirmed it.

'I'll meet you downstairs,' I said, and closed the door quietly behind me.

*

We drove back to the Upper East Side in silence. Agnes called Mr Gopnik and apologized, she hadn't realized her phone was off, a design fault – the thing was always shutting down without her doing it – she really needed a different one. *Yes, darling. We're headed back now. Yes, I know . . .*

She did not look at me. In truth, I could barely look at her. My mind was humming, marrying up the events of the last months with what I now understood.

When we finally reached home I walked a few paces behind her through the lobby, but as we got to the lift, she swivelled, stared at the floor, and then turned back towards the door. 'Okay. Come with me.'

We sat in a dark, gilded hotel bar, the kind where I imagined rich Middle Eastern businessmen entertained their clients and waved away bar bills without looking. It was nearly empty. Agnes and I sat in a dimly lit corner booth, waiting as the server ostentatiously offloaded two vodka tonics and a pot of glossy green olives, trying and failing to catch Agnes's eye.

'She's mine,' Agnes said, as he walked away.

I took a sip of my drink. It was ferociously strong and I was glad. It felt useful to have something to focus on.

'My daughter.' Her voice was tight, oddly furious. 'She lives with my sister in Poland. She is fine – she was so young when I went that she barely remembers when her mama lived with her – and my sister is happy because she cannot have children, but my mother is very angry at me.'

'But –'

'I didn't tell him when I met him, okay? I was so . . . so happy that someone like him liked me. I didn't think for one minute we would be together. It was like a dream, you know? I thought, I will just have this little adventure, and then my work visa will finish and I will go back to Poland and I will remember this thing always. And then everything happened so fast and he leaves his wife for me. I couldn't think how to tell him. Every time I meet him I think, *This is the time, this is the time* . . . and then when we are together he tell me – he tells me that he doesn't want any more children. He is *done*, he says. He feels he has made big mess with his own family and he does not want to make it worse with step-families, half-brothers, half-sisters, all this business. He loves me but the no-children thing is deal-breaker for him. So how can I tell him then?'

I leant forward so that nobody else could hear. 'But . . . but this is batshit crazy, Agnes. You already have a daughter!'

'And how can I tell him this now after two years? You think he will not think I am bad woman? You think he will not see this as terrible, terrible deceit? I have made huge problem for myself, Louisa. I know this.' She took a swig of her drink.

'I think all the time – *all* the time – how I can fix this? But there is nothing to fix. I lied to him. For him, trust is everything. He would not forgive me. So is simple. This way he is happy, I am happy, I can provide for everyone. I try to convince my sister to come to live in New York one day. Then I can see Zofia every day.'

'But you must miss her terribly.'

Her jaw tightened. 'I am providing for her future.' She spoke as if reading from a long-rehearsed mental list. 'Before, our family had not so much. My sister now lives in very good house – four bedrooms, everything new. Very nice area. Zofia will go to best school in Poland, play best piano, she will have everything.'

'But no mother.'

Her eyes suddenly brimmed. 'No. I have to leave Leonard or I have to leave her. So is my . . . my . . . oh, what is word? . . . my penance to live without her.' Her voice cracked a little.

I sipped my vodka. I didn't know what else to do. We both stared at our glasses.

'I am not bad person, Louisa. I love Leonard. Very much.'

'I know.'

'I had this idea that maybe when we had been married, when we had been together a while, I could tell him. And he would be little bit upset but maybe he could come round. Or I could go backwards and forwards to Poland, you know? Or maybe she could come stay for a bit. But things just get so – so complicated. His family hate me so much. You know what would happen if they found out about her now? You know what would happen if Tabitha knew this thing about me?'

I could guess.

'I love him. I know you think many things about me. But I love him. He is good man. Sometimes I find it very hard because he is working so much and because nobody cares for me in his world . . . and I get so lonely and maybe . . . I do not always behave perfectly, but when I think of being without him I cannot bear it. He is truly my soulmate. From first day, I knew this.'

She traced a pattern on the table with a slim finger. 'But then I think of my daughter growing up for next ten, fifteen years without me and I . . . I . . .'

She let out a shuddering sigh, loud enough to draw the attention of the barman. I reached into my bag, and when I couldn't find a handkerchief I passed her a cocktail napkin. When she looked up there was a softness to her face. It was an expression I hadn't seen before, radiant with love and tenderness.

'She is so beautiful, Louisa. She is nearly four years old now and so clever. And so bright. She knows days of the week and she can point out countries on the globe and she can sing. She knows where New York is. She can draw a line on map between Kraków and New York without anybody showing her. And every time I visit she hangs onto me and says, "Why do you have to go, Mama? I don't want you to go." And a little bit of my heart, it breaks . . . Oh, God, it breaks . . . Sometimes now I don't even want to see her because the pain when I have to leave is . . . it is . . .' Agnes hunched over her drink, her hand lifting mechanically to wipe the tears that fell silently onto the shiny table.

I handed her another cocktail napkin. 'Agnes,' I said softly, 'I don't know how long you can keep this up.'

She dabbed at her eyes, her head bowed. When she looked up it was impossible to tell she had been crying. 'We are friends, yes? Good friends.'

'Of course.'

She glanced behind her and leant forward over the table. 'You and I. We are both immigrants. We both know it is hard to find your place in this world. You want to make your life better, work hard in country that is not your own – you make new life, new friends, find new love. You get to become new person! But is never a simple thing, never without cost.'

I swallowed, and pushed away a hot, angry image of Sam in his railway carriage.

'I know this – nobody gets everything. And we immigrants know this more than anyone. You always have one foot in two places. You can never be truly happy because, from the moment you leave, you are two selves, and wherever you are one half of you is always calling to the other. This is our price, Louisa. This is the cost of who we are.'

She took a sip of her drink and then another. Then she took a deep breath and shook her hands out across the table, as if she were ridding herself of excess emotion through her fingertips. When she spoke again her voice was steely. 'You must not tell him. You must not tell him what you see today.'

'Agnes, I don't know how you can hide this for ever. It's too big. It –'

She reached out a hand and laid it on my arm. Her fingers closed firmly around my wrist. 'Please. We are friends, yes?'

I swallowed.

There are no real secrets among the rich, it turns out. Just people paid to keep them. I walked up the stairs, this new burden unexpectedly heavy on my heart. I thought of a little girl across the world with everything but the thing she wanted most in the world, and a woman who probably felt the same, even if she was only just beginning to realize it. I thought about calling my sister – the only person left with whom I might be able to discuss it – but knew without speaking to her what her judgement would be. She would no more have left Thom in another country than she would have cut off her own arm.

I thought about Sam, and the bargains we make with ourselves to justify our choices. I sat in my room that evening until my thoughts hung low and black around my head and I pulled out my phone. *Hey, Josh, is that offer still open? But for, like, a drink-drink instead of coffee?*

Within thirty seconds the answer pinged back: *Just say where and when, Louisa.*

21

In the end, I met Josh at a dive bar he knew off Times Square. It was long and narrow, covered with photographs of boxers, and the floor was tacky underfoot. I wore black jeans and scraped my hair into a ponytail. Nobody looked up as I squeezed my way past the middle-aged men and autographed pictures of flyweights and men whose necks were wider than their heads.

He was seated at a tiny table at the end of the bar in a waxed dark brown jacket – the kind you buy to look like you belong in the countryside. When he saw me, his smile was sudden and infectious and made me briefly glad that someone uncomplicated was pleased to see me in a world that felt impossibly messy.

'How you doing?' He stood and looked like he wanted to step forward and hug me but something – perhaps the circumstances of our last meeting – prevented him. He touched my arm instead.

'I've had a bit of a day. A bit of a week, actually. And I really need a friendly face to have a drink or two with. And – guess what – yours was the first name I pulled out of my New York hat!'

'What do you want? Bear in mind they do about six drinks here.'

'Vodka tonic?'

'I'm pretty sure that's one of them.'

He was back within minutes with a bottled beer for himself and a vodka tonic for me. I had shed my coat and was oddly nervous to be opposite him.

'So . . . this week of yours. What happened?'

I took a sip of my drink. It sat too comfortably on top of the one I'd had that afternoon. 'I . . . I found out something today. It's kind of knocked me sideways. I can't tell you what it is, not because I don't trust you but because it's so big that it would affect all sorts of people. And I don't know what to do about it.' I shifted in my seat. 'I think I just need to kind of swallow it and learn how not to let it give me indigestion. Does that make sense? So I was hoping I could see you and have a couple of drinks and hear a bit about your life – a nice life without big dark secrets, assuming you don't have any big dark secrets – and remind myself that life can be normal and good, but I really don't want you to try and get me to talk about mine. Like if I happen to drop my defences and stuff.'

He put his hand on his heart. 'Louisa, I do not want to know about your thing. I'm just happy to see you.'

'I honestly would tell you if I could.'

'I have no curiosity about this gigantic, life-altering secret whatsoever. You're safe with me.' He took a swig of his drink and smiled his perfect smile at me, and for the first time in two weeks I felt a tiny bit less lonely.

Two hours later the bar was overheated and three-deep, exhausted tourists, marvelling at three-dollar beers, and regulars rammed along its narrow length, the vast majority focused on a boxing match on the TV in the corner. They cried out in unison at a swift uppercut, and roared as one when their man, his face pulped and misshapen, went down against the ropes. Josh was the only man in the whole place not watching it, leaning quietly over his bottle of beer, his eyes on mine.

I, in turn, was slumped over the table and telling him at length the story of Treena and Edwina on Christmas Day, one of the few stories I could legitimately share, along with that of Granddad's stroke, the story of the grand piano (I said it was for Agnes's niece) and – in case I sounded too gloomy – my lovely upgrade from New York to London. I don't know how many vodkas I'd had by then – Josh tended to magic them in front of me before I'd realized I was done with the last one – but some distant part of me was aware that my voice had acquired a weird, sing-song quality, sliding up and down not always in accordance with what I was saying.

'Well, that's cool, right?' he said, when I reached Dad's speech about happiness. I may have made it a little more Lifetime movie than it had been. In my latest version Dad had become Atticus Finch delivering his closing speech to the courtroom in *To Kill a Mockingbird*.

'It's all good,' Josh went on. 'He just wants her to be happy. When my cousin Tim came out to my uncle he didn't speak to him for, like, a year.'

'They're so happy,' I said, stretching my arms across the table just so I could feel the cool bits on my skin, trying to not mind that it was sticky. 'It's great. It really is.' I took another sip of my drink. 'It's like you look at them both together and you're so glad because, you know, Treena's been on her own for a million years but honestly . . . it would be really nice if they could just be a teeny tiny bit less glowy and radiant around each other. Like not *always* gazing into each other's eyes. Or doing that secret smile which is all about the private shared jokes. Or the one that means they just had really, really great sex. And maybe Treena could just stop sending me pictures of the two of them together. Or text messages about every amazing thing that Eddie says or does. Which apparently is pretty much anything she says or does.'

'Ah, c'mon. They're newly in love, right? People do that stuff.'

'I never did. Did you do that stuff? Seriously, I have never sent anyone pictures of me kissing someone. If I'd sent a picture of me snuggling with a boyfriend to Treena she would have reacted like I'd sent her a dick pic. I mean, this is the woman who found all displays of emotion *disgusting*.'

'Then it's the first time she's been in love. And she'll be delighted to get the next picture you send her of you being nauseatingly happy with your boyfriend.' He looked like he was laughing at me. 'Maybe not the dick pic.'

'You think I'm a terrible person.'

'I don't think you're a terrible person. Just a fairly . . . refreshed one.'

I groaned. 'I know. I'm a terrible person. I'm not asking them not to be happy, just to be a teeny bit sensitive to those of us who might not be . . . just at this . . .' I'd run out of words.

Josh had settled back in his chair and was now watching me.

'Ex-boyfriend,' I said, my voice slurring slightly. 'He's now an ex-boyfriend.'

He raised his eyebrows. 'Woah. Quite the couple of weeks, then.'

'Oh, man.' I rested my forehead on the table. 'You have no idea.'

I was conscious of a silence falling gently between us. I wondered briefly if I might just take a little power nap right there. It felt so nice. The sounds of the boxing match briefly receded. My forehead was only a little bit wet. And then I felt his hand on mine. 'Okay, Louisa. I think it's time we got you out of here.'

I said goodbye to all the nice people on my way out, high-fiving as many as I could (some seemed to miss my hand – idiots). For some reason, Josh kept apologizing out loud. I think maybe he was bumping into them as we walked. He put my jacket on me when we got to the door and I got the giggles because he couldn't get my arms into my sleeves, and when he did, it was the wrong way round, like a strait-jacket. 'I give up,' he said eventually. 'Just wear it like that.' I heard someone shout, 'Take a little water with it, lady.'

'I *am* a lady!' I exclaimed. 'An English lady! I am Louisa Clark the First, aren't I, Joshua?' I turned to face them and air-punched. I was leaning against the wall of photographs and brought a few clattering down on top of me.

'We're going, we're going,' Josh said, raising his hands towards the barman. Someone started shouting. He was still apologizing to everyone. I told him it wasn't good to apologize – Will had taught me that. You had to hold your head up.

And suddenly we were out in the brisk cold air. Then, before I knew it, I tripped on something and suddenly I was on the icy pavement, my knees smacking onto the hard concrete. I swore.

'Oh, boy,' said Josh, who had his arm firmly round my waist and was hauling me upright. 'I think we need to get you some coffee.'

He smelt so nice. He smelt like Will had – expensive, like the men's section of a posh department store. I put my nose against his neck and inhaled as we staggered along the pavement. 'You smell lovely.'

'Thank you very much.'

'Very expensive.'

'Good to know.'

'I might lick you.'

'If it makes you feel better.'

I licked him. His aftershave didn't taste as nice as it smelt but it was kind of nice to lick someone. 'It does make me feel better,' I said, with some surprise. 'It really does!'

'Oooh-*kay*. Here's the best spot to get a cab.' He manoeuvred himself so that he was facing me and put his hands on my shoulders. Around us Times Square was blinding and dizzying, a glittering neon circus, its leviathan images looming down at me with impossible brightness. I turned slowly, gazing up at the lights and feeling like I might fall over. I went round and round while they blurred, then staggered slightly. I felt Josh catch me.

'I can put you in a cab home, because I think you might need to sleep this off. Or we can walk to mine and get some coffee down you. Your choice.' It was after one in the morning yet he had to shout to be heard over the noise of the people around us. He was so handsome in his shirt and jacket. So clean cut and crisp-looking. I liked him so much. I turned in his arms and blinked at him. It would have been helpful if he'd stopped swaying.

'That's very kind of you,' he said.

'Did I say all that out loud?'

'Yup.'

'Sorry. But you really are. Terrifically handsome. Like American handsome. Like an actual movie star. Josh?'

'Yeah?'

'I think I might sit down. My head has gone kind of fuzzy.' I was halfway to the ground when I felt him sweep me up again.

'And there we go.'

'I really want to tell you the thing. But I can't tell you the thing.'

'Then don't tell me the thing.'

'You'd understand. I know you would. You know . . . you look so like someone I loved. Really loved. Did you know that? You look just so like him.'

'That's . . . nice to know.'

'It is nice. He was terrifically handsome. Just like you. Movie-star handsome . . . Did I say that already? He died. Did I tell you he died?'

'I'm sorry for your loss. But I think we need to get you out of here.' He walked me down two blocks, hailed a cab and, with some effort, helped me in. I fought my way upright on the back seat and held onto his sleeve. He was half in, half out of the taxi door.

'Where to, lady?' The driver looked behind him.

I looked at Josh. 'Can you stay with me?'

'Sure. Where are we going?'

I saw the wary glance of the driver in his rear-view mirror. A television blared from the back of his seat and a television studio audience burst into applause. Outside, everyone started to honk their horns at once. The lights were too bright. New York was suddenly too loud, too everything. 'I don't know. Your house,' I said. 'I can't go back. Not yet.' I looked at him and felt suddenly tearful. 'Do you know I have two legs in two places?'

He tilted his head towards me. His face was kind. 'Somehow, Louisa Clark, that doesn't surprise me.'

I let my head rest on his shoulder and felt his arm slide gently around me.

I woke to the sound of a phone ringing, shrill and insistent. The blessed relief of it stopping, then a man's voice murmuring. The welcome bitter smell of coffee. I shifted, trying to lift my head from the pillow. The resulting pain through my temples was so intense and unforgiving that I let out a little animal sound, like a dog whose tail had just been trapped in a door. I closed my eyes, took a breath, then opened them again.

This was not my bed.

It was still not my bed when I opened them a third time.

This indisputable fact was enough to prompt me to attempt to lift my head again, this time ignoring the thumping pain long enough to focus. Nope, this was definitely not my bed. This was also not my bedroom. In fact, it was no bedroom I had ever seen before. I took in the clothes – men's clothes – folded neatly over the back of a chair, the television in the corner, the desk and the wardrobe, and became aware of the voice growing nearer. And then the door opened and Josh walked in, fully suited, holding a mug with one hand, his phone pressed to his ear with the other. He caught my eye, raised an eyebrow, and placed the mug on the bedside table, still talking.

'Yeah, there's been a problem with the subway. I'm going to grab a cab and I'll be there in twenty . . . Sure. No problem . . . No, she's on that already.'

I pushed myself upright, discovering as I did so that I was in a man's T-shirt. The ramifications of this took a couple of minutes to seep in, and I felt the blush start from somewhere around my chest.

'No, we already talked about that yesterday. He's got all the paperwork ready to go.'

He turned away, and I wriggled back down, so that the duvet was around my neck. I was wearing knickers. That was something.

'Yeah. It'll be great. Yup – lunch sounds good.' Josh rang off and shoved his phone into his pocket. 'Good morning! I was just going to get you a side order of Advil. Want me to find you a couple? I'm afraid I have to go.'

'Go?' My mouth tasted rank, as dry as if it had been lightly powdered. I opened and closed it a couple of times, noting it made a faintly disgusting smacking sound.

'To work. It's Friday?'

'Oh, God. What time is it?'

'A quarter of seven. I have to shoot. Already running late. Will you be okay letting yourself out?' He rummaged in a drawer and withdrew a blister pack, which he placed beside me. 'There. That should help.'

I pushed my hair back from my face. It was slightly damp with sweat and astonishingly matted. 'What – what happened?'

'We can talk about it later. Drink your coffee.'

I took a sip obediently. It was strong and restorative. I suspected I would need another six. 'Why am I in your T-shirt?'

He grinned. 'That would be the dance.'

'The dance?' My stomach lurched.

He stooped and kissed my cheek. He smelt of soap and cleanliness and citrus and all things wholesome. I was aware that I was giving off hot waves of stale sweat and alcohol and shame. 'It was a fun night. Hey – just make sure you give the door a really good slam when you leave, okay? Sometimes it doesn't catch properly. I'll call you later.'

He saluted from the doorway, turned and was gone, patting his pockets as if to reassure himself of something as he left.

'Hold on – where am I?' I yelled, a minute later, but he was already gone.

I was in SoHo, it turned out. One giant angry traffic jam away from where I was meant to be. I caught the subway from Spring Street to 59th Street, trying not to sweat gently into yesterday's crumpled shirt and grateful for the small mercy that I was not in my usual glittery evening clothes. I had never really understood the term 'grubby' until that morning. I could remember almost nothing from the previous evening. And what I did remember came to me in unpleasant hot flashbacks.

Me sitting down in the middle of Times Square.

Me licking Josh's neck. I had actually licked his neck.

What was that about dancing?

If I hadn't been hanging onto the subway pole for dear life, I would have held my head in my hands. Instead I closed my eyes, lurched my way through the stations, shifted to avoid the backpacks and the grumpy commuters locked into their earphones, and tried not to throw up.

Just get through today, I told myself. If life had taught me one thing, it was that the answers would come soon enough.

I was just opening the door to my room when Mr Gopnik appeared. He was still dressed in his workout gear – unusual for him after seven – and lifted a hand when he saw me, as if he had been trying to locate me for some time. 'Ah. Louisa.'

'I'm sorry I –'

'I'd like to talk to you in my study. Now.'

Of course you would, I thought. Of course. He turned and walked back up the corridor. I cast an anguished look at my room, which held my clean clothes, deodorant and toothpaste. I thought longingly about a second coffee. But Mr Gopnik was not the kind of man you kept waiting.

I glanced down at my phone, then jogged after him.

I walked into the study to find him already seated. 'I'm really sorry I was ten minutes late. I'm not normally late. I just had to . . .'

Mr Gopnik was behind his desk, his expression unreadable. Agnes was on the upholstered chair by the coffee table in her workout gear. Neither of them asked me to sit down. Something in the atmosphere made me feel suddenly horribly sober.

'Is . . . is everything okay?'

'I'm hoping you can tell me. I had a call from my personal account manager this morning.'

'Your what?'

'The man who handles my banking operations. I wondered if you could explain this.'

He pushed a piece of paper towards me. It was a bank statement, with the totals blacked out. My eyesight was a little blurry but just one thing was visible, a trail of figures, five hundred dollars a day under 'cash withdrawals'.

It was then that I noticed Agnes's expression. She was staring fixedly at her hands, her mouth compressed into a thin line. Her gaze flickered towards me and away again. I stood, a fine trickle of sweat running down my back.

'He told me something very interesting. Apparently in the run-up to Christmas a considerable sum of money was removed from our joint bank account. It was removed day by day from a nearby ATM in amounts that were – perhaps – designed not to be noticed. He picked it up because they have anti-fraud software designed to identify strange patterns of use in any of our bank cards and this was flagged up as unusual. Obviously this was a little concerning so I asked Agnes and she told me it wasn't anything to do with her. So I asked Ashok to provide the CCTV for the days concerned and my security people matched it up with the times of the withdrawals and it turns out, Louisa,' here he looked at me directly, 'the only person going in and out of the building at those times was you.'

My eyes widened.

'Now, I could go to the banks concerned and ask them to provide the CCTV from their ATMs at the times the amount was taken, but I'd rather not put them to that trouble. So really I wanted to know whether you could explain what was going on here. And why almost ten thousand dollars was removed from our joint account.'

I looked at Agnes but she was still looking away from me. My mouth had dried even more than it had that morning.

'I had to do some . . . Christmas shopping. For Agnes.'

'You have a card to do that. Which clearly shows which shops you've been in and you provide the receipts for all purchases. Which, up to now, I gather from Michael, you have done. But cash . . . cash is rather less transparent. Do you have the receipts for this shopping?'

'No.'

'And can you tell me what you bought?'

'I . . . No.'

'So what has happened to the money, Louisa?'

I couldn't speak. I swallowed. And then I said, 'I don't know.'

'You don't know?'

'I – I didn't steal anything.' I felt the colour rising to my cheeks.

'So Agnes is lying?'

'No.'

'Louisa – Agnes knows that I would give her anything she wanted. To be frank, she could spend ten times that in a day and I wouldn't bat an eyelid. So she has no reason to sneak around withdrawing cash sums from the nearest ATM. So I'm asking you again, what happened to the money?'

I felt flushed, panicky. And then Agnes looked up at me. Her face was a silent plea.

'Louisa?'

'Perhaps I – I might have taken it.'

'You *might have* taken it?'

'For shopping. Not for me. You can check my room. You can check my bank account.'

'You spent ten thousand dollars on "shopping". Shopping for what?'

'Just . . . bits and pieces.'

He lowered his head briefly, as if he were trying to control his temper.

'Bits and pieces,' he repeated slowly. 'Louisa, you realize your being in this household is a matter of trust.'

'I do, Mr Gopnik. And I take that very seriously.'

'You have access to the most inner workings of this household. You have keys, credit cards, intimate knowledge of our routines. You are well rewarded for that – because we understand this is a position of responsibility and we rely on you to not betray that responsibility.'

'Mr Gopnik. I love this job. I wouldn't . . .' I cast an anguished look at Agnes, but she was still staring down. One of her hands, I saw, was holding the other, her fingernail digging deep into the flesh of the ball of her thumb.

'You really can't explain what has happened to that money?'

'I – I didn't steal it.'

He looked at me intently for a long moment, as if waiting for something. When it didn't come his expression hardened. 'This is disappointing, Louisa. I know Agnes is very fond of you and feels you have been very helpful to her. But I cannot have someone in my household whom I do not trust.'

'Leonard –' Agnes began, but he held up a hand.

'No, darling. I've been through this before. I'm sorry, Louisa, but your employment is terminated with immediate effect.'

'Wh-what?'

'You will be given an hour to clear your room. You will leave a forwarding address with Michael and he will be in touch regarding whatever is owed to you. I would take this opportunity to remind you of the non-disclosure element of your contract. The details of this conversation will go no further. I hope you can see that this is for your benefit as much as ours.'

The colour had drained from Agnes's face. 'No, Leonard. You can't do this.'

'I am not discussing this further. I have to go to work. Louisa, your hour starts now.'

He stood. He was waiting for me to leave the room.

I emerged from the study with my head spinning. Michael was waiting for me, and it took me a couple of seconds to grasp that he was not there to see if I was okay but to escort me to my room. That from now on I really was not trusted in this house.

I walked silently down the corridor, vaguely conscious of Ilaria's stunned face at the kitchen door, the sound of impassioned conversation somewhere at the other end of the apartment. I couldn't see Nathan anywhere. As Michael stood in the doorway I pulled my case from under my bed and began to pack, messily, chaotically, pulling out drawers, hauling things in as quickly as I could, conscious that I was working against some capricious clock. My brain hummed – shock and outrage tempered by the need not to forget anything: *had I left laundry in the laundry room? Where were my trainers?* And then, twenty minutes later, I was done. All my belongings were packed into a suitcase, a holdall and a large checked shopping bag.

'Here, I'll take that,' said Michael, reaching for my wheelie case as he saw me struggling to get the three bags to the bedroom door. It took me a second to realize this was less an act of kindness than efficiency.

'iPad?' he said. 'Work phone? Credit card.' I handed them over, along with the door keys, and he put them into his pocket.

I walked along the hallway, still struggling to believe this was happening. Ilaria was standing in the kitchen doorway, her apron on, her plump hands pressed together. As I passed her, I glanced sideways, expecting her to curse me in Spanish, or to give me the kind of withering look that women of her age reserve for alleged thieves. But instead she stepped forward and silently touched my hand. Michael turned away, as if he hadn't seen. And then we were at the front door.

He passed me the handle of my case.

'Goodbye, Louisa,' he said, his expression unreadable. 'Good luck.'

I stepped out. And the huge mahogany door closed firmly behind me.

I sat in the diner for two hours. I was in shock. I couldn't cry. I couldn't rage. I just felt paralysed. I thought at first that Agnes would sort this out. She would find a way to convey to her husband that he was wrong. We were friends, after all. So I sat and waited for Michael to appear, looking slightly awkward, ready to pull my cases back to the Lavery. I gazed at my mobile phone, waiting for a text message – *Louisa, there has been terrible misunderstanding.* But none came.

When I realized it probably wasn't going to come, I thought about simply heading back to the UK, but to do so would wreak havoc on Treena's life – the last thing she and Thom needed was me turfing them out of the flat. I couldn't return to Mum and Dad's – it wasn't just the soul-destroying thought of moving back to Stortfold but I thought I might die if I had to go home as a failure twice, the first time broken after drunkenly falling from a building, the second fired from the job I had loved.

And, of course, I could no longer stay with Sam.

I cradled my coffee cup with fingers that still trembled and saw that I had effectively boxed myself out of my own life. I considered calling Josh, but I didn't feel it was appropriate to ask him if I could move in, given I wasn't sure we'd even had a first date.

And if I did find accommodation, what was I going to do? I had no job. I didn't know if Mr Gopnik could revoke my work permit. Presumably that only existed as long as I worked for him.

Worst of all, I was haunted by the way he had looked at me, his expression of utter disappointment and faint contempt when I had failed to come up with a satisfactory answer. His quiet approval had been one of the many small satisfactions of my life there – that a man of such stature had thought I was doing a good job had boosted my confidence, had left me feeling capable, professional, in a way I hadn't since looking after Will. I wanted so badly to explain myself to him, to regain his goodwill, but how could I? I saw Agnes's face, eyes wide, pleading. She would call, wouldn't she? Why hadn't she called?

'You want a refill, sweetheart?' I looked up at the middle-aged waitress with tangerine-coloured hair holding the coffee jug. She eyed my belongings like she had seen this scenario a million times before. 'Just got here?'

'Not exactly.' I tried to smile but it came out as a kind of grimace.

She poured the coffee, and stooped, lowering her voice. 'My cousin runs a hostel in Bensonhurst if you're stuck for somewhere to stay. There are cards over by the till. It ain't pretty, but it's cheap and it's clean. Call sooner rather than later, you know what I'm saying? Places fill up.' She put a hand briefly on my shoulder and walked on to the next customer.

That small act of kindness almost did for my composure. For the first time I felt overwhelmed, crushed by the knowledge that I was alone in a city that no longer welcomed me. I didn't know what I was supposed to do now that my bridges were apparently pushing out thick black smoke on two continents. I tried to picture myself explaining to my parents what had happened, but found myself once again butting up against the vast wall of Agnes's secret. Could you tell even one person without the truth slowly creeping out? My parents would be so outraged on my behalf that I couldn't put it past Dad not to ring Mr Gopnik just to set him straight about his deceitful wife. And what if Agnes denied everything? I thought about Nathan's words – ultimately we were staff, not friends. What if she lied and said I had stolen the money? Wouldn't that make things worse?

For perhaps the first time since I had arrived in New York I wished I hadn't come. I was still in last night's clothes, stale and crumpled, which made me feel even worse. I sniffed quietly and wiped my nose with a paper napkin while staring at the mug in front of me. Outside, life in Manhattan continued, oblivious, fast-moving, ignoring the detritus that piled up in the gutter. *What do I do now, Will?* I thought, a huge lump rising in my throat.

As if on cue my phone pinged.

What the bloody hell is going on? wrote Nathan. *Call me, Clark.*

And, despite myself, I smiled.

Nathan said there was no bloody way I was going to stay in a bloody hostel in bloody God knew where, with the rapists and the drug-dealers and God knew what. I was to wait until seven thirty when the bloody Gopniks had left for bloody dinner and I was to meet him at the service entrance and we would work out what the hell to do next. There was quite a lot of swearing for three text messages.

When I arrived his anger was uncharacteristically undimmed.

'I don't get it. It's like they just ghosted you. Like a ruddy Mafiosi code of silence. Michael wouldn't tell me anything other than it was a "matter of dishonesty". I told him I'd never met a more honest person in my bloody life and they all needed their heads looking at. What the hell happened?'

He had shepherded me into his room off the service corridor and closed the door behind us. It was such a relief to see him it was all I could do not to hug him. I didn't, though. I thought I'd probably clutched enough men in the last twenty-four hours.

'For Chrissakes. People. You want a beer?'

'Sure.'

He cracked open two cans and handed one to me, sitting down on his easy chair. I perched on the bed and took a sip.

'So . . . well?'

I pulled a face. 'I can't tell you, Nathan.'

His eyebrows shot somewhere towards the ceiling. 'You too? Oh, mate. Don't tell me you –'

'Of course not. I wouldn't steal a teabag from the Gopniks. But if I told you what really happened it would . . . it would be disastrous. For other people in the house . . . It's complicated.'

He frowned. 'What? Are you saying you took the blame for something you didn't do?'

'Sort of.'

Nathan rested his elbows on his knees, shaking his head. 'This isn't right.'

'I know.'

'Someone's got to say something. You know he was thinking about calling the cops?'

My jaw might have dropped.

'Yeah. She persuaded him not to, but Michael said he was mad enough to do it. Something about an ATM?'

'I didn't do it, Nathan.'

'I know that, Clark. You'd make a crap criminal. Worst poker face I ever saw.' He took a swig of his beer. 'Dammit.

You know, I love my job. I like working for these families. I like Old Man Gopnik. But every now and then it's like they remind you, you know? You're basically just expendable. Doesn't matter how much they say you're their mate and how great you are, how much they depend on you, yada-yada-yada, the moment they don't need you any more or you've done something they don't like, *bang*. You're out the door. Fairness doesn't even come into it.'

It was the longest thing I'd heard Nathan say since I got to New York.

'I hate this, Lou. Even knowing so little it's clear to me you're being shafted. And it stinks.'

'It's complicated.'

'Complicated?' He gazed at me steadily, shook his head again and took a long swig of his beer. 'Mate, you're a better person than I am.'

We were going to order takeout but just as Nathan was climbing into his jacket to head off to the Chinese restaurant there was a knock at the door. We looked at each other in horror and he motioned me into the bathroom. I skidded in and closed the door silently behind me. But as I stood wedged up against his towel rail I heard a familiar voice.

'Clark, it's okay. It's Ilaria,' said Nathan, a moment later.

She was in her apron, holding a pot with a lid on it. 'For you. I hear you talking.' She held the pot towards me. 'I made it for you. You need to eat. It's the chicken you like, with the pepper sauce.'

'Aw, mate.' Nathan clapped Ilaria on the back. She stumbled forwards, recovered and placed the pot carefully on Nathan's desk.

'You made this for me?'

Ilaria was prodding Nathan in the chest. 'I know she does

not do this thing they say. I know plenty. Plenty that goes on this apartment.' She tapped her nose. 'Oh, yes.'

I briefly lifted the lid – delicious smells seeped out. I suddenly remembered I had barely eaten all day. 'Thanks, Ilaria. I don't know what to say.'

'Where you go now?'

'I haven't got a clue.'

'Well. You're not staying in a hostel in bloody Bensonhurst,' Nathan said. 'You can stay here for a night or two to sort yourself out. I'll lock my door. You won't say anything, will you, Ilaria?'

She pulled an incredulous face, like it was stupid of him even to ask.

'She's been cursing your woman out all afternoon like you wouldn't believe. Says she sold you down the river. She made them a fish thing for dinner that she knows they both hate. I tell you, mate, I've learnt a whole new bunch of swear words today.'

Ilaria muttered something under her breath. I could only make out the word *puta*.

The easy chair was too small for Nathan to sleep in and he was too old fashioned to countenance me sleeping in it so we agreed to share his double bed with an arrangement of cushions down the middle to protect us from accidentally touching each other in the night. I'm not sure who was more ill-at-ease. Nathan made a great show of shepherding me into the bathroom first, making sure I'd locked the door, and waiting for me to get into bed before he emerged from his ablutions. He was in a T-shirt and striped cotton pyjama bottoms, and even then I didn't know where to look.

'Bit weird, eh?' he said, climbing in.

'Um, yes.' I don't know if it was shock or exhaustion or just the surreal turn of events but I started to giggle. And then the giggle turned into tears. And before I knew it I was sobbing, hunched over in a strange bed, my head in my hands.

'Aw, mate.' Nathan plainly felt awkward hugging me while we were actually in bed together. He kept patting my shoulder and leaning in towards me. 'It'll be all right.'

'How can it be? I've lost my job and my place to live and the man I loved. I'll have no references, because Mr Gopnik thinks I'm a thief, and I don't even know which country I belong in.' I wiped my nose on my sleeve. 'I've messed up everything again and I don't know why I even bother trying to be something more than I was because every time I do it ends in disaster.'

'You're just tired. It'll be all right. It will.'

'Like it was with Will?'

'Aw . . . that was completely different. Come on . . .' Nathan hugged me then, pulling me into his shoulder, his big arm around me. I cried until I couldn't cry any more and then, just as he said, exhausted by the day's – and night's – events, I must have fallen asleep.

I woke eight hours later to find myself alone in Nathan's room. It took me a couple of minutes to work out where I was and then the previous day's events hit me. I lay under the duvet for a while, curled up in a foetal ball, wondering idly if I could just stay there for a year or two until my life had somehow sorted itself out.

I checked my phone: two missed calls and a series of messages from Josh that seemed to have come through in a clump late the previous evening.

Hey, Louisa – hope you're feeling okay. Kept thinking about your dance and bursting out laughing at work! What a night! Jx

You okay? Just checking you did make it home and didn't take another nap in Times Square ;-) Jx

Okay. So it's now gone ten thirty. I'm going to guess you headed to bed to sleep it off. Hope I didn't offend you. I was just kidding around. Give me a call x

That night, with its boxing match and the glittering lights of Times Square, already seemed a lifetime ago. I climbed out of bed, showered and dressed, setting my belongings in the corner of the bathroom. It limited the space somewhat but I thought it was safer, just in case a stray Gopnik happened to poke a head around Nathan's door.

I texted him to ask when it would be safe for me to go out and he sent back *NOW. Both in study.* I slipped out of the apartment and down to the service entrance, walking swiftly past Ashok with my head low. He was talking to a delivery man but I saw his head spin and heard his 'Hey! Louisa!' but I had already gone.

Manhattan was frozen and grey, one of those bleak days when ice particles seem to hang in the air, the chill pierces your bones, and only eyes, occasionally noses, are visible. I walked with my head down and my hat rammed low, not sure where I was going. I ended up back at the diner, reasoning that everything looked better after breakfast. I sat in a booth by myself and looked out at the commuters with somewhere to go and forced down a muffin, because it was the cheapest, most filling thing on the menu, trying to ignore the fact that it was claggy and tasteless in my mouth.

At nine forty a text arrived. Michael. My heart leapt. *Hi, Louisa. Mr Gopnik will pay you to the end of the month in lieu of notice. All your healthcare benefits cease at that point. Your green card is unaffected. I'm sure you understand this is obviously beyond what he was required to do, given the violation of your contract, but Agnes intervened on your behalf.*

Best, Michael

'Nice of her,' I muttered. *Thank you for letting me know*, I typed. He didn't respond further.

And then my phone pinged again. *Okay, Louisa. Now I'm worried I did do something to upset you. Or maybe you got lost headed back to Central Park? Please give me a call. JX*

I met Josh near his office, one of those buildings in Midtown that are so tall that if you stand on the sidewalk and look up, a little part of your brain suggests you should probably topple over. He came striding towards me, a soft grey scarf wrapped around his neck. As I climbed off the small wall I had been sitting on he walked straight up and gave me a hug.

'I can't believe this. C'mon. Ah, boy, you're freezing. Let's go grab something warm for you to eat.'

We sat in a steamy, cacophonous taco bar two blocks away while a constant stream of office workers filed through and servers barked orders. I told him, as I had Nathan, the bare bones of the story. 'I can't really say any more, just that I didn't steal anything. I wouldn't. I've never stolen anything. Well, apart from once when I was eight. Mum still brings it up occasionally, if she needs an example of how I nearly ended up on a path to a life of crime.' I tried to smile.

He frowned. 'So does this mean you're going to have to leave New York?'

'I don't really know what I'm going to do. But I can't imagine the Gopniks are going to give me a reference, and I don't know how I can support myself here. I mean, I don't have a job and Manhattan hotels are a little out of my price range . . .' I had looked online in the diner at local rentals and nearly spat out my coffee. The tiny room I had felt so ambivalent about when I had first arrived with the Gopniks turned out to be affordable only with an executive salary. No wonder that cockroach hadn't wanted to move.

'Would it help you to stay at mine?'

I looked up from my taco.

'Just temporarily. It doesn't have to mean a whole boyfriend-girlfriend thing. I have a sofa-bed in the front room. You probably don't remember.' He gave me a small smile. I had forgotten how Americans actually genuinely invited people into their homes. Unlike English people, who would issue an invitation but emigrate at short notice if you said you were going to take them up on it.

'That's really kind. But, Josh, it would complicate things. I think I might have to go home, for now at least. Just till another position comes up.'

Josh stared at his plate. 'Timing sucks, huh?'

'Yup.'

'I was looking forward to more of those dances.'

I pulled a face. 'Oh, God. The dance thing. I . . . Do I . . . want to ask you what happened the other night?'

'You really don't remember?'

'Only the Times Square bits. Maybe getting into a taxi.'

He raised his eyebrows. 'Oho! Oh, Louisa Clark. It's pretty tempting to start teasing you here, but nothing happened. Like *that*, anyway. Unless licking my neck is really your thing.'

'But I wasn't wearing my clothes when I woke up.'

'That's because you insisted on removing them during your dance. You announced, once we got to my building, that you would like to express your last few days through the medium of freeform dance, and while I followed on behind, you shed items of clothing from the lobby to the living room.'

'I took my own clothes off?'

'And very charmingly too. There were . . . flourishes.'

I had a sudden image of myself twirling, a coy leg thrust

out from behind a curtain, the feel of cool window glass on my backside. I didn't know whether to laugh or cry. My cheeks a furious red, I covered my face with my hands.

'I have to say, as a drunk you make a highly entertaining one.'

'And . . . when we got into your bedroom?'

'Oh, by that stage you were down to your underwear. And then you sang a crazy song – something about a monkey, or a molahonkey or something? Then you fell asleep very abruptly in a little heap on the floor. So I put a T-shirt on you and put you in my bed. And I slept on the sofa-bed.'

'I'm so sorry. And thank you.'

'My pleasure.' He smiled, and his eyes twinkled. 'Most of my dates are not half that entertaining.'

I dipped my head over my mug. 'You know, these last few days I've felt like I'm permanently about two degrees from either laughing or crying and right now I slightly want to do both.'

'Are you staying at Nathan's tonight?'

'I think so.'

'Okay. Well, don't do anything hasty. Let me put a few calls in before you book that ticket. See if there are any openings anywhere.'

'You really think there might be?' He was always so confident. It was one of the things that most reminded me of Will.

'There's always something. I'll call you later.'

And then he kissed me. He did it so casually that I almost didn't register what he was doing. He leant forward and kissed me on the lips, like it was something he'd done a million times before, like it was the natural end to all our lunch dates. And then, before I had time to be startled, he let go of my fingers and wound his scarf around his neck. 'Okay. I gotta go. Couple of big meetings this afternoon. Keep your chin up.' He smiled, his high-wattage perfect smile, and headed back to his office, leaving me on my high plastic stool, my mouth hanging open.

I didn't tell Nathan what had happened. I checked in with him by text that it was okay to come home, and he told me the Gopniks were headed out again at seven so I should probably leave it till a quarter past. I walked in the cold and sat in the diner and finally returned home to find Ilaria had left me some soup in a Thermos and two of the soft scones they called biscuits. Nathan was out on a date that evening and gone in the morning when I woke. He left me a note to say he hoped I was okay and reassured me that it was fine for me to stay. I only snored a little bit, apparently.

I had spent months wishing I had more free time. Now that I had it, I found the city was not a friendly place without money to burn. I left the building when it was safe to do so and walked the streets until my toes grew too cold, then had a cup of tea in a Starbucks, stretching that out for a couple of hours and using the free WiFi to search for jobs. There wasn't much for someone with no references, unless I was experienced in the food industry.

I began to layer up, now that my life did not involve mere minutes spent in the open air between heated lobbies and warm limousines. I wore a blue fisherman's jumper, my workman's dungarees, heavy boots and a pair of tights and socks underneath. Not elegant, but that was no longer my priority.

At lunchtime I headed for a fast-food joint where the burgers were cheap and nobody noticed a solitary diner eking out a bun for another hour or two. Department stores were a depressing no-no, as I no longer felt able to spend money, although there were good Ladies and WiFi. Twice I headed down to the Vintage Clothes Emporium, where the girls commiserated with me but exchanged the slightly tense looks of those who suspect they are going to be asked a favour. 'If you hear of any jobs going – especially like yours – can you let me know?' I said, when I could no longer browse the rails.

'Sweetheart, we barely make rent or we'd have you here like a shot.' Lydia blew a sympathetic smoke ring at the ceiling and looked to her sister, who batted it away.

'You'll make the clothes stink. Look, we'll ask around,' Angelica said. She said it in a way that made me think I was not the first person who had asked.

I trudged out of the shop feeling despondent. I didn't know what to do with myself. There was nowhere quiet where I could just sit for a while, nowhere that offered space where I could work out what to do next. If you didn't have money in New York, you were a refugee, unwelcome anywhere for too long. Perhaps, I mused, it was time to admit defeat and buy that plane ticket.

And then it hit me.

I took the subway up to Washington Heights and got off a short walk from the library. It felt, for the first time in days, like I was somewhere familiar, somewhere that welcomed me. This would be my refuge, my springboard to a new future. I headed up the stone steps. On the first floor I found an unoccupied computer terminal. I sat down heavily, took a breath and, for the first time since the Gopnik debacle, I closed my eyes and just let my thoughts settle.

I felt some long-held tension ease away from my shoulders and allowed myself to float on the low murmur of people around me, a world away from the chaos and bustle of outside. I don't know if it was just the joy of being surrounded by books, and quiet, but I felt like an equal here, inconspicuous, a brain, a keyboard, just another person searching for information.

And there, for the first time, I found myself asking what the hell had just happened anyway. Agnes had betrayed me. My months with the Gopniks suddenly felt like a fever dream, time out of time, a strange, compacted blur of limousines and gilded interiors, a world onto which a curtain had been briefly drawn back, then abruptly closed again.

This, in contrast, was real. This, I told myself, was where I could come each day until I had worked out my strategy. Here I would find the steps to forge a new route upwards.

Knowledge is power, Clark.

'Ma'am.'

I opened my eyes to find a security guard in front of me. He stooped so that he was looking directly into my face. 'You can't sleep in here.'

'What?'

'You can't sleep in here.'

'I wasn't sleeping,' I said indignantly. 'I was thinking.'

'Maybe think with your eyes open then, huh? Or you got to leave.' He turned away, murmuring something into a walkie-talkie. It took me a moment to register what he had really been saying to me. Two people at a nearby table looked up at me and then away. My face flushed. I saw the awkward glances of other library users around me. I looked down at my clothes, at my denim dungarees with the fleece-lined workman's boots and my woollen hat. Not quite Bergdorf Goodman but hardly Vagrant City.

'Hey! I'm not homeless!' I called out at his departing back. 'I have protested on behalf of this place! Mister! I AM NOT HOMELESS!' Two women looked up from their quiet conversation, one raising an eyebrow.

And then it occurred to me: I was.

22

Dear Ma,

Sorry it's been a while since I've been in contact. We're working round the clock on this Chinese deal here, and I'm often up all night coping with different time zones. If I sound a bit jaded, it's because I feel it. I got the bonus, which was nice (am sending Georgina a chunk so she can buy that car she wants), but over the last few weeks I've realized ultimately I'm not really feeling it here any more.

It's not that I don't like the lifestyle – and you know I've never been afraid of hard work. I just miss so many things about England. I miss the humour. I miss Sunday lunch. I miss hearing English accents, at least the non-phoney kind (you would not believe how many people end up plummier than Her Maj). I like being able to pop across for weekends in Paris or Barcelona or Rome. And the expat thing is pretty tedious. In the goldfish bowl of finance here you just end up running into the same faces whether you're in Nantucket or Manhattan. I know you think I have a type, but here it's almost comical: blonde hair, size zero, identikit wardrobes, off to the same Pilates classes . . .

So here's the thing: do you remember Rupe? My old friend from Churchill's? He says there's an opening at his firm. His boss is flying out in a couple of weeks and wants to meet me. If all goes well I might be back in England sooner than you think.

I've loved New York. But everything has its time, and I think I've had mine.

Love, W x

Over the next few days I rang up about numerous jobs on Craigslist, but the nice-sounding woman with the nanny job put the phone down on me when she heard I had no references, and the food-server jobs were already gone by the time I called. The shoe-shop assistant position was still available but the man I spoke to told me the wage would be two dollars an hour lower than advertised because of my lack of relevant retail experience, and I calculated that would barely leave me enough for travel. I spent my mornings in the diner, my afternoons in the library at Washington Heights, which was quiet and warm and, apart from that one security guard, nobody eyed me like they were waiting for me to start singing drunkenly or pee in a corner.

I would meet Josh for lunch in the noodle bar by his office every couple of days, update him on my job-hunting activities and try to ignore that, next to his immaculately dressed, go-getting presence, I felt increasingly like a grubby, sofa-hopping loser. 'You're going to be fine, Louisa. Just hang in there,' he would say, and kiss me as he left, like somehow we had already agreed to be boyfriend and girlfriend. I couldn't think about the significance of this along with everything else I had to think about so I just figured that it was not actually a *bad* thing, like so much in my life was, and could therefore be parked for now. Besides, he always tasted pleasingly minty.

I couldn't stay in Nathan's room much longer. The previous morning I had woken with his big arm slung over me and something hard pressing into the small of my back. The cushion wall had apparently gone awry, migrating to a chaotic heap at our feet. I froze, attempted to wriggle discreetly out of his sleeping grasp and he had opened his eyes, looked at me, then leapt out of bed as if he had been stung, a pillow clutched in front of his groin. 'Mate. I didn't mean – I wasn't trying to –'

'No idea what you're talking about!' I insisted, pulling a sweatshirt over my head. I couldn't look at him in case it –

He hopped from foot to foot. 'I was just – I didn't realize I . . . Ah, mate. Ah, Jeez.'

'It's fine! I needed to get up anyway!' I bolted and hid in the tiny bathroom for ten minutes, my cheeks burning, while I listened to him crashing around and getting dressed. He was gone before I came out.

What was the point in trying to stay after all? I could only sleep in Nathan's room for a night or two more at most. It looked like the best I could expect elsewhere, even if I was lucky enough to find alternative employment, was a minimum-wage job and a cockroach- and bedbug-infested flat-share. At least if I went home I could sleep on my own sofa. Perhaps Treen and Eddie were besotted enough with each other that they would move in together and then I could have my flat back. I tried not to think about how that would feel – the empty rooms and the return to where I had been six months earlier, not to mention the proximity to Sam's workplace. Every siren I heard passing would be a bitter reminder of what I had lost.

It had started to rain, but I slowed as I approached the building and glanced up at the Gopniks' windows from under my woollen hat, registering that the lights were still on, even though Nathan had told me they were out at some gala event. Life had moved on for them as smoothly as if I had never existed. Perhaps Ilaria was up there now, vacuuming, or tutting at Agnes's magazines scattered over the sofa cushions. The Gopniks – and this city – had sucked me in and spat me right out. Despite all her fond words, Agnes had discarded me as comprehensively and completely as a lizard sheds its skin – and not cast a backward look.

If I had never come, I thought angrily, I might still have a home. And a job.

If I had never come, I would still have Sam.

The thought caused my mood to darken further and I hunched my shoulders and thrust my freezing hands into my pockets, prepared to head back to my temporary accommodation, a room I had to sneak into, and a bed I had to share with someone who was terrified of touching me. My life had become ridiculous, a looping bad joke. I rubbed my eyes, feeling the cold rain on my skin. I would book my ticket tonight and I would go home on the next available flight. I would suck it up and start again. I didn't really have a choice.

Everything has its time.

It was then that I spotted Dean Martin. He was standing on the covered carpet that led up to the apartment building, shivering without his coat on and glancing around as if deciding where to go next. I took a step closer, peering into the lobby, but the night man was busy sorting through some packages and hadn't seen him. I couldn't see Mrs De Witt anywhere. I moved swiftly, leant down and scooped him up before he had time to grasp what I was doing. Holding his wriggling body at arms' length, I ran in and swiftly up the back stairs to take him back to her, nodding at the night man as I went.

It was a valid reason for being there, but I emerged from the stairs onto the Gopniks' corridor with trepidation: if they returned unexpectedly and saw me, would Mr Gopnik conclude I was up to no good? Would he accuse me of trespass? Did it count if I was on their corridor? These questions buzzed around my head as Dean Martin writhed furiously and snapped at my arms.

'Mrs De Witt?' I called softly, peering behind me. Her front door was ajar again and I stepped inside, lifting my voice. 'Mrs De Witt? Your dog got out again.' I could hear the television blaring down the corridor and took a few steps further inside.

'Mrs De Witt?'

When no answer came, I closed the door gently behind me and put Dean Martin on the floor, keen not to hold him for any longer than I had to. He immediately trotted off towards the living room.

'Mrs De Witt?'

I saw her leg first, sticking out on the floor beside the upright chair. It took me a second to register what I was seeing. Then I ran round to the front of the chair and threw myself to the floor, my ear to her mouth. 'Mrs De Witt?' I said. 'Can you hear me?'

She was breathing. But her face was the blue-white of marble. I wondered briefly how long she had been there.

'Mrs De Witt? Wake up! Oh, God . . . wake up!'

I ran around the apartment, looking for the phone. It was in the hallway, situated on a table that also housed several phone books. I rang 911 and explained what I had found.

'There's a team on its way, ma'am,' came the voice. 'Can you stay with the patient and let them in?'

'Yes, yes, yes. But she's really old and frail and she looks like she's out cold. Please come quickly.' I ran and fetched a quilt from her bedroom and placed it over her, trying to remember what Sam had told me about treating the elderly who had taken a fall. One of the biggest risks was their growing chilled from lying undiscovered for hours. And she felt so cold, even with the full blast of the building's central heating. I sat on the floor beside her and took her icy hand in mine, stroking it gently, trying to let her know somebody was there. A sudden thought crossed my mind: if she died, would they blame me? Mr Gopnik would testify that I was a criminal, after all. I wondered briefly about whether to run, but I couldn't leave her.

It was during this tortured train of thought that she opened an eye.

'Mrs De Witt?'

She blinked at me, as if trying to work out what had happened.

'It's Louisa. From across the corridor. Are you in pain?'

'I don't know . . . My . . . my wrist . . .' she said weakly.

'The ambulance is coming. You're going to be okay. It's all going to be okay.'

She looked blankly at me, as if trying to piece together who I was, whether what I was saying made any sense. And then her brow furrowed. 'Where is he? Dean Martin? Where's my dog?'

I scanned the room. Over in the corner the little dog was parked on his backside, noisily investigating his genitals. He looked up when he heard his name and adjusted himself back into a standing position. 'He's right here. He's okay.'

She closed her eyes again, relieved. 'Will you look after him? If I have to go to the hospital? I am going to the hospital, aren't I?'

'Yes. And of course.'

'There's a folder in my bedroom that you need to give them. On my bedside table.'

'No problem. I'll do that.'

I closed my hands around hers, and while Dean Martin eyed me warily from the doorway – well, me and the fireplace – we waited in silence for the paramedics to come.

I travelled to the hospital with Mrs De Witt, leaving Dean Martin in the apartment as he wasn't allowed in the ambulance. Once her paperwork was done and she was settled, I headed for the Lavery, reassuring her that I would look after the dog. I would be back in the morning to let her know how he was doing. Her tiny blue eyes filled with tears as she issued croaking instructions as to his food, his walks, his various likes and dislikes, until the paramedic shushed her, insisting that she needed to rest.

I caught the subway back to Fifth Avenue, simultaneously bone-weary and buzzing with adrenalin. I let myself in, using the key Mrs De Witt had given me. Dean Martin was waiting in the hallway, standing four-square in the middle of the floor, his compact body radiating suspicion.

'Good evening, young man! Would you like some supper?' I said, as if I were his old friend and not someone vaguely expecting to lose a chunk out of one of my lower legs. I walked past him with simulated confidence to the kitchen, where I tried to decipher the instructions as to the correct amount of cooked chicken and kibble that I had scribbled on the back of my hand.

I placed the food in his dish and pushed it towards him with my foot.

'There you go! Enjoy!'

He stared at me, his bulbous eyes sullen and mutinous, forehead rippling with wrinkles of concern.

'Food! Yum!'

Still he stared.

'Not hungry yet, huh?' I said. I edged my way out of the kitchen. I needed to work out where I was going to sleep.

Mrs De Witt's apartment was approximately half the square footage of the Gopniks', but that wasn't to say it was small. It comprised a vast living room with floor-to-ceiling windows overlooking Central Park, its interior decorated in bronze and smoked glass, as if it had last been done some time around the days of Studio 54. There was a more traditional dining room, packed with antiques sporting a layer of dust, which suggested it hadn't been used in generations, a melamine and Formica kitchen, a utility room, and four bedrooms, including the main bedroom, which had a bathroom and sizeable dressing room leading off it. The bathrooms were even older than the Gopniks' and let loose unpredictable torrents of spluttering water. I walked round the apartment with the peculiar silent reverence that comes with being in the uninhabited house of a person you don't know very well.

When I reached the main bedroom, I drew a breath. It was filled, three and a half walls of it, with clothes neatly stacked on racks, hanging in plastic from cushioned hangers. The dressing room was a riot of colour and fabric, punctuated above and below by shelves with piles of handbags, boxed hats and matching shoes. I walked slowly around the perimeter, running my fingertips along the materials, pausing occasionally to tug gently at a sleeve or push back a hanger to see each outfit better.

And it wasn't just these two rooms. As the little pug trotted suspiciously after me, I walked through two of the other bedrooms and found more – row upon row of dresses, trouser suits, coats and boas, in long, air-conditioned cupboards. There were labels from Givenchy, Biba, Harrods and Macy's, shoes from Saks Fifth Avenue and Chanel. There were labels I had never heard – French, Italian, even Russian – clothes from multiple eras: neat little Kennedy-esque boxy suits, flowing kaftans, sharp-shouldered jackets. I peered into boxes and found pillbox hats and turbans, huge jade-framed sunglasses and delicate strings of pearls. They were not arranged in any particular order so I simply dived in, pulling things out at random, unfolding tissue paper, feeling the cloth, the weight, the musty scent of old perfume, lifting them out to admire cut and pattern.

On what wall space was still visible above the shelves I could just make out framed clothes designs, magazine covers from the fifties and sixties with beaming, angular models in psychedelic shift dresses, or impossibly trim shirt-waisters. I must have been there an hour before I realized I hadn't located another bed. But in the fourth bedroom there it was, covered with discarded items of clothing – a narrow single, possibly dating back to the fifties, with an ornate walnut headboard, a matching wardrobe and chest of drawers. And there were four more racks, of the more basic kind you would find in a changing room, and alongside them, boxes and boxes of accessories – costume jewellery, belts and scarves. I moved some carefully from the bed and lay down, feeling the mattress give immediately as exhausted mattresses do, but I didn't care. I would basically be sleeping in a wardrobe. For the first time in days I forgot to be depressed.

For one night at least, I was in Wonderland.

The following morning I fed and walked Dean Martin, trying not to be offended by the way he travelled the whole way down Fifth Avenue at an angle, one eye permanently trained on me as if waiting for some transgression, and then I left for the hospital, keen to reassure Mrs De Witt that her baby was fine, if permanently braced for savagery. I decided I probably wouldn't tell her that the only way I'd been able to persuade him to eat was to grate Parmigiano-Reggiano onto his breakfast.

When I arrived at the hospital I was relieved to find her a more human pink, although oddly unformed without her familiar make-up and set hair. She had indeed fractured her wrist and was scheduled for surgery, after which she would be in the hospital for another week, due to what they called 'complicating factors'. When I revealed that I wasn't a member of her family they declined to say more.

'Can you look after Dean Martin?' she said, her face creased with anxiety. He had plainly been her main concern in the hours I had been gone. 'Perhaps they could let you pop in and out to see him in the day? Do you think Ashok could take him for walks? He'll be terribly lonely. He's not used to being without me.'

I had wondered whether it was wise to tell her the truth. But truth had been in short supply in our building lately and I wanted everything out in the open.

'Mrs De Witt,' I began, 'I have to tell you something. I – I don't work for the Gopniks any more. They fired me.'

Her head moved back against her pillow a little. She mouthed the word as if it were unfamiliar. '*Fired?*'

I swallowed. 'They thought I had stolen money from them. All I can tell you is that I didn't. But I feel it's only right to tell you because you may decide that you don't want my help.'

'Well,' she said weakly. And again. 'Well.'

We sat there in silence for a while.

Then she narrowed her eyes. 'But you didn't do it.'

'No, ma'am.'

'Do you have another job?'

'No, ma'am. I'm trying to find one.'

She shook her head. 'Gopnik is a fool. Where are you living?'

I looked sideways. 'Uh . . . I'm . . . well, I'm actually staying in Nathan's room for now. But it's not ideal. We're not – you know – romantically involved. And obviously the Gopniks don't exactly know . . .'

'Well, it sounds like an arrangement that might suit us both rather well. Would you look after my dog? And perhaps conduct your job-hunting from my side of the corridor? Just till I come home?'

'Mrs De Witt, I'd be delighted.' I couldn't hide my smile.

'You'll have to look after him better than you did before, of course. I'm going to give you notes. I'm sure he's terribly unsettled.'

'I'll do whatever you say.'

'And I'll need you to come here daily to let me know how he is. That's very important.'

'Of course.'

With that decided, she seemed to subside a little with relief. She closed her eyes. 'No fool like an old fool,' she murmured. I wasn't sure if she was talking about Mr Gopnik, herself or someone else entirely, so I waited until she had fallen asleep, then headed back to her apartment.

All that week I devoted myself to the care of a boggle-eyed, suspicious, cranky, six-year-old pug. We walked four times a day, I grated Parmesan onto his breakfast, and several days in, he ceased his habit of standing in any room I was in and staring at me with his brow furrowed, as if waiting for me to do something unmentionable, and simply lay down a few feet away, panting gently. I was still a little wary of him but I felt sorry for him too – the only person he loved had vanished abruptly and there was nothing I could do to reassure him that she would be coming home again.

And, besides, it was kind of nice to be in the building without feeling like a criminal. Ashok, who had been away for a few days, listened to my description of this turn of events with shock, outrage, then delight. 'Man, it's lucky you found him! He could have just wandered off and then nobody would have known she was even on the floor!' He shuddered theatrically. 'When she's back I'm gonna start checking in on her every day, making sure she's okay.'

We looked at each other.

'Nothing would make her more furious,' I said.

'Yup, she'd hate it,' he said, and went back to work.

Nathan pretended to be sad that he had his room back to himself, and brought my stuff over with almost unseemly haste to 'save me a journey' of approximately six yards. I think he just wanted to be sure I was really going. He dropped my bags and peered around the apartment, gazing in amazement at the walls of clothes. 'What a load of junk!' he exclaimed. 'It's like the world's biggest Oxfam shop. Boy, I'd hate to be the house-clearance company having to go through this lot when the old lady pops her clogs.' I kept my smile fixed and level.

He told Ilaria, who knocked on my door the next day for news of Mrs De Witt, then asked me to take her some muffins she had baked. 'The food in these hospitals would make you sick,' she said, patted my arm, and left at a brisk trot before Dean Martin could bite her.

I heard Agnes playing the piano from across the hall, once a beautiful piece that sounded relaxed and melancholy, once something impassioned and anguished. I thought of the many times Mrs De Witt had hobbled across and furiously demanded an end to the noise. This time the music ended abruptly without her intervention, Agnes seemingly slamming her hands down on the keys. Occasionally I would hear raised voices, and it took me a few days to convince my body that my own adrenalin didn't need to rise with them, that they no longer had anything to do with me.

I passed Mr Gopnik just once, in the main lobby. He didn't see me, then performed a double-take, apparently primed to object to my presence there. I lifted my chin and held up the end of Dean Martin's lead. 'I'm helping Mrs De Witt with her dog,' I said, with as much dignity as I could manage. He glanced down at Dean Martin, set his jaw, then turned away as if he hadn't heard me. Michael, at his side, glanced at me, then turned back to his mobile phone.

Josh came on Friday night after work, bringing takeout and a bottle of wine. He was still in his suit – working late all week, he said. He and a colleague were competing for a promotion so he was there for fourteen hours a day, and planned to go in on Saturday too. He peered around the apartment, raising his eyebrows at the décor. 'Well, dog-sitting was one job opening I certainly hadn't considered,' he observed, as Dean Martin trailed suspiciously at his heels. He walked around the living room slowly, picking up the onyx ashtray and the sinuous African-woman sculpture, putting them down, peering intently at the gilded artwork on the walls.

'It wasn't top of my list either.' I laid a trail of doggy treats to the main bedroom and shut the little dog in until he'd calmed down. 'But I'm really okay with it.'

'So how you doing?'

'Better!' I said, heading to the kitchen. I had wanted to show Josh I was more than the scruffy, intermittently drunk jobseeker he had been meeting the past week so I had dressed up in my black Chanel-style dress with the white collar and cuffs and my emerald fake-crocodile Mary Janes, my hair sleek and blow-dried into a neat bob.

'Well, you look cute,' he said, following me. He put his bottle and bag on the side in the kitchen, then walked over to me, standing just a couple of inches away, so that his face filled my vision. 'And, you know, not homeless. Which is always a good look.'

'Temporarily, anyway.'

'So does this mean you'll be sticking around a little longer?'

'Who knows?'

He was mere inches from me. I had a sudden sensory memory of burying my face in his neck a week previously.

'You're going pink, Louisa Clark.'

'That's because you're extremely close to me.'

'I do that to you?' His voice dropped, his eyebrow lifted. He took a step closer, then put his hands on the worktop, at either side of my hips.

'Apparently,' I said, but it came out as almost a cough. And then he dropped his lips to mine and kissed me. He kissed me and I leant back against the kitchen units and closed my eyes, absorbing the mint taste of his mouth, the slightly strange feel of his body against mine, the unfamiliar hands closing over my own. I wondered if this was what it would have been like to kiss Will before his accident. And then I thought that I would never kiss Sam again. And then I thought that it was quite bad form to think about kissing other men when you had a perfectly nice one kissing you at that very moment. And I pulled my head back a little, and he stopped and looked into my eyes, trying to gauge what it meant.

'I'm sorry,' I said. 'It's – it's just all kind of soon. I really like you but –'

'But you only just broke up with the other guy.'

'Sam.'

'Who is clearly an idiot. And not good enough for you.'

'Josh . . .'

He let his forehead tip forward so that it rested against mine. I didn't let go of his hand.

'It just all feels a bit complicated still. I'm sorry.'

He closed his eyes for a moment, then opened them again. 'Would you tell me if I was wasting my time?' he said.

'You're not wasting your time. It's just . . . it was barely two weeks ago.'

'There's a lot that's happened in those two weeks.'

'Well, then, who knows where we'll be in another two weeks?'

'You said "we".'

'I suppose I did.'

He nodded, as if this were a satisfactory answer. 'You know,' he said, almost to himself, 'I have a feeling about us, Louisa Clark. And I'm never wrong about these things.'

And then, before I could respond, he let go of my hand and walked over to the cupboards, opening and closing them in search of plates. When he turned round, his smile was brilliant. 'Shall we eat?'

I learnt a lot about Josh that evening. I learnt about his Boston upbringing, the baseball career his half-Irish businessman father had made him give up because he felt that sport would not secure a long-lasting income. His mother, unusually among her peers, was an attorney who had held on to her job throughout his childhood and, in their retirement years, both his parents were adjusting to being in the house together. It was, apparently, driving them completely nuts. 'We're a family of doers, you know? So Dad has already taken on some executive role at the golf club and Mom is mentoring kids at the local high school. Anything so they don't have to sit there looking at each other.' He had two brothers, both older, one who ran a Mercedes dealership just outside Weymouth, Massachusetts, and another who was an accountant, like my sister. They were a close family, and competitive, and he had hated his brothers with the impotent fury of a tortured youngest sibling until they left home, after which he found he missed them with a gnawing and unexpected pain. 'Mom says it was because I lost my yardstick, the thing I judged everything by.'

Both brothers were now married and settled with two

kids apiece. The family converged for holidays and every summer rented the same house in Nantucket. In his teens he had resented it, but now it was a week he looked forward to more each year.

'It's great. The kids and the hanging out and the boat . . . You should come,' he said, casually helping himself to more *char siu bau*. He talked without self-consciousness, a man used to things working out the way he wanted them to.

'To a family thing? I thought men in New York were all about casual dating.'

'Yeah, well, I've done all that. And, besides, I'm not from New York.'

He was a man who seemingly threw himself at everything. He worked a million hours a week, was hungry for promotion, and went to the gym before six a.m. He played baseball with the office team, and was thinking about volunteering to mentor at a local high school, like his mother did, but was worried that his work schedule meant he couldn't commit to a regular time. He was shot through with the American dream, like a stick of rock – you worked hard, you succeeded and then you gave back. I tried not to keep drawing comparisons with Will. I listened to him and felt half admiring, half exhausted.

He drew a picture of his future in the air between us – an apartment in the Village, maybe a weekend place in the Hamptons if he could get his bonuses to the right level. He wanted a boat. He wanted kids. He wanted to retire early. He wanted to make a million dollars before he was thirty. He punctuated much of this talk with the waving of chopsticks and the phrase 'You should come!' or 'You'd love it!' and I was partly flattered, but mostly grateful that this implied he wasn't offended by my earlier reticence.

He left at ten thirty, since he planned to get up at five, and we stood in the hallway by the front door, with Dean Martin on guard a few feet away.

'So, are we going to be able to squeeze in lunch? What with the whole dog-and-hospital thing?'

'We could perhaps see each other one evening?'

'"We could perhaps see each other one evening,"' he mimicked softly. 'I love your English accent.'

'I haven't got an accent,' I said. 'You have.'

'And you make me laugh. Not many girls make me laugh.'

'Ah. Then you've just not met the right girls.'

'Oh, I think I have.' He stopped talking then, and looked up at the heavens, as if he were trying to prevent himself doing something. And then he smiled, as if acknowledging the slight ridiculousness of two adults nearing their thirties trying not to kiss in a doorway. And it was the smile that did it for me.

I reached up and touched the back of his neck, very lightly. And then I went up on tiptoe and kissed him. I told myself there was no point in dwelling on something that was gone. I told myself two weeks was certainly long enough to make a decision, especially when you had barely seen that other person for months beforehand and had pretty much been single anyway. I told myself I had to move on.

Josh didn't hesitate. He kissed me back, his hands sliding slowly up my spine, manoeuvring me against the wall, so that I was pinned, pleasurably, against him. He kissed me and I made myself stop thinking and just give in to sensation, his unfamiliar body, narrower and slightly harder than the one I had known, the intensity of his mouth on mine. This handsome American. We were both a little dazed when we came up for air.

'If I don't go now . . .' he said, stepping back, and blinked hard, raising his hand to the back of his neck.

I grinned. I suspected my lipstick was halfway across my face. 'You have an early start. I'll speak to you tomorrow.' I opened the door and, with a last kiss on my cheek, he stepped out into the main corridor.

When I closed it, Dean Martin was still staring at me. 'What?' I said. 'What? I'm single.'

He lowered his head in disgust, turned, and pottered towards the kitchen.

23

To: MrandMrsBernardClark@yahoo.com
From: BusyBee@gmail.com

Hi Mum,

Lovely to hear that you and Maria had such a nice tea at Fortnum & Mason on Maria's birthday. Although, yes, I agree, that is a LOT for a packet of biscuits and I'm sure both you and Maria could do better scones at home. Yours are very light. And, no, the toilet thing in the theatre was not good. I'm sure as an attendant herself she has a very keen eye for things like that. I'm glad someone is looking out for all your . . . hygiene needs.

All fine here. New York is pretty chilly right now, but you know me, clothing for every occasion! There are a few things up in the air at work but hopefully all will be sorted by the time we speak. And, yes, I'm totally fine about Sam. Just one of those things, indeed.

Sorry to hear about Granddad. I hope when he's feeling better you can start your night classes again.

I miss you all. A lot.

Lots of love,

Lou xx

PS Probably best if you email or write to me via Nathan just now as we're having some issues with the post.

Mrs De Witt came out of hospital ten days after she was admitted, squinting in the unfamiliar daylight, her right arm in a plaster cast that seemed too heavy for her thin frame. I brought her home in a taxi. Ashok met her at the kerb and helped her slowly up the steps. For once she didn't crab at him or bat him away, but walked gingerly, as if balance were no longer a given. I had brought the outfit she'd demanded – a 1970s pale blue Céline trouser suit, a daffodil yellow blouse and a pale pink wool beret – with some of the cosmetics that were on her dresser and sat on the side of her hospital bed to help her apply them. She said her own attempts with her left hand made her look like she had drunk three Sidecars for breakfast.

Dean Martin, delighted, jogged and snuffled at her heels, looking up at her, then back at me pointedly, as if to tell me I could leave now. We had reached something of a truce, the dog and I. He ate his meals and curled up on my lap every evening, and I think he had even started to enjoy the slightly faster pace and longer reach of our walks because his little tail wagged wildly whenever he saw me pick up the lead.

Mrs De Witt was overjoyed to see him, if joyousness could be conveyed by a series of complaints about my obvious mismanagement of his care, by the fact that within a space of twelve hours she had deemed him both over- and underweight, and by an ongoing, crooning apology to him for leaving him in my inadequate hands. 'My poor baby. Did I leave you with a stranger? I did? And she didn't care for you properly? It's okay. Momma's home now. It's all okay.'

She was plainly delighted to be home, but I can't pretend I wasn't anxious. She seemed to require a prodigious number of pills – even by American standards – and I wondered if she had some kind of brittle-bone syndrome: it seemed an awful lot just for a broken wrist. I told Treena, who said in England you would have been prescribed a couple of painkillers and told not to lift anything heavy, and laughed heartily.

But Mrs De Witt, I felt, had been left even frailer by her time in hospital. She was pale and coughed repeatedly, and her tailored clothes gaped in odd places around her body. When I cooked her macaroni cheese, she ate four or five neat mouthfuls and pronounced it delicious but declined to eat any more. 'I think my stomach shrank in that awful place. Probably trying to shut itself off from their abysmal food.'

She took half a day to reacquaint herself fully with her apartment, tottering slowly from room to room, reminding and reassuring herself that everything was as it should be – I tried not to view this as her checking I hadn't stolen anything. Finally she sat down on her tall, upholstered chair and let out a little sigh. 'I can't tell you how good it is to be home.' She said it as if she had half expected not to make it back. And then she nodded off. I thought for the hundredth time about Granddad and how lucky he was to have Mum caring for him.

Mrs De Witt was plainly too frail to be left alone, and apparently in no hurry to see me go. So, with no actual discussion between us, I simply stayed on. I helped her wash and dress and cooked her meals and, for the first week at least, walked Dean Martin several times a day. Towards the end of that week, I found she had cleared me a little space in the fourth bedroom, moving books and items of clothing one at a time to reveal a bedside table that was usable or a shelf on which I could put my things. I commandeered her guest bathroom for myself, scrubbing it thoroughly and running the taps until the water was clear. Then, discreetly, I set about cleaning all those areas of her own bathroom and kitchen that her failing eyesight had begun to miss.

I took her to the hospital for her follow-up appointments, and sat outside with Dean Martin until I was asked to return for her. I booked her an appointment at her hairdresser and waited while her thin, silvery hair was returned to its former neat waves, a small act that seemed to be more restorative than any of the medical attention she had received. I helped her with her make-up, and located her various pairs of glasses. She would thank me quietly and emphatically for my help in the way you might a favoured guest.

Conscious that, as she'd lived alone for years, she might need her space, I would often go out for a few hours in the day, sit in the library and look for jobs but without the urgency I had felt previously and, in truth, there was nothing I wanted to do. She would usually be either sleeping or propped in front of her television when I returned. 'Now, Louisa,' she would say, pushing herself upright, as if we had been mid-conversation, 'I'd been wondering where you were. Would you be kind enough to take Dean Martin for a little stroll? He's been looking rather concerned . . .'

On Saturdays I went with Meena to the library protests. The crowds had grown thinner now, the library's future dependent not just on public support but a crowd-funded legal challenge. Nobody seemed to hold out much hope for it. We stood, less chilled as each week passed, waving our bat-tered placards and accepting with thanks the hot drinks and snacks that still arrived from neighbours and local shopkeep-ers. I'd learnt to look out for familiar faces – the grandmother I'd met on my first visit, whose name was Martine and now greeted me with a hug and a broad smile. A handful of others waved or said hi, the security guard, the woman who brought pakoras, the librarian with the beautiful hair. I never saw the old woman with the ripped epaulettes again.

I had been living in Mrs De Witt's apartment for thirteen

days when I bumped into Agnes. Given our proximity to each other, I suppose it was surprising that it hadn't happened earlier. It was raining heavily and I was wearing one of Mrs De Witt's old raincoats – a yellow and orange 1970s plastic one with bright circular flowers all over it – and she had put a little mackintosh with an elevated hood on Dean Martin, which made me snort with laughter every time I looked at it. We ran along the corridor, me giggling at the sight of his bulbous little face under the plastic hood, and I stopped suddenly as the lift doors opened and Agnes stepped out, tailed by a young woman with an iPad, her hair scraped back into a tight ponytail. She stopped and stared at me. Something not quite readable passed across her face – something that might have been awkwardness, a mute apology or even suppressed fury at my being there, it was hard to tell. Her eyes met mine, she opened her mouth as if to speak, then pressed her lips together and walked past me as if she hadn't seen me, her glossy blonde hair swinging and the girl close behind.

I stood watching as the front door closed emphatically after them, my cheeks burning like a spurned lover's.

I had a vague memory of us laughing in a noodle bar.

We are friends, yes?

And then I took a deep breath, called the little dog to me to fasten his lead, and headed out into the rain.

In the end, it was the girls at the Vintage Clothes Emporium who offered me paid employment. A container of stuff was arriving from Florida – several wardrobes' worth – and they needed an extra pair of hands to go over each item before it hit the shelves, sew on missing buttons and make sure everything that went out on the rails was steam-pressed and clean in time for a vintage clothes fair at the end of April. (Articles that didn't smell fresh were the most commonly returned.) The pay was minimum wage but the company was good, the coffee free, and they would give me a 20 per cent discount on anything I wanted to buy. My appetite for purchasing new clothes had diminished along with my lack of accommodation, but I said yes gladly and, once I was sure Mrs De Witt was stable enough to walk Dean Martin at least to the end of the block and back by herself, I would head to the store every Tuesday at ten a.m. and spend the day in their back room, cleaning, sewing and chatting to the girls during their cigarette breaks, which seemed to happen every fifteen minutes or so.

Margot – I was forbidden to call her Mrs De Witt any more: 'You're living in my home, for goodness' sake' – listened carefully when I told her of my new role, then asked what I was using to repair the clothes. I described the huge plastic box of old buttons and zips but added that the whole thing was such a chaotic mess that I often couldn't find a match, and rarely more than three of the same type of button. She rose heavily from her chair and motioned to me to follow. I walked very close to her, these days – she didn't seem completely steady on her feet, and frequently listed to one side, like a badly loaded ship in high seas. But she made it, her hand trailing the wall for extra stability.

'Under that bed, dear. No, there. There are two chests. That's it.' I knelt and wrenched out two heavy wooden boxes with lids. Opening them, I found them filled to the brim with rows of buttons, zips, tapes and fringes. There were hooks and eyes, fastenings of every type, all neatly separated and labelled, brass naval buttons and tiny Chinese ones, covered with bright silk, bone and shell, sewn neatly onto little strips of card. In the cushioned lid sat sprays of pins, rows of different-sized needles, and an assortment of silk threads on tiny pegs. I ran my fingers across them reverently.

'I was given those for my fourteenth birthday. My

grandfather had them shipped from Hong Kong. If you get stuck you can check in there. I used to take the buttons and zippers from everything I didn't wear any more, you know. That way if you lose a button from something nice, and can't replace it, you always have a full set that you can sew on instead.'

'But won't you need them?'

She waved her good hand. 'Oh, my fingers are far too clumsy for sewing now. Half the time I can't even work the button-holes. And so few people bother with fixing buttons and zippers these days – they just throw their clothes in the trash and buy something awful from one of those discount stores. You take them, dear. It would be nice to feel they were useful.'

So, by luck and perhaps a little by design, I now had two jobs that I loved. And with them I found a kind of contentment. Every Tuesday evening I would bring home a few items of clothing in a chequered laundry bag of plastic webbing, and while Margot napped, or watched television, I would care-fully remove all the remaining buttons on each item and sew on a new set, holding them up afterwards for her approval.

'You sew quite nicely,' she remarked, peering at my stitches through her spectacles, as we sat in front of *Wheel of Fortune*. 'I thought you'd be as dreadful at it as you are at every-thing else.'

'At school needlework was pretty much the only thing I was any good at.' I smoothed out the creases on my lap, and prepared to refold a jacket.

'I was just the same,' she said. 'By thirteen, I was making all my own clothes. My mother showed me how to cut a pattern and that was it. I was away. I became obsessed with fashion.'

'What was it you did, Margot?' I put down my stitching.

'I was fashion editor of the *Ladies' Look*. It doesn't exist now – never made it into the nineties. But we were around for thirty years or more, and I was fashion editor for most of that.'

'Is that the magazine in the frames? The ones on the wall?'

'Yes, those were my favourite covers. I was rather sentimental and kept a few.' Her face softened briefly, and she tilted her head, casting me a confiding look. 'It was quite the job back then, you know. The magazine company wasn't terribly keen on having women in senior roles but there was the most dreadful man in charge of the fashion pages and my editor – a wonderful man, Mr Aldridge – argued that having an old fuddy-duddy, who still wore suspenders to hold up his socks, dictating what fashion meant simply wouldn't work with the younger girls. He thought I had an eye for it, promoted me, and that was that.'

'So that's why you have so many beautiful clothes.'

'Well, I certainly didn't marry rich.'

'Did you marry at all?'

She looked down and picked at something on her knee. 'Goodness, you do ask a lot of questions. Yes, I did. A lovely man. Terrence. He worked in publishing. But he died in 1962, three years after we married, and that was it for me.'

'You never wanted children?'

'I had a son, dear, but not with my husband. Is that what you wanted to know?'

I flushed. 'No. I mean, not like that. I – gosh – having children is – I mean I wouldn't presume to –'

'Stop flapping, Louisa. I fell in love with someone unsuitable when I was grieving my husband and I became pregnant. I had the baby but it caused a bit of a stir, and in the end it was considered better for everyone if my parents brought him up in Westchester.'

'Where is he now?'

'Still in Westchester. As far as I know.'

I blinked. 'You don't see him?'

'Oh, I did. I saw him every weekend and vacation for the whole of his childhood. But once he reached adolescence he grew rather angry with me for not being the kind of mother he thought I should be. I had to make a choice, you see. In those days it wasn't common to work if you married or had children. And I chose work. I honestly felt I would die without it. And Frank – my boss – supported me.' She sighed. 'Unfortunately my son has never really forgiven me.'

There was a long silence.

'I'm so sorry.'

'Yes. So am I. But what's done is done and there's no point dwelling.' She began to cough so I poured her a glass of water and handed it to her. She motioned towards a bottle of pills that she kept on the sideboard and I waited while she swallowed one. She settled herself again, like a hen that had ruffled her feathers.

'What is his name?' I asked, when she had recovered.

'More questions . . . Frank Junior.'

'So his father was –'

'– my editor at the magazine, yes. Frank Aldridge. He was significantly older than I was and married, and I'm afraid that was my son's other great resentment. It was rather hard for him at school. People were different about these things, then.'

'When did you last see him? Your son, I mean.'

'That would be . . . 1987. The year he married. I found out about it after the event and wrote him a letter telling him how hurt I was that he hadn't included me, and he told me in no uncertain terms that I had long since relinquished any right to be included in anything to do with his life.'

We sat in silence for a moment. Her face was perfectly still and it was impossible to tell what she was thinking, or even if she was now simply focused on the television. I didn't know what to say to her. I couldn't find any words that were up to a hurt that great. But then she turned to me.

'And that was it. My mother died a couple of years later and she was my last point of contact with him. I do sometimes wonder how he is – if he's even alive, whether he had children. I wrote to him for a while. But over the years I suppose I've become rather philosophical about the whole thing. He was quite right, of course. I had no right to him, really, to anything to do with his life.'

'But he was your son,' I whispered.

'He was, but I hadn't really behaved like a mother, had I?'

She took a shaky breath. 'I've had a very good life, Louisa. I loved my job and I worked with some wonderful people. I travelled to Paris, Milan, Berlin, London, far more than most women my age ... I had my beautiful apartment and some excellent friends. You mustn't worry about me. All this nonsense about women having it all. We never could and we never shall. Women always have to make the difficult choices. But there is a great consolation in simply doing something you love.'

We sat in silence, digesting this. Then she placed her hands squarely on her knees. 'Actually, dear girl, would you help me to my bathroom? I'm feeling quite tired and I think I might take myself to bed.'

That night I lay awake, thinking about what she had told me. I thought about Agnes and the fact that these two women, living yards away from each other, both cloaked in a very specific sadness, might, in another world, have been a comfort to each other. I thought about the fact that there seemed to be such a high cost to anything a woman chose to do with her life, unless she simply aimed low. But I knew that already, didn't I? I had come here and it had cost me dear.

Often in the small hours I conjured Will's voice telling me not to be ridiculous and melancholy but to think instead of all the things I'd achieved. I lay in the dark and ticked off my achievements on my fingers. I had a home – for the time being at least. I had paid employment. I was still in New York, and I was among friends. I had a new relationship, even if sometimes I wondered how I had ended up in it. Could I really say that I would have done things any differently?

But it was the old woman in the next room I was thinking of when I finally slept.

There were fourteen sporting trophies on Josh's shelf, four of them the size of my head, for American football, baseball, something called track-and-field, and a junior trophy for a spelling bee. I had been there before but it was only now, sober and unhurried, that I was able to take in my surroundings and the scale of his achievements. There were pictures of him in sporting garb, preserved at the moment of his triumphs, his arms clasped around his teammates, those perfect teeth in a perfect smile. I thought of Patrick and the multitude of certificates on the wall of his apartment, and wondered at the male need to display achievements, like a peacock permanently shimmering his tail.

When Josh put down the phone, I jumped. 'It's only take-out. I'm afraid with everything at work I don't have time for anything else right now. But this is the best Korean food south of Koreatown.'

'I don't mind,' I said. I had no other Korean food experiences to judge it by. I was just enjoying the prospect of coming to see him. Walking to catch the subway south, I had relished the novelty of heading Downtown without battling either Siberian winds, deep snow or torrential, icy rain.

And Josh's apartment was not quite the rabbit hutch he'd

described, unless your rabbit had decided to move into a renovated loft in an area that had apparently once housed artists' studios but now formed a base for four different versions of Marc Jacobs, punctuated by artisan jewellers, specialist coffee shops and boutiques that employed men with earpieces on the doorstep. It was all whitewashed walls and oak floors, with a modernistic marble table and a distressed leather sofa. The smattering of a few carefully chosen ornaments and pieces of furniture suggested everything had been carefully considered, sourced and earned, perhaps through the services of an interior designer.

He had brought me flowers, a delicious mix of hyacinths and freesias. 'What are these for?' I said.

He shrugged as he shepherded me in. 'I just saw them on the way home from work and thought you might like them.'

'Wow. Thank you.' I inhaled deeply. 'This is the nicest thing that's happened to me in ages.'

'The flowers? Or me?' He raised an eyebrow.

'Well, I suppose you are *quite* nice.'

His face fell.

'You're amazing. And I love them.'

He smiled broadly then and kissed me. 'Well, you're the nicest thing that's happened to me in ages,' he said, softly, when he pulled back. 'Feels like I waited a long time for you, Louisa.'

'We only met in October.'

'Ah. But we live in an age of instant gratification. And we're in the city where anything you want you get yesterday.'

There was a strange potency to being wanted as much as Josh seemed to want me. I wasn't quite sure what I'd done to deserve it. I wanted to ask him what he saw in me but I suspected it would sound oddly needy to say it aloud so I tried to work it out in other ways.

'Tell me about the other women you've dated,' I said, from the sofa, as he moved around the little kitchenette, pulling out plates and cutlery and glasses. 'What were they like?'

'Aside from Tinder hook-ups? Smart, pretty, usually successful . . .' He stooped to pull a bottle of fish sauce from the back of a cupboard. 'But honestly? Like self-obsessed,' he said. 'Like they couldn't be seen without perfect make-up, or they would have a full-on meltdown if their hair wasn't right, and everything had to be Instagrammed or photographed or reported on social media and presented in the best light. Including dates with me. Like they could never drop their guard.'

He straightened up, holding bottles. 'You want chilli sauce? Or soy? I dated one girl who used to check what time I was getting up each day and set her alarm for half an hour before just so she could fix her hair and make-up. Just so I would never see her not looking perfect. Even if it meant getting up at, like, four thirty.'

'Okay. I'm going to warn you now, I'm not that girl.'

'I know that, Louisa. I've put you to bed.'

I kicked off my shoes and folded my legs under me. 'I suppose it's kind of impressive that they put in so much effort.'

'Yeah. But it can be a little exhausting. And you never feel quite like . . . like you know what's really underneath. With you, I have to say, it's all pretty much out there. You are who you are.'

'Should I take that as a compliment?'

'Sure. You're like the girls I grew up with. You're honest.'

'The Gopniks don't think so.'

'Fuck them.' His voice was uncharacteristically harsh. 'You know, I've been thinking about it. You can prove you didn't do what they said you did – right? So you should sue them for unfair dismissal and loss of reputation and hurt feelings and –'

354

I shook my head.

'Seriously. Gopnik trades on this reputation of being a decent, old-fashioned good guy in business and he's always doing stuff for charity, but he fired you for *nothing*, Louisa. You lost your job and your home with no warning and no compensation.'

'He thought I was stealing.'

'Yeah, but he must know there was something not quite right about what he was doing or he would have called the cops. Given who he is, I'd bet there's some lawyer who would take this on a no-win-no-fee basis.'

'Really. I'm fine. Lawsuits aren't my style.'

'Yeah, well. You're too nice. You're being *English* about it.'

The doorbell rang. Josh held up a finger, as if to say we would continue this conversation. He disappeared into the narrow hallway and I heard him paying the delivery boy while I finished laying the little table.

'And you know what?' he said, bringing the bag into the kitchen. 'Even if you didn't have evidence I'd bet Gopnik would pay a lump sum just to stop the whole thing getting into the papers. Think what that could do for you. I mean, a couple of weeks ago you were sleeping on someone's floor.' (I hadn't told him about sharing Nathan's bed.)

'This could get you a decent deposit on a rental. Hell, you get a good enough lawyer, this could buy you an apartment. You know how much money Gopnik has? Like, he is *famously* rich. In a city of seriously rich people.'

'Josh, I know you mean well but I just want to forget it.'

'Louisa, you –'

'*No.*' I put my hands down on the table. 'I'm not suing anybody.'

He waited for a minute, perhaps frustrated by his inability to push me further, and then he shrugged and smiled.

'Okay – well, dinner time! You don't have any allergies, right? Have some chicken. Here – you like eggplant? They do this eggplant chilli dish that's just the greatest.'

I slept with Josh that night. I wasn't drunk and I wasn't vulnerable and I wasn't breathless with need for him. I think I just wanted my life to feel normal again. We had eaten and drunk and talked and laughed until late into the night, and he had pulled the drapes and turned down the lights and it seemed like a natural progression, or at least I could think of no reason not to. He was so beautiful. He had skin without a blemish and cheekbones you could actually see, and his hair was soft and chestnut-coloured and tinged with tiny flecks of gold, even after the long winter. We kissed on his sofa, first sweetly and then with increasing fervour, and he lost his shirt and then I lost mine and I made myself focus on this gorgeous, attentive man, this prince of New York, and not on all the rambling things my imagination tended to focus on, and I felt need grow in me, like a distant, reassuring friend, until I was able to block out everything but the sensations of him against me, and then, some time later, inside me.

Afterwards he kissed me tenderly and asked me if I was happy, then murmured that he had to get some sleep and I lay there and tried to ignore the tears that inexplicably trickled from the corners of my eyes into my ears.

What was it Will had told me? You had to seize the day. You had to embrace opportunities as they came. You had to be the kind of person who said yes. If I had turned Josh away, wouldn't I have regretted it for ever?

I turned silently in the unfamiliar bed and studied his profile as he slept, the perfect straight nose and the mouth that looked like Will's. I thought of all the ways Will would have approved of him. I could even picture them together, laughing with each other, a competitive edge to their jokes. They might have been friends. Or enemies. They were almost too similar.

Perhaps I was meant to be with this man, I thought, albeit via a strange, unsettling route. Perhaps this was Will, come back to me. And with this thought I wiped my eyes and fell into a brief, disjointed sleep.

24

To: KatClark!@yahoo.com
From: BusyBee@gmail.com

Dear Treen,

I know you think it's too soon. But what did Will teach me? You only get one life, right? And you're happy with Eddie? So why can't I be happy? You'll get it when you meet him, I promise.

So this is the kind of man Josh is: yesterday he took me to the best bookshop in Brooklyn and bought me a bunch of paperbacks he thought I might like, then at lunchtime he took me to a posh Mexican restaurant on East 46th and made me try fish tacos – don't pull a face, they were absolutely delicious. Then he told me he wanted to show me something (no, not that). We walked to the Grand Central Terminal and it was packed, as usual, and I was thinking, Okay, bit weird – are we going on a trip? then he told me to stand with my head in the corner of this archway, just by this Oyster Bar. I laughed at him. I thought he was joking. But he insisted, told me to trust him.

So there I am, standing with my head in the corner of this huge masonry archway, with all the commuters coming and going around me, trying not to feel like a complete eejit, and when I look round he's walking away from me. But then he stops diagonally across from me, maybe fifty feet away, and he puts his own face in the corner and suddenly, above all the noise and chaos and rumbling trains, I hear – murmured into my ear, like he was right beside me – 'Louisa Clark, you are the cutest girl in the whole of New York City.'

Treen, it was like witchcraft. I looked up and he turned around and smiled, and I have no idea how it worked, but he walked across and just took me in his arms and kissed me in front of everyone and someone whistled at us and it was honestly the most romantic thing that has ever happened to me.

So, yes, I'm moving on. And Josh is amazing. It would be nice if you could be pleased for me.

Give Thom a big kiss.
Lx

Weeks passed and New York, as it did with most things, careered into spring at a million miles an hour, with little subtlety and a lot of noise. The traffic grew heavier, the streets were thicker with people, and each day the grid around our block became a cacophony of noise and activity that barely dimmed until the small hours. I stopped wearing a hat and gloves to the library protests. Dean Martin's padded coat was laundered and went into the cupboard. The park grew green. Nobody suggested I move out.

Margot, in lieu of any kind of helper's wage, pressed so many items of clothing on me that I had to stop admiring things in front of her because I became afraid she would feel obliged to give me more. Over the weeks, I observed that she might share an address with the Gopniks but that was where the similarity between them ended. She survived, as my mother would have said, on shirt buttons.

'Between the healthcare bills and the maintenance fees I don't know where they think I'm meant to find the money to feed myself,' she remarked, as I handed her another letter hand-delivered by the management company. The envelope said 'OPEN – LEGAL ACTION PENDING'. She wrinkled her nose and put it neatly in a pile on the sideboard, where it would stay for the next couple of weeks unless I opened it.

She grumbled often about the maintenance fees, which totalled thousands of dollars a month, and seemed to have reached a point at which she had decided to ignore them because there was nothing else she could do.

She told me she had inherited the apartment from her grandfather, an adventurous sort, the only person in her family who didn't believe that a woman should restrict her sights to husband and children. 'My father was furious that he had been bypassed. He didn't talk to me for years. My mother tried to broker an agreement but by then there were the . . . other issues.' She sighed.

She bought her groceries from a local convenience store, a tiny supermarket that operated on tourist prices, because it was one of the few places she could walk to. I put a stop to that and twice a week headed over to a Fairway on East 86th Street where I loaded up on basics to the tune of about a third of what she had been spending.

If I didn't cook, she ate almost nothing sensible herself, but bought good cuts of meat for Dean Martin or poached him white fish in milk 'because it's good for his digestion'.

I think she had become accustomed to my company. Plus she was so wobbly that I think we both knew she couldn't manage alone any more. I wondered how long it took someone of her age to get over the shock of surgery. I also wondered what she would have done if I hadn't been there.

'What will you do?' I said, motioning towards the pile of bills.

'Oh, I'll ignore those.' She waved a hand. 'I'm leaving this apartment in a box. I have nowhere to go and no one to leave it to, and that crook Ovitz knows it. I think he's just sitting tight until I die and then he'll claim the apartment under the non-payment of maintenance fees clause and make a fortune selling it to some dotcom person or awful CEO, like that fool across the corridor.'

'Maybe I could help? I have some savings from my time with the Gopniks. I mean, just to get you through a couple of months. You've been so kind to me.'

She hooted. 'Dear girl. You couldn't meet the maintenance fees on my guest bathroom.'

For some reason this made her laugh so heartily that she coughed until she had to sit down. But I sneaked a look at the letter after she went to bed. Its 'late payment charges', its 'direct contravention of the terms of your lease' and 'threat of compulsory eviction' made me think that Mr Ovitz might not be as beneficent – or patient – as she seemed to think.

I was still walking Dean Martin four times a day, and during those trips to the park I tried to think what could be done for Margot. The thought of her being evicted was appalling. Surely the managing agent wouldn't do that to a convalescent elderly woman. Surely the other residents would object. Then I remembered how swiftly Mr Gopnik had evicted me, and how insulated the inhabitants of each apartment were from each other's lives. I wasn't entirely sure they'd even notice.

I was standing on Sixth Avenue peering at a wholesale underwear store when it hit me. The girls at the Emporium might not sell Chanel and Yves St Laurent but they would if they could get it – or would know some dress agency that could. Margot had innumerable designer labels in her collection, things I was sure that collectors would pay serious money for. There were handbags alone that must be worth thousands of dollars.

I took Margot to meet them under the guise of an outing. I told her it was a beautiful day and that we should go further than usual and build up her strength with fresh air. She told me not to be so ridiculous and nobody had breathed fresh air in Manhattan since 1937, but she climbed into the taxi without too much complaint and, Dean Martin on her lap, we made our way to the East Village, where she frowned up at the concrete storefront as if somebody had asked her to enter a slaughterhouse for fun.

'What *have* you done to your arms?' Margot paused at the checkout and gazed at Lydia's skin. Lydia was wearing an emerald green puffed-sleeve shirt, and her arms displayed three neatly traced Japanese koi carp in orange, jade and blue.

'Oh, my tatts. You like 'em?' Lydia put her cigarette in her other hand and raised her arm towards the light.

'If I wanted to look like a navvy.'

I began to shepherd Margot to a different part of the shop. 'Here, Margot. See they have all their vintage clothes in different areas – if you have clothes from the 1960s they go here, and over there the 1950s. It's a little like your apartment.'

'It's nothing like my apartment.'

'I just mean they trade in outfits like yours. It's quite a successful line of business, these days.'

Margot pulled at the sleeve of a nylon blouse, then peered at the label over the top of her spectacles. 'Amy Armistead is an awful line. Never could stand the woman. Or Les Grandes Folies. Their buttons always fell off. Cheap on thread.'

'There are some really special dresses back here, under plastic.' I walked over to the cocktail-gown section where the best of the women's pieces were displayed. I pulled out a Saks Fifth Avenue dress in turquoise, trimmed with sequins and beads at the hem and cuffs, and held it up against myself, smiling.

Margot peered at it, then turned the price tag in her hand. She pulled a face at the figure. 'Who on earth would pay this?'

'People who love good clothes,' said Lydia, who had appeared behind us. She was chewing noisily on a piece of gum and I could see Margot's eyes flicker slightly every time her jaws met.

'There's an actual market for them?'

'A good market,' I said. 'Especially for things in immaculate condition, like yours. All Margot's outfits have been kept in plastic and air conditioning. She has things that date back to the 1940s.'

'Those aren't mine. Those are my mother's,' she said stiffly.

'Seriously? Whaddaya got?' said Lydia, giving Margot's coat a visible up and down. Margot was in a Jaeger three-quarter-length wool coat, and a black fur hat the shape of a large Victoria sponge. Even though the weather was almost balmy, she still appeared to feel the cold.

'What do I have? Nothing I want to send here, thank you.'

'But, Margot, you have some really fine suits – the Chanels and the Givenchys that no longer fit you. And you have scarves, bags – you could sell those to specialist dealers. Auction houses even.'

'Chanel makes serious money,' said Lydia, sagely. 'Especially purses. If it's not too shabby, a decent Chanel double flap in caviar leather will make two and a half to four thousand. A new one's not going to cost you much more, you know what I'm saying? Python, woah, the sky's the limit.'

'You have more than one Chanel handbag, Margot,' I pointed out.

Margot tucked her Hermès alligator bag more tightly under her arm.

'You got more like that? We can sell 'em for you, Mrs De Witt. We got a waiting list for the good stuff. I got a lady in Asbury Park will pay up to five thousand for a decent Hermès.' Lydia reached out to run a finger down the side of it and Margot pulled away as if she'd assaulted her.

'It's not stuff,' she said. 'I don't own "stuff".'

'I just think it might be worth considering. There seems to be quite a bit you don't use any longer. You could sell it, pay the maintenance fees, and then you could, you know, relax.'

'I am relaxed,' she snapped. 'And I'll thank you not to discuss my financial affairs in public, as if I'm not even here. Oh, I don't like this place. It smells of old people. Come on, Dean Martin. I need some fresh air.'

I followed her out, mouthing an apology at Lydia, who shrugged, unconcerned. I suspected that even the faint possibility of Margot's wardrobe coming her way had softened any natural tendency towards combativeness.

We caught a taxi back in silence. I was annoyed with myself for my lack of diplomacy and simultaneously irritated with Margot for her out-and-out rejection of what I had thought was quite a sensible plan. She refused to look at me during the whole journey. I sat beside her, Dean Martin panting between us, and rehearsed arguments in my head until her silence became unnerving. I glanced sideways and saw an old woman, who had recently come out of hospital. I had no right to pressure her into anything.

'I didn't mean to upset you, Margot,' I said, as I helped her out in front of her building. 'I just thought it might be a way forward. You know, with the debts and everything. I just don't want you to lose your home.'

Margot straightened up and adjusted her fur hat with a brittle hand. Her voice was querulous, almost tearful, and I realized she had also been rehearsing an argument in her head for the entire fifty or so blocks. 'You don't understand, Louisa. These are my *things*, my babies. They may be old clothes, potential financial assets, to you but they are *precious* to me. They are my history, beautiful, prized remnants of my life.'

'I'm sorry.'

'I wouldn't send them to that grubby second-hand shop if I were on my *knees*. And the thought of seeing a perfect stranger walking towards me on the street in an outfit I'd loved! I would feel utterly wretched. No. I know you were trying to help, but no.'

She turned and waved off my outstretched hand, waiting instead for Ashok to help her to the lift.

Despite our occasional misfires, Margot and I were quite content that spring.

In April, as promised, Lily came to New York, accompanied by Mrs Traynor. They stayed at the Ritz Carlton, a few blocks away, and invited Margot and me for lunch. Having them there together made me feel as if a threaded darning needle was quietly drawing the different parts of my life together.

Mrs Traynor, with her diplomat's good manners, was delightful to Margot, and they found common ground over the history of the building and of New York in general. At lunch, I saw another Margot: quick-witted, knowledgeable, enlivened by new company. Mrs Traynor, it emerged, had come here for her honeymoon in 1978 and they discussed restaurants, galleries and exhibitions of the time. Mrs Traynor talked of her time as a magistrate, and Margot discussed the office politics of the 1970s, and they laughed heartily in a way that suggested we younger people couldn't possibly understand. We ate salad and a small portion of fish wrapped in prosciutto. I noticed that Margot had a tiny forkful of everything, sliding the rest to one side, and despaired quietly of ever getting her to fill any of her clothes again.

Lily, meanwhile, leant into me and quizzed me about where she could go that didn't involve either old people or any kind of cultural improvement.

'Granny has packed these four days absolutely full of educational crap. I've got to go to the Museum of Modern Art and some botanical gardens and all sorts, which is fine, blah-blah, if you like all that, but I really want to go clubbing and get wrecked and go shopping. I mean, this is New York!'

'I've already spoken with Mrs Traynor. And I'm taking you out tomorrow while she catches up with a cousin of hers.'

'Seriously? Thank God. I'm going backpacking in Vietnam in the long vac. Did I tell you? I want to get some decent cut-off shorts. Something I can wear for weeks and it won't matter if they don't get washed. And maybe an old biker jacket. Something good and battered.'

'Who are you going with? A friend?' I raised an eyebrow.

'You sound like Granny.'

'Well?'

'A boyfriend.' And then, as I opened my mouth, 'But I don't want to say anything about him.'

'Why? I'm delighted you have a boyfriend. It's lovely news.' I lowered my voice. 'You know the last person who got cagey like that was my sister. And she was basically hiding the fact that she was about to come out.'

'I am not coming out. I do not want to go rooting about in someone's lady-garden. Bleurgh.'

I tried not to laugh. 'Lily, you don't have to keep everything close to your chest. We all just want you to be happy. It's okay if people know your business.'

'Granny does know my business, as you so quaintly call it.'

'Then why can't you tell me? I thought you and I could tell each other anything!'

Lily bore the resigned expression of someone cornered. She sighed theatrically and put down her knife and fork. She looked at me as if braced for a fight. 'Because it's Jake.'

'Jake?'

'Sam's Jake.'

The restaurant ground to a gentle halt around me. I forced my face into a smile. 'Okay! . . . Wow!'

She scowled. 'I knew you'd react like that. Look, it just happened. And it's not like we talk about you all the time or anything. I just ran into him a couple of times – you know we met at that Letting Go thing for that cringy grief counselling group you used to go to and we got on okay and we liked each other? Well, we sort of get each other's situations so we're going backpacking together in the summer. No biggie.'

My brain was spinning. 'Has Mrs Traynor met him?'

'Yes. He comes to ours and I go to his.' She looked almost defensive.

'So you see a lot of –'

'His dad. I mean I do see Ambulance Sam but I mostly see Jake's dad. Who is okay, but still quite depressed and eats about a ton of cake a week, which is stressing Jake out a lot. That's partly why we want to get away from everything. Just for six weeks or so.'

She kept talking but a low hum had started somewhere in the back of my head and I couldn't quite register what she was saying. I didn't want to hear about Sam, even vicariously. I didn't want to hear about people I loved playing Happy Families without me while I was thousands of miles away. I didn't want to know about Sam's happiness or Katie with her sexy mouth or how they were no doubt living in his house together in a newly built den of passion and tangled matching uniforms.

'So how's your new boyfriend?' she said.

'Josh? Josh! He's great. Totally great.' I put my knife and fork neatly to the side of my plate. 'Just . . . dreamy.'

'So what's going on? I need to see pictures of you with him. You're massively annoying not sharing any photos on Facebook. Don't you have any pictures of him on your phone?'

'Nope,' I said, and she wrinkled her nose as if that were a completely inadequate response.

I wasn't telling the truth. I had one of the two of us at a pop-up rooftop restaurant, taken a week earlier. But I didn't want her to know that Josh was the spitting image of her father. It would either unbalance her or, worse, having her acknowledge it out loud would unbalance me.

'So when are we heading out of this funeral parlour? We can leave the olds here to finish their lunch, surely.' Lily nudged me. The two women were still chatting. 'Did I tell you I've been winding Grandpa up massively about Granny's imaginary heart-throb boyfriend? I told him they were going on holiday to the Maldives and that Granny had been to Rigby and Peller to stock up on new underwear. I swear he's about to break down and declare he still loves her. It's making me *die* laughing.'

Much as I loved Lily, I was grateful that Mrs Traynor's packed schedule of cultural improvements over the next few days meant that, aside from our shopping trip, we had limited time together. Her presence in the city – with her intimate knowledge of Sam's life – had created a vibration in the air that I didn't know how to dispel. I was grateful that Josh was flat out with work and didn't notice if I was down or distracted. But Margot noticed and one night, when her beloved *Wheel of Fortune* had finished and I rose to take Dean Martin for his last walk of the day, she asked me straight out what the matter was.

I told her. I couldn't think of a reason not to.

'You still love the other one,' she said.

'You sound like my sister,' I said. 'I don't. I just – I just loved him so much when I did. And the end of it was so awful and I thought that being over here and living a different life would insulate me from it. I don't do social media any more. I don't want to keep tabs on anyone. And yet somehow information about your ex will always end up finding its way to you. And it's like I can't concentrate while Lily's here because she's now part of his life.'

'Perhaps you should just get in touch with him, dear. It sounds as if you still have things to say.'

'I have nothing to say to him,' I said. My voice grew impassioned. 'I tried so hard, Margot. I wrote to him and sent him emails and called. Do you know he didn't write me one letter? In three months? I asked if he would write because I thought it would be a really lovely way for us to stay connected and we could learn things about each other and look forward to speaking and have something to remind us of our time apart and he just . . . he just wouldn't.'

She sat and watched me, her hands folded across the remote control.

I straightened my shoulders. 'But it's fine. Because I've moved on. And Josh is just terrific. I mean, he's handsome, and he's kind, and he has this great job, and he's ambitious – oh, he is *so* ambitious. He's really going places, you know. He has things he wants – houses and a career and giving things back. He wants to give back! And he hasn't even really got anything to give back yet!'

I sat down. Dean Martin stood in front of me, confused. 'And he's totally clear that he wants to be with me. No ifs and no buts. He literally called me his girlfriend from our first date. And I've heard all about the serial daters in this town. Do you know how lucky that makes me feel?'

She gave a small nod.

I stood again. 'So I don't really give a monkey's about Sam. I mean, we hardly even knew each other when I came over here. I suspect if it hadn't been for each of us requiring emergency medical help we might not have been together at all. In fact, I'm sure of it. And I plainly wasn't right for him or he would have waited, right? Because that's what people do. So all in all, it's great. And I'm actually really happy with how everything has turned out. It's all good. All good.'

There was a short silence.

'So I see,' said Margot, quietly.

'I'm really happy.'

'I can see that, dear.' She watched me for a moment, then placed her hands on the arms of her chair. 'Now. Perhaps you could take that poor dog out. His eyes have started to bulge.'

25

It took me two evenings to locate Margot's grandson. Josh was busy with work and Margot went to bed most nights by nine so one evening I sat on the floor by the front door – the one place where I could pick up the Gopniks' WiFi – and I started googling her son, testing the name Frank De Witt, and when nothing of that name came up, Frank Aldridge Junior. There was nobody who could have been him, unless he'd moved to a different part of the country, but even then the dates and nationalities of all the men who came up under that name were wrong.

On the second night, on a whim, I looked up Margot's married name in some old papers that were in the chest of drawers in my room. I found a card for a funeral service for Terrence Weber, so I tried Frank Weber and discovered, with some wistfulness, that she had named her son after her beloved husband, who had died years before he was even born. And that some time further down the line she had changed her name back to her maiden name – De Witt – and reinvented herself completely.

Frank Weber Junior was a dentist who lived somewhere called Tuckahoe in Westchester. I found a couple of references to him on LinkedIn and on Facebook through his wife, Laynie. The big news was that they had a son, Vincent, who was a little younger than me. He worked in Yonkers at a not-for-profit educational centre for underprivileged children and it was he who decided it for me. Frank Weber Junior might be too angry with his mother to rebuild a relationship, but what harm would there be in trying Vincent? I found his profile, took a breath, sent him a message, and waited.

Josh took a break from his never-ending round of corporate jockeying and had lunch with me at the noodle bar, announcing there was a corporate 'family day' the following Saturday at the Loeb Boathouse and that he'd like me to come as his plus-one.

'I was planning on going to the library protest.'

'You don't want to keep doing that, Louisa. You're not going to change anything standing around with a bunch of people shouting at passing cars.'

'And I'm not really family,' I said, bristling slightly.

'Close enough. C'mon! It'll be a great day. Have you ever been to the boathouse? It's gorgeous. My firm really knows how to lay on a party. You're still doing your "say yes" thing, right? So you have to say yes.' He did puppy eyes at me. 'Say yes, Louisa, please. Go on.'

He had me and he knew it. I smiled resignedly. 'Okay. Yes.'

'Great! Last year apparently they had all these inflatable sumo suits and people wrestled on the grass and there were family races and organized games. You're going to love it.'

'Sounds amazing,' I said. The words 'organized games' held the same appeal to me as the words 'compulsory smear test'. But it was Josh and he looked so pleased at the thought of my accompanying him that I didn't have the heart to say no.

'I promise you won't have to wrestle my workmates. You might have to wrestle me afterwards, though,' he said, kissed me, and left.

I checked my inbox all week, but there was nothing, other than an email from Lily asking if I knew the best place to get an underage tattoo, a friendly hello from someone who was supposedly at school with me but whom I didn't remember at all, and one from my mother sending me a GIF of an over-weight cat apparently talking to a two-year-old and a link to a game called Farm Fun Fandango.

'Are you sure you'll be okay by yourself, Margot?' I said, as I gathered my keys and purse into my handbag. I was wear-ing a white jumpsuit with gold lamé epaulettes and trim that she'd given me from her early eighties period and she clasped her hands together. 'Oh, that looks magnificent on you. You must have almost exactly the measurements that I had at the same age. I used to have a bust, you know! Terribly unfash-ionable in the sixties and seventies but there you go.'

I didn't like to tell her that it was taking everything I had not to burst the seams but she was right – I had lost a few pounds since I'd moved in with her, mostly because of my efforts to cook her things that were nutritionally useful. I felt lovely in the jumpsuit and gave her a twirl. 'Have you taken your pills?'

'Of course I have. Don't fuss, dear. Does that mean you won't be back later?'

'I'm not sure. I'll take Dean Martin for a quick walk before I go, though. Just in case.' I paused, as I reached for the dog's lead. 'Margot? Why did you call him Dean Martin? I never asked.'

The tone of her response told me it was an idiotic ques-tion. 'Because Dean Martin was the most terrifically handsome man, and he's the most terrifically handsome dog, of course.'

The little dog sat obediently, his bulging, mismatched eyes rolling above his flapping tongue.

'Silly of me to ask,' I said, and let myself out of the front door.

*

'Well, look at you!' Ashok whistled as Dean Martin and I ran down the last flight of stairs to the ground floor. 'Disco diva!'

'You like it?' I said, throwing a shape in front of him. 'It was Margot's.'

'Seriously? That woman is full of surprises.'

'Watch out for her, will you? She's pretty wobbly today.'

'Kept back a piece of mail just so I have an excuse to knock on her door at six o'clock.'

'You're a star.'

We jogged outside to the park and Dean Martin did what dogs do and I did what you do with a little bag and a certain amount of shuddering and various passers-by stared in the way you do if you see a girl in a lamé-trimmed jumpsuit running around with an excitable dog and a small bag of poo. It was as we sprinted back in, Dean Martin yapping delightedly at my heels, that we bumped into Josh in the lobby. 'Oh, hey!' I said, kissing him. 'I'll be two minutes, okay? Just have to wash my hands and grab my handbag.'

'Grab your handbag?'

'Yes!' I gazed at him. 'Oh. Purse. You call it a purse.'

'I just meant – you're not getting changed?'

I looked down at my jumpsuit. 'I am changed.'

'Sweetheart, if you wear that to our office day out they're going to wonder if you're the entertainment.'

It took me a moment to realize he wasn't joking. 'You don't like it?'

'Oh. No. You look great. It's just it's kind of a bit . . . drag queeny? We're an office full of suits. Like, the other wives and girlfriends will be in shift dresses or white pants. It's just . . . smart casual?'

'Oh.' I tried not to feel disappointed. 'Sorry. I don't really get US dress codes. Okay. Okay. Wait there. I'll be right back.'

I took the stairs two at a time and burst into Margot's apartment, throwing Dean Martin's lead towards Margot, who had got up out of her chair for something and now followed me down the hallway, one thin arm braced against the wall.

'Why are you in such a tearing hurry? You sound like a herd of elephants charging around the apartment.'

'I have to change.'

'Change? Why?'

'I'm not suitable, apparently.' I rattled my way through my wardrobe. Shift dresses? The only clean shift dress I had was the psychedelic one Sam had given me and it felt somehow disloyal to wear that.

'I thought you looked very nice,' said Margot, pointedly.

Josh appeared at the open front door, having made his way up behind me. 'Oh, she does. She looks great. I just – I just want her to be talked about for the right reasons.' He laughed. Margot didn't laugh back.

I rifled through my wardrobe, throwing things onto my bed, until I found my navy Gucci-style blazer and a striped silk shirt dress. I threw that over my head and slid my feet into my green Mary Janes.

'How's that?' I said, as I ran into the hallway, trying to straighten my hair.

'Great!' he said, unable to hide his relief. 'Okay. Let's go.'

'I'll leave the door unlocked, dear,' I heard Margot mutter, as I ran after Josh, who was headed out. 'Just in case you want to come back.'

The Loeb Boathouse was a beautiful venue, sheltered by its position from the noise and chaos outside Central Park, its vast windows offering a panoramic view of the lake glinting in the afternoon sun. It was packed with smartly dressed men in identikit chinos, women with professionally blow-dried hair and was, as Josh had predicted, a sea of pastels and white trousers.

I took a glass of champagne from a tray being proffered by a waiter and watched quietly while Josh worked the room, glad-handing various men, who all seemed to look the same, with their short neat haircuts and square jaws with even white teeth. I had a brief memory of events I had been to with Agnes: I had fallen into my other New York world again, a world away from the vintage clothes stores and mothballed jumpers and cheap coffee I had been immersed in more recently. I took a long sip of my champagne, deciding to embrace it.

Josh appeared beside me. 'Quite something, isn't it?'

'It's very beautiful.'

'Better than sitting in some old woman's apartment all afternoon, huh?'

'Well, I don't think I –'

'My boss is coming. Okay. I'm going to introduce you. Stay with me. Mitchell!'

Josh lifted an arm and the older man walked over slowly, a statuesque brunette woman at his side, her smile oddly blank. Perhaps if you had to be nice to everyone all the time that was what eventually happened to your face.

'Are you enjoying the afternoon?'

'Very much so, sir,' Josh said. 'What a truly beautiful setting. May I introduce my girlfriend? This is Louisa Clark, from England. Louisa, this is Mitchell Dumont. He's head of Mergers and Acquisitions.'

'English, eh?' I felt the man's huge hand close over mine and shake it emphatically.

'Yes. I –'

'Good. Good.' He turned back to Josh. 'So, young man, I hear you're making quite a splash in your department.'

Josh couldn't hide his delight. His smile spread across his

face. His eyes flickered to me and then to the woman beside me, and I realized he was expecting me to make conversation with her. Nobody had bothered to introduce us. Mitchell Dumont put a paternal arm around Josh's shoulders and walked him a few feet away.

'So . . .' I said. I raised my eyebrows and lowered them again.

She smiled blankly at me.

'I love your dress,' I said, the universal smoother for two women who have absolutely nothing to say to each other.

'Thank you. Cute shoes,' she said. But she said it in the way that meant they weren't cute at all. She glanced over, plainly wondering if she could find someone else to talk to. She had taken one look at my outfit and deemed herself way beyond my pay grade.

There was nobody else nearby, so I tried again. 'So do you come here a lot? To the Loeb Boathouse, I mean?'

'It's Lobe,' she said.

'Lobe?'

'You pronounced it Lerb. It's Loeb.'

Looking at her perfectly made-up, suspiciously plump lips repeatedly saying the word made me want to giggle. I took a swig of my champagne to disguise it. 'So do you cerm to the Lerb Berthouse often?' I said, unable to help myself.

'No,' she said. 'Although one of my friends got married here last year. That was such a beautiful wedding.'

'I'll bet. And what do you do?'

'I'm a homemaker.'

'A herm-maker! My merther is also a herm-maker.' I took another long sip of my drink. 'Herm-making is perfectly lervely.' I saw Josh, his face focused intently on his boss's, reminding me briefly of Thom's when he was pleading with Dad to give him some of his crisps.

The woman's expression had become faintly concerned – or as far as a woman who couldn't move her brow could express concern. A bubble of giggles had started to build in my chest and I pleaded with some unseen deity to keep them under control.

'Maya!' Her voice tinged with relief, Mrs Dumont (at least, I assumed that was whom I'd been talking to) waved at a woman approaching us, her perfect figure neatly pinned into a mint-coloured shift dress. I waited while they air-kissed.

'You look simply gorgeous.'

'As do you. I love that dress.'

'Oh, it's so old. And you're so sweet. How's that darling husband of yours? Always talking business.'

'Oh, you know Mitchell.' Mrs Dumont plainly couldn't ignore my presence any longer. 'This is Joshua Ryan's girl-friend. I'm so sorry, I missed your name. Terribly noisy in here.'

'Louisa,' I said.

'How lovely. I'm Chrissy. I'm Jeffrey's other half. You know Jeffrey in Sales and Marketing?'

'Oh, everyone knows Jeffrey,' said Mrs Dumont.

'Oh, Jeffrey . . .' I said, shaking my head. Then nodding. Then shaking my head again.

'And what do you do?'

'What do I do?'

'Louisa's in fashion.' Josh appeared at my side.

'You certainly do have an individual look. I love the British, don't you, Mallory? They are so *interesting* in their choices.'

There was a brief silence, while everyone digested my choices.

'Louisa's about to start work at *Women's Wear Daily*.'

'You are?' said Mallory Dumont.

'I am?' I said. 'Yes. I am.'

'Well, that must be just thrilling. What a wonderful magazine. I must find my husband. Do excuse me.' With another bland smile she walked off on her vertiginous heels, Maya beside her.

'Why did you say that?' I said, reaching for another glass of champagne. 'It sounds better than *I house-sit an old lady*?'

'No. You – you just look like you might work in fashion.'

'You're still uncomfortable with what I'm wearing?' I looked over at the two women, in their complementary dresses. I had a sudden memory of how Agnes must have felt at such gatherings, the myriad subtle ways women can find to let other women know they do not fit in.

'You look great. It's just it makes it easier to explain your – your particular . . . unique sensibility if they think you're in fashion. Which you kind of are.'

'I'm perfectly happy with what I do, Josh.'

'But you want to work in fashion, don't you? You can't look after an old woman for ever. Look, I was going to tell you after – my sister-in-law, Debbie, she knows a woman in the marketing department at *Women's Wear Daily*. She said she's going to ask them to find out if they have any entry-level vacancies. She seems pretty confident she can do something for you. What do you say?' He was beaming, like he'd presented me with the Holy Grail.

I took a swig of my drink. 'Sure.'

'There you go. Exciting!' He kept looking at me, eyebrows raised.

'Yay!' I said finally.

He squeezed my shoulder. 'I knew you'd be happy. Right. Let's get back out there. It's the family races next. Want a lime and soda? I don't think we can really be seen to be drinking more than one glass of the champagne. Here, let me take that for you.' He put my glass on the tray of a passing waiter and we headed out into the sunshine.

Given the elegance of the occasion and the spectacular nature of the setting, I should really have enjoyed the next couple of hours. I had said yes to a new experience, after all. But in truth I felt increasingly out of place among the corporate couples. The conversational rhythms eluded me so that when I was pulled into a casual group I ended up seeming either mute or stupid. Josh moved from person to person, like a guided managerial missile, at every stop his face eager and engaged, his manner polished and assertive. I found myself watching him and wondering again what on earth he saw in me. I was nothing like these women, with their glowing peach-coloured limbs and their uncreasable dresses, their tales of impossible nannies and holidays in the Bahamas. I followed in his wake, repeating his lie about my nascent fashion career and smiling mutely and agreeing that *yes, yes it is very beautiful and thank you, ooh, yes, I'd love another glass of champagne* and trying not to notice Josh's bobbing eyebrow.

'How are you enjoying the day?'

A woman with a red-haired bob so shiny it was almost mirrored stood beside me as Josh laughed uproariously at the joke of some older man in a pale blue shirt and chinos.

'Oh. It's great. Thank you.'

I had become very good by then at smiling and saying nothing at all.

'Felicity Lieberman. I work two desks away from Josh. He's doing really well.'

I shook her hand. 'Louisa Clark. He certainly is.' I stepped back and took another sip of my drink.

'He'll make partner within two years. I'm certain of it. You two been dating long?'

'Uh, not that long. But we've known each other a lot longer.'

She seemed to be waiting for me to say more.

'Well, we were sort of friends before.' I had drunk too much and found myself talking more than I had intended. 'I was actually with someone else, but Josh and I, we kept bumping into each other. Well, he says he was waiting for me. Or waiting until me and my ex split up. It was actually kind of romantic. And a bunch of stuff happened, then – bang! Suddenly we were in a relationship. You know how these things go.'

'Oh, I do. He's very persuasive, is our Josh.'

There was something in her laugh that unsettled me. '"Persuasive"?' I said, after a moment.

'So did he do the whispering gallery on you?'

'Did he what?'

She must have caught my look of shock. She leant towards me. *Felicity Lieberman, you are the cutest girl in New York.* She glanced at Josh, then backtracked. 'Oh, don't look like that. We weren't serious. And Josh really does like you. He talks about you *a lot* at work. He's definitely serious. But, Jeez, these men and their moves, right?'

I tried to laugh. 'Right.'

By the time Mr Dumont had made a self-congratulatory speech and couples had begun to float off to their homes I was sinking under an early hangover. Josh held open the door of a waiting taxi but I said I'd walk.

'You don't want to come back to mine? We could grab a bite to eat.'

'I'm tired. And Margot has an appointment in the morning,' I said. My cheeks were aching from all the fake smiling.

His eyes searched my face. 'You're mad at me.'

'I'm not mad at you.'

'You're mad at me because of what I said about your job.' He took my hand. 'Louisa, I didn't mean to upset you, sweetheart.'

'But you wanted me to be someone else. You thought I was beneath them.'

'No. I think you're great. It's just you could do better, because you have so much potential and I –'

'Don't say that, okay? The potential thing. It's patronizing and it's insulting and . . . Well, I don't want you to say it to me. Ever. Okay?'

'Woah.' Josh glanced behind him, perhaps checking to see if any work colleagues were watching. He took my elbow. 'Okay, so what is really going on here?'

I stared at my feet. I didn't want to say anything, but I couldn't stop myself. 'How many?'

'How many what?'

'How many women have you done that thing to? The whispering gallery?'

It threw him. He rolled his eyes and briefly turned away. 'Felicity.'

'Yeah. Felicity.'

'So you're not the first. But it's a nice thing, right? I thought you'd enjoy it. Look, I just wanted to make you smile.'

We stood on each side of the door as the taxi meter ticked, and the driver raised his eyes to the rear-view mirror, waiting.

'And it did make you smile, right? We had a moment. Didn't we have a moment?'

'But you'd already had that moment. With someone else.'

'C'mon, Louisa. Am I the only man you've ever said nice things to? Dressed up for? Made love to? We're not teen-agers. We've got history.'

'And tried and tested moves.'

'That's not fair.'

I took a breath. 'I'm sorry. It's not just the whispering-gallery thing. I find these events a little tricky. I'm not used to having to pretend to be someone I'm not.'

His smile returned, his face softening. 'Hey. You'll get there. They're nice people once you know them. Even the ones I've dated.' He tried to smile.

'If you say so.'

'We'll go on one of the softball days. That's a bit lower key. You'll love it.'

I raised a smile.

He leant forward and kissed me. 'We okay?' he said.

'We're okay.'

'You sure you don't want to come back with me?'

'I need to check on Margot. Plus I have a headache.'

'That's what you get for knocking it back! Drink lots of water. It's probably dehydration. I'll speak to you tomorrow.' He kissed me, climbed into the taxi and closed the door. As I stood there watching, watching, he waved, then tapped twice on the screen to send the taxi forward.

I checked the clock in the lobby when I arrived back and was surprised to find it was only six thirty. The afternoon seemed to have lasted several decades. I removed my shoes, feeling the utter relief that only a woman knows when pinched toes are finally allowed to sink into deep pile carpet, and walked up to Margot's apartment barefoot with them dangling from my hand. I felt weary and cross in a way I couldn't quite articulate, like I'd been asked to play a game whose rules I didn't understand. I'd actually felt as if I'd rather be anywhere else than where I was. And I kept thinking about Felicity Lieberman's *Did he do the whispering gallery on you?*

As I walked through the door I stooped to greet Dean Martin, who bounced his way up the hall to me. His squished little face was so delighted at my return that it was hard to stay grumpy. I sat down on the hall floor and let him jump around me, snuffling to reach my face with his pink tongue until I was smiling again.

'It's just me, Margot,' I called.

'Well, I hardly thought it was George Clooney,' came the response. 'More's the pity for me. How were the Stepford Wives? Has he converted you yet?'

'It was a lovely afternoon, Margot,' I lied. 'Everyone was very nice.'

'That bad, huh? Would you mind fetching me a nice little vermouth if you happen to be passing the kitchen, dear?'

'What the hell is vermouth?' I murmured to the dog, but he sat down to scratch one of his ears with his hind leg.

'Have one yourself, if you like,' she added. 'I suspect you'll be in need of it.'

I was just climbing to my feet when my phone rang. I felt a momentary dismay – it would probably be Josh and I wasn't quite ready to talk to him, but when I checked the screen it was my home number. I pressed the phone to my ear.

'Dad?'

'Louisa? Oh, thank goodness.'

I checked my watch. 'Is everything okay? It must be the middle of the night there.'

'Sweetheart, I've got bad news. It's your granddad.'

26

In Memory of Albert John Compton, 'Granddad'

Funeral service: St Mary and All Saints Parish Church,
Stortfold Green
23 April 12.30 p.m.

All welcome for refreshments afterwards at the Laughing
Dog public house on Pinemouth Street

No flowers, but any donations welcome to the Injured
Jockeys Fund.

'Our hearts are empty, but we are blessed to have
loved you.'

Three days later I flew home in time for the funeral. I cooked
Margot ten days' worth of meals, froze them, and left instructions with Ashok that he was to sneak up to her apartment at
least once a day on a pretext and make sure that she was okay,
or that if she wasn't, I wouldn't walk in a week later to a
health hazard. I postponed one of her hospital appointments, made sure she had clean sheets, that Dean Martin had
enough food and paid Magda, a professional dog-walker, to
come twice a day. I told Margot firmly that she was not to

sack her on day one. I told the girls at the Vintage Clothes Emporium that I would be away. I saw Josh twice. I let him stroke my hair and tell me he was sorry and that he remembered how it felt to lose his own grandfather. It was only when I was finally on the plane that I realized the myriad ways I had made myself busy had been a way not to acknowledge the truth of what had just happened.

Granddad was gone.

Another stroke, Dad said. He and Mum had been sitting in the kitchen chatting while Granddad watched the racing and she had come in to ask if he wanted a top-up of tea and he had slipped away, so quietly and peacefully that fifteen minutes had passed before it had dawned on them that he wasn't just asleep.

'He looked so relaxed, Lou,' he said, as we travelled back from the airport in his van. 'His head was just on one side and his eyes were closed, like he was taking a nap. I mean, God love him, we none of us wanted to lose him, but that would be the way to go, wouldn't it? In your favourite chair in your own house with the old telly on. He didn't even have a bet on that race so it's not like he'd be headed up to the hereafter feeling gutted that he missed out on his winnings.' He tried to smile.

I felt numb. It was only when I followed Dad into our house and saw the empty chair that I was able to convince myself it was true. I would never see him again, never feel that curved old back under my fingertips as I hugged him, never again make him a cup of tea or interpret his silent words or joke with him about cheating at Sudoku.

'Oh, Lou.' Mum came down the corridor and pulled me to her.

I hugged her, feeling her tears seep into my shoulder while Dad stood behind her patting her back and muttering, 'There

there, love. You're all right. You're all right,' as if saying it enough times would make it so.

Much as I loved Granddad I had sometimes wondered abstractly if when he finally went Mum would feel in some way freed from the responsibility of caring for him. Her life had been so firmly tied to his for so long that she had only ever been able to carve out little bits of time for herself – his last months of poor health had meant she could no longer even go to her beloved night classes.

But I was wrong. She was bereft, permanently on the edge of tears. She berated herself for not having been in the room when he had gone, welled up at the sight of his belongings, and fretted constantly over whether she could have done more. She was restless, lost without someone to care for. She got up and she sat down, plumping cushions, checking a clock for some mythical appointment. When she was really unhappy she cleaned manically, wiping non-existent dust from skirting and scrubbing floors until her knuckles were red and raw. In the evenings we sat around the kitchen table while Dad went to the pub – supposedly to sort the last of the arrangements for the funeral tea – and she tipped away the fourth cup she had made by accident for a man who was no longer there, then blurted out the questions that had haunted her since he had died.

'What if I could have done something? What if we had taken him to the hospital for more tests? They might have been able to pick up on the risk of more strokes.' Her hands twisted together over her handkerchief.

'But you did all those things. You took him to millions of appointments.'

'Do you remember that time he ate two packets of chocolate Digestives? That might have been the thing that did it.

Sugar's the devil's work now, by all accounts. I should have put them on a higher shelf. I shouldn't have let him eat those wretched cakes . . .'

'He wasn't a child, Mum.'

'I should have made him eat his greens. But it was hard, you know? You can't spoon-feed an adult. Oh, Lord, no offence. I mean with Will, obviously, it was different . . .'

I put my hand over hers and watched her face crumple. 'Nobody could have loved him more, Mum. Nobody could have cared for Granddad better than you did.'

In truth, her grief made me uncomfortable. It was too close to a place I had been, and not that long ago. I was wary of her sadness, as if it was contagious, and found myself looking for excuses to stay away from her, trying to keep myself busy so that I didn't have to absorb it too.

That night, when Mum and Dad sat going over some paper-work from the solicitor, I went to Granddad's room. It was still just as he'd left it, the bed made, the copy of the *Racing Post* on the chair, two races for the following afternoon cir-cled with blue biro.

I sat on the side of the bed, tracing the pattern on the candlewick counterpane with my index finger. On the bedside table stood a picture of my grandmother in the 1950s, her hair set in rolled waves, her smile open and trusting. I had only fleeting memories of her. But my grandfather had been a constant fixture in my childhood, first in the little house along the street (Treena and I would run down there for sweets on Saturday afternoon as my mother stood at the gate), and then, for the last fifteen years, in a room at our house, his sweet, wavering smile the punctuation to my day, a permanent presence in the living room with his newspaper and a mug of tea.

I thought about the stories he would tell us when we were small of his time in the navy (the ones about desert islands and monkeys and coconut trees might not have been entirely true), about the eggy bread he would fry in the blackened pan – the only thing he could cook – and how, when I was really small, he would tell my grandmother jokes that made her weep with laughter. And then I thought about his later years when I'd treated him almost as a part of the furniture. I hadn't written to him. I hadn't called him. I had just assumed he would be there for as long as I wanted him to be. Had he minded? Had he wanted to speak to me?

I hadn't even said goodbye.

I remembered Agnes's words: that we who travelled far from home would always have our hearts in two places. I placed my hand on the candlewick bedspread. And, finally, I wept.

On the day of the funeral I came downstairs to find Mum cleaning furiously in preparation for the funeral guests, even though to my knowledge nobody was coming back to the house. Dad sat at the table looking faintly out of his depth – not an unusual expression when he was talking to my mother, these days.

'You don't need to get a job, Josie. You don't need to do anything.'

'Well, I need something to do with my time.' Mum took off her jacket and folded it carefully over the back of a chair before going down on her knees to get at some invisible speck of dirt behind a cupboard. Dad wordlessly pushed a plate and knife towards me.

'I was just saying, Lou, love, your mother doesn't need to jump into anything. She's saying she's headed to the Job Centre after the service.'

'You looked after Granddad for years, Mum. You should just enjoy having some time to yourself.'

'No. I'm better if I'm doing something.'

'We'll have no cupboards left if she keeps scrubbing them at this rate,' Dad muttered.

'Sit down. Please. You need to eat something.'

'I'm not hungry.'

'For God's sake, woman. You'll give *me* a stroke if you carry on like this.' He winced as soon as he'd said it. 'I'm sorry. I'm sorry. I didn't mean . . .'

'Mum.' I walked over to her when she didn't appear to hear me. I put my hand on her shoulder and she briefly stilled. 'Mum.'

She pushed herself to her feet and looked out of the window. 'What use am I now?' she said.

'What do you mean?'

She adjusted the starched white net curtain. 'Nobody needs me any more.'

'Oh, Mum, I need you. We all need you.'

'But you're not here, are you? None of you is. Not even Thom. You're all miles away.'

Dad and I exchanged a look.

'Doesn't mean we don't need you.'

'Granddad was the only one who relied on me. Even you, Bernard, you'd be fine with a pie and a pint up the road every evening. What am I supposed to do now? I'm fifty-eight years old and I'm good for nothing. I've spent my whole life looking after someone else and now there's nobody left who even needs me.'

Her eyes brimmed with tears. I thought, for one terrifying minute, that she was about to howl.

'We'll always need you, Mum. I don't know what I'd do if you weren't here. It's like you're like the foundations of a building. I might not see you all the time, but I know you're there. Supporting me. All of us. I bet you Treena would say the same.'

She looked at me, her eyes troubled, as if she weren't sure what to believe.

'You are. And this – this is a weird time. It's going to take a while to adjust. But remember what happened when you started your night classes? How excited you felt? Like you were discovering bits of yourself? Well, that's going to happen again. It's not about who needs you – it's about finally devoting some time to you.'

'Josie,' said Dad, softly, 'we'll travel. Do all those things we thought we couldn't do because it would have meant leaving him. Maybe we'll come and see you, Lou. A trip to New York! See, love, it's not that your life is over, just that it's going to be a different sort of life.'

'New York?' said Mum.

'Oh, my God, I'd love that,' I said, pulling a piece of toast from the rack. 'I could find you a nice hotel and we could do all the sights.'

'You would?'

'Perhaps we can meet that millionaire fella you work for,' said Dad. 'He can give us a few tips, right?'

I'd never actually told them about my change in circumstances. I kept eating my toast, my face blank.

'Us? Go to New York?' said Mum.

Dad reached for a box of tissues and handed them to her. 'Well, why not? We have savings. You can't take it with you. The old man knew that at least. Don't be expecting any expensive bequests, eh, Louisa? I'm frightened to pass the bookie in case he jumps out and says Granddad owes him a fiver.'

Mum straightened up, her cloth in her hand. She looked to one side.

'You and me and Dad in New York City. Well, wouldn't that be a thing?'

'We can look up flights this evening, if you like.' I wondered, briefly, if I could persuade Margot to say her surname was Gopnik.

Mum put a hand to her cheek. 'Oh, gracious, listen to me making plans and Granddad not cold in his grave yet. What would he think?'

'He'd think it was wonderful. Granddad would love the thought of you and Dad coming to America.'

'You really think so?'

'I know so.' I reached across and hugged her. 'He travelled the world in the navy, didn't he? And I also know he'd like to think of you starting back at the adult education centre. No point wasting all that knowledge you've gained over the past year.'

'Though I'm also pretty sure he'd like to think you were still leaving me some dinner in the oven before you went,' said Dad.

'C'mon, Mum. Just get through today and then we can start planning. You did everything you could for him, and I know Granddad would feel you deserved the next stage of your life to be an adventure.'

'An adventure,' Mum mused. She took a tissue from Dad and dabbed at the corner of her eye. 'How did I raise daughters with so much wisdom, eh?'

Dad raised his eyebrows and, with a deft move, slid the toast off my plate.

'Ah. Well, that would be the fatherly influence, you see.' He yelped as Mum flicked her tea-towel at the back of his head and then, as she turned, he smiled at me with a look of utter relief.

*

The funeral passed, as funerals do, with varying degrees of sadness, some tears, and a sizeable percentage of the congregation wishing they knew the tunes to the hymns. It was not an *excessive* gathering, as the priest put it politely. Granddad had ventured out so rarely by the end that few of his friends even seemed to know that he'd passed, even though Mum had put a notice in the *Stortfold Observer*. Either that or most of them were dead too (with a couple of the mourners it was quite hard to tell the difference).

At the graveside I stood beside Treena, my jaw tense, and felt a very particular kind of sibling gratitude when her hand crept into mine and squeezed it. I looked behind me to where Eddie was holding Thom's hand, and he was kicking quietly at a daisy in the grass, perhaps trying not to cry, or perhaps thinking about Transformers or the half-eaten biscuit he had wedged into the upholstery of the funeral car.

I heard the priest murmur the familiar recitation about dust and ashes and my eyes filled with tears. I wiped them away with a handkerchief. And then I looked up, and across the grave at the back of the small throng of mourners stood Sam. My heart lurched. I felt a hot flush, somewhere between fear and nausea. I caught his eye briefly through the crowd, blinked hard and looked away. When I looked back, he had gone.

I was at the buffet at the pub when I turned to find him beside me. I had never seen him in a suit and the sight of him looking both so handsome and so unfamiliar briefly knocked my breath from my chest. I decided to handle the situation in as mature a way as possible and simply refused to acknowledge his presence, peering intently instead at the plates of sandwiches, in the manner of someone who had only recently been introduced to the concept of food.

He stood there, perhaps waiting for me to look up, and then said softly, 'I'm sorry about your granddad. I know what a close family you are.'

'Not that close, clearly, or I would have been here.' I busied myself arranging the napkins on the table, even though Mum had paid for waiting staff.

'Yes, well, life doesn't always work like that.'

'So I've gathered.' I closed my eyes briefly, trying to remove the spike from my voice. I took a breath, then finally looked up at him, my face arranged carefully into something neutral. 'So how are you?'

'Not bad, thanks. You?'

'Oh. Fine.'

We stood for a moment.

'How's your house?'

'Coming on. Moving in next month.'

'Wow.' I was briefly startled from my discomfort. It seemed improbable to me that someone I knew could build a house from nothing. I had seen it when it was just a patch of concrete on the ground. And yet he had done it. 'That's – that's amazing.'

'I know. I'll miss the old railway carriage, though. I quite liked being in there. Life was . . . simple.'

We looked at each other, then away.

'How's Katie?'

The faintest of pauses. 'She's fine.'

My mother appeared at my shoulder with a tray of sausage rolls. 'Lou, sweetheart, would you see where Treen is? She was going to hand these round for me – oh, there she is. Perhaps you could take them to her. There's people over there haven't had anything to eat ye–' She suddenly grasped who I was talking to. She snatched the tray away from me. 'Sorry. I'm sorry. Didn't mean to interrupt.'

'You weren't,' I said, slightly more emphatically than I'd intended. I took hold of the tray's edge.

'I'll do it, love,' she said, pulling it towards her waist.

'I can do it.' I held tight, my knuckles glowing white.

'Lou. Let. Go,' she said firmly. Her eyes burnt into mine. I finally relinquished my grip and she hurried away.

Sam and I stood by the table. We smiled awkwardly at each other but the smiles fell away too quickly. I picked up a plate and put a carrot stick on it. I wasn't sure I could eat anything but it seemed odd to stand there with an empty plate.

'So. Are you back for long?'

'Just a week.'

'How's life treating you over there?'

'It's been interesting. I got the sack.'

'Lily told me. I see a fair bit of her now with the whole Jake thing.'

'Yeah, that was . . . surprising.' I wondered briefly what Lily had told him about her visit.

'Not to me. I could see it from the first time they met. You know, she's great. They're happy.'

I nodded, as if in agreement.

'She talks a lot. About your amazing boyfriend and how you picked yourself up after the firing thing and found another place to live and your job at that Vintage Clothes Emporium.' He was apparently as fascinated as I was by the cheese straws. 'You got it all sorted, then. She's in awe of you.'

'I doubt that.'

'She said New York suits you.' He shrugged. 'But I guess we both knew that.'

I snuck a look at him while his gaze was elsewhere, marvelling with the small part of me that wasn't actually dying that two people who were once so comfortable with each other could now barely work out how to string a sentence together in conversation.

'I have something for you. In my room at home,' I said abruptly. I wasn't entirely sure where it came from. 'I brought it back last time but . . . you know.'

'Something for me?'

'Not you exactly. It's, well, it's a Knicks baseball cap. I bought it . . . a while back. That thing you told me about your sister. She never made it to 30 Rock but I thought, well, maybe Jake might like it.'

He stared at me.

It was my turn to look down at my feet. 'It's probably a stupid idea, though,' I said. 'I can give it to someone else. It's not like I can't find a home for a Knicks cap in New York. And it might be a bit weird, me giving you stuff.'

'No. No. He'd love it. That's very kind of you.' Someone beeped a horn outside and Sam glanced towards the window. I wondered idly if Katie was waiting in the car for him.

I didn't know what to say. There didn't seem to be a right answer to any of it. I tried to fight the lump that had risen to my throat. I thought back to the Strager ball – I'd assumed that Sam would hate it, that he wouldn't have a suit. Why did I think that? The one he was wearing today looked like it had been made for him. 'I'll – I'll send it. Do you know what?' I said, when I couldn't bear it any longer. 'I think I'd better help Mum with those – with the – there are sausages that . . .'

Sam took a step backwards. 'Sure. I just wanted to pay my respects. I'll leave you to it.'

He turned away and my face crumpled. I was glad I was at a wake where nobody would think this particular expression worthy of attention. And then, before I could straighten my face, he turned back to me.

'Lou,' he said quietly.

I couldn't speak. I just shook my head. And then I watched him as he made his way through the mourners and out through the pub door.

That evening Mum handed me a small parcel.

'Is this from Granddad?' I said.

'Don't be daft,' she said. 'Granddad never gave anyone a present for the last ten years of his life. This is from your man, Sam. Seeing him today reminded me. You left it here the last time you came. I wasn't sure what you wanted me to do with it.'

I held the little box and had a sudden memory of our argument at the kitchen table. *Happy Christmas*, he'd said, and dropped it there as he left.

Mum turned away and began washing up. I opened it carefully, peeling off the layers of wrapping paper with exaggerated care, like someone opening an artefact from a previous age.

Inside the little box lay an enamel pin in the shape of an ambulance, perhaps from the 1950s. Its red cross was made of tiny jewels that might have been rubies, or might have been paste. Either way, it glittered in my hand. A tiny note was folded in the roof of the box. *To remind you of me while we're apart. All my love, Your Ambulance Sam. Xxx*

I held it in the palm of my hand and Mum came to look over my shoulder. It's rare that my mother chooses not to speak. But this time she squeezed my shoulder, dropped a kiss on the top of my head and went back to the washing-up.

27

Dear Louisa Clark,

My name is Vincent Weber – grandson of Margot Weber, as I
know her. But you seem to know her by her maiden name of
De Witt.

Your message came as a surprise because my dad doesn't really
talk about his mom – to be honest, for years I was led to believe
that she wasn't even alive, although I realize now that nobody ever
put it in those exact terms.

After I got your message I asked my mom and she said there had
been some big falling-out way before I was born, but I've been
thinking and have decided that's really nothing to do with me, and
I would love to know some more about her (you seemed to hint
that she'd been unwell?). Can't believe I have another grandma!

Please email back. And thank you for your efforts.

Vincent Weber (Vinny)

He came at the agreed time on a Wednesday afternoon, the first
really warm day of May when the streets were full of abruptly
exposed flesh and newly purchased sunglasses. I didn't tell
Margot because (a) I knew she'd be furious and (b) I had a
strong feeling she would simply go out for a walk until he
had left. I opened the front door and there he stood – a tall
blond man with his ear pierced in seven places, wearing a

pair of 1940s-style baggy trousers with a bright scarlet shirt, highly polished brown brogues and a Fair Isle sweater draped around his shoulders.

'Are you Louisa?' he said, as I stooped to pick up the flailing dog.

'Oh, my,' I said, looking him slowly up and down. 'You two are going to get on like a house on fire.'

I walked him down the corridor and we whispered a conversation. It took a full two minutes of Dean Martin barking and snarling before she called, 'Who was at the door, dear? If it's that awful Gopnik woman you can tell her her piano playing is showy, sentimental tripe. And that's from someone who once saw Liberace.' She started to cough.

Walking backwards, I beckoned him towards the living room. I pushed open the door. 'Margot, you have a visitor.'

She turned, frowning slightly, her hands resting on the arm of her chair and surveyed him for a full ten seconds. 'I don't know you,' she said decisively.

'This is Vincent, Margot.' I took a breath. 'Your grandson.'

She stared at him.

'Hey, Mrs De Witt . . . Grandma.' He walked forward and smiled, then stooped and crouched in front of her, and she studied his face.

Her expression was so fierce that I thought she was going to shout at him, but then she gave what sounded like a little hiccup. Her mouth dropped open a half-inch and her bony old hands closed on his sleeves. 'You came,' she said, her voice a low croon, cracking as it emerged from somewhere deep in her chest. 'You came.' She stared at him, her eyes flickering over his features as if she were already seeing similarities, histories, prompting memories long forgotten. 'Oh, but you're so, so like your father.' She reached out a hand and touched the side of his face.

'I like to think I have slightly better taste,' Vincent said, smiling, and Margot gave a yelp of laughter.

'Let me look at you. Oh, my goodness. Oh, you're so handsome. But how did you find me? Does your father know about . . . ?' She shook her head, as if it were a jumble of questions, and her knuckles were white on his sleeves. Then she turned to me, as if she had forgotten I was even there. 'Well, I don't know what you're staring at, Louisa. A normal person would have offered this poor man a drink by now. Goodness. Some days I have no idea what on earth you're doing here.'

Vincent looked startled, but as I turned and walked to the kitchen I was beaming.

28

This was it, Josh said, clapping his hands together. He was sure he was going to get the promotion. Connor Ailes hadn't been invited to a dinner. Charmaine Trent, who had recently been brought across from Legal, hadn't been invited to a dinner. Scott Mackey, the accounts manager, had been invited to a dinner before he became accounts manager, and he'd said he was pretty sure Josh was a shoo-in.

'I mean I don't want to get too confident, but it's all about the social thing, Louisa,' he said, examining his reflection. 'They only ever promote people if they think they can mix with them socially. It's not what you know, right? I was wondering if I should take up golf. They all play golf. But I haven't played since I was, like, thirteen. What do you think of this tie?'

'Great.' It was a tie. I didn't really know what to say. They all seemed to be blue anyway. He knotted it with swift, sure strokes.

'I called Dad yesterday and he said the key thing was to look like you're not dependent on it, right? Like – like I'm ambitious and I'm totally a company man, but equally I could move to another firm at any time because I'd be so much in demand. They have to feel a sense of threat that you might go somewhere else if they don't give you your due, you know what I'm saying?'

'Oh, yes.'

It was the same conversation we had had fourteen times over the past week. I wasn't sure it even required answers on my side. He checked his reflection again, and then, apparently satisfied, walked over to the bed and leant across to run a hand down the back of my hair. 'I'll pick you up just before seven, okay? Make sure you've walked that dog so we don't get held up. I don't want to be late.'

'I'll be ready.'

'Have a nice day. Hey, it was great what you did with the old lady's family, you know? Really great. You did a good thing.'

He kissed me emphatically, already smiling at the thought of the day ahead, and then he was gone.

I stayed in his bed in the exact position he had left me, dressed in one of his T-shirts and hugging my knees. Then I got up, dressed and let myself out of his apartment.

I was still distracted when I took Margot to her morning hospital appointment, leaning my forehead against the taxi window and trying to sound like I understood what she was talking about.

'Just drop me here, dear,' said Margot, as I helped her out. I let go of her arm as she reached the double doors and they slid open as if to swallow her.

This was our pattern for every appointment. I would stay outside with Dean Martin, she would make her way in slowly and I would come back in an hour, or whenever she chose to call me.

'I don't know what's got into you this morning. You're all over the place. Useless.' She stood in the entrance and handed me the lead.

'Thanks, Margot.'

'Well, it's like travelling with a halfwit. Your brain is clearly somewhere else and you're no company at all. Why, I've had to speak to you three times just to get you to do a thing for me.'

'Sorry.'

'Well, make sure you devote your full attention to Dean Martin while I'm inside. He gets very distressed when he knows he's being ignored.' She lifted a finger. 'I mean it, young lady. I'll *know*.'

I was halfway to the coffee shop with the outside tables and the friendly waiter when I found I was still holding her handbag. I cursed and ran back up the street.

I raced into Reception, ignoring the pointed stares of the waiting patients, who glared at the dog, as if I had brought in a live hand grenade. 'Hi! I need to give a bag – a *purse* – to Mrs Margot De Witt. Can you tell me where I might find her? Please. I'm her carer.'

The woman didn't look up from her screen. 'You can't call her?'

'She's in her eighties. She doesn't do cell-phones. And if she did it would be in her purse. Please. She will need this. It's got her pills and her notes and stuff.'

'She has an appointment today?'

'Eleven fifteen. Margot De Witt.' I spelt it out, just in case.

She went through the list, one extravagantly manicured finger tracing the screen. 'Okay. Yeah, I got her. Oncology is down there, through the double doors on the left.'

'I'm sorry, what?'

'Oncology. Down this main corridor, through the double doors on the left. If she's in with the doctor you can leave her purse with one of the nurses there. Or just leave a message with them to tell her where you'll be waiting.'

I stared at her, waiting for her to tell me she'd made a mistake. Finally she looked up at me, her face a question, as if waiting to hear why I was still standing, stupefied, in front of her. I gathered the appointment card off the desk and turned away. 'Thank you,' I said weakly, and walked Dean Martin out into the sunshine.

'Why didn't you tell me?'

Margot sat in the taxi, turned mulishly away from me, Dean Martin panting on her lap. 'Because it's none of your business. You would have told Vincent. And I didn't want him to feel he has to come and see me just because of some stupid cancer.'

'What's your prognosis?'

'None of your business.'

'How . . . how do you feel?'

'Exactly how I felt before you started asking all these questions.'

It all made sense now. The pills, the frequent hospital visits, the diminished appetite. The things I had thought were simply evidence of old age, of over-attentive private US medical care, had all been disguising the much deeper fault line. I felt sick. 'I don't know what to say, Margot. I feel like –'

'I'm not interested in your feelings.'

'But –'

'Don't you dare get all goopy on me now,' she snapped. 'What happened to that English stiff upper lip? Yours made of marshmallow?'

'Margot –'

'I'm not discussing it. There is nothing to discuss. If you're going to insist on getting all wishy-washy with me you can go stay in someone else's apartment.'

When we arrived at the Lavery, she was out of the taxi with unusual vigour. By the time I had finished paying the driver, she was already inside the lobby without me.

*

I wanted to talk to Josh about what had happened but when I texted him he said he was flat out and I could fill him in that evening. Nathan was busy with Mr Gopnik. Ilaria might freak out or, worse, would insist on stopping by all the time and smothering Margot with her own brand of brusque care and reheated pork casseroles. There was really nobody else I could talk to.

While Margot had her afternoon nap I moved quietly into the bathroom and, under pretext of cleaning, I opened the cabinet and looked at the shelf of drugs, noting down the names, until I found the confirmation: morphine. I looked up the other drugs in the cabinet and searched them online until I got my answers.

I felt shaken to the core. I wondered how it must feel to be looking death so squarely in the face. I wondered how long she had left. I realised that I loved the old woman, with her sharp tongue and her sharper mind, like I loved my family. And some tiny part of me, selfishly, wondered what it meant for me: I had been happy in Margot's apartment. It might not have felt permanent, but I'd thought I might have a year or more there at least. Now I had to face the fact that I was on shifting sands again.

I had pulled myself together a little by the time the doorbell rang, promptly, at seven. I answered, and there was Josh, immaculate. Not even a hint of five o'clock shadow.

'How?' I said. 'How do you look like that after a whole day at work?'

He leant forward and kissed my cheek. 'Electric razor. And I left another suit at the dry-cleaner's and changed at work. Didn't want to turn up creased.'

'But surely your boss will be in the same suit he's been in all day.'

'Maybe. But he's not the one angling for a promotion. You think I look okay?'

'Hello, Josh, dear.' Margot walked past on her way to the kitchen.

'Good evening, Mrs De Witt. How are you doing today?'

'I'm still here, dear. That's about as much as you need to know.'

'Well, you look wonderful.'

'And you talk a lot of old bobbins.'

He grinned and turned back to me. 'So what are you wearing, shortcake?'

I looked down. 'Uh, this?'

A short silence.

'Those . . . pantyhose?'

I glanced at my legs. 'Oh, *those*. I've had a bit of a day. They're my feel-better tights, my equivalent of a fresh suit from the dry-cleaner's.' I smiled ruefully. 'If it helps, I only wear them on the *most* special occasions.'

He stared at my legs a moment longer, then dragged a hand slowly over his mouth. 'Sorry, Louisa, but they're not really appropriate for this evening. My boss and his wife are pretty conservative. And it's a really upscale restaurant. Like, Michelin-starred.'

'This dress is Chanel. Mrs De Witt lent it to me.'

'Sure, but the whole effect is just a little bit . . .' he pulled a face '. . . Crazytown?'

When I didn't move he reached out his hands and took hold of my upper arms. 'Sweetheart, I know you love dressing up, but could we keep it a little straighter just for my boss? This evening is really important for me.'

I looked down at his hands and flushed. I felt suddenly ridiculous. Of course my bumblebee tights were wrong for dinner with a financial CEO. What had I been thinking? 'Sure,' I said. 'I'll go and change.'

'You don't mind?'

'Of course not.'

He almost deflated with relief. 'Great. Can you make it super quick? I really don't want to be late and the traffic is backed up all the way down Seventh. Margot, would it be all right if I used your bathroom?'

She nodded wordlessly.

I ran into my bedroom and started hauling my way through my belongings. What did one wear to a posh dinner with finance people? 'Help me, Margot,' I said, hearing her behind me. 'Do I just change the tights? What should I wear?'

'Exactly what you have on,' she said.

I turned to her. 'But he said it's not suitable.'

'For who? Is there a uniform? Why aren't you allowed to be yourself?'

'I –'

'Are these people such fools that they can't cope with someone who doesn't dress exactly like them? Why do you have to pretend to be someone you're so clearly not? Do you want to be one of "those" women?'

I dropped the hanger I was holding. 'I – I don't know.'

Margot lifted a hand to her newly set hair. She gave me what my mother would have called an old-fashioned look. 'Any man lucky enough to be your date shouldn't give a fig if you come out in a trash bag and galoshes.'

'But he –'

Margot sighed, and pressed her fingers to her mouth, like people do when they have a lot more they'd like to say but won't. A moment passed before she spoke again. 'I think at some point, dear, you're going to have to work out who Louisa Clark really is.' She patted my arm. And with that she walked out of the bedroom.

I stood, staring at the space where she had been. I looked down at my stripy legs and back up at the clothes on my rail. I thought of Will, and the day he had given the tights to me.

A moment later Josh appeared in the doorway, straightening his tie. *You're not him*, I thought suddenly. *In fact you're really nothing like him at all.*

'So?' he said, smiling. Then his face fell. 'Uh, I thought you were going to be ready?'

I stared at my feet. 'Actually . . .' I said.

29

Margot told me I should go away for a few days to clear my head. When I said I wouldn't, she asked me why ever not and added that I plainly hadn't been thinking straight for a while: I needed to sort myself out. When I admitted that I didn't want to leave her by herself, she told me I was a ridiculous girl and that I didn't know what was good for me. She watched me from the corner of her eye for a while, her bony old hand tapping irritably on the arm of her chair, then raised herself heavily and disappeared, returning minutes later with a Sidecar so strong that the first sip made my eyes burn. Then she told me to sit my backside down, that my sniffling was getting irritating and I should watch *Wheel of Fortune* with her. I did as I was told and tried not to hear Josh's voice, outraged and uncomprehending, echoing in my head.

You're dumping me over a pair of pantyhose?

When the programme had finished, she looked at me, tutted loudly, told me this really wouldn't do, and that we would go away together instead.

'But you haven't got any money.'

'Goodness, Louisa. It's immensely vulgar to discuss financial matters,' she scolded. 'I'm shocked by the way you young women are brought up to talk about these things.' She told me the name of the hotel on Long Island that she wanted me to call, instructed me to tell them specifically that I was calling on behalf of Margot De Witt in order to get the preferential 'family' rate. She added that she had been thinking about it, and if it really upset me so much, I could pay for both of us. And there, didn't I feel better now?

Which was how I ended up paying for me, Margot and Dean Martin to go on a trip to Montauk.

We caught a train out of New York to a small shingle-clad hotel on the shore that Margot had travelled to every summer for decades until frailty – or finance – had stopped her. As I stood, they welcomed her on the doorstep as if she was, indeed, long-lost family. We picked at a lunch of griddled prawns and salad and I left her talking to the couple who ran the place while I walked down the path to the wide, wind-swept beach, breathed the ozone-infused air and watched Dean Martin skittering happily around in the sand dunes. There, I started to feel, under the giant sky, for the first time in months, as if my thoughts were not infinitely cluttered by everyone else's needs and expectations.

Margot, exhausted by the train journey, spent much of the rest of the next two days in the little drawing room, watching the sea or chatting with the elderly patriarch of the hotel, a weather-beaten Easter Island statue of a man called Charlie, who nodded along to her uninterrupted flow of conversation, and shook his head and said that, no, things weren't what they were, or, yes, things sure were changing fast around there, and the two of them would exhaust this topic over small cups of coffee, then sit, satisfied by how awful everything had become and to have this view confirmed by each other. I realized very quickly that my role had simply been to get her here. She barely seemed to need me at all, except to help with fiddly items of clothing and to walk the dog. She smiled more than I had seen her smile for the entire time I'd known her, which was a useful distraction in itself.

So, for the next four days I had breakfast in my room, read

the books in the little hotel bookshelf, gave in to the slower rhythms of Long Island life and did as instructed. I walked and walked until I had an appetite again and could quell the thoughts in my head with the roar of the waves and the sound of the gulls in the endless leaden sky and the yapping of a small, overexcited dog who couldn't quite believe his luck.

On the third afternoon I sat on my hotel bed, called my mother and told her the truth about my last few months. For once she didn't talk but listened, and at the end of it, she said she thought I had been very wise and very brave, and those two affirmations made me cry a little. She put Dad on and he told me he'd like to kick the arses of those ruddy Gopniks, I wasn't to talk to strangers and to let them know as soon as Margot and I were back in Manhattan. He added that he was proud of me. 'Your life – it's never quiet, is it, love?' he said. And I agreed that, no, it was not, and I thought back two years to my life before Will, when the most exciting thing that happened to me was someone demanding a refund at the Buttered Bun and realized I quite liked it this way, despite everything.

On the last night Margot and I had supper in the hotel's dining room, at her behest. I dressed up in my dark pink velvet top and my three-quarter-length silk culottes and she wore a frilled green floral shirt and matching slacks (I had sewn an extra button in the waistline so that they didn't slip down over her hips) and we quietly enjoyed the widening eyes of the other guests as we were shown to our seats at the best table by the big window.

'Now, dear. It's our last night, so I think we should push the boat out, don't you?' she said, lifting a regal hand to wave at the guests who were still staring. I was just wondering whose particular boat was being pushed when she added, 'I think I'll have the lobster. And perhaps some champagne. I suspect this is the last time I shall come here, after all.'

I started to protest, but she cut me off: 'Oh, for goodness' sake. It's a fact, Louisa. A bald fact. I thought you British girls were made of sterner stuff.'

So we ordered a bottle of champagne and two lobsters, and as the sun set we picked at the delicious, garlicky flesh and I cracked open the claws that Margot was too frail to manage and handed them back to her; she sucked at them with little delighted noises and passed tiny bits of flesh down to where Dean Martin was being diplomatically ignored by everyone else. We shared a huge bowl of French fries (I ate most of them and she scattered a few on her plate and said they were really quite good).

We sat in companionable, overstuffed silence as the restaurant slowly emptied, and she paid with a seldom-used credit card ('I'll be dead before they come looking for payment, hah!'). Then Charlie walked over stiffly and put a giant hand on her tiny shoulder. He said he would be getting off to bed but he hoped he would see her in the morning before she left and that it had been a true pleasure to see her again after all these years.

'The pleasure was all mine, Charlie. Thank you for the most wonderful stay.' Her eyes wrinkled with affection, and they clutched each other's hands until he released hers reluctantly and turned away.

'I went to bed with him once,' she said, as he walked off. 'Lovely man. No good for me, of course.'

As I coughed out my last French fry, she gave me a weary look. 'It was the seventies, Louisa. I'd been alone for a long time. It's been rather nice seeing him again. Widowed now, of course.' She sighed. 'At my age everybody is.'

We sat in silence for a while, gazing out at the endless, inky black ocean. A long way off you could just make out the tiny winking lights of the fishing vessels. I wondered how it would feel to be out there, on your own, in the middle of nowhere.

And then Margot spoke. 'I didn't expect to come back here,' she said quietly. 'So I should thank you. It's been . . . it's been something of a tonic.'

'For me too, Margot. I feel . . . unscrambled.'

She smiled at me before reaching down to pat Dean Martin. He was stretched out under her chair, snoring quietly. 'You did the right thing, you know, with Josh. He wasn't for you.'

I didn't respond. There was nothing to say. I had spent three days thinking of the person I might have become if I had stayed with Josh – affluent, semi-American, mostly happy even, and had discovered that, after a few short weeks, Margot understood me better than I understood myself. I would have moulded myself to fit him. I would have shed the clothes I loved, the things I cared most about. I would have transformed my behaviour, my habits, lost in his charismatic slipstream. I would have become a corporate wife, blaming myself for the bits of me that wouldn't fit, never-endingly grateful for this Will in American form.

I didn't think about Sam. I'd become very good at that.

'You know,' she said, 'when you get to my age, the pile of regrets becomes so huge it can obscure the view terribly.'

She kept her eyes fixed on the horizon and I waited, wondering who she was addressing.

Three weeks passed uneventfully after we returned from Montauk. My life no longer felt as if it held any real certainties at all, so I had decided to live as Will had told me, simply existing in each moment, until my hand was forced again. At some point, I supposed, Margot would be either unwell enough or in debt enough that our contented little bubble would pop and I would have to book my flight home.

Until then, it was not an unpleasant way to live. The routines that punctuated my day gave me pleasure – my runs around Central Park, my strolls with Dean Martin, preparing the evening meal for Margot, even if she didn't eat much, and our now joint nightly viewing of *Wheel of Fortune*, shouting letters at the Mystery Wedges. I upped my wardrobe game, embracing my New York self with a series of looks that left Lydia and her sister slack-jawed in admiration. Sometimes I wore things that Margot lent me, and sometimes I wore things I had bought from the Emporium. Every day I stood in front of the mirror in Margot's spare room and surveyed the racks I was allowed to pick from, and a part of me sparked with joy.

I had work, of sorts, doing shifts for the girls at the Vintage Clothes Emporium while Angelica was away doing a sweep of a women's garment factory in Palm Springs that had apparently kept samples of every item it had made since 1952. I manned the till alongside Lydia, helping pale-skinned young girls into vintage prom dresses and praying the zips would hold, while she reorganized the layout of the racks and fretted noisily about the amount of wasted space in their outlet. 'You know what square footage costs now, around here?' she said, shaking her head at our lone rotating rail in the far corner. 'Seriously. I would be letting that corner as valet parking if we could work out how to get the cars in.'

I thanked a customer who had just bought a sequined tulle bolero and slammed the till drawer shut. 'So why don't you let it? To a shop or something? It would give you more income.'

'Yeah, we've talked about it. It's complicated. As soon as you've got other retailers involved you need to build a partition and separate access and get insurance, and then you don't know who you got coming in at all hours . . . Strangers in our stuff. It's too risky.' She chewed her gum and blew a bubble, popping it absently with a purple-nailed finger. 'Plus, you know, we don't like anybody.'

*

'Louisa!' Ashok was standing on the carpet and clapped his gloved hands together as I arrived home. 'You coming to ours next Saturday? Meena wants to know.'

'Is the protest still on?'

The two previous Saturdays I couldn't help but notice there had been a distinct dwindling of the numbers. The hopes of local residents were almost non-existent now. The chanting had become half-hearted as the city's budgets tightened, the seasoned protesters slowly drifting away. Months after the action had started, just our little core remained, Meena rallying everyone with bottles of water and insisting it wasn't over till it was over.

'It's still happening. You know my wife.'

'Then I'd love to. Thank you. Tell her I'll bring dessert.'

'You got it.' He made a happy mm-mm sound to himself at the prospect of good food, and called as I reached the elevator, 'Hey!'

'What?'

'Nice threads, lady.'

That day I was dressed in homage to *Desperately Seeking Susan*. I wore a purple silk bomber jacket with a rainbow embroidered on the back, leggings, layered vests and an armful of bangles, which had made a pleasing jangle each time I'd whacked the till drawer shut (it wouldn't close properly unless you did).

'You know,' he said, shaking his head. 'I can't believe you used to wear that golf shirt combo when you were working for the Gopniks. That was so not you.'

I hesitated as the lift door opened. I refused to use the service lift, these days. 'You know what, Ashok? You're so right.'

Out of deference to her status as homeowner, I always knocked before I let myself into Margot's apartment, even though I had had a key for months. There was no response the first time and I had to check my reflexive panic, telling myself that she often had the radio on loudly, that Ashok would have let me know if anything was wrong. Finally I let myself in. Dean Martin came skittering up the hallway to greet me, his eyes askew with joy at my arrival. I picked him up, and let his wrinkled nose snuffle all over my face.

'Yes, hello, you. Hello, you. Where's your mum, then?' I put him down and he yapped and ran in excited circles. 'Margot? Margot, where are you?'

She came out of the living room in her Chinese silk dressing-gown.

'Margot! Are you not well?' I dropped my bag and ran to her, but she held up a palm.

'Louisa, something miraculous has happened.'

My response popped out of my mouth before I had a chance to stop it. 'You're getting better?'

'No, no, no. Come in. Come in! Come and meet *my son*.' She turned before I could speak and disappeared back into the living room. I walked in behind her and a tall man in a pastel sweater, the beginnings of a belly straining over his belt buckle, rose from a chair and reached across to shake my hand.

'This is Frank Junior, my son. Frank, this is my dear friend Louisa Clark, without whom I could not have made it through the past few months.'

I tried to cover my feeling of wrong-footedness. 'Oh. Uh. It – it was mutual.' I leant over to shake the hand of the woman beside him, who wore a white roll-neck sweater and had the kind of pale candyfloss hair that she might have spent a lifetime trying to control.

'I'm Laynie,' she said, and her voice was high, like one of those women who had never been able to let go of girlishness. 'Frank's wife. I believe we have you to thank for our little family reunion.' She dabbed at her eyes with an embroidered handkerchief. Her nose was tinged pink, like she had recently been crying.

Margot reached out a hand to me. 'So it turns out Vincent, the deceitful little wretch, told his father about our meetings and my – my situation.'

'Yes, the deceitful little wretch would indeed be me,' said Vincent, appearing at the door with a tray. He looked relaxed and happy. 'Nice to see you again, Louisa.' I nodded, a half smile now fixed on my face.

It was so odd seeing people in the apartment. I was used to the quiet, to it being just me, Margot and Dean Martin, not Vincent in his checked shirt and Paul Smith tie coming through bearing our dinner tray, and the tall man with his legs concertinaed against the coffee table and the woman who kept gazing around the living room with slightly startled eyes, as if she had never been anywhere like this before.

'They surprised me, you know.' Margot told me, her voice croaking a little, like someone who had already talked too much. 'He called up to say he was passing and I thought it was just Vincent and then the door opened a little wider and, well, I can't . . . You must all think me so shocking. I hadn't even got round to getting dressed, had I? I'd quite forgotten until just now. But we have had the loveliest afternoon. I can't begin to tell you.' Margot reached out her other hand and her son took it, and squeezed it. His chin quivered a little with suppressed emotion.

'Oh, it really has been magical,' said Laynie. 'We have so much to catch up on. I honestly think this was the Lord's work bringing us all together.'

'Well, Him and Facebook,' said Vincent. 'Would you like some coffee, Louisa? There's some left in the pot. I just brought some cookies out in case Margot wanted to eat something.'

'She won't eat those,' I said, before I could stop myself.

'Oh, she's quite right. I don't eat cookies, Vincent dear. Those are really for Dean Martin. The chocolate drops aren't actual chocolate, see?'

Margot barely drew breath. She seemed completely transformed. It was as if she'd lost a decade overnight. The brittle light behind her eyes had gone, replaced by something soft, and she couldn't stop talking, her tone babbling and merry.

I backed towards the door. 'Well, I . . . don't want to get in the way. I'm sure you all have a lot to discuss. Margot, give me a shout when you need me.' I stood, waving my hands uselessly. 'It's lovely to meet you all. I'm so pleased for you.'

'We think it would be the right thing if Mom came back with us,' said Frank Junior.

There was a brief silence.

'Came back where?' I said.

'To Tuckahoe,' said Laynie. 'To our home.'

'For how long?' I said.

They looked at each other.

'I mean how long will she be staying? Just so I can pack for her.'

Frank Junior was still holding his mother's hand. 'Miss Clark, we've lost a lot of time, Mom and I. And we both think it would be a fine thing if we could make the most of what we have. So we need to make . . . arrangements.' The words held a hint of possession, as if he were already telling me of his greater claim over her.

I looked at Margot, who looked back at me, clear-eyed and serene. 'That's right,' she said.

'Hold on. You want to leave . . .' I said, and, when nobody spoke, '. . . here? The apartment?'

Vincent's expression was sympathetic. He turned to his father. 'Why don't we head out for now, Dad?' he said.

'Everyone has a lot to process. We certainly have a lot to work out. And I think Louisa and Grandma need to have a talk too.'

He touched my shoulder lightly as he left. It felt like an apology.

'You know, I thought Frank's wife was actually quite pleasant, though not a *clue* how to dress, poor thing. He had such awful girlfriends when he was younger, according to my mother. She wrote me letters for a while describing them. But a white cotton turtle-neck. Can you imagine the horror? A *white turtle-neck*.'

The memory of this travesty – or perhaps the speed at which Margot was talking – brought on a bout of coughing. I fetched a glass of water and waited until she recovered. They had left within minutes after Vincent had spoken up. I got the feeling it was done at his urging, and that neither of his parents really wanted to leave Margot.

I sat down on the chair. 'I don't understand.'

'This must all seem very sudden to you. It was just the most extraordinary thing, Louisa dear. We talked and talked, and we may even have shed a tear or two. He's just the same! It was like we'd never been apart. He's the same – so serious and quiet but actually quite gentle, just as he was as a boy. And that wife of his is just the same – but then, out of the blue, they asked me to come and stay with them. I got the distinct feeling they had all discussed it before they came. And I said I would.' She looked up at me. 'Oh, come on, you and I know it won't be for ever. There is a very nice place two miles from their home that I can move to when it all becomes too difficult.'

'Difficult?' I whispered.

'Louisa, don't get all sappy on me again, for heaven's sake. When I can't do things for myself. When I'm properly unwell. Honestly, I don't imagine I'll be with my son for more than a few months. I suspect that's why they felt so comfortable asking me.' She let out a dry chuckle.

'But – but I don't understand. You said you'd never leave this place. I mean, what about all your things? You can't just go.'

She gave me a look. 'That's exactly what I can do.' She took a breath, her bony old chest lifting painfully underneath the soft fabric. 'I'm dying, Louisa. I'm an old woman and I'm not going to get an awful lot older, and my son, who I thought was lost to me, has been gracious enough to swallow his pain and his pride and reach out. Can you imagine? Can you imagine what it is to have someone do that for you?'

I thought of Frank Junior, his eyes on his mother, their chairs pressed together, his hand holding hers tightly.

'Why on earth would I choose to stay in this place a moment longer if I have a chance to spend time with him? To wake up and see him over breakfast and chat about all the things I've missed and see his children ... and *Vincent* ... dear Vincent. Do you know he has a brother? I have two grandchildren. *Two!* Anyway. I got to say sorry to my son. Do you know how important that was? I got to say sorry. Oh, Louisa, you can hang on to your hurt out of some misplaced sense of pride, or you can just let go and relish whatever precious time you have.'

She placed her hands firmly on her knees. 'So that's what I plan to do.'

'But you can't. You can't just go.' I had started to cry. I'm not sure where it came from.

'Oh, darling girl, I do hope you're not going to fuss about it. Now, now. No tears, please. I have a favour to ask.'

I wiped my nose.

'This is the difficult bit.' She swallowed, with some effort. 'They won't take Dean Martin. They're very apologetic but there are allergies or some such. And I was going to tell them not to be ridiculous and that he had to come with me but, to be honest, I've been rather anxious about what will happen to him, you know, after I've gone. He's got years left, after all. Certainly a lot longer than I have.

'So . . . I wondered whether you would take him for me. He seems to like you. Goodness knows why after how dreadfully you used to cart the poor creature around. The animal must be the very soul of forgiveness.'

I stared at her through my tears. 'You want me to take Dean Martin?'

'I do.'

I looked down at the little dog, who waited expectantly at her feet.

'I'm asking you, as my friend, if . . . if you would consider it. For me.'

She was peering at me intently, her pale eyes scanning mine, her lips pursed. My face crumpled. I was glad for her, but I felt heartbroken at the thought of losing her. I didn't want to be on my own again.

'Yes.'

'You will?'

'Of course.' And then I started to cry again.

Margot sagged with relief. 'Oh, I knew you would. I knew it. And I know you'll take care of him.' She smiled, for once not scolding me for my tears, and leant forward, her fingers closing over my hand. 'You're that kind of person.'

They came two weeks later to take her away. I had thought it faintly indecent haste, but I supposed that none of us was sure quite how much time she had left.

Frank Junior had paid off the mountain of management charges – a situation that could be seen as only slightly less altruistic when you realized that this meant he could inherit

the apartment rather than it being claimed by Mr Ovitz –
but Margot chose to see it as an act of love and I had no
reason not to do the same. He certainly seemed happy to
have her with him again. The couple fussed over her, checking she was okay, that she had all her medication, that she
wasn't too tired or dizzy or feeling unwell or in need of water,
until she flapped her hands and rolled her eyes in mock irritation. But she was going through the motions. She had
barely stopped talking about him since she had told me.

I was to stay and look after the place 'for the foreseeable',
according to Frank Junior. I think that meant until Margot
died, although nobody said it out loud. Apparently the real-
tor had said that nobody would want to rent it as it stood,
and it was a little unseemly to gut it before the 'foreseeable' so
I had been awarded the role of temporary caretaker. Margot
also made the point several times that it would help Dean
Martin to have some stability while he adjusted to his new
situation. I'm not sure Frank Junior felt that the dog's mental
wellbeing was quite as high on his own list of concerns.

She took only two suitcases and wore one of her favourite
suits to travel, the jade bouclé jacket and skirt with the matching pillbox hat. I dressed it with a midnight blue Saint-Laurent
scarf knotted around her narrow neck, to disguise the way it
now emerged, painfully bony, from her collar, and dug out
the turquoise cabochon earrings as a final touch. I worried
that she might be too hot but she seemed to have grown ever
tinier and frailer and complained of cold even on the warmest of days. I stood on the sidewalk outside, Dean Martin in
my arms, watching as her son and Vincent oversaw the packing up of her cases. She checked that they had her jewellery
boxes – she planned to give some of the more valuable items
to Frank Junior's wife, and some to Vincent 'for when he gets
married' and then, apparently satisfied that they were safely

stowed, she walked over to me slowly, leaning heavily on her stick. 'Now. Dear. I've left you a letter with all my instructions. I haven't told Ashok I'm going – I don't want any fuss. But I have left a little something for him in the kitchen. I'd be grateful if you could pass it on once we're gone.'

I nodded.

'I've written everything you need for Dean Martin in a separate letter. It's very important that you stick to his routine. It's how he likes things.'

'You mustn't worry. I'll make sure he's happy.'

'And none of those liver treats. He begs for them but they do make him sick.'

'No liver treats.'

Margot coughed, perhaps with the effort of talking, and waited for a moment until she could be sure of her breath. She steadied herself on her cane and looked up at the building that had housed her for more than half a century, holding up a frail hand to shield her eyes from the sun. Then she turned stiffly and surveyed Central Park, the view that had been hers for so long.

Frank Junior was calling from the car, stooping so that he could see us more clearly. His wife stood beside the passenger door in her pale blue windbreaker, her hands pressed together with anxiety. She was apparently not a woman who liked the big city.

'Mom?'

'One moment, thank you, dear.'

Margot moved so that she stood directly in front of me. She reached out a hand, and as I held him, she stroked his head, three, four times with her thin, marbled fingers. 'You're a good fellow, aren't you, Dean Martin?' she said softly. 'A very good fellow.'

The dog gazed back at her, rapt.

'You really are the most handsome boy.' Her voice cracked on the last word.

The dog licked her palm and she stepped forward and kissed his wrinkled forehead, her eyes closing and her lips pressed to him just a moment too long so that his wonky eyes bulged and his paws paddled against her. Her face sagged momentarily.

'I – I could bring him to see you.'

She kept her face to his, her eyes shut, oblivious to the noise and the traffic and the people around her.

'Did you hear what I said, Margot? I mean once you're settled we could get the train out and –'

She straightened up and opened her eyes, glancing down for a moment.

'No. Thank you.'

Before I could say anything else, she turned away. 'Now, take him for a walk, please, dear. I don't want him to see me go.'

Her son had climbed out of the car and stood on the sidewalk, waiting. He offered her a hand but she waved him away. I thought I saw her blink back tears, but it was hard to tell as my own eyes seemed to be streaming.

'Thank you, Margot,' I called. 'For everything.'

She shook her head, her lips set. 'Now go. Please, dear.' She turned towards the car just as her son approached, his hand outstretched towards her, and I don't know what she did next because I put Dean Martin on the sidewalk as she had told me and walked briskly towards Central Park, my head down, ignoring the stares of the curious people wondering why a girl in glittery hot-pants and a purple silk bomber jacket was crying openly at eleven o'clock in the morning.

I walked for as long as Dean Martin's little legs could stand. And then when he stopped, mutinously, near the Azalea

Pond, his tiny pink tongue hanging out and one eye drooping slightly, I picked him up and carried him, my eyes swollen with tears, my chest one breath away from another racking sob.

I have never really been an animal person. But I suddenly understood what comfort could be gained from burying your face in the soft pelt of another creature, the consolation of the many small tasks that you're obliged to perform for its welfare.

'Mrs De Witt off on vacation?' Ashok was behind his desk as I entered, my head down and my blue plastic sunglasses on.

I didn't have the energy to tell him just yet. 'Yup.'

'She never told me to cancel her papers. I'd better get on to it.' He shook his head, reaching for a ledger. 'Know when she's coming home?'

'Let me get back to you.'

I walked upstairs slowly, the little dog not moving in my arms, as if he were afraid that if he did he might be asked to use his legs again. And then I let myself into the apartment.

It was dead silent, already shot through with her absence in a way it had never been when she was in the hospital, dust motes settling in the still, warm air. In a matter of months, I thought, somebody else would live here, tearing off the 1960s wallpaper, scrapping the smoked-glass furniture. It would be transformed, redesigned, a bolthole for busy executives or a terrifyingly wealthy family with small children. The thought of it made me feel hollow inside.

I gave Dean Martin some water and a handful of kibble as a treat, then made my way slowly through the apartment, with its clothes and its hats and its walls of memories, and told myself not to think about the sad things but about the delight on the old woman's face at the prospect of living out her days with her only child. It was a joy that had been trans-formative, lifting her tired features and making her eyes shine. It made me wonder how much all this stuff, all this memorabilia, had been her way of insulating herself from the lengthy pain of his absence.

Margot De Witt, style queen, fashion editor extraordi-naire, woman ahead of her time, had built a wall, a lovely, gaudy, multi-coloured wall, to tell herself it had all been for *something*. And the moment he had returned to her she had demolished it without a backward glance.

Some time later, when my tears had slowed to intermittent hiccups, I picked the first envelope off the table and opened it. It was written in Margot's beautiful, looping script, a rem-nant of an age when children were judged by their penmanship. As promised, it contained details of the little dog's preferred diet, times of eating, veterinary needs, vac-cinations, flea-prevention and worming schedules. It told me where to find his various winter coats – there were different ones for rain, wind and snow – and his favourite brand of shampoo. He would also require his teeth descaling, his ears cleaning and – I winced – his anal glands emptying.

'She didn't tell me *that* when she asked me to take you on,' I said to him, and he lifted his head, groaned and lowered it again.

Further on, she gave details of where any post should be forwarded, the contact details for the packing company – the items they were not to take were to remain in her bedroom and I should write a note and pin it to the door to tell them not to enter. All the furniture, the lamps, the cur-tains could go. Her son's and daughter-in-law's cards were in the envelope, should I wish to reach them for further clarification.

And now to the important things. Louisa, I didn't thank you in person for finding Vincent – the act of civil disobedience that has brought me so much unexpected happiness – but I'd like to thank you now. And for looking after Dean Martin. There are few people I would trust to do as I ask, and love him as I do, but you are one of them.

Louisa, you are a treasure. You were always too discreet to tell me the details but do not let whatever happened with that foolish family next door dim your light. You are a courageous, gorgeous, tremendously kind little creature and I shall be for ever grateful that their loss has been my gain. Thank you.

It is in the spirit of thanks that I'd like to offer you my wardrobe. To anyone else – except perhaps your rather mercenary friends at that disgusting clothes store – this would be junk. I am well aware of that. But you see my clothes for what they are. Do with them what you want – keep some, sell some, whatever. But I know you will take pleasure in them.

Here are my thoughts – though I'm well aware nobody really wants the thoughts of an old woman. Set up your own agency. Hire them out, or sell them. Those girls seemed to think there was money in it – well, it strikes me that this would be the perfect career for you. There should be enough there for you to start some sort of enterprise. Though, of course, you may have other ideas for your future, far better ones. Will you let me know what you decide?

Anyway, dear roommate, I will look forward to receiving news. Please kiss that little dog for me. I miss him so terribly already.

With fondest regards,
Margot

I put down the letter and sat motionless in the kitchen for a while, then walked through to Margot's bedroom and the dressing room beyond it, surveying the bulging racks, outfit after outfit.

A clothes agency? I knew nothing about business, nothing about premises or accounts or dealing with the public. I was living in a city whose rules I didn't entirely understand, with no permanent address, and I had failed in pretty much every job I had ever held. Why on earth would Margot believe that I could set up a whole new enterprise?

I ran my fingers down a midnight blue velvet sleeve, then pulled out the garment: Halston, a jumpsuit, slashed almost to the waist, with a mesh insert. I put it back carefully and took out a dress – white broderie anglaise, its skirts a mass of ruffles. I walked along that first rail, stunned, daunted. I had only just begun to absorb the responsibility of owning a dog. What was I supposed to do with three rooms full of clothes?

That night I sat in Margot's apartment and turned on *Wheel of Fortune*. I ate the remains of a chicken I had roasted for her last dinner (I suspect she had sneaked most of hers under the table to the dog). I didn't hear what Vanna White said, or shout out letters at the Mystery Wedges. I thought about what Margot had said to me, and wondered about the person she had seen.

Who was Louisa Clark, anyway?

I was a daughter, a sister, a kind of surrogate mother for a time. I was a woman who cared for others but who seemed to have little idea, even now, how to care for herself. As the glittering wheel spun in front of me, I tried to think about what I really wanted, rather than what everyone else seemed to want for me. I thought about what Will had really been telling me – not to live some vicarious idea of a full life but to live my own dream. The problem was, I don't think I'd ever really worked out what that dream was.

I thought of Agnes across the corridor, a woman trying to convince everyone that she could shoehorn herself into a new life while some fundamental part of her refused to stop mourning the role she had left behind. I thought of my sister, her new-found contentment once she had taken the step of understanding who she really was. The way she had stepped so easily into love once she allowed herself to do so. I thought of my mother, a woman so moulded by looking after other people that she no longer knew what to do when she was freed.

I thought of the three men I had loved, and how each of them had changed me, or tried to. Will had left himself indubitably imprinted on me. I had seen everything through the prism of what he had wanted for me. *I would have changed for you too, Will. And now I understand – you probably knew that all along.*

Live boldly, Clark.

'Good luck!' shouted the *Wheel of Fortune* host, and spun again.

And I realised what I really wanted to do.

I spent the next three days collating Margot's wardrobe, sorting the clothing into different sections: six different decades, and within those, daywear, evening wear, special occasion. I took out everything that needed repairing in any small way – buttons missing, gaps in lace, tiny holes – marvelling at how she had managed to avoid moths, and how many seams were not stretched, still perfectly aligned. I held pieces up against myself, tried things on, lifting off plastic covers and letting out little noises of delight and awe that made Dean Martin prick up his ears, then walk away in disgust. I went to the public library and spent half a day looking up everything to do with starting a small business, tax requirements, grants, paperwork, and printed out a file that grew day by day. Then I took a trip to the Vintage Clothes Emporium with Dean Martin and sat down with the girls to ask the best places to get delicate items dry-cleaned, and the names of the best haberdashers to find silk lining fabric for repair.

They were agog at the news of Margot's gift. 'We could take the whole lot off you,' said Lydia, blowing a smoke ring upwards. 'I mean, for something like that we could get a bank loan. Right? We'd give you a good price. Enough for a deposit on a really nice rental! We've had a lot of interest from this television company in Germany. They've got a twenty-four-episode multigenerational series that they want to –'

'Thanks, but I haven't decided what I want to do with it all yet,' I said, trying not to notice their faces fall. I already felt a little protective about those clothes. I leant forward over the counter. 'But I have had another idea . . .'

The following morning I was trying on a 1970 green 'Judy' Ossie Clark trouser suit, checking for rotting seams or tiny holes, when the doorbell rang. 'Hold on, Ashok. Hold on! Let me just grab the dog,' I called, scooping him up as he barked furiously at the door.

Michael stood in front of me.

'Hello,' I said, coldly, when I had recovered from the shock. 'Is there a problem?'

He struggled not to raise an eyebrow at my outfit. 'Mr Gopnik would like to see you.'

'I'm here legitimately. Mrs De Witt invited me to stay on.'

'It's not about that. I don't know what it is, to tell you the truth. But he wants to talk to you about something.'

'I don't really want to talk to him, Michael. But thanks anyway.' I made to close the door but he put his foot in it, stopping me. I looked down at it. Dean Martin let out a low growl.

'Louisa. You know what he's like. He said I wasn't to leave until you agreed.'

'Tell him to walk down the corridor himself then. It's hardly far.'

He lowered his voice. 'He doesn't want to see you here. He

wants to see you at his office. In private.' He looked uncharacteristically uncomfortable, as someone might, who had professed they were your best friend, then dropped you like a hot stone.

'Tell him I might come by later this morning then. When Dean Martin and I have had our walk.'

Still he didn't move.

'What?'

He looked almost pleading. 'The car is waiting outside.'

I brought Dean Martin. He was a useful distraction from my vague sense of anxiety. Michael sat beside me in the limousine and Dean Martin glared at him and at the back of the driver's seat simultaneously. I sat in silence, wondering what on earth Mr Gopnik was going to do now. If he had decided to press charges surely he would have sent the police, rather than his car. Had he waited deliberately until Margot had gone? Had he uncovered other things I was about to be blamed for? I thought of Steven Lipkott and the pregnancy test and wondered what my response would be if he asked point blank what I knew. Will had always said I had the worst poker face. I practised in my head, *I know nothing*, until Michael shot me a sharp look and I realized I'd started saying it out loud.

We were discharged in front of a huge glass building. Michael walked briskly through the cavernous, marble-clad lobby, but I refused to hurry and instead let Dean Martin amble along at his own pace even though I could tell it infuriated Michael. He collected a pass from security, handed it to me, then directed me towards a separate lift near the back of the lobby – Mr Gopnik was plainly too important to travel up and down with the rest of his staff.

We went up to the forty-sixth floor, travelling at a speed that made my eyes bulge almost as much as Dean Martin's, and I tried to hide the slight wobble in my legs as I stepped out into the hushed silence of the offices. A secretary, immaculately dressed in a tailored suit and spiked heels, did a double-take at me – I guessed they didn't get too many people dressed in 1970s emerald Ossie Clark trouser suits with red satin trim, clutching furious small dogs. I followed Michael along a corridor to another office, in which sat another woman, also immaculately dressed in her office uniform.

'I have Miss Clark to see Mr Gopnik, Diane,' he said.

She nodded, and lifted a phone, murmuring something into it. 'He'll see you now,' she said, with a small smile.

Michael pointed me towards the door. 'Do you want me to take the dog?' he said. He was plainly desperate for me not to take the dog.

'No. Thank you,' I said, holding Dean Martin a little tighter to me.

The door opened and there stood Leonard Gopnik in his shirtsleeves.

'Thank you for agreeing to see me,' he said, closing the door behind him. He gestured towards a seat on the other side of the desk and walked slowly around it. I noticed his limp was pronounced and wondered what Nathan was doing with him. He always was too discreet to discuss it.

I said nothing.

He sat down heavily in his chair. He looked tired, I noticed, the expensive tan unable to hide the shadows under his eyes, the strain lines at their edges.

'You're taking your duties very seriously,' he said, gesturing at the dog.

'I always do,' I said, and he nodded, as if that were a fair comeback.

Then he leant forward over the desk and steepled his fingers. 'I'm not someone, Louisa, used to finding myself lost for words, but ... I confess I am right now. I discovered something two days ago. Something which has left me rather shaken.'

He looked up at me. I looked steadily back at him, my expression a study in neutrality.

'My daughter Tabitha had become ... suspicious about some things she'd heard and put a private investigator on the case. This is not something I'm particularly happy about – we are not, as a family, prone to investigating each other. But when she told me what the gentleman had found, it was not something I could ignore. I talked to Agnes about it and she has told me everything.'

I waited.

'The child.'

'Oh,' I said.

He sighed. 'During these rather – extensive discussions, she also explained about the piano, the money for which, I understand, you were under instruction to remove in increments, day by day, from a nearby ATM.'

'Yes, Mr Gopnik,' I said.

He lowered his head as if he had hoped against hope that I might dispute the facts, tell him it was all nonsense, that the private investigator was talking rubbish.

Finally he sat back heavily in his chair. 'We appear to have done you a great wrong, Louisa.'

'I'm not a thief, Mr Gopnik.'

'Plainly. And yet, out of loyalty to my wife, you were prepared to let me believe you were.'

I wasn't sure if it was a criticism. 'I didn't feel like I had a choice.'

'Oh, you did. You absolutely did.'

We sat in the cool office in silence for a few moments. He tapped on his desk with his fingers.

'Louisa, I have spent much of the night trying to figure out how I can put this situation right. And I'd like to make you an offer.'

I waited.

'I'd like to give you your job back. You will, of course, receive better terms – longer holidays, a pay rise, significantly improved benefits. If you would rather not live on site, we can arrange accommodation nearby.'

'A job?'

'Agnes hasn't found anyone she likes half as much as she liked you. You have more than proven yourself, and I'm immensely grateful for your . . . loyalty and your continued discretion. The girl we took on after you has been . . . well, she's not up to it. Agnes doesn't like her. She considered you more of . . . of a friend.'

I looked down at the dog. He looked up at me. He seemed distinctly unimpressed. 'Mr Gopnik, that's very flattering but I don't think I would feel comfortable working as Agnes's assistant now.'

'There are other positions, positions within my organization. I understand that you do not have another job yet.'

'Who told you that?'

'There's not a lot goes on in my building that I don't know about, Louisa. Usually, at least.' He allowed himself a wry smile. 'Look, we have openings in our marketing and administrative departments. I could ask Human Resources to bypass certain entry requirements and we could offer you training. Or I would be prepared to create a position in my philanthropic arm if you felt that was something you were interested in. What do you say?' He sat back, one arm on his desk, his ebonized pen loose in his hand.

An image of this alternative life swam before my eyes – me, dressed in a suit, headed to work each day in these vast glass offices. Louisa Clark, earning a big salary, living somewhere I could afford. A New Yorker. Not looking after anyone, for once, just pushing upwards, the sky limitless above me. It would be a whole new life, a real shot at the American Dream.

I thought of my family's pride if I said yes.

I thought of a scruffy warehouse downtown, filled to the brim with other people's old clothes. 'Mr Gopnik, again, I'm very flattered. But I don't think so.'

His expression hardened. 'So you do want money.'

I blinked.

'We live in a litigious society, Louisa. I am conscious that you hold highly sensitive information about my family. If it's a lump sum you're after, we'll talk about it. I can bring my lawyer into the discussion.' He leant over and put his finger on the intercom. 'Diane, can you —'

It was at this point that I stood. I lowered Dean Martin gently to the floor. 'Mr Gopnik, I don't want your money. If I'd wanted to sue you or — or make money from your secrets I would have done it weeks ago, when I was left without a job or anywhere to live. You've misjudged me now as you misjudged me back then. And I'd like to leave now.'

He took his finger off the phone. 'Please . . . sit. I didn't mean to offend you.' He motioned to the chair. 'Please, Louisa. I need to get this matter sorted out.'

He didn't trust me. I saw now that Mr Gopnik lived in a world where money and status were prized so far above everything else that it was inconceivable to him that somebody wouldn't try to extract some, given the opportunity.

'You want me to sign something,' I said coolly.

'I want to know your price.'

And then it occurred to me. Perhaps I did have one, after all.

I sat down again, and after a moment I told him, and for

the first time in the nine months that we'd met, he looked properly surprised. 'That's what you want?'

'That's what I want. I don't care how you do it.'

He leant back in his chair, and placed his hands behind his head. He looked off to the side, thinking for a moment, then turned back to me. 'I rather wish you would come back and work for me, Louisa Clark,' he said. And then he smiled, for the first time, and reached across the desk to shake my hand.

'Letter for you,' said Ashok, as I walked in. Mr Gopnik had instructed that the car should bring me home and I had asked the driver to drop me two blocks away so that Dean Martin could stretch his legs. I was still shaking from the encounter. I felt light-headed, elated, as if I were capable of anything. Ashok had to call twice before I registered what he'd said.

'For me?' I stared down at the address – I couldn't think who knew I was living at Mrs De Witt's aside from my parents, and my mother always liked to email me to tell me that she'd written me a letter just so I could keep a look out.

I ran upstairs, gave Dean Martin a drink, then sat down to open it. The handwriting was unfamiliar so I flicked the letter over. It was written on cheap copier paper, in black ink, and there were a couple of crossings-out, as if the writer had struggled with what he wanted to say.

Sam.

30

Dear Lou,

I wasn't entirely truthful when we last met. So I'm writing to you now, not because I think it will change anything but because I deceived you once and it's important to me that you know I will never mislead or deceive you again.

I'm not with Katie. I wasn't when I last saw you. I don't want to say too much but it became clear pretty quickly that we are very different people, and that I had made a huge mistake. If I'm honest, I think I knew it from the start. She has put in for a transfer and although they don't like it much at head office it looks like they'll go ahead with it.

I'm left feeling like a fool, and rightly so. Not a day goes by when I don't wish I'd just written you a few lines every day, like you asked, or sent the odd postcard. I should have hung on tighter. I should have told you what I felt when I felt it. I should have just tried a bit harder instead of throwing myself a pity party at the thought of all the people who had left me behind.

Like I said, I'm not writing to change your mind. I know you've moved on. I just wanted to tell you I'm sorry, and that I'll always regret what happened, and that I really hope you're happy (it's kind of hard to tell at a funeral).

Take care of yourself, Louisa.

Love always,
Sam

I felt giddy. Then I felt a bit sick. And then I gulped, swallowing a huge sob of an emotion I couldn't quite identify. And then I screwed the letter up in a ball and, with a roar, hurled it with force into the bin.

I sent Margot a picture of Dean Martin and wrote her a short letter updating her on his wellbeing, just to calm my nerves. I walked up and down the empty apartment and swore a bit. I poured myself a sherry from Margot's dusty drinks cabinet and drank it in three gulps, although it wasn't even lunchtime. And then I pulled the letter out of the bin, opened my laptop, sat on the hall floor with my back to Margot's front door so that I could use the Gopniks' WiFi, and emailed Sam.

> What kind of bullshit letter is that? Why would you send me that now? After all this time?

The answer came back within minutes, as if he had been sitting waiting at his computer.

> I get your anger. I'd probably be angry too. But Lily said you were thinking of getting married and the whole looking at apartments in Little Italy thing just made me think if I didn't tell you now it was going to be too late.

I stared at my screen, frowning. I reread what he'd written, twice. Then I typed:

> Lily told you that?

> Yes. And the thing about you thinking it was a bit soon and not wanting him to think you were doing it for the residency. But how his proposal made it impossible for you to say no.

438

I waited a few minutes, then I typed, carefully:

Sam, what did she tell you about the proposal?

That Josh had gone down on one knee at the top of the Empire State Building? And about the opera singer he hired? Lou, don't be angry with her. I know I shouldn't have made her tell me. I know it's none of my business. But I just asked her how you were the other day. I wanted to know what was going on in your life. And then she kind of knocked me sideways with all this stuff. I told myself to just be glad you were happy. But I kept thinking: What if I had been that guy? What if I had – I don't know – seized the moment?

I closed my eyes.

So you wrote to me because Lily told you I was about to get married?

No. I wanted to write to you anyway. Have done since I saw you in Stortfold. I just didn't know what to say. But then I figured once you were married – especially if you were getting married so quickly – it was going to be impossible for me to say anything afterwards. Maybe that's old-fashioned of me.

Look, I basically just wanted you to know I was sorry, Lou. That's it. I'm sorry if this is inappropriate.

It took a while before I wrote again.

Okay. Well, thanks for letting me know.

I shut the lid and leant back against the front door and closed my eyes for a long time.

I decided not to think about it. I was quite good at not thinking about things. I did my household errands, and I took

Dean Martin on his walks and I travelled to the East Village on the subway in the stifling heat and discussed square footage and partitions and leases and insurances with the girls. I did not think about Sam.

I did not think about him when I walked the dog past the vomitous ever-present garbage trucks, or dodged the honking UPS vans, or twisted my ankles on the cobbles of SoHo, or lugged holdalls of clothing through the turnstiles of the subway. I recited Margot's words and I did the thing I loved, which had now grown from a tiny germ of an idea into a huge oxygenated bubble, which inflated from the inside of me, steadily pushing out everything else.

I did not think about Sam.

His next letter arrived three days later. I recognized the handwriting this time, scrawled across an envelope that Ashok had pushed under my door.

> So I thought about our email exchange and I just wanted to talk to you about a couple more things. (You didn't say I couldn't so I hope you're not going to rip this up.)
>
> Lou, I never knew you even wanted to get married. I feel stupid for not asking you about that now. And I didn't realize you were the kind of girl who secretly wanted big romantic gestures. But Lily has told me so much about what Josh does for you – the weekly roses, the fancy dinners and stuff – and I'm sitting here thinking . . . Was I really so static? How did I just sit there and expect that everything was going to be okay if I didn't even try?
>
> Lou, did I get this so wrong? I just need to know if the whole time we were together you were waiting for me to make some grand gesture, if I misread you. If I did, I'm sorry, again.
>
> It's kind of odd to have to think about yourself so much, especially if you're a bloke not massively prone to introspection. I like doing stuff,

*not thinking about it. But I guess I need to learn a lesson here and I'm
asking you if you'd be kind enough to tell me.*

I took one of Margot's faded notelets with the address at
the top. I crossed out her name. And I wrote:

*Sam, I never wanted anything grand from you. Nothing.
Louisa*

I ran down the stairs, handed it to Ashok for posting and
ran away again just as quickly, pretending I couldn't hear him
asking if everything was okay.

The next letter arrived within days. Each was Express Delivery. It had to be costing him an absolute fortune.

*You did, though. You wanted me to write. And I didn't do it. I was
always too tired or, I'm being honest, I felt self-conscious. It didn't feel
like I was talking to you, just chuntering away on paper. It felt fake.*
*And then the more I didn't do it, and the more you started
adapting to your life there and changing, I felt like – well, what the
hell do I have to tell her anyway? She's going to these fancy balls and
country clubs and riding around in limousines and having the time of
her life, and I'm riding around in an ambulance in east London,
picking up drunks and lonely pensioners who have fallen out of bed.*
*Okay, I'm going to tell you something else now, Lou. And if you
never want to hear from me again I will understand but now we're
talking again I have to say it: I'm not glad for you. I don't think you
should marry him. I know he's smart and handsome and rich and hires
string quartets for when you're eating dinner on his roof terrace and stuff,
but there's something there I don't trust. I don't think he's right for you.*
*Ah, crap. It's not even just about you. It's driving me nuts. I hate
thinking of you with him. Even the thought of him with his arm*

441

around you makes me want to punch things. I don't sleep properly any more because I've turned into this stupid jealous guy who has to train his mind to think about other stuff. And you know me – I sleep anywhere.

You are probably reading this now and thinking, Good, you dickhead, serves you right. And you'd be entitled.

Just don't rush into anything, okay? Make sure he really is all the things you deserve. Or, you know, don't marry him at all.

Sam

x

I didn't respond for a few days that time. I carried the letter around with me and I looked at it in the quiet moments at the Vintage Clothes Emporium and when I stopped for coffee in the dog-friendly diner near Columbus Circle. I reread it when I was getting into my sagging bed at night and thought about it when I was soaking in Margot's little salmon-coloured bathtub.

And then, finally, I wrote back:

Dear Sam,

I'm not with Josh any more. To use your phrase, we turned out to be very different people.

Lou

PS For what it's worth, the thought of a violinist hovering over me while I'm trying to eat makes my toes curl.

31

Dear Louisa,

So I had my first decent night's sleep in weeks. I found your letter when I got back from a night shift at six a.m. and I have to tell you it made me so bloody glad that I wanted to shout like a crazy person and do a dance, but I'm crap at dancing and I had nobody to talk to so I went and let the hens out and sat on the step and told them instead (they were not massively impressed. But what do they know?).

So can I write?

I have stuff to say now. I also have a really stupid grin on my face for about eighty per cent of my working day. My new partner (Dave, forty-five, definitely not about to bring me French novels) says I'm scaring the patients.

Tell me what's going on with you. Are you okay? Are you sad? You didn't sound sad. Maybe I just want you not to be sad.

Talk to me.

Love,
Sam x

The letters arrived most days. Some were long and rambling, some just a couple of lines, a few scribbles, or a photo of him showing different parts of his now-completed house. Or hens. Sometimes the letters were long, exploratory, fervent.

We went too fast, Louisa Clark. Perhaps my injury accelerated it all. You can't play hard to get with someone after they've literally held your insides with their bare hands, after all. So maybe this is good. Maybe now we get to really talk to each other.

I was a mess after Christmas. I can tell you that now. I like to feel I've done the right thing. But I didn't do the right thing. I hurt you and it haunted me. There were so many nights when I just gave up on sleep and went to work on the house instead. I'd fully recommend behaving like an arse if you want to get a building project completed.

I think about my sister a lot. Mostly what she'd say to me. You don't have to have known her to imagine what she'd be calling me right now.

Day after day they came, sometimes two in twenty-four hours, sometimes supplemented by email but most often just long, handwritten essays, windows into the inside of Sam's head and heart. Some days I almost didn't want to read them – afraid to renew an intimacy with the man who had so comprehensively broken my heart. On others I found myself running downstairs barefoot in the mornings, Dean Martin at my heels, standing in front of Ashok and bouncing on my toes as he flicked through the wedge of post on his desk. He would pretend there was nothing, then pull one from his jacket and hand it over with a smile as I bolted back upstairs to enjoy it in private.

I read them over and over, discovering with each one how little we had really known each other before I left, building a new picture of this quiet, complicated man. Sometimes his letters made me sad:

Really sorry. No time today. Lost two kids in an RTA. Just need to go to bed.

X

PS I hope your day was full of good things.

444

But mostly they did not. He talked of Jake and how Jake had told him that Lily was the only person who really understood how he felt, and how each week Sam would take Jake's dad on a walk along the canal path or make him help paint the walls of the new house just to try to get him to open up a bit (and to stop eating cake). He talked of the two hens he had lost to a fox, the carrots and beetroot that were growing in his vegetable patch. He told me how he had kicked his bike exhaust in desperation and fury on Christmas Day after he had left me at my parents' and hadn't had the dent repaired because it was a useful reminder of how miserable he had felt when we weren't talking. Every day he opened up a little more, and every day I felt I understood him a little better.

Did I tell you Lily stopped by today? I finally told her that you and I had been in touch and she went bright pink and coughed out a piece of gum. Seriously. I thought I was going to have to do the Heimlich on her.

I wrote back in the hours when I was neither working nor walking Dean Martin. I drew him little vignettes of my life, my careful cataloguing and repairing of Margot's wardrobe, sending photographs of items that fitted me as if they had been made for me (he told me he pinned these up in his kitchen). I told him of how Margot's idea of the dress agency had taken root in my imagination and how I couldn't let it go. I told him of my other correspondence – spidery little cards from Margot, still radiant with joy at her son's forgiveness, and from her daughter-in-law, Laynie, who sent me sweet flowered cards updating me on Margot's deteriorating condition and thanking me for bringing her husband some closure, expressing her sadness that it had taken so long for it to happen.

I told Sam how I had begun to look for apartments, how I had headed, with Dean Martin, into unfamiliar new neighbourhoods – Jackson Heights, Queens, Park Slope, one eye trying to assess the risk of being murdered in my bed, the other trying not to balk at the terrifying differential between square footage and cost.

I told him of my now weekly dinners with Ashok's family, how their casual insults and evident love for each other made me miss my own. I told him how my thoughts returned again and again to Granddad, far more so than when he was alive, and how Mum, freed from all responsibility, was still finding it impossible to stop grieving him. I told him how, despite spending more time by myself than I had in years, despite living in the vast, empty apartment, I felt, curiously, not lonely at all.

And, gradually, I let him know what it meant to me to have him in my life again, his voice in my ear in the small hours, the knowledge that I meant something to him. The sense of him as a physical presence, despite the miles that separated us.

Finally I told him I missed him. And realized almost as I pressed *send* that that really didn't solve anything at all.

Nathan and Ilaria came for dinner, Nathan bringing a clutch of beers and Ilaria a spicy pork and bean casserole that nobody had wanted. I had thought about how often Ilaria seemed to cook dishes that nobody wanted. The previous week she had brought over a prawn curry, which I distinctly remembered Agnes telling her never to serve again.

We sat with our bowls on our laps, side by side on Margot's sofa, mopping up the rich tomato sauce with chunks of cornbread and trying not to belch at each other as we talked over the television. Ilaria asked after Margot, crossing herself and shaking her head sadly when I told her of Laynie's updates. In turn she told me Agnes had banned Tabitha from the apartment, a cause of some stress for Mr Gopnik, who had chosen to deal with this particular family fracture by spending even more time at work.

'To be fair, there's a lot going on at the office,' said Nathan.

'There's a lot going on across the corridor.' Ilaria raised an eyebrow at me.

'The *puta* has a daughter,' she said quietly, when Nathan got up to visit the bathroom, wiping her hands on a napkin.

'I know,' I said.

'She is coming to visit, with the *puta's* sister.' She sniffed, picked at a loose thread on her trousers. 'Poor child. It is not her fault she is coming to visit with a family of crazies.'

'You'll look out for her,' I said. 'You're good at that.'

'Colour of that bathroom!' said Nathan, arriving back in the room. 'I didn't think anyone did cloakroom suites in mint green. You know there's a bottle of body lotion in there dated 1974?'

Ilaria raised her eyebrows and compressed her lips.

Nathan left at a quarter past nine, and as the door closed behind him Ilaria lowered her voice, as if he could still hear, and told me he was dating a personal trainer from Bushwick who wanted him to visit at all hours of the day and night. Between the girl and Mr Gopnik he barely had time to talk to anybody these days. What could you do?

Nothing, I said. People were going to do what they were going to do.

She nodded, as if I had imparted some great wisdom, and padded back down the corridor.

'Can I ask you something?'

'Sure! Nadia, baby, take that through to Grandma, will you?' Meena stooped to give the child a small plastic cup of iced water. It was a sweltering evening and every window in Ashok

447

and Meena's apartment was open. Despite the two fans that whirred lazily, the air was still stubbornly resistant to movement. We were preparing supper in the tiny kitchen and every motion seemed to make a bit of me stick to something.

'Has Ashok ever hurt you?'

Meena turned swiftly from the stove to face me.

'Not physically, I mean. Just . . .'

'My feelings? As in messing me around? Not too much, to be honest. He's not really built that way. He did once joke that I looked like a whale when I was forty-two weeks pregnant with Rachana, but after I got past the hormones and stuff I kind of had to agree with him. And, boy did he pay for that one!' She let out a honking laugh at the memory, then reached into a cupboard for some rice. 'Is this your guy in London again?'

'He writes to me. Every day. But I . . .'

'You what?'

I shrugged. 'I'm afraid. I loved him so much. And it was so awful when we split up. I guess I'm just afraid that if I let myself fall again I'll be setting myself up for more hurt. It's complicated.'

'It's always complicated.' She wiped her hands on her apron. 'That's life, Louisa. So show me.'

'What?'

'The letters. Come on. Don't pretend you don't carry them around all day. Ashok says your whole face goes kinda mushy when he hands one over.'

'I thought doormen were meant to be discreet!'

'That man has no secrets from me. You know that. We are *highly invested* in the twists and turns of your life down there.' She laughed and held out her hand, waggling her fingers impatiently. I hesitated just a moment, then pulled the letters carefully from my handbag. And, oblivious to the comings and goings of her small children, to the muffled laughter of her mother at the television comedy next door, to the noise and the sweat and the rhythmic click-click-click of the overhead fan, Meena bent her head over my letters and read them.

The strangest thing, Lou. So I've spent three years building this damn house. Obsessing over the right window frames and which kind of shower cubicle and whether to go with the white plastic power sockets or the polished nickel. And now it's done, or as done as it will ever be. And I sit here alone in my immaculate front room with the perfect shade of pale grey paint and the reconditioned wood-burner and the triple-pleat interlined curtains that my mum helped me choose, and I wonder, well, what was the bloody point? What did I build it for?

I think I needed a distraction from the loss of my sister. I built a house so I didn't have to think. I built a house because I needed to believe in the future. But now it's done and I look around these empty rooms, I feel nothing. Maybe some pride that I actually finished the job but apart from that? Nothing at all.

Meena stared at the last few lines for a long moment. Then she folded the letter, placed it carefully in the pile and handed them back to me. 'Oh, Louisa,' she said, her head cocked to one side. 'Come *on*, girl.'

1442 Lantern Drive
Tuckahoe
Westchester, NY

Dear Louisa,

I hope you are well and that the apartment is not proving too trouble-some. Frank says the contractors are coming to look round in two weeks – could you be there to let them in? We'll give you the firm details nearer the time.

Margot isn't up to writing too much these days – she finds a lot of things tiring and those drugs do make her a little woozy – but I thought you'd like to know that she is being well cared for. We have decided, despite everything, we cannot bear to move her into the home so she will stay with us, with some help from the very kind medical staff. She still has plenty to say to Frank and me, oh, yes! She has us running round like headless chickens most days! I don't mind. I quite like having someone to look after, and on her good days it's lovely hearing all the stories of when Frank was a boy. I think he likes hearing them too, even though he won't admit as much. Two peas in a pod, those two!

Margot asked me to ask you would you mind sending another picture of the dog? She did so like the other one you sent. Frank has put it in a lovely silver frame beside her bed and I know it is a great comfort to her as she spends so much time resting now. I can't say I find the little fellow quite as pleasing to look at as she plainly does, but each to her own.

She sends you her love and says she hopes you're still wearing those gorgeous stripy pantyhose. I'm not sure if that's the pharmaceuticals talking, but I know she means well!

With warmest wishes,

Laynie G. Weber

'Did you hear?'

I was headed out with Dean Martin to work. Summer had begun to assert its presence forcefully, every day warmer and more humid, so that the short walk to the subway left my shirt stuck to my lower back, and delivery boys exposed pale, sunburnt flesh on their bikes and swore at jaywalking tourists. But I was wearing my 1960s psychedelic dress that Sam had bought me and a pair of cork wedge shoes with pink flowers over the strap, and after the winter I'd had, the sun on my arms was like a balm.

'Did I hear what?'

'The library! It's been saved! Its future has been secured for the next ten years!' Ashok thrust his phone at me. I stopped on the carpet and lifted my sunglasses to read the text message from Meena. 'I can't believe it. An anonymous donation in honour of some dead guy. The – hang on, I got it here.' He scanned the message with a finger. 'The William Traynor Memorial Library. But who cares who it is! Funding for ten years, Louisa! And the city council has agreed! Ten years! Oh, man. Meena is over the *moon*. She was so sure we'd lost it.'

I peered at the phone then handed it back to him. 'It's a nice thing, right?'

'It's amazing! Who knew, Louisa? Huh? Who knew? One for the little people. Ohhh, yes!' Ashok's smile was enormous.

I felt something rise inside me then, a feeling of joy and anticipation so great that it seemed as if the world had briefly stopped turning, like there was just me and the universe and a million good things that could happen if you only hung on in there.

I looked down at Dean Martin, then back at the lobby. I waved to Ashok, adjusted my sunglasses and set off down Fifth Avenue, my own smile growing wider with every step.

I had only asked for five.

32

So, I guess at some point we have to talk about the fact that your year is nearly up. Do you have a date in mind to come home? I'm guessing you can't stay in the old woman's place for ever.

I've been thinking about your dress agency – Lou, you could use my house as a base if you wanted, got a lot of spare room here, completely free. If you fancied it, you could stay too.

If you think it's too soon for that but you don't want to disrupt your sister's life by moving back to the flat, you could have the railway carriage? This is not my preferred option, by the way, but you always loved it and there is something quite appealing in the thought of having you just across the garden . . .

There is, of course, another option, which is that this is all too much and you don't want anything to do with me, but I don't much like that one. It's a crappy option. I hope you think so too.

Thoughts?
Sam x

PS Picked up a couple who had been married fifty-six years tonight. He had breathing difficulties – nothing too serious – and she wouldn't let go of his hand. Fussed over him until they got to hospital. I don't usually notice these things but tonight? I don't know.

I miss you, Louisa Clark.

I walked the length of Fifth Avenue, with its clogged artery of traffic and its brightly coloured tourists blocking the side-walks, and I thought how lucky you might be to find not one but two extraordinary men to love – and what a fluke it was if they happened to love you back. I thought about how you're shaped so much by the people who surround you, and how careful you have to be in choosing them for this exact reason, and then I thought, despite all that, in the end maybe you have to lose them all in order to truly find yourself.

I thought about Sam and a couple who had been married for fifty-six years, whom I would never meet, and his name in my head became the drumbeat of my footfall as I walked past the Rockefeller Plaza, past the gaudy glitz of Trump Tower, past St Patrick's, past the huge glowing Uniqlo, with its dazzling pixellated screens, past Bryant Park, the vast and ornate New York Public Library with its vigilant masonry lions, the shops, the hoardings, the tourists, the street vendors and rough sleepers – all the daily features of a life I loved in a city that he didn't inhabit, and yet, above the noise and the sirens and the blare of the horns, I realised he was there at every step.

Sam.

Sam.

Sam.

And then I thought about how it would feel to go home.

28 October 2006

Mum,

In haste, but I'm coming back to England! I got the job with Rupe's firm, so I'll be handing in my notice tomorrow and no doubt headed out of the office with my belongings in a box minutes later – these Wall Street firms don't like to hang on to people out here if they think you might plunder the client lists.

So, come the New Year, I'll be executive director in Mergers and Acquisitions back in London. Really looking forward to a new challenge. Thought I'd take a little break first – might do that month-long Patagonian trek I've been going on about – and then I'll have to find somewhere to live. If you get the chance, could you sign me up with some estate agents? Usual postcodes, very central, two/three beds. Underground parking for the bike if possible (yes, I know you hate me using it).

Oh, and you'll like this. I met someone. Alicia Deware. She's actually English but she was out here visiting friends and I met her at a bloody awful dinner and we went out a few times before she had to head back to Notting Hill. Proper dating, not the New York kind. Early days but she's good fun. I'll be seeing a bit of her when I come back. Don't go looking at wedding hats just yet, though. You know me.

So that's it! Give my love to Dad – tell him I'll be buying him a pint or two at the Royal Oak very soon.

To new beginnings, eh?

With love, your son
Will x

I read and reread Will's letter, with its hints of a parallel universe, and what-might-have-been landed gently around me like falling snow. I read between the lines at the future that could have been his and Alicia's – or even his and mine. More than once William John Traynor had pushed the course of my life off its predetermined rails – not with a nudge but with an emphatic shove. By sending me his correspondence, Camilla Traynor had inadvertently ensured he did it again.

To new beginnings, eh?

I read his words once more, then folded the letter carefully back with the others and sat, thinking. Then I poured myself the last of Margot's vermouth, stared into space for a bit, sighed, walked to the front door with my laptop, sat on the floor and wrote:

Dear Sam,

I'm not ready.

I know it's been almost a year and I originally said that was it – but here's the thing: I'm not ready to come home.

All my life I've ended up looking after other people, fitting myself around what they need, what they wanted. I'm good at it. I do it before I even realize what I'm doing. I'd probably do it to you too. You have no idea how much right now I want to book a flight and just be with you.

But these last couple of months something has happened to me – something that stops me doing just that.

I'm opening my dress agency here. It's going to be called the Bee's Knees and it's going to be based at the corner of the Vintage Clothes Emporium and clients can buy from the girls or rent from me. We're pooling contacts, stumping up for some advertising, and I hope we'll help each other get business. I open my doors on Friday and I've been writing to everyone I can think of. Already we've had a whole lot of interest from film-production people and fashion magazines and even women who just want to hire something for fancy dress. (You would not believe the number of Mad Men themed parties in Manhattan.)

It's going to be hard and I'm going to be broke, and when I'm home each night I pretty much fall asleep on my feet, but for the first time in my life, Sam, I wake up excited. I love meeting the customers and working out what is going to look good on them. I love stitching these beautiful old clothes to make them as good as new. I love the fact that every day I get to reimagine who I want to be.

You once told me you'd wanted to be a paramedic from when you were a boy. Well, I've waited nearly thirty years to work out who I'm meant to be. This dream of mine might last a week or it might last a year, but every day I head down to the East Village with my holdalls full of clothes and my arms ache and I feel like I'll never be ready and, well, I just feel like singing.

I think about your sister a lot. I think about Will too. When people we love die young it's a nudge, reminding us that we shouldn't take any of it for granted, that we have a duty to make the most of what we have. I feel like I finally get that.

So here it is: I've never really asked anyone for anything. But if you love me, Sam, I want you to join me – at least while I see if I can make this thing happen. I've done some research and there's an exam you'd need to pass and apparently hiring in New York State is seasonal but they do need paramedics.

You could rent out your house for an income, and we could get a little apartment in Queens, or maybe the cheaper reaches of Brooklyn, and every day we would wake up together and, well, nothing would make me happier. And I would do everything I could – in the hours that I'm not covered with dust and moths and stray sequins – to make you glad you were here with me.

I guess I want it all.

You only get one life, right?

You once asked me if I wanted a grand gesture. Well, here it is: I'll be where your sister always wanted to be, the evening of

25 July at seven p.m. You know where to find me if the answer's yes. If not, I'll stand there for a while, take a long view, and just be glad that, even if it was only in this way, we found each other again.

All my love always,
Louisa xxx

33

I saw Agnes once more before I finally left the Lavery. I had staggered in with two armfuls of clothing that I was bringing home for repair, the plastic covers sticking uncomfortably to my skin in the heat. As I walked past the front desk two dresses slid to the floor. Ashok leapt forward to pick them up for me and I struggled to keep hold of the rest.

'You got your work cut out this evening.'

'I certainly have. Getting this lot back on the subway was an absolute nightmare.'

'I can believe it. Oh, excuse me, Mrs Gopnik. I'll just get those out of your way.'

I looked up as Ashok swept my dresses from the carpet with a fluid movement and took a step back to allow Agnes through unimpeded.

I straightened as she passed, as far as I could with my armful of clothes. She was wearing a simple shift dress with a wide scoop neck, and flat pumps, and looked, as she always did, as if somehow the prevailing weather conditions – whether extreme heat or cold – simply didn't apply to her. She was holding the hand of a small girl, around four or five years old, in a pinafore dress, who slowed to peer up at the brightly coloured garments I was holding in front of me. She had honey-blonde hair, which tapered to fine curls, combed back neatly into two velvet bows, and her mother's slanting eyes, and as she looked at me she allowed herself a small, mischievous smile at my predicament.

I couldn't help but grin back, and as I did, Agnes turned

to see what the child was looking at and our eyes locked. I froze briefly, made to straighten my face, but before I could, the corners of her mouth twitched, like her daughter's, almost as if she couldn't help herself. She nodded at me, a gesture so small that it's possible only I could have seen it. And then she stepped through the door that Ashok was holding back, the child already breaking into a skip, and they were gone, swallowed by the sunlight and the ever-moving human traffic of Fifth Avenue.

34

From: MrandMrsBernardClark@yahoo.com
To: BusyBee@gmail.com

Dear Lou,

Well. I had to read that twice just to check I'd got it right. I looked at the girl in those newspaper pictures and I thought can this possibly be my little girl in an actual New York newspaper?

Those are wonderful pictures of you with all your dresses, and you look so gorgeous dressed up with your friends. Did I tell you how proud Daddy and I are? We've cut out the ones from the free-sheet and Daddy has screen-shotted all the ones we could find on the internet (did I tell you he's started a computer course at the adult education centre? He'll be Stortfold's Bill Gates next). We're sending you all our love and I know you'll make a success of it, Lou. You sounded so upbeat and bold on the telephone – when you rang off I sat there staring at the phone and I couldn't believe this was my little girl, full of plans, calling from her own business across the Atlantic. (It is the Atlantic, isn't it? I always get it mixed up with the Pacific.)

So here's OUR big news. We're going to come and see you later in the summer! We'll come when it cools down a bit – didn't much like the sound of that heat-wave of yours: you know your daddy chafes in unfortunate places. Deirdre from the travel agents is letting us use her staff discount and we're booking the flights at the end of this week. Could we stay with you in the old lady's flat?

If not, could you tell us where to go? NOWHERE WITH BEDBUGS.

Let me know what dates suit you. I'm so excited!!

Ever so much love,
Mum xxx

PS Did I tell you Treena got a promotion? She always was such a smart girl. You know, I can see why Eddie is so keen on her.

25 July

'Wisdom and Knowledge Shall Be the Stability of Thy Times.'

I stood in the epicentre of Manhattan in front of the towering building, letting my breathing slow, and stared at the gilded sign above the vast entrance to 30 Rockefeller Plaza. Around me New York teemed in the evening heat, the sidewalks solid with meandering tourists, the air thick with blaring horns and the ever-present scent of exhaust and overheated rubber. Behind me a woman with a 30 Rock golf shirt, her voice struggling to be heard over the racket, was giving a well-rehearsed tour speech to a group of Japanese sightseers. *The building project was completed in 1933 by noted architect Raymond Hood in the art deco style – Sir, please stay together, sir. Ma'am? Ma'am? – and was originally named the RCA building before becoming the GE building in – ma'am? Over here please . . .* I gazed up at its sixty-seven floors and took a deep breath.

It was a quarter to seven.

I had wanted to look perfect for this moment, had planned to head back to the Lavery at five to give myself time to shower and pick an appropriate outfit (I was thinking Deborah Kerr in *An Affair To Remember*). But Fate had intervened in the form of a stylist from an Italian fashion magazine, who had arrived at the Vintage Clothing Emporium at four thirty and wanted to look at all the two-piece suits for a feature she was planning, then needed her colleague to try some on so she could take pictures and come back to me. Before I knew what was happening it was twenty to six and I barely had time to run Dean Martin home and feed him before heading down here. So here I was, sweaty and a little frazzled, still in my work clothes, about to find out which way my life was about to go next.

Okay, ladies and gentlemen, this way to the observation deck, please.

I had stopped running several minutes previously, but still felt breathless as I made my way across the plaza. I pushed at the smoked-glass door and noted with relief that the queue for tickets was short. I had checked on TripAdvisor the night before and been warned that queues could be lengthy but felt somehow too superstitious to buy one in advance. So I waited my turn, checking my reflection in my compact, glancing around me surreptitiously on the off-chance he had turned up early, then bought a ticket that gave me access between the hours of six fifty and seven ten, followed the velvet rope and waited while I was shepherded with a group of tourists towards a lift.

Sixty-seven floors, they said. So high that the ride up was meant to make your ears pop.

He would come. Of course he would come.

What if he didn't?

This was the thought that had crossed my mind ever since his one-line response to my email. 'Okay. I hear you.' Which really could have meant anything. I waited to see if he wanted to ask questions about my plan, or say anything else that hinted at his decision. I reread my own email, wondering if perhaps I had sounded off-putting, too bold, too assertive, whether I had conveyed my own strength of feeling. I loved Sam. I wanted him with me. Did he understand how much? But having issued the most enormous of ultimata it seemed weird to start double-checking that it had been understood properly, so I simply waited.

Six fifty-five p.m. The lift doors opened. I held out my ticket and stepped in. Sixty-seven floors. My stomach tightened.

The lift began to move upwards slowly and I felt a sudden panic. What if he didn't come? What if he'd got it, but changed his mind? What would I do? Surely he wouldn't do that to me, not after all this. I found myself taking an audible gulp of air, and pressed my hand to my chest, trying to steady my nerves.

'It's the height, isn't it?' A kindly woman next to me reached out and touched my arm. 'Sixty-seven floors up is quite a distance.'

I tried to smile. 'Something like that.'

If you can't leave your work and your house and all the things that make you happy I will understand. I'll be sad, but I'll get it.

You'll always be with me one way or the other.

I lied. Of course I lied. *Oh, Sam, please say yes. Please be waiting when the doors open again.* And then the lift stopped.

'Well, that wasn't sixty-seven floors,' someone said, and a couple of people laughed awkwardly. A baby in a pram gazed at me with wide brown eyes. We all stood for a moment, then someone stepped out.

'Oh. That wasn't the main elevator,' said the woman beside me, pointing. '*That*'s the main elevator.'

And there it was. At the far end of an endless snaking horseshoe of people.

I stared at it in horror. There must have been a hundred visitors, two hundred even, milling quietly, staring up at the museum exhibits, the laminated histories on the wall. I looked at my watch. It was already one minute to seven. I texted Sam, watching in horror as the message refused to send. I started to push my way through the crowd, muttering, 'I'm sorry. I'm sorry,' as people tutted loudly and yelled, 'Hey lady, we're all waiting here.' Head down, I made my way past the wallboards that told the story of the Rockefeller building, of its Christmas trees, the video exhibit of NBC, bobbing and weaving, muttering my apologies. There are few grumpier people than overheated tourists who have found themselves waiting in an unexpected queue. One grabbed at my sleeve. 'Hey! You! We're all waiting!'

'I'm meeting someone,' I said. 'I'm so sorry. I'm English. We're normally *very good* at queuing. But if I'm any later I'm going to miss him.'

'You can wait like the rest of us!'

'Let her go, baby,' said the woman beside him, and I mouthed my thanks, pushing on through the morass of sunburnt shoulders, of shifting bodies and querulous children and 'I HEART NY' T-shirts, the lift doors coming slowly closer. But less than twenty feet away the queue came to a solid stop. I hopped, trying to see over the top of people's heads, and came face to face with a fake iron girder. It rested against a huge black and white photographic backdrop of the New York skyline. Visitors were seating themselves in groups on the structure, mimicking the iconic photograph of workmen eating their lunch during the tower's construction, while a young woman behind a camera yelled at them: 'Put your hands in the air, that's it, now thumbs up for New York, that's it, now pretend to push each other off, now kiss. Okay. Pictures available when you leave. Next!' Time after time she repeated her four phrases as we shifted gradually closer. The only way to get past would mean ruining someone's possibly once-in-a-lifetime 30 Rock novelty photograph. It was four minutes past seven. I made to push through, to see if I could edge behind her, but found myself blocked by a group of teenagers with rucksacks. Someone shoved my back and we were moving.

'On the girder, please. Ma'am?' The way through was blocked by an immovable wall of people. The photographer beckoned. I was going to do whatever would make this move fastest. Obediently I hoisted myself up onto the girder, muttering under my breath, 'Come on, come on, I need to move.'

'Put your hands in the air, that's it, now thumbs up for New York!' I put my hands in the air, forced my thumbs up. 'Now pretend to push each other off, that's it . . . Now kiss.' A teenage boy with glasses turned to me, surprised, and then delighted.

I shook my head. 'Not this one, bud. Sorry.' I leapt off the girder, pushed past him and ran to the final queue waiting in front of the lift.

It was nine minutes past seven.

It was at this point that I wanted to cry. I stood, squashed in the hot, grumbling queue, shifting from foot to foot and watching as the other lift disgorged people, cursing myself for not doing my research. This was the problem with grand gestures, I realized. They tended to backfire in spectacular fashion. The guards observed my agitation with the indifference of service workers who have seen every kind of human behaviour. And then, finally, at twelve minutes past, the elevator door opened and a guard herded people towards it, counting our heads. When he got to me, he pulled the rope across. 'Next elevator.'

'Oh, come *on*.'

'It's the rules, lady.'

'Please. I have to meet someone. I'm so, so late. Just let me squeeze in? Please. I'm begging you.'

'Can't. Strict on numbers.'

But as I let out a small moan of anguish, a woman a few yards away beckoned to me. 'Here,' she said, stepping out of the lift. 'Take my place. I'll get the next one.'

'Seriously?'

'Gotta love a romantic meeting.'

'Oh, thank you, thank you!' I said, as I slid past. I didn't like to tell her that the chance of it being romantic, or even a meeting, was growing slimmer by the second. I wedged myself into the lift, conscious of the curious glances of the other passengers, and clenched my fists as the lift started to move.

This time the lift flew upwards at warp speed, causing children to giggle and point as the glass ceiling betrayed how fast we were going. Lights flashed overhead. My stomach turned somersaults. An elderly woman beside me in a floral hat nudged me. 'Want a breath mint?' she said, and winked. 'For when you finally see him?'

I took one and smiled nervously.

'I wanna know how this goes,' she said, and tucked the packet back into her bag. 'You come find me.' And then, as my ears popped, the lift began to slow and we were stopping.

Once upon a time there was a small-town girl who lived in a small world. She was perfectly happy, or at least she told herself she was. Like many girls, she loved to try different looks, to be someone she wasn't. But, like too many girls, life had chipped away at her until, instead of finding what truly suited her, she camouflaged herself, hid the bits that made her different. For a while she let the world bruise her until she decided it was safer not to be herself at all.

There are so many versions of ourselves we can choose to be. Once, my life was destined to be measured out in the most ordinary of steps. I learnt differently from a man who refused to accept the version of himself he'd been left with, and an old lady who saw, conversely, that she could transform herself, right up to a point when many people would have said there was nothing left to be done.

I had a choice. I was Louisa Clark from New York or Louisa Clark from Stortfold. Or there might be a whole other Louisa I hadn't yet met. The key was making sure that anyone you allowed to walk beside you didn't get to decide which you were, and pin you down like a butterfly in a case. The key was to know that you could always somehow find a way to reinvent yourself again.

I would survive if he wasn't there, I reassured myself. After all, I had survived worse. It would just be another reinvention. I told myself this several times as I waited for the lift doors to open. It was seventeen minutes past seven.

I walked swiftly to the glass doors, telling myself that surely if he'd come this far he would wait twenty minutes. Then I ran across the deck, spinning and weaving my way through the sightseers, the chatting tourists and selfie-takers to see if he was there. I ran back through the glass door and across the vast internal lobby until I came to a second deck. He must be on this side. I moved swiftly, in and out, turning to peer into the faces of strangers, eyes trained for one man, slightly taller than everyone around him, his hair dark, his shoulders square. I criss-crossed the tiled floor, the evening sun beating down on my head, sweat starting to bloom across my back as I looked, and looked, and observed, with a sick feeling, that he wasn't there.

'Did you find him?' said the elderly woman, grabbing my arm.

I shook my head.

'Go upstairs, honey.' She pointed towards the side of the building.

'Upstairs? There's an upstairs?'

I ran, trying not to look down, until I came to a small escalator. This led to yet another observation deck, this one even more packed with visitors. I felt despairing, had a sudden vision of him moving downstairs on the opposite side, even as we spoke. And I would have no way of knowing.

'Sam!' I yelled, my heart thumping. 'Sam!'

A few people glanced at me but most continued looking outwards, taking selfies or posing against the glass screen.

I stood in the middle of the deck and shouted, my voice hoarse, '*Sam?*'

I jabbed at my phone, trying to send the message again and again.

'Yeah, cell-phone coverage is patchy up here. You lost someone?' said a uniformed guard, appearing beside me. 'You lost a kid?'

'No. A man. I was meant to meet him here. I didn't know there were two levels. Or so many decks. Oh, God. Oh, God. I don't think he's on either of them.'

'I'll radio over to my colleague, see if he can give him a shout.' He lifted his walkie-talkie to his ear. 'But you do know there's actually three levels, lady?' He pointed upwards. At this point I let out a muffled sob. It was twenty-three minutes past seven. I would never find him. He would have left by now. If he was ever even here in the first place.

'Try up there.' The guard took my elbow and pointed to the next set of steps. And turned away to speak into his radio.

'That's it, right?' I said. 'No more decks.'

He grinned. 'No more decks.'

There are sixty-seven steps between the doors to the second deck of 30 Rockefeller Plaza and the final, uppermost, viewing deck, more if you are wearing vintage satin dancing heels in fuchsia pink with the elastic straps cut off that really weren't made for running in, especially in a heat-wave. I walked slowly this time. I mounted the narrow flight of steps and, halfway up, when I felt something in me might actually burst with anxiety, I turned and looked behind me at the view. Across Manhattan the sun glowed orange, the endless sea of glittering skyscrapers reflecting back a peach light, the centre of the world, going about its business. A million lives below me, a million heartbreaks big and small, tales of joy and loss and survival, a million little victories every day.

There is a great consolation in simply doing something you love.

In those last few steps I considered all the ways in which my life was still going to be wonderful. I steadied my breath and thought of my new agency, my friends, my unexpected little dog with his wonky, joyful face. I thought of how in less than twelve months I had survived homelessness and joblessness in one of the toughest cities on earth. I thought of the William Traynor Memorial Library.

And when I turned and looked up again, there he was, leaning on the ledge and looking out across the city, his back to me, hair ruffling slightly in the breeze. I stood for a moment as the last of the tourists pushed past me, and I took in his broad shoulders, the way his head tipped forward, the soft dark hair at his collar, and something altered in me – a recalibrating of something deep within so that I was calm, just at the sight of him.

I stood and I stared and a great sigh escaped me.

And, perhaps conscious of my gaze, at that moment he turned slowly and straightened, and the smile that spread slowly across his face matched my own.

'Hello, Louisa Clark,' he said.

Acknowledgements

Huge thanks to Nicole Baker Cooper and Noel Berk for their generosity and wisdom relating Central Park and the Upper East Side, and for giving me such a clear window into these very specific worlds. Any deviation from the facts are entirely my responsibility and there to serve the purposes of the plot.

Huge gratitude also to Vianela Rivas of the New York Library service for taking the time to show me around Washington Heights public library. My fictional library is not an exact replica, but its creation has certainly been informed by the invaluable public service the real version and its staff provide. Long may it continue.

Thank you, as ever, to my agent, Sheila Crowley, and my publisher, Louise Moore, for their continuing faith and endless support. Thanks also to the many hardworking people at Penguin Michael Joseph who help shape this raw material into something publishable, particularly: Maxine Hitchcock, Hazel Orme, Matilda McDonald, Clare Parker, Liz Smith, Lou Jones and Claire Bush, Ellie Hughes and Sarah Harwood. Thanks also to Chris Turner, Anna Curvis and Sarah Munro as well as Beatrix McIntyre, and Lee Motley for cover design. Thank you also to Tom Weldon, and beyond that, all the unsung heroes in bookshops who help get us authors out there.

Massive gratitude to everyone who works alongside Sheila at Curtis Brown for your continued support, especially Claire Nozieres, Katie McGowan, Enrichetta Frezzato, Mairi Friesen-Escandell, Abbie Greaves, Felicity Blunt, Martha Cooke, Nick

Marston, Raneet Ahuja, Alice Lutyens, and of course Jonny Geller. In the US, thank you yet again to Bob Bookman.

Thank you for enduring friendship, professional advice, lunch, tea and inappropriate beverages to Cathy Runciman, Monica Lewinsky, Maddy Wickham, Sarah Millican, Ol Parker, Polly Samson, David Gilmour, Damian Barr, Alex Heminsley, Wendy Byrne, Sue Maddix, Thea Sharrock, Jess Ruston, Lisa Jewell, Jenny Colgan and all at Writersblock.

Closer to home, thank you to Jackie Tearne, Claire Roweth, Chris Luckley, Drew Hazell, the staff at Bicycletta, and everyone who helps me do what I do.

Love and thanks to my parents – Jim Moyes and Lizzie Sanders – Guy, Bea and Clemmie, and most of all to Charles, Saskia, Harry and Lockie and BigDog (whose inclusion in 'family' will surprise nobody who knows her).

Final thanks to Jill Mansell and her daughter Lydia, whose generous donation to the Authors for Grenfell appeal mean that Lydia is now immortalized as a gum-chewing, cigarette-smoking vintage clothes-store owner.

Reading Group Discussion Questions

1. Discuss the role that New York plays in shaping Lou's career, her love life and her relationship with her family.

2. Do you think Agnes was ultimately a force for good or destruction in Lou's life? Did her reasons justify her treatment of Lou?

3. How much was distance to blame for Sam and Lou's relationship difficulties? What other factors were there?

4. Was there anything about Josh's character that surprised you? Do you think meeting Josh helped Lou in any way, or did it hold her back?

5. The Gopniks were often unhappy despite their wealth and status. To what extent do you think money can buy happiness?

6. What influence do you think Will Traynor has over Lou? Discuss whether you think Lou has truly overcome his loss, or not.

7. First impressions are often deceiving. Were there any characters you changed your mind about over the course of the book?

8. Lou and Sam both meet other people in *Still Me*. How do the ways in which they each handle this differ? Do you agree with their choices?

9. Discuss the role Mrs De Witt played in the story. Was she more of a saviour to Lou or someone who needed saving?

10. How do you think Lou changed throughout the book? Do you think she fulfilled Will's entreaty to 'live boldly'?

Don't miss the new standalone novel coming from Jojo in 2019 . . .

Follow Jojo online to find out more:

Discover the love story that has captured
millions of hearts around the world . . .

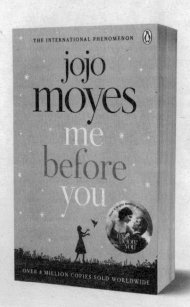

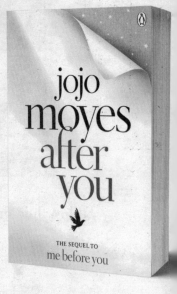

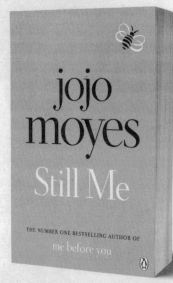